Love Past The Moment

Darrien Lee

Dedication

This novel is dedicated to all the brave souls who have been touched by cancer, especially those sisters who are breast cancer survivors.

Hope. Courage. Strength.

"For I know the plans I have for you," says the Lord, "plans to prosper you and not to harm you, plans to give you hope and a future."

Jeremiah 29: 11

Acknowledgements

The journey since my last novel has been one filled with undeniable blessings, trials and tribulations but God. I would like to thank my friends and family for supporting me over the years, especially my husband, Wayne and daughters, Alyvia and Marisa. The love I have for you is unmeasured and indescribable. You are my heart and soul and I do this is for you. I hope I have made you proud. A special thank you goes out to my fabulous editor, Melissa Forbes Bennett. I do not trust my beloved stories with anyone else and you know this. You know how I think and I appreciate your honesty. I have mad love for you and your skills! Kiss Amaya for me. Words also can't express the love and affection I have for two beloved friends and fellow authors, Tina Brooks McKinney and V. Anthony Rivers. V., you and I have a brotherly/sisterly bond and love for each other that is unbreakable and our friendship is priceless and forever. You had lifted me up when I was down and kept me encouraged during some very tough times in my life. Tina, thank you for keeping me motivated and encouraged and for your love and friendship. You were also there for me when I needed to be lifted up and I am forever grateful. There is also a host of people who have been extremely supportive of me over the years. There are too many to name individually, but you know who you are. To the Literary Divas in Nashville, I love you guys and all the support you have shown me over the years. Mad love also goes out to the Sip 'n Swirl Girlz, I love you dearly and I look forward to our future adventures. WINE UP! To my loyal fans, thanks for your love, support and patience. I know it has been awhile since I shared my stories with you. Without you, I could not do this. I'm forever grateful for your trust in me. I hope I made you proud with this new novel and characters.

PROLOGUE

It was Saturday morning and Ky and Yale had just finished doing what they did on most Saturday mornings—having sex. Ky had a reasonable and healthy sexual appetite, but Yale knew how to take it to a higher level. If she had it her way they would have sex three times a day, seven days a week. She had the strongest sexual appetite of any woman he had ever dated, and while he tried to oblige her most of the time, there were moments he just wanted to chill and enjoy her company. While most men would have killed to have a woman like Yale at their beck and call, Ky wasn't most men. He wanted a woman who wasn't so insecure and full of jealousy.

After thinking more about his relationship with Yale while showering, Ky decided it was time to end things. Even Ky's family and friends had started to notice that he didn't seem to be happy with his relationship. Ky knew their relationship had hit a dead end. All Yale ever wanted to do was shop, have sex, and party. That was about as deep as her personality ran at the moment, although Ky knew she had the potential of being so much more. Ky wanted more, but he realized that Yale wasn't going to mature any time soon, and he didn't have time to wait. He had a business to run, and what he wanted was a woman by his side who was supportive and loved him for more than what he could provide financially and physically.

Ky decided to head into his office to catch up on some paperwork, but when he was finished, he knew he would finally tell her their relationship was over. As he gathered his wallet and keys he turned to Yale. "I'll be back in a few hours. When I get back I want to talk to you about a few things."

She rolled over in the bed, still naked, and sighed. "OK, but do you really have to go into the office today? Can we go shopping or drive up to the casino or something?"

He frowned. This was typical Yale, and one of the prime reasons he was breaking up with her. "All you think about is spending money," he said.

"You want me to look good, don't you, baby?"

"That's just the outside, Yale," he said as he opened his bedroom door. "You need to work on the inside too."

"What do you mean?" she asked as she sat up.

"We'll talk about it later," he replied. "Let my sister know when you're leaving. She's upstairs in her room."

"No worries," she purred as she climbed out of bed and made her way into the bathroom to shower as Ky left the room.

He ran upstairs to let his sister know that Yale was still in the house, and that he was leaving for the office. Savoy was home from college for the weekend and staying with him. Just as Ky pulled his car to the edge of the driveway, he realized he forgot his cell phone. He pulled back to the front of the house and made his way inside to his bedroom. When he entered the room he found Yale sitting on the bed going through his cell phone. She was so engrossed in what she was doing that she didn't even hear him come in.

"What the hell are you doing?" he yelled, startling her.

Stuttering, she answered, "Nothing, baby. I just noticed you forgot your phone."

He ripped his phone out of her hand. "This is the kind of bullshit I hate about you! You're a gold digger that can't be trusted, and you have no respect for other people's privacy."

Still wrapped in a towel from her quick shower, she tried to explain her case, but it was falling on deaf ears. The things Ky wanted to talk to her about couldn't be held back any longer. It wasn't the first time he had caught her snooping through his personal belongings, but this was the last straw. He couldn't take it anymore. He wasn't happy, and he knew he didn't want to be with a woman he couldn't trust.

"Get your clothes on and get the hell out of my house!" he yelled as he threw her clothes at her. Yale tried to hug his waist to plead her case, but Ky shoved her away. "I said get out! It's over! I'm done with you and your trifling ways."

All the yelling caused Savoy, and his black lab, Samson, to run to the bedroom to see what was happening. As soon as the dog entered the bedroom he started growling and barking at Yale.

Samson had never warmed up to Yale, and when she was over Ky always had to keep them separated. Ky knew dogs had a sense about people, and it was clear that Samson didn't like the vibe Yale was giving off now. He should have known from the start that Yale was not right for him when Samson never liked her.

"You better get that damn dog!" Yale yelled.

Ky held his dog by the collar to keep him from attacking Yale.

"What's going on?" Savoy asked her brother as she entered his bedroom.

"It's OK, Savoy. Yale is leaving and she won't be back," he said as he continued to restrain his dog.

"About time," Savoy mumbled as she folded her arms and stood in support of her brother. She had never liked his girlfriend, and was glad he was finally getting rid of her.

Ky asked Savoy to step out into the hallway as he continued to hold on to his dog.

"Take Samson and go back upstairs. I have to take care of this."

"Are you sure?" she asked as she grabbed the dog's collar. Savoy wanted to stay and help her brother in case Yale decided to get physical. She knew he wouldn't hit her because he was a man and wasn't raised that way, but Savoy would knock her out and not give it a second thought.

"Yeah, I'm sure," he said to reassure his sister.

Savoy turned on her heels with a sly smile on her face and made her way back upstairs to her room.

Ky returned to his bedroom where he watched Yale get dressed.

"I can't believe you're doing this to me," she said as she slid into her clothing. "You act like looking through your phone is a crime. I'm sorry, OK?"

He shook his head. "It's over. I wasted enough time with you. Hurry up so you can get out of here."

Yale slowly picked up her belongings. "You'll be sorry you ever treated me like this."

"You did this to yourself," he said as he walked her to the front door and opened it. "I'll send the rest of your things to your house later."

She opened the door to her car and set her purse and belongings on the seat. Instead of getting inside, though, she reached inside the car's side panel and pulled out a gun.

"Don't think I won't pull this trigger, you bastard. I refuse to let you throw me out like yesterday's trash."

Ky smiled and shook his head in disbelief. He knew very well that Yale carried a gun, but he never thought she would have the nerve to point it at him.

He took a step toward her and pulled his own gun out of his back waistband and held it down by his thigh. "I wish you would."

She started laughing when she saw the gun in his hand and the look on his face. She loved him and didn't want to hurt him; however, she was sick of people mistreating her. Yale lowered her gun. "Baby, you know I was just playing. I love you. I could never hurt you."

Ky wasn't stupid and would never underestimate her or anybody with a gun, especially when that gun was pointed at him.

"Sweetheart, never point a gun at anyone unless you're ready to use it. Now get your ass off my property."

Yale could clearly see that Ky wasn't playing with her, and now she regretted ever pointing her gun at him. He continued to stare at her with a look that could kill and it sent shivers over her body. She realized he wouldn't think twice about shooting her if she pushed him. He always did have an explosive temper.

With tears in her eyes, she repeated, "I'm sorry, baby. I'm just hurt and upset. Can't we work this out?"

Ky slammed the front door without responding and put the gun back into his waistband. When he turned around he found his sister coming down the stairs applauding him. She didn't see the gun exchange and he was glad. Savoy had a temper too, and she could've easily made the situation quickly escalate.

"It's about damn time you kicked that skank to the curb. You're too nice of a guy to waste your time with someone like her. She never loved you, Ky."

"I know," he replied as he peeped out the door to make sure she was gone.

"Don't worry. You'll find the right woman one day."

He put his arm around his sister's shoulders and said, "I appreciate your support. Look, I need you to do me a favor. I'm going to call a locksmith to come out and change the locks, and I'm changing the alarm code. Can you stick around the house until they get here? I don't know if she snuck around and made a copy of my keys or somehow learned the alarm code. It'll give me peace of mind getting everything changed. She's not allowed on this property. Got it?"

"You don't have to tell me twice, and you know Samson will tear her ass up if she tries to come up in here. He's never liked her and he usually likes everybody. That should've told you something from the beginning."

"You're right," he answered solemnly.

"Why were y'all arguing anyway?" she asked as she followed him back into his bedroom.

"I caught her going through my phone." He examined his phone to see what Yale could've possibly seen.

"Wow! Well, let me know if there's anything else you need me to do," she said as she played with Samson.

"I'm glad you asked. Can you box up the few clothes and accessories she has in here? I want every trace of her gone."

Savoy gave her brother a kiss on the cheek. "Of course. Keep your head up, bro. You'll get your blessings soon enough." Savoy didn't waste any time pulling all of Yale's belongings out of the closet, drawers, and bathroom.

Savoy knew her brother was ready to settle down and find that special woman to love, and from what all her friends told her, Ky was one of the sexiest and most handsome men they'd ever seen. Because of his kind nature and good looks, there had been many women who had tried to lock him down permanently, but were unsuccessful. It wasn't that he was picky. He just wanted a woman with the full package—brains, beauty, a sense of humor, a nurturing nature, sexy, self-sufficient, God fearing, and one who liked music, sports, and fishing. He didn't feel like he was asking for anything unreasonable, but he had yet to find a woman who met those requirements. He knew she was out there, and he wasn't about to lose hope. Ky was confident that God would put her in his life in due time. He just had to stay in faith and be patient.

"Go on to the office, Ky. I got this," Savoy urged her brother. "I'll take this box by Yale's place later so you won't have to deal with her."

He hugged her. "Thanks, sis. I'll be back in a couple of hours so we can grab some lunch. Call me when the locksmith gets here."

"Will do and be careful, Ky. You know Yale can be a little unstable. I think she's bipolar if you ask me."

He laughed and walked out of the room. He didn't want his sister to know that Yale had already pointed a gun at him and it wasn't that far-fetched to think she might be bipolar. That would take the situation to a whole other level, but he didn't want Savoy worrying. He could take care of himself, and he could definitely handle Yale.

As Yale sped angrily across town she mumbled to herself, "You may have won the battle, you son of a bitch, but you damn sure haven't won the war. I'm not worried, because I was prepared for you to pull this one on me. Payback is a bitch."

CHAPTER 1

It has been nearly six months since Ky's breakup with Yale and today was one of Ky's most challenging days at work. Supplies didn't come in as scheduled, an employee got hurt on the job, and a lucrative deadline was fast approaching. As a successful boat and yacht builder, he wasn't sure if they would meet the deadline, but he would do everything within his power to satisfy his valued clients. So he retreated to a place that brought him immediate comfort, which was the local record store. These types of establishments had become almost extinct over the years, but music lovers like Ky helped breathe new life into the vinyl record industry. Spending time in the record store always allowed Ky to unwind from the stresses of his day. Vinyl records were making a comeback, but for Ky they had always been a part of his life. He usually purchased a couple albums per week to add to his personal collection. Ky's grandmother always said he had an old soul and he found it comical, but she meant it with all seriousness. His favorite artists were singers from the sixties, seventies, and eighties—eras he felt were filled with true musicianship. He enjoyed hearing not only the talented voices, but the talent of the musicians as well.

Ky flipped through several selections before he settled on a legend. He closed his eyes while listening to none other than the late, great Donny Hathaway. It didn't take long for his concentration to be interrupted when he got a whiff of a heavenly perfume. He opened his eyes and was mesmerized by the beauty of a woman dressed to perfection in a navy business suit. She was stunning. As she thumbed through the classical music section a row down from him, he noticed her perfectly groomed nails and hair, and her body that was curvy in all the right places. It was hard for him to tear his eyes away from her, but he didn't want to get caught staring.

The store clerk walked over to the young woman and offered assistance. Ky couldn't hear their conversation, but he figured she was looking for a specific classical artist. She already had an Aretha

Franklin gospel album, Nina Simone, and Earth, Wind and Fire albums under her arm. Her eclectic music tastes, along with her shared love for vinyl interested him even more. Seconds later the store clerk returned from their stock room with the album she had been looking for, and her appreciative smile lit up the room.

Ky was so engrossed in their exchange that he didn't even realize the Donny Hathaway song had ended. He clumsily fumbled with the stereo, causing him to knock over a stack of albums on display. As he picked up the scattered albums and placed them back on display, his eyes briefly locked with the young lady's.

As she walked by, she pointed at the Donny Hathaway album in his hand and said, "Great choice."

Ky smiled. "Thank you."

He continued to watch as the clerk rang up her purchases. He felt a strong urge to introduce himself, but at the last minute he changed his mind.

After paying for her purchases, she smiled at the clerk and said, "See you next time."

"Thank you, Ms. Miller. Hopefully I will have that other album for you by next Friday."

"I hope so too. It's really important to me. You have my number so call me as soon as you find it," she replied before she disappeared out the door.

Ky watched as the young woman climbed into a white Lexus SUV and pulled away from the curb. With his trance broken, he placed his stack of albums on the checkout counter and pulled out his wallet. He was one of the store's best customers and had a great relationship with the owner and clerks.

"How are you doing today, Trey?" he asked the clerk.

With a huge smile on his face he gazed out the window and answered, "I haven't seen anything that fine in a long time, so I'm doing fantastic."

Ky laughed. "I agree. How much do I owe you today?"

The clerk thumbed through the stack albums and said, "Forty bucks."

Ky handed over his cash and said, "Here's sixty. Dinner is on me tonight."

"Thanks, Ky!" he said as he folded the extra money and slid it into his pocket. "You know you don't have to buy me dinner for doing my job."

Ky tucked his wallet back in his pocket and said, "I know, but you've helped me more times than I can count, and you have an advanced knowledge and love of music. I like your enthusiasm too. That goes a long way with me."

The clerk slid Ky's purchases into a bag and handed the bag to him.

"It's always my pleasure. Thanks again."

"You're welcome. See you next week," Ky replied as he walked out the door.

Ky couldn't wait to get home to pour himself a glass of brown liquor and listen to his latest purchases. As he drove down the street, he glanced over into a strip mall parking lot and noticed a familiar white SUV parked there with a couple of teens he knew standing on each side of the vehicle. He quickly pulled into the parking lot and exited his truck.

The teens looked over at Ky approaching and one of them said, "Damn! Let's go. Here comes Ky."

"What are you guys doing?" Ky asked as he got closer to the vehicle.

They walked toward him and one of the teens named Kelvon said, "We were just trying to help that lady. She has a flat tire."

Ky passed the teens, and as he looked over his shoulder, he said, "Sure you were. I know better."

Andre`, the other teen who just happened to be his ex-girlfriend's cousin mumbled, "Fuck you, Ky."

"Shut up, Dre`!" Kelvon yelled. "You know Ky don't play."

Before the teen could respond, Ky turned and said, "Dre`, you need to watch your mouth and stop trying to see who you can rip off. Get a job."

Andre` waved Ky off and said, "Whatever, man."

"I have a job for you guys when you're ready to be real men," Ky announced.

Kelvon opened the driver's side door of his car and said, "You're lucky he didn't fuck you up."

"Please! He's a preacher's kid," Andre` joked.

"I know he's a preacher's kid, but he's not one to mess with," Kelvon replied. "There must be some truth to his reputation because he gets respect from some of the baddest dudes in the streets. My uncle said Ky used to get in fights all the time because people teased him about being a biracial preacher's kid. He's also friends with Pepto and you know his rep. That dude use to be hardcore."

Ky watched as the teens drove off and then he approached the SUV. When he walked over to the car he locked eyes with the gorgeous woman from the record store. She was talking on her cell phone with a fearful look in her eyes. He tapped on the window, startling her.

"Are you OK?"

She cracked her window and said, "I'm on the phone with the police."

"Really?" he asked. "Did those kids hurt you?"

"No, but they were trying to get me out of my car. I don't need to get out of the car for them to change a flat. They could've carjacked, robbed, or raped me."

He could clearly see that she was scared and he wanted to calm her down and let her know that she was safe.

He smiled. "That's true. You did the right thing by staying in the car. You can tell the police the kids are gone and I will change your tire for you."

The young woman reluctantly told the dispatcher that the teenagers were gone and someone was changing her tire. The dispatcher informed her they would send a police officer by just to make sure she was OK.

She hung up the cell phone and said, "You don't have to change my tire. I have roadside service I can call."

Ky looked around the area at the people hanging out in front of a nearby corner store and said, "Yeah, you can, but it'll probably be an hour or so before they get here. This is not the neighborhood you need to be stranded in alone, especially driving a Lexus."

She thought for a moment and then said, "Look, I'm new in town and I just want to get back to my place without getting murdered."

He laughed and said, "Well, I can assure you that I can change your tire and have you on your way without laying a hand on you."

She blushed at the handsome stranger and said, "I would appreciate that. Thank you. Wait, didn't I just see you in the record store?"

"Yes, that would be me." He reached inside his wallet. "Here's my card. If you would feel more comfortable talking to a family member while I'm changing your tire, you can let them know who you're with."

She took the card from him through the cracked window and said, "Thank you. By the way, my name is Reece."

"That's a nice name," he said before asking her to pop the hatch. "As you can see on the card, my name is Ky."

He pulled her jack and spare tire out of the car and was about to start jacking up the vehicle when a police cruiser pulled up. Relieved, Reece stepped out of the car to talk to the officer as he approached her car. Ky started jacking up her vehicle and waited a few seconds before making his way over to them. The officer immediately recognized Ky as one of his church members and greeted him with a friendly handshake.

"Miss Miller, you're in great hands. I know Ky very well. I'm glad he came by when he did to assist you. If you feel more comfortable, though, I can stay here and help him change your tire."

She glanced over at Ky and then said, "No, if you can vouch for him, I'm sure I'll be fine. I appreciate you coming by to check on me. I wouldn't want to waste your valuable time."

"It wouldn't waste my time. Making sure our citizens are safe is my job," he said before shaking her hand. "Ky, do you know who the teenagers were that were here hassling her?"

He nodded. "It was Andre` and Kelvon. I told them I had a job for them when they were ready, but they don't want any honest work."

"That's unfortunate. We need more men like you to reach out to these kids," the officer said. "Don't give up on them. Hopefully they'll wake up before they end up in the backseat of my car."

"I agree."

"Well, I'll let you get back to Miss Miller's tire. Have a great day and I'll see you this weekend."

Ky gave the officer a brotherly handshake and said, "Will do. Be safe out there, Officer Wayman."

"Miss Miller, you have a great day as well," he said before walking away.

"Thank you," she replied before dialing her brother Alston's number. As she chatted with him she watched Ky change her tire. Alston was her best friend and she couldn't ask for a better brother. She looked up to him on so many levels. He had always been supportive of her, and she admired and loved him so much. She was also happy he was finally engaged to his girlfriend of two years, Gabriella, whose family originated from the island of Trinidad. With a dual citizenship, the former beauty queen now worked as a financial consultant for a major bank in D.C. They met at a black tie event and it was practically love at first sight. The couple had been inseparable ever since.

Moments later, Reece noticed that the handsome stranger had finished changing the tire, so she ended her call with Alston. She stood back and watched as he put her flat tire in the back of the vehicle and closed the hatch.

He turned to her and said, "You're all set to go. You have a nail in it so it shouldn't be a big expense to get it fixed."

"Thank you so much, and my brother thanks you as well."

He pulled a tiny tissue out of his pocket to wipe the dirt off his hands and said, "I have some important women in my life as well. I would expect someone to help them out in a situation like this."

Reece nodded. "I have some hand sanitizer and napkins in my car for you to clean your hands better."

Ky happily accepted the items. As he cleaned his hands he pointed to the street and said, "There's a tire store about a half mile down the street that will fix the tire for you."

She put the hand sanitizer back in her car and said, "Again, I can't thank you enough for running those young boys off and for changing my tire."

He threw the napkin in the trash. "It was my pleasure, Reece. Is there anything else I can help you with?"

She looked into his handsome eyes and said, "I don't think so. You've done more than enough for me, and I appreciate it so much."

He opened her car door for her so she could climb inside. "It was my pleasure. Drive safely and have a nice day."

After closing her door, Reece said, "You too."

Reece watched as Ky walked back to his truck. She admired how handsome and sexy he was before finally driving away.

At the tire store, as Reece waited for her car, she couldn't help but stare at the business card Ky had given her. She ran her fingertips over the embossed lettering and read each line again. *Coastal Yacht Builders, Owner & Designer, Ky G. Parker.* He didn't look like a businessman, but he was. He owned his own business and seemed to be a true Southern gentleman. As she sat there, she tried not to think about him, but she couldn't help but remember his broad chest, huge biceps, and how sexy he looked in his jeans. She would guess he was around six feet, two inches tall with emerald green eyes that seemed to look right through her. He also had a bronze complexion and muscles in all the right places. He wore his hair short and had perfect lips and a smile with dimples that could light up a room. He was sexy all right, and had the body of a well-toned athlete. Thinking about him did make her blood pressure rise, but he had mentioned important women in his life. He wasn't wearing a wedding band but a drop dead gorgeous man like him would not be single for sure. He must have a girlfriend, if not two. He was *that* sexy.

As she reminisced over their casual exchange she realized she was fanning herself with his card. It had been a long time since a man had stirred her body like this, and she wanted the opportunity to at least thank him for his kindness. If he hadn't come along when he had, God only knew what could've happened with those teens. She had his card with his address and phone number on it, and she made a mental note to do something special to thank him for his assistance.

"Miss Miller, we have your car ready," the tire repairman said as he entered the waiting area.

Reece gathered her belongings and was finally on her way.

Ky set his groceries on the table, put his Donny Hathaway record on the player, and grabbed a beer out of the refrigerator. He took a sip and thought about Reece. She was even more beautiful when he saw her up close in natural light. He was taken aback by her beauty. Her eyes were dark brown with light brown specks. Her caramel brown skin looked smooth and soft. She had full, luscious lips with peach lip gloss and her hair was dark auburn with reddish highlights and large natural curls. He could tell she had a very curvaceous body under her business suit and she seemed to be thick in all the right places. It was difficult for him not to stare at her when she was standing outside her car because she was just that beautiful. Trey at the record store was right. He hadn't seen a woman that fine in a while.

He was kicking himself for forgetting to ask her for her number or at least invite her to dinner. It was too late now. All he could hope for was to run into her again at the record store, or see if Trey could possibly give him her contact information.

CHAPTER 2

Ky yawned as he walked through the warehouse to check on the progress of a couple projects he had in the works. He hadn't gotten much sleep since he'd met Reece two weeks earlier. Her beautiful face and soft voice were cemented in his mind and he was still kicking himself for not getting her number. He walked over to a table and stared down at the design plans for his next project and yawned again.

The foreman walked over and jokingly asked, "Long night, boss?"

Ky chuckled. "Restless night, that's all. Are we still on schedule with the Lanbeau yacht?"

"As much as we can be. The wife called again this morning with another design change."

Ky frowned. "What now?"

"She wants to add a small area to store their wine collection."

"This is the third design change since we've started. I'm calling them in for a meeting this afternoon because this has to stop. If they keep this up we'll never finish it."

"I agree," the foreman responded. "How do you want us to proceed?"

Ky stared at the design and found the only place to put the wine room. He drew out the dimensions and gave the foreman the authorization to proceed.

Over the intercom Ky's assistant called for him to return to the office. Once he finished checking on a couple of other projects in progress he made his way back to his office and was stunned by what he saw.

"Reece," he said as he greeted her with a huge smile.

She was sitting in his office holding an edible fruit design. She stood. "You remembered my name."

"How could I forget?" he asked.

She blushed. "I hope I didn't catch you at a bad time."

He was trying to regain his composure as he walked closer to her, but it was difficult. His prayers had been answered and now he had the second chance he had hoped for.

He motioned for her to sit back down. "No, it's not a bad time. In fact, I couldn't ask for a nicer interruption. How did you find me?"

"You gave me your business card, remember?"

He smiled again. "I forgot about that. Can I get you something to drink?"

She shook her head. "No, but thanks for offering."

He pointed at the fruit. "What do you have there?"

She handed the fruit to him. "I've been meaning to bring this over as a token of my appreciation for everything you did for me. I didn't think flowers were appropriate, so this was the next best thing. I'm sorry it took me so long to come by. I've been extremely busy getting settled in at my new job."

Ky took the fruit out of her hands. "I totally understand. It looks delicious, but you didn't have to do this. I was honored to change your tire."

Reece crossed her shapely legs and he couldn't help but glance at them.

"You were more than kind to me. I had to thank you somehow."

Ky called his assistant into the office so she could refrigerate his gift. While she was there he discreetly instructed her to set up a meeting with the Lanbeaus. Once she was out of the room, he turned his attention back to Reece. "Excuse me for that interruption."

"It's OK. I know you're at work. I should get out of your way."

"You're not in my way, and I really appreciate the gift. I can't wait to taste it. It looks delicious."

She blushed at the sensual tone of Ky's statement. "Well I hope you enjoy it," she said as she stood and looked at her watch.

"Do you have time to grab some breakfast?" Ky asked as he also stood. "I haven't eaten yet and I'm starving."

She pulled her purse strap up onto her shoulder and said, "I really have to get to work. Maybe some other time. I still have a ton of meetings and some other work to do as well. I'm also trying to learn my way around the city."

As they exited Ky's office together he walked her out to her car. He opened her car door and said, "Well, I would love to show you around town. We have some of the best restaurants, shopping, parks, and waterfronts in the area. If you're not up for that yet, at least let me take you to dinner."

She slid into the car and said, "I'm not sure what my work load is going to be or how much free time I'm going to have. Can I get back with you?"

Ky put his hand up to stop her and said, "There's no pressure, Reece, but at some point you will have to eat."

She sighed and then smiled. "You're right. I guess I'm just a little apprehensive about everything. New city, new job, new people, I don't want you to think . . ."

"It's OK. I would never think anything inappropriate about you. I totally understand about being busy. This place keeps me running from sun up to sun down and it can get stressful. I try to do things to relax so it won't get the best of me."

"I can imagine and you're right. It's a lot for me to take in all at once."

He smiled, revealing his sexy dimples. "I can understand that."

There was an awkward silence between them for a few seconds until Reece said, "Well, I'd better get going."

He closed her car door and said, "I'm really glad you stopped by and thanks again for the fruit. I was really hoping I would get the chance to see you again."

"Me too, and I don't see any reason why we can't have lunch or dinner sometime soon."

Ky smiled, feeling he had finally made some headway with his beautiful new friend.

"I'd like that, but I'm at a disadvantage since I don't have any way to reach you."

She pulled out her cell phone and punched a series of numbers. Ky's cell phone rang and he pulled it off his belt clip and stared down at the screen.

Reece started her car and said, "Now you have my number. Give me a call in a day or two and maybe we can do something."

He quickly saved her number in his phone and said, "Most definitely. Drive safely and have a great day."

Reece put the car in reverse and said, "You too."

Ky watched as Reece pulled out of the parking lot and disappeared down the street. When he returned to his office his assistant followed close behind.

She mumbled, "It's about time."

He sat down at his desk and said, "Don't start, Trish."

She handed him a slip of paper. "No, don't you start. We had a chance to talk before you came into the office. I really like her."

"I just met the woman a few weeks ago," he replied as he stared at the slip of paper. "You're already planning my wedding."

Trish folded her arms and said, "I know you, Ky Parker. You're feeling this woman and it doesn't hurt that she's intelligent and absolutely gorgeous. Did you see the legs on her? I go to the gym three times a week to try and get legs like hers. It's been over six months since you've dated anyone seriously. It's time!"

Ky twirled around in his chair and laughed but he had to agree with his assistant. Reece was stunningly beautiful and he couldn't wait to see her again. In just those few minutes, Ky found himself in a daze reliving every second of Reece's visit. The sound of her voice, her smile, and the scent of her perfume during this short interaction had stirred something deep inside him.

"Ky!" Trish yelled. "Are you listening to me?"

He snapped back to reality, picked up his ink pen, and scooted his chair up to the desk.

"Why are you yelling?" he asked.

She put her hands on his desk and leaned closer to him. "I asked you a question three times and you ignored me. It's obvious your lady friend made a strong impression on you. I asked you if you wanted me to confirm that carpet shipment for the Kingsley's motor yacht."

He tapped his pen on the desk and in a monotone voice said, "Yeah, go ahead, I'm sorry. Thanks."

She stared at him and asked, "Are you OK?"

"I'm fine," he answered in his normal tone as he started typing on his laptop. "I'm going back out into the warehouse. Let me know when the Lanbeaus get here."

She let out a loud sigh and said, "I will. Can I get you anything before they arrive?"

"Yes, can you please go pick up breakfast for the crew?"

She pulled out her notepad and said, "Sure. What do you want me to get?"

"Get them whatever they want. All I want is turkey sausage, cheesy hash browns, egg whites and toast."

Trish wrote down his request and asked, "Anything else, boss?"

He glanced up at her and laughed. "No, that's all."

She made her way towards the door and said, "Call my cell if you think of anything else."

He nodded without looking up from the computer screen.

Reece felt a great sense of accomplishment after leaving her meeting with the school superintendent. She was encouraged and excited about him giving her his blessing over the work she had done in her short two weeks there. He also gave her his approval to implement her strategy in improving the inner city school systems. Now all she had do was meet with the principals to make sure they understood the mission after they received her memo. Making sure the children of the city got an adequate education in a safe and healthy environment was the primary focus for her and her team. It was a six-month plan, but if she could reach her goal sooner, she would be able to get back to her life in Washington D.C. sooner as well. She served on a lot of executive boards and was on staff at the U.S. Department of Education. She was extremely successful by most standards, but as far as her personal life, she wasn't emotionally ready for a relationship.

Thinking of her personal life, Reece's thoughts drifted to Geno Matthews, a handsome young executive whom she dated while in college. He was a couple of years older than her and had given her an engagement ring during her junior year. Their plan was to marry after her graduation, but everything changed her senior year when Geno was murdered in a case of mistaken identity. He was out having a good time with one of his friends who had been having an affair with a married woman. The husband found out and tracked him down to the bar where they had been watching a football game. Geno was shot as he sat behind the wheel of his friend's car as they were leaving the parking lot. He had taken the car keys from his friend and was driving him home since the friend was too drunk to drive.

Reece's world crumbled and she felt like a piece of her soul had died along with Geno. She was so devastated over his death that she nearly dropped out of school. Her brother, Alston, who worked as a high level civilian employee at the Pentagon, helped bring her out of the darkness and get her back on track.

Since the tragedy, she had tried her luck at relationships a couple of times, but each time they ended before they could really get started. She had only come close to finding love again once since losing Geno, and even that relationship ended in pain. It had been hard for her to find anyone who lived up to Geno's memory or the standards she expected from a mate. It had been six years since that horrible night, and she was still psychologically and emotionally wearing black.

As she entered her office while shaking her head to clear her thoughts of the past, her cell phone rang. She looked at the caller ID she smiled.

"Hello, Daddy."

"Hello, baby. Can you talk?"

She sat down at her desk. "Yes, I just got out of a meeting. What's up?"

"Oh, nothing, I was just checking on you to see how things are going so far with the job."

She eased her feet out of her heels. "Well, the job is going great, and the people here are really friendly. I have my work cut out for me, but it's getting off to a great start."

"You're being careful, aren't you? I don't want you letting your guard down. And make sure you're not too trusting with people."

"I'm being careful, Daddy."

"Make sure you pay attention to your surroundings when you're coming in at night."

Reece smiled. "Daddy, I've been living by myself for how many years now?"

"I don't care. You're still my baby girl, so you're going to get this speech regardless of your age."

Reece could feel the love through the telephone as she chatted with her father. She was a daddy's girl, and she couldn't love him more. Her dad was very protective of her, but Alston was worse, and kept a close eye on her always, especially when she was in college. He didn't ease up until Geno entered her life and got his brotherly stamp of approval.

"How's Momma?"

"She's fine. She's gone to her Zumba class."

Reece laughed. "Momma's getting it in, isn't she?"

"She always has."

"Give her my love and let her know I'll call her tomorrow. I'm getting ready to get out of here, grab some dinner, and call it a day."

"OK. I won't hold you. Send me a text when you get to your place so I know you made it in safely."

"Will do, Daddy. I love you."

"I love you too."

Reece hung up the telephone, slipped back into her heels, and gathered her belongings before heading out of her office. It had been a good day and she looked forward to the rest of her assignment and having the chance to get input from some of the students.

Ky's meeting that afternoon with the Lanbeaus was heated, but successful. This was the second yacht Ky's family business had built for them, so they already had a standing relationship.

"Mrs. Lanbeau, all I'm saying is once the design is approved, it's difficult to alter it once work has begun."

"All I asked for was the wine room," she explained.

"Yes, but before that you wanted a few other changes, and that's not how we work here."

Mr. Lanbeau put his hands up to try to calm the conversation.

"Ky, my wife and I understand that you have deadlines to meet and that we're not your only clients, but we have been good clients. Making my wife happy is my main goal, so if there's some minor change she suggested, it would please me if you could accommodate her."

Ky rolled out the blueprint so they could finalize the design. Once the Lanbeaus was gone, he retrieved the fruit from Reece, and notified the crew to call it a day.

On the way home, Ky decided to stop by one of his favorite restaurants to get a bite to eat. It wasn't that he wasn't a great cook, but he was tired and he loved their food. As he got out of the truck, he was greeted by a couple of guys he grew up with who were hanging around outside.

"What's up, Pepto?" Ky asked as he shook the man's hand. "I see you're keeping your Benz nice and clean."

"You know how I roll," he answered proudly.

He was nicknamed Pepto because he suffered from ulcers and was always taking a sip of Pepto Bismol to relieve his pain.

"You're the man. I see business is still doing well for you too. New truck?" he asked, admiring Ky's new Ford F-150 Platinum Series truck.

"Yeah. I thought I would reward myself a little bit," Ky answered as he greeted the other man known as Domino who was somewhat of a dominos game champion in the neighborhood and was proud of his nickname. They were a couple of men from the streets with somewhat of a shady past, but they had known each other all their lives. They had taken different paths. Pepto now owned a small club in town that featured various genres of music and comedy acts, depending on the night. Ky and his friends would go on jazz night and R&B night. They even attended some nights when certain comedy acts came to town.

Ky turned to Pepto. "I hear the club is doing well."

"Yeah, it is, and you haven't been through in a while either."

Ky laughed. "I've been on that grind, but I'm going to come by soon."

Pepto shook his hand. "I'll be looking for you. What you up to tonight?"

"Nothing. Just picking up some dinner because I'm too tired to cook," he answered before opening the door to the restaurant.

Pepto laughed. "I hear you. If you get yourself a sexy lady you wouldn't have to cook."

Ky shook his head. "Been there, done that. Besides, half the women I dated lacked in that department."

They laughed as Ky reached for the door to the restaurant.

Pepto stopped him. "Speaking of sexy ladies, before you go in you might want to know that your girl's inside."

Ky froze. The last thing he wanted to do was run into his ex since their one of their last encounter almost took a violent turn. They often saw each other around town and at church, but Ky tried to make it a point to keep some distance between them.

"Who's with her?" Ky asked.

"Her usual crew of messy females," Pepto replied. "You're about to walk into a hornet's nest, my friend."

"I can handle her. I'm going to be in and out anyway. Come on in. Dinner's on me."

Domino laughed. "Cool! I'm starving and this I have to see."

"Me too," Pepto said in agreement as they followed their friend into the restaurant.

As soon as Ky and his friends walked up to the counter to place his order, Yale immediately spotted them and jumped up from her seat.

She slid in between Ky and Pepto and said, "Well hello, Ky."

Pepto jokingly said, "Hide the knives."

This caused Domino to let out a loud laugh. Yale glared at Pepto angrily and then turned her attention back to her ex.

"Hello, Yale," Ky replied without making eye contact with her as he paid the waitress for his order.

She stroked his arm. "Damn, baby! You're looking fine as ever."

Ky finally turned to her and looked her up and down.

"Thank you. You look nice too. Then again you always do."

Yale twirled around to give Ky a bird's eye view of her sexy physique in her white, linen pantsuit. She stroked his arm again. "So, are you ready to kiss and make up yet? I know you miss all this."

Ky chuckled. "Sweetheart, you know we're done. I'll pass."

"You really don't mean that. We had a good thing going. Stop being so stubborn. I've given you some space to think it over. I know you still have feelings for me. I still love you."

Pepto and Domino started laughing at Yale's admission. She ignored them and kept trying to convince Ky of her love for him.

"I'm not stubborn, but I am realistic. As I told you a hundred times before, you ruined whatever we had by being so manipulative, jealous, conniving, greedy, and possessive, and you had the nerve to pull a gun on me. So you have no one to blame for our breakup but yourself. It's time for you to move on, because I definitely have."

Angry, Yale put her hands on her hips and asked, "Are you seeing someone?"

"If I am, it's definitely none of your business," he explained as the waitress handed him the bags filled with their order.

Yale took a step back from him and pointed her finger at him in anger. "You're going to regret treating me like this."

"I've heard it all before," he replied.

Pepto and Domino laughed again. She pointed her finger at them as well. "You two thugs need to get a life."

"We have one," Pepto said, "and I have a couple of partners I can introduce you to if you're interested."

"Go to hell, Pepto!" she said before saluting them with the middle finger as she made her way back over to her table of friends.

"That girl is crazy," Pepto said as they all walked out together. "You better watch your back with her, especially since she's strapped. It's going on a year and she's still trying to get back with you."

"Yale's persistent, I'll give her that, but she's not the only one with a gun. If she steps to me crazy, she's going to be dealt with," Ky replied. "Here's your dinner. Enjoy. I'm out of here."

"Thanks again for dinner, bro," Domino said as they walked out together. "Next time it's on me."

Yale took a sip of her lemonade and stared at Ky as he walked out of the restaurant with his friends.

"What did he say?" one of her girlfriends asked.

"Not much, but I'll get him back. He's not going to know what hit him."

CHAPTER 3

Reece knew her way around the kitchen and she had enjoyed cooking ever since she was a little girl. Tonight it would be a quick meal of salad and spaghetti with garlic bread and some red wine. She was pleased with her day at work and glad she got to thank Ky for his generosity. He was appreciative of the fruit and clearly seemed to be a nice guy. It'd been a long time since she had allowed herself to lower her guard and date. She realized that it couldn't hurt having a friend in a new city.

As she ate her dinner she picked up her cell phone and glanced down at Ky's number. Having dinner with him would give her a chance to get to know him. Her heart wasn't ready to love again, and she wasn't even sure if she would ever be able to love again. Thinking about love made her sad so she tried to keep her mind focused on work and family. After a yawn or two she finished up her dinner, cleaned the kitchen, ran a hot bath, and soaked while enjoying another glass of wine. Before calling it a night, she lay in bed watching one of her favorite TV shows, and then finally drifted off to sleep.

Ky lay in bed staring at the ceiling. He was more mentally exhausted than physically, but somehow he felt emotionally charged. Seeing Reece up close and personal awakened emotions in him that he hadn't felt in a long time. His relationship with Yale was good while it lasted, but she was immature and insecure, something he didn't want or need in his life. It was obvious Reece was intelligent, mature, and professional, and she was absolutely gorgeous. He was anxious to get the opportunity to show her around the city and get to know her better.

As he was contemplating where he would take Reece on a first date, his telephone rang. When he looked at the caller ID he saw Yale's name on the screen and sighed. Instead of ignoring the call he answered because he knew she would keep calling.

"What do you want, Yale?"

"You know what I want. I want us," she replied as she pleaded with him.

He sat up in bed and said, "Well, it's not going to happen. Look, I'm tired and it's getting late and we have nothing more to talk about. Have a good evening."

Ky immediately ended the conversation and sat on the side of the bed. He needed a drink but before he could get up, his cellphone rang again. This time when he looked at the screen a smile immediately graced his face.

"I know you're not in bed," the young female voice said in a joking manner.

"As a matter of fact, I am, little sister."

"What are you, an eighty-year-old man? It's early."

He laughed. "I have a job, girl. I'm tired. What's up with you? You OK?"

"I'm good. I was calling to make sure you're still coming to the game on the thirteenth."

"I wouldn't miss it for the world," he announced. "How are your classes coming along?"

Savoy made a gagging noise before answering, "As good as can be. I'm so ready to graduate."

"Don't rush it, because you know you're going to be in the real world once you do. Enjoy college life as long as you can."

"I guess you're right."

Savoy was Ky's heart, and he loved her dearly. Making sure she was safe and happy was his priority.

"So, how's Patrick? He better be treating you good."

"Patrick is perfect and he definitely treats me good."

Ky frowned. "I don't like what you're insinuating, Savoy."

Savoy laughed. "I know you don't think I'm a virgin."

"I don't want to hear it. Stop it!"

Savoy continued to laugh. "OK, I'm sorry. I really didn't mean for it to come out like that. You're the one who went there. If it makes you feel better, I want you to know that Patrick is always a perfect gentleman with me. He loves me and I love him."

Hearing his sister profess her love for her boyfriend tugged at his heart. He had met Patrick, who was a football player, and he approved of him dating his sister. Ky didn't see him as anything but a well-mannered and respectful young man. Of course he also knew that Patrick, like any other college student including his sister, would always be on his best behavior anytime he was around. The truth was that he was a handsome and stellar athletic, and she was a beautiful dancing majorette with curves and shapely legs, and they both had hormones raging off the charts.

"I'm happy that you're happy, and you make sure you call me if you need anything."

"Thanks, Ky. Oh! Guess who called me today?"

"Who?" he asked curiously.

"Yale," she revealed. "She left a message on my cell phone asking me if I would talk you into giving her a second chance."

"You have got to be kidding me!" Ky yelled into the telephone.

"She knows I can't stand her ass, so I don't know why she's reaching out to me. I called her back and told her I can't influence you or tell you what to do because you're a grown ass man. I don't know about that girl, Ky. She's strange. I'm just glad you're not with her anymore."

"Me too. I just hung up with her right before you called."

"What did she want?" Savoy asked.

"She was begging me to take her back. She probably called you because I ran into her today at Miss Katie's restaurant. I don't know how many times I've told that girl it's over."

"I'm sorry you have to go through that. Maybe you need to consider changing your number?"

"No, what she need to do is stop calling me. Look, I don't want to talk about Yale anymore. It's giving me a headache. Tell Patrick I said hello and I'll see you on the thirteenth. I love you, sis."

"I love you too, Ky. Goodnight and hang in there."

"I will. Goodnight."

Ky hung up the telephone and tried to calm his anger at Yale for dragging his sister into her drama. She had no right to reach out to Savoy, and he made a mental note to confront her about it the next opportunity he had. In the meantime, he said his prayers, turned out the light, and finally went to sleep.

Over the next week, Ky engrossed himself in his work. With a couple of projects in the works and more on standby, he was adamant about staying on schedule. He was also looking forward to seeing Savoy dance with the band, and to get a chance to do some fishing. Being out on the water was what relaxed him the most, and he hoped to get the chance to introduce Reece to one of his favorite past times. As Ky worked side by side with his crew, he was interrupted by Trish when she called him over the intercom to come to the office. Ky put down his tools and immediately headed for his office. When he entered he stopped in his tracks when he saw that his visitor was Yale.

"What the hell are you doing here?" he asked in a calm yet slightly irritated tone.

Yale, dressed in a tight fitted, short, black dress with matching high heels walked over to Ky and said, "I don't like the way things ended between us. It's been six months and you're still so angry with me. I don't want that, and I know you don't either."

Ky walked over to his desk and casually glanced over some paperwork. Yale was stunning in her dress and there used to be a time when her beauty would arouse him, but he could see her beyond the beauty now, and he almost despised her.

"The only thing we need to talk about is for you to stop calling me, my sister and any other friends and family about our past relationship."

She folded her arms. "Can't you tell I'll do anything to get you back? I didn't know I was bothering them, but—"

"But nothing!" Ky yelled. "Leave my sister alone and don't call her anymore."

"Why are you so angry? You act like I screwed somebody or something! All I did was go through your damn cell phone."

"I'm not angry. And you going through my personal things wasn't the only reason we're not together."

Yale walked over to him and wrapped her arms around his waist. She snuggled up to him and ran her hand down towards his groin in a desperate act to try and break him.

He immediately pushed her away. "Goddamnit, Yale! That shit doesn't work on me anymore! Get out of here, and while you're getting yourself together, you need to tell your trifling ass cousin, Andre`, to get himself together before he ends up dead or in jail."

"I'm not his momma," she replied as she tugged on her tight dress. "I tried to talk to him, but he's hard headed."

Ky laughed. "It must run in your family, huh?"

She smiled. "Touché."

He walked over to his door and opened it. "Good-bye, Yale."

"I'm not giving up on us. I have my ways to get you back. You're a good man, Ky, and I know you have a forgiving heart," she said before walking out of his office.

Emotionally drained, he closed the door and sat down in his chair. He covered his face with his hands and said a short prayer.

His assistant Trish walked into the room and asked, "What the hell? Are you OK?"

"I'm fine," he replied softly. "Thanks for asking."

"You were yelling so loudly that I thought I was going to have to run in here and cut that crazy woman. Do you want me to tell the guard not to let her on the grounds anymore, because if she comes back up in here acting like that, I will cut her."

Ky couldn't help but laugh. Trish was not only a great employee, but she was also very devoted to him and his business. She was a young, Latino wife and mother of two young children, and her role at the company was very important to him.

"No, it's OK. Put your knife back in your purse. Trish, you are hilarious. I don't know what I would do without you."

She grabbed a stack of papers off Ky's desk, and with her thick Latino accent said, "I know, and I'm not going to let you find out either. What do you want for lunch?"

He walked around his desk and gave her a friendly hug. "Surprise me."

"Consider it done," she answered before leaving his office, mumbling in Spanish, still upset over Yale's visit.

Ky sat back down at his desk and pulled out his cell phone. He stared at Reece's number for a second before sending her a text message to invite her to dinner. He needed to get his altercation with Yale out of his mind, and start thinking about more pleasant things.

Seconds letter he received a response accepting his invitation, along with a request for him to call her around four o'clock. With a huge smile on his face, Ky quickly answered the text before clipping his phone back on his belt and rejoining his crew in the warehouse.

Reece sat at her desk feeling anxious and nervous about her dinner date with Ky. This time she would be face to face, and one on one with an extremely handsome man. She just hoped she didn't make a fool of herself or show her nervousness. In reality, she was looking forward to getting to know him a little better. As she sat in her office she wondered what she should wear. She didn't want to come off too sexy or too casual. She would just have to wait until she spoke to him to find out where they were going before choosing her attire. For now she would bury herself in her work and wait for her date to call her with the details.

Yale called out sick from work. After her meeting with Ky, she was too upset to go in. She earned a decent salary, and she didn't want to lose her job because she was accustomed to a particular lifestyle. But if she went into work and someone said something to her that she didn't like, she knew she would lose her mind.

Since Ky had broken up with her, she had gone out with a few men, but she was unable to find the love connection she had felt with Ky. Seeing him this morning, feeling his strong, hard body against hers excited her emotions.

Back at home, she kicked off her heels, unzipped her dress, pulled out a bottle of wine, and poured herself a glass. She eased down on her sofa, turned on the TV, and sent her best friend a text message. Anniston would be leaving her job at the hospital at three o'clock. Even though it was a weekday, hopefully she would want to hit the town for happy hour and possibly some dancing so they could wash away the drama of the day.

It only took a few seconds for Anniston to respond to Yale's message. She informed her she was game for drinks but wouldn't be able to hang out too late. That was OK with Yale. She just wanted to get out and drink something stronger than her pinot grigio so she could try to get Ky off her mind. After finishing off her glass of wine she lay down on the sofa and took a nap.

Ky and his crew had been working extremely hard and he hadn't even noticed the time. It was nearly four o'clock and he needed to call Reece regarding their dinner plans. He put his tools down and told his crew to call it a day. They normally worked until five, and sometimes six, but today he wanted to get out early. Inside his office he sat down at his desk and picked up the telephone to dial Reece's number.

She picked up on the second ring. "Hello, Ky."

Hearing her voice put a huge smile on his face. "Hello, Reece. Is this a good time?"

"It's actually perfect timing. I was on my way out. Are we still on for dinner tonight?"

"Yes. I was calling you to get some information. Where can I pick you up?"

Reece hesitated for a couple of seconds as a little fear crept up on her.

"Reece? Are you there?" Ky asked.

She cleared her throat. "I'm here. You can pick me up at the Extended Stay hotel on Main Street downtown. I'm staying there until I can get my own place. I hope to have something in the next week or two."

"I know exactly where that is, and if you need help looking for a place, I can help you with your search."

"I appreciate it, but I have a Realtor doing the leg work for me."

"Great, but if the Realtor can't find anything you like, I might know of some locations he or she might not think about."

She smiled. "I'll keep that in mind."

"Good. Now will it be OK if I pick you up at six o'clock?"

"Yes, that's fine, but how should I dress? Casual or fancy?"

"It's a come as you are restaurant, so I'm sure whatever you wear will be fine."

She thanked him for the information then said, "Just give me a call when you get to my hotel, and I'll meet you in the lobby."

"Sounds like a plan," Ky replied. "I'll see you soon."

"I'm looking forward to it," Reece answered before hanging up the telephone.

On the drive back to her hotel, panic started to set in as her mind started second guessing her date. Maybe it was too early to be going out with someone so soon after arriving in town. Ky was, after all, a stranger, and she didn't know anything about him.

"Get yourself together, Reece," she said to herself. "He's just a man, and this is how you'll get to know him."

She felt herself starting to calm down as she pulled into the hotel parking lot. She needed a night of fun in the company of a handsome man. She had almost forgotten what that felt like, and tonight she planned to make the most of it. Hopefully she would gain a nice companion to hang out with while on her temporary assignment.

CHAPTER 4

Reece stared at herself in the mirror. She wanted to make sure she looked nice for her first date with Ky. Tonight she chose a pair of skinny jeans, a yellow tank top with an off the shoulder knitted top, and some wedge heeled sandals. Feeling satisfied with her outfit, she applied her lipstick and within seconds her cell phone rang.

"Hello?"

"Hello, Reece," Ky said. "I'm downstairs if you're ready."

She smiled. "I'm on my way down."

Ky paced in the lobby of the hotel as he waited for Reece. He wasn't nervous, just anxious. The elevator doors opened and Reece stepped out with a huge smile on her face. She was stunning. Her jeans fit her body like a glove and showed off all her curves.

He gave her a warm hug. "You look nice. I appreciate you accepting my dinner invitation."

"Thank you, and I appreciate you inviting me. By the way, you look nice too."

Ky was dressed casually in a white button down shirt, jeans, and a pair of navy blue casual canvas shoes. His broad shoulders and chiseled features clearly showed the stature of a man who worked out and took care of himself. As he escorted her through the lobby, he placed his hand on the small of her back. He opened the door to his black Audi so Reece could slide in on the leather seats. She inhaled the scent of his cologne, which permeated the car. It was subtle and not overpowering.

He climbed in beside her and said, "The restaurant's not far. I hope you're as hungry as I am. They have an excellent menu."

"I'm starving too, and I'm anxious to try some of these gulf coast specialties."

"In that case you're in for a treat. They have some of the best seafood and steaks I've ever had. Maybe I can get you to try some gator."

She frowned. "I don't know about that, but we'll see."

He laughed. "It's actually delicious. I like it grilled and fried."

As Ky drove through the downtown streets he gave Reece a short tour of the downtown district, pointing out not only businesses she might be interested in, but also historical aspects of the city. Minutes later, they pulled up to the front of the restaurant. A valet quickly opened the door for Reece and then made his way around to Ky to give him a valet ticket.

Ky handed over his keys. "Thank you."

Inside, the couple was shown to their table. Reece looked around at the décor and noticed a lot of Southern nostalgic items decorating the restaurant, along with pictures of famous Southerners. Some of these celebrities had visited the establishment and it had also been featured on the Food Network for its delicious entrees.

Reece picked up her menu. "I love the way they have it decorated. It has that warm feeling like you're at home."

"Wait until you taste the food," Ky answered as he quickly scanned the menu. He already knew exactly what he wanted. When the waitress came to their table he allowed Reece to order first. She chose grilled tilapia with mango salsa over rice, sweet potatoes and steamed asparagus. Ky ordered some crab legs for them to share, chicken marsala, steamed mixed vegetables and roasted potatoes. Ky requested a bottle of wine with Reece's approval and they chatted while they waited for their meals.

He took a sip of the Riesling and asked, "So, Reece, tell me a little about yourself. Where are you from and how did you make it all the way to the Gulf Coast?"

"You go first," she suggested with a smile.

"OK, that's fair," he replied. "Well, I grew up here and I really never wanted to live anywhere else. I'm single with no kids. My sister, Savoy, is a senior in college. My dad's a local pastor and my mom is a former school teacher, but now she's involved with community affairs and a lot of the social scene around here, and she also organizes church activities. My grandmother is the matriarch of our family. She's a retired jazz singer with a big personality."

Reece smiled and said, "I can tell you and your family are very close and I can see the love you have for them by the way you talk about them."

Ky stared into Reece's beautiful eyes and answered, "You're very observant and you're correct. I live for my family. They're the most important people in my life."

Reese took a sip of her wine and asked, "That's so sweet, Ky."

"Thank you," he replied.

"So how did you get started in the boat business?" She asked as she butter a piece of bread.

"My two uncles, who are my dad's brothers, started the company. I started hanging around my uncles and the shop when I was a kid. I love being out on the water. When I got old enough, I started working at the company until I left for college. I majored in marine engineering and architectural design. After graduation, I came back and continued to work at the company. Once they retired, my uncles sold the business to me because their kids weren't interested. This is all I ever wanted to do, so keeping it as a family business seemed right. I guess you can say the rest is history."

"Impressive and honorable for you to do that for your family," Reece acknowledged.

"It helps that I'm my own boss and I love what I do."

"Wow! You're a hard act to follow," she joked.

He smiled. "I gave you the chance to go first."

She put down her wine glass. "I know. I'm just teasing you."

Just then the waitress returned with their entrees. After making sure they didn't need anything else at the moment, she excused herself. Ky asked Reece if she would like him to blessed their food. Impressed she nodded and closed her eyes and lowered her head. She was extremely impressed that Ky was a Christian and this one gesture gave him high points on her scale.

"OK, your turn," he answered as he picked up his fork.

Reece also picked up her fork and said, "Well, I'm originally from Charlotte, North Carolina, but my family moved to D.C. when I was still in grade school. I went to college at Howard University where I double majored in education and finance."

"Wow! A double major. You go girl."

Reese giggled and then said, "I played volleyball in high school and college. After I graduated I started working in D.C. with the Department of Education and I love my job as well."

"Good for you," Ky replied. "What about your family? Any brothers or sisters?"

"I have an older brother named Alston, who works at the Pentagon. He's getting married in the spring. My mom works in real estate and my dad is a retired police officer. I'm single and no kids."

"Nice resume and the fact that you love what you do."

"Exactly! I get to travel and interact with the administrators and teachers who work the front lines with our children each and every day. Teachers don't get the pay or respect they should, dealing with children with different personalities and demographics. They're basically raising a lot of the children they teach. Some children come from single family homes or from homes where the parents work multiple jobs and are not at home as much as they would like to be. Others are not getting the love, attention, and nutrition they should, and it's disheartening. I travel around to school districts to review and implement plans to make schools better. For me, it's all about the children and supporting the teachers. That pretty much sums it up."

Ky poured Reese and himself another glass of wine. "That's great, Reece. My mother was a great teacher and the kids loved her. Our teachers and school systems need someone like you to help get these schools back on track. With all the school shootings and teachers sleeping with students they need an educational crusader like you, huh?"

"I guess in a way I am," she answered. "I would hope that someone would do the same for my children one day."

"So you definitely want kids?" he asked curiously.

"Most definitely! I think they're a blessing from God. I look forward to being a mom."

"Well, I think you'll be a good one from what I can tell already."

Reece dipped a piece of crab into the butter and with a smile asked, "Are you planning on having a family one day too?"

"Yes, if I ever meet the right woman."

Reece saw the perfect opportunity to quiz her date on the statement he made a couple of weeks ago about having important women in his life.

"A couple of weeks ago you mentioned you had some important women in your life. Are you saying you haven't met Miss Right yet?"

Ky couldn't believe she remembered that. It let him know she was at least interested in his availability.

"When I said I had important women in my life, I meant my mother, sister, grandmother, and a few other females I care about."

She giggled. "You don't look like the kind of man who's not at least dating someone."

He chuckled. "Reece, I'm single. I'm not dating anyone, but I'll take that as a compliment, thank you. I'm sure you know it's not about looks. At least it's not for me. Of course I appreciate an attractive woman, but she has to be much deeper than just a pretty face. I want a woman who's nurturing, supportive, strong willed, God fearing, not afraid to take chances, and intelligent."

"You have some nice standards in place. Are those qualities hard to find around here?" she asked just as the waitress arrived to check on them and refresh their water.

"I don't go looking for it. So far it hasn't happened yet. If it's meant to be, it'll happen."

Reece nodded and they continued to talk about their lives over dinner and wine. Once they were finished, Ky paid the bill and they walked out completely satisfied.

As they waited for the valet to return the car, Reece said, "That was delicious. I can see why you brought me here. I will be returning because I saw a few more items on the menu I would like to try."

He turned to her and looked into her beautiful brown eyes and said, "This is just one of many great restaurants in the city. If you're up for it, I would like to show you a few more spots you might be interested in for shopping, eating, etcetera."

"I'd like that," she answered as she held onto his arm. The valet arrived with Ky's car and they climbed in and made their way out onto the city streets.

Yale and Anniston were finishing up happy hour when they decided to go for a walk down Market Street to see what else they could get into. They had consumed a lot of alcohol and were feeling pretty good at this point. Both would be taking a taxi home when the night ended. For now, they wanted to see what else they could get into as they headed toward the pedestrian mall. The two women loved the area because it consisted of bars, restaurants, boutiques, and so much more. It even had an amphitheater at the end for outdoor concerts. On this night, they would walk around and enjoy the evening.

The two ladies had just bought some food from one of the food trucks parked nearby. They sat down at one of the tables to eat and started scanning through their social media pages That's when Anniston noticed that Yale's total demeanor changed.

"Son of a bitch," she mumbled as she sat her cell phone down.

"What's wrong, Yale?" Anniston asked before turning around to see what had distracted her best friend. What she saw made her gasp, because she had no idea how Yale was going to react to seeing Ky walking arm in arm with another woman. And the couple was heading in their direction.

Anniston looked at her friend and asked, "Are you cool?"

"Hell, no, I'm not cool. Who's that bitch?"

"I've never seen her before," Anniston replied. "Don't do anything stupid."

Yale stood up and sarcastically said, "Now would I do anything stupid?"

"Here we go," Anniston said before getting up to accompany her friend.

"Well, well, well," Yale said, drawing Ky's attention her way. "I see it didn't take you long to find some new bitch to take my place."

"Is she talking about me?" Reece asked Ky under her breath.

Ky gave Reece's hand a gentle squeeze and said, "That's my ex. I'm sorry about this. I'll handle her."

He took a deep breath and said, "Yale, this is my friend, Reece. Reece, this is Yale, my ex."

Yale looked Reece up and down. "Friends, huh?"

"Yes, friends," Reece repeated.

"Enjoy the rest of your evening, ladies," Ky stated, and with Reece's hand in his, he led her around the two women so they could continue on their way.

"Friends my ass! You're not fooling me, Ky!" Yale yelled.

Anniston grabbed her friend by the arm and led her back over to their table. As they sat down, Anniston noticed the tears forming in her girlfriend's eyes.

"Damn, sis. You OK? I hate to see you keep doing this to yourself. You're a bad bitch. You can have any man you want. Forget about Ky."

Yale dabbed her tears with a napkin. "I can't, Anniston. I'm still in love with him."

She put her hand over her friend's hand and said, "I know you are, but you'll never get him back being confrontational like that. Men don't respond to drama like that. If you guys have any chance to get back together, you're going to have to stop making a scene every time you see him."

"I hear what you're saying, but it's not easy to do," Yale admitted. "I miss being with him, and then to see him with another woman kills me."

"They said they were just friends. Maybe that's all they are."

"You're full of shit, Anniston!" She yelled as she immediately tweeted her angry on Twitter. "Did you not see their body language?"

"Yes, and I didn't see anything that looked romantic between them."

"They were walking arm in arm, Anniston!"

"What did you just tweet?" Anniston asked as she checked her cell phone. Yale had tweeted that her ex was a liar and couldn't be trusted but thankfully she didn't mention Ky's name.

Anniston rubbed her friend's arm. "So what if they were walking arm in arm? Friends do that all the time. Look, Yale, let's forget about Ky for now and stay off social media. We're out having a great time, eating some delicious food. After we're done here, we'll hit one more bar, do a little dancing, and you can stay at my place tonight."

Yale looked at her friend and eventually smiled. Anniston had always been her ride or die friend, and with her emotions being on edge after seeing Ky with another woman, she decided to take up Anniston on her offer.

"I don't have any clothes at your house."

Anniston popped a piece of shrimp in her mouth and said, "Girl, please! You know we wear the same size. Just borrow something of mine, or if you want to, just get up a little earlier in the morning and swing by your place. You know you can come and go as you please at your job."

"True," she answered. "Thanks, sis. You're the best friend a girl could have, and I'm sorry I yelled at you."

"It's OK. I love you too," Anniston replied. "I know you're in pain over Ky. Just tone it down a little and think about moving on."

About that time a man walked over. "Excuse me, ladies, but aren't you Yale Spencer from channel seven news?"

"Yes, she is!" Anniston replied answering for her friend.

"Wow!" he said as he pulled out his cell phone. "Will you take a picture with me? My friends won't believe it. You're more beautiful in person than you are on TV."

Yale stood with a smile. "Thank you. I don't mind taking pictures with my fans."

The man moved in close to Yale and snapped a couple of pictures. He reviewed the pictures, shook her hand, and said, "Perfect! Thank you so much, and I didn't mean to interrupt your dinner."

In unison the two women said, "You're welcome."

After the man walked off, Anniston said, "He's fine. You should've asked him for his number."

Yale sat down. "No, he should've asked me for mine so I could turn him down. Did you see his ashy ass hands?"

"You're pitiful. You find something wrong with every man," Anniston pointed out. "There is no perfect man, and if he has ashy hands it might mean he's a hard working guy."

"Ky works hard and he never has ashy hands," Yale said before taking a bite of her po'boy sandwich.

"You're hopeless."

Yale laughed as they continued to enjoy their meals.

Further down the mall, Ky took Reece into a pastry shop for dessert. He knew he needed to sit down and talk to her about Yale and explain her outburst. He just hoped that Yale hadn't scared Reece away. They walked up to the counter to view their choices.

"Everything looks so delicious," Reece pointed out. "It's going to be hard to select one."

Ky knew Reece was trying to avoid the conversation, so he wanted to make his selection quickly so he could sit down and talk to her. Ky chose a strawberry cheesecake and Reece selected a slice of key lime pie. Once they took their seats, Ky immediately filled Reece in on Yale.

"Reece, I want to apologize to you for that ignorant scene outside. I ended my relationship with Yale over six months ago, and for some reason she refuses to move on. She has so much potential, but she can be extremely childish at times."

Reece took a bite of her pie and listened to Ky explain his past relationship to her.

"She's very pretty. Why did you break up with her if you don't mind me asking?" she asked as she wiped her mouth with her napkin.

Ky put down his fork. "She crossed some boundaries. For one, I caught her going through my cell phone, and later I found out she had installed some type of spyware on my laptop. She was very insecure. Any time she would see me talking to another woman she would always get confrontational just like she did tonight. She wouldn't allow herself to trust me."

"Wow!" Reece replied. "Is she that insecure, or did you give her a reason not to trust you?"

Ky was surprised by Reece's question. Hopefully she was curious because she wanted to get his relationship history before determining if she would consider dating him.

He leaned in closer. "No, I didn't give her a reason not to trust me. We both grew up here. I know a lot of people, many of whom are women. Just because I talk to them or give them a hug doesn't mean I'm trying to hook up. At times I felt like I had a stalker more than a relationship. She would show up at my house or other places like she was checking to see if I was with someone. It got stressful and ridiculous so I knew I had to get out. She has issues from her childhood that she really needs to deal with before she can have a healthy relationship. In reality, we really didn't have a lot in common."

"This sounds like a bestseller plot," Reece joked.

"You would be amazed at some of the things she's done," he revealed before picking up his fork and finishing off his cheesecake.

"You seem a little sad when you talk about her," she pointed out.

He let out a deep breath. "It is sad. She has so much potential if she would just get her life in order."

"She's obviously still in love with you."

He laughed and said, "I'm not sure she capable of that. What I do know is she has issues."

"Listen, Ky, I know we just met, but do I have anything to worry about? That woman is very angry."

He thought for a second, contemplating whether Yale would ever take her anguish out on anyone besides him.

"No, you're fine. She's a spoiled drama queen. I just think she needs a little more time to realize it's really over between us."

"Well, you obviously mean a lot to her for her to embarrass herself like that."

"Don't get me wrong. I cared about her at one time, but her juvenile antics started making me feel less and less," he revealed. "I would never put you in an awkward position, so I wanted you to know the truth."

Reece smiled. "I appreciate your honesty."

"This is a relatively small town, so if by chance you ever run into her and she starts in on you, ignore her and then let me know so I can take care of it."

She finished off her pie. "Don't worry. I know how to handle myself with women like her, but thanks for the head's up."

Ky felt somewhat reassured that Yale hadn't ruined his chances with Reece, and he figured there was no better time than now to ask her about her personal life.

"So, you've seen my crazy ex. Do you have one too, or someone special waiting for you to return to D.C.?"

She blushed. "No, there's no crazy ex, and there's no one special. I work so much I really haven't allowed myself to date that much."

"That's hard to believe," he replied. "You're so attractive. I'm sure you can't get through the day without someone asking you out."

"That's sweet of you to say," she answered. "Most of the time if I go out it's with friends or relatives. My romantic life has been on hold for a while."

He stood to dispose of their containers. "Well, I'm glad you accepted my dinner invitation."

"I am too," she answered with a smile as she also stood. "It's getting late, and we both have work tomorrow. I guess we better go."

"You're right," he answered as he opened the door for her. "I enjoyed spending time with you tonight. You're really easy to talk to."

"I feel the same way. I also appreciate you showing me around town."

"It's my pleasure, and that was just a short tour. There's a lot more to see."

"In that case, I look forward to the extended tour," she said as she linked her arm with his once more and they made their way back through the pedestrian mall to his waiting car.

On the ride back to the hotel they talked about their favorite sports teams. Ky found out that Reece knew a lot about the NFL and the players as well as their backgrounds, which surprised and excited him. He thought about how cool it would be to watch sports with a woman he was attracted to and who also knew a lot about the game.

Minutes later they pulled up in front of Reece's hotel. He quickly exited his vehicle, walked around the car, and opened the door for his lovely date. She took his hand and climbed out, then leaned against the car. She had enjoyed spending the evening with Ky so much that she really wasn't ready for it to end, but it was their first date and she didn't want to appear desperate. It had been difficult to look into his emerald eyes all night because he was so handsome. When he smiled and showed those sexy dimples, she couldn't help but melt.

"If I had my own place, I would invite you in for some coffee or something. Hopefully that will change soon once I find a place to lease."

"It's OK. It is our first date," he replied. "Hopefully you'll let me take you out again on a night when we don't have to work the next day."

"I would like that. Are you free this weekend?" she asked with a smile.

He shoved his hands into his pockets. "As a matter of fact, I am, as long as you're up for some fun."

Reece giggled. "What do you have in mind?"

He winked. "You'll have to wait and see, but I can assure you, you won't be disappointed."

"I love a mystery," she said before taking a few steps toward the entrance to the hotel.

"Would you like me to walk you in?" he asked. He wanted to spend as much time with her as possible.

She smiled. "If you like."

"I like," he replied with a chuckle.

They slowly made their way through the lobby and over to the elevator where Reece pushed the button and turned to him.

"Thanks again for a great evening and for walking me in."

He took a step closer to her and said softly, "It was my pleasure."

Reece felt her heart beating wildly in her chest. He was staring at her with those eyes and his scent was intoxicating.

The doors of the elevator opened and she let out a breath, and then gave him a warm hug. Ky wrapped his arms around her waist and held her tightly against his body.

Her body felt heavenly in his arms and he couldn't resist giving her a kiss on the forehead. "Have a good night, Reece."

Shivers ran over her body at the sensation of his lips on her skin. She looked up at him and said, "You have a good night as well. Drive safely."

He watched as she stepped onto the elevator and the view was amazing. She had an incredible body, but it was her smile and personality that had him in awe. He waited until the elevator doors closed before walking away. Once she was out sight, he slowly made his way back to his car and drove off.

Reece felt like she could finally breathe as she made her way up in the elevator. Once in her room she replayed the events of the evening in her head. Ky was an extremely handsome man with strong sex appeal and lots of confidence. A woman could easily get lost in his mesmerizing eyes, and she recognized a good man when she saw one. No wonder his ex was still bitter about their breakup and upset that she had ruined their relationship. She peeled out of her clothes and made a mental note to take it slow with her new friend. She could easily see it go from zero to one hundred if she wasn't careful, and she wasn't sure if she was ready for a relationship. Only time would tell, although she was looking forward to their date this weekend.

Ky pulled into the garage at his lakefront home. It had been a great night with Reece and he was glad that Yale's outburst hadn't caused Reece to retreat. He had really enjoyed her company and could see their friendship quickly going to the next step, but he didn't want to rush her. He wanted to learn a little more about her life in D.C. Being honest was very important to him, and he was willing to answer any questions she asked, and hoped she would do the same. He felt drawn to her and he would be kidding himself if he didn't admit that he wanted more with her. He hoped this weekend would give him that opportunity.

As he made his way into his kitchen, Samson met him at the door. After a few seconds of play, he opened the back door to let him out while he retrieved a beer from the refrigerator. He walked outside onto his patio and took a seat at the table while Samson ran around the huge backyard. He had a beautiful property designed for not only privacy but for entertaining as well. It consisted of an in ground pool, hot tub, and an outdoor kitchen area for some serious grilling. There was a large outdoor living area equipped with a fireplace, which was the perfect spot to enjoy a drink and watch the sunset. Closer to the lake was another seating area with a fire pit, perfect for chilling with friends. It was his place of serenity after a hard week at work and he enjoyed every inch of it. Listening to nature's symphony of crickets chirping, frogs croaking, and owls hooting was music to his ears.

Out on the water was where he loved to be, and he hoped to share his love of nature with Reece. At that moment he received a text message. When he pulled out his cell phone he noticed it was from Reece. She was texting him to make sure he had made it home safely. He quickly texted her back to confirm his safe arrival and thanked her for checking on him. He stood, finished off the rest of his beer, and whistled for Samson, who ran full speed in his direction. They re-entered the house and Ky proceeded to secure his home and set the alarm before going to bed.

Reece settled into bed, but she was unable to sleep after her evening with Ky. She had all sorts of emotions running through her mind and she couldn't help but think about her beloved Geno. She turned to a picture of them that she had on her nightstand. He had been the only man she had ever loved, and losing him continued to affect her. She wanted to be happy and love again, but the pain from his death had been too great. In reality, she was afraid to open up her heart completely to any man again, and only attempted it once since. Her family and church pastor counseled her about moving on with her life, but it was easier said than done. All the relationships she had since her fiancé's death felt awkward except one, and that one had ended because of lies. It was going to take a miracle for her to get over her loss. In the meantime she would bury herself in her work and take life one day at a time. Before calling it a night she kissed Geno's picture, said a prayer, and turned out the light.

CHAPTER 5

It was finally the weekend and Ky surprised Reece by taking her fishing on the Gulf. He packed a delicious lunch and hoped she didn't think a fishing date was lame. Luckily for him she was extremely excited because she used to go fishing with her dad, but she hadn't been able to enjoy it since she entered the corporate world. Ky could never get Yale to do anything he loved to do, and she wouldn't be caught dead baiting a hook with a cricket or worm. Reece was a natural and wasn't squeamish at all about handling the slimy bait.

It was a warm, breezy day and she looked heavenly in her denim shorts, Pittsburgh Steelers tank top, and matching hat. It was hard for him not to stare at her legs, cleavage, and backside. He didn't want to creep her out way out in the middle of the Gulf, but she was breathtaking.

The peaceful art of fishing gave them another opportunity to get to know each other and to talk about their lives. They spent a few hours fishing and releasing, but decided to keep a couple fish to eat at a later date. At one point Reece caught a good size mackerel and needed Ky's help to bring it in. After he put their catch on ice, Ky drove the boat into a shady cove where they ate lunch. Reece couldn't remember the last time she had this much fun or felt so relaxed. They enjoyed their lunch, more conversation, laughs, and great music, but things got a little more adventurous when Reece announced that she had to use the restroom. The last thing she wanted to do was go into the woods and squat. Lucky for her, Ky knew where everything was along the coast and was able to drive his boat right up to a restaurant a few minutes away.

As the day wore on, the couple decided to call it a day. Reece helped Ky tie off the boat at his company's dock and then said, "OK, Ky, you've showed me one of your favorite past times. Now you have to go with me to one of mine."

He sat their belongings on the dock and asked, "And where is that?"

She did a silly little dance and in a singing voice she said, "Karaoke, baby."

"Oh, no!" he said with a chuckle.

"Come on, Ky. It will be fun."

"I don't sing, Reece, especially in front of people."

She picked up the lunch basket. "Why not? Is it too corny for you?"

They walked side by side up the dock and back to his truck. He put the items in the bed of the truck and closed it. He turned to her and sighed.

"No, it's not corny. It's just not my thing. The only singing I do is in the shower."

She playfully pretended to hold a microphone to her mouth and asked, "Are you afraid you might lose a few cool points with your friends?"

He laughed again. "You really want to do this?"

She smiled. "Yes, I do. It's not about having a great voice. It's about having fun and doing something outside your comfort zone. I'll make a deal with you. If we get there and you really don't want to do it, you don't have to."

He opened the truck door for her. "I'll think about it. What time do you want me to pick you up?"

She clapped with excitement. "Seven o'clock will be perfect."

He dropped her off at her hotel and went home to relax for a few hours before picking her back up for their karaoke date.

Later that evening, Ky picked up Reece and he nearly cursed out loud when she walked out dressed in an extremely short lime green dress with spaghetti straps. He was still in awe of her shapely body. For a moment he couldn't speak because he was trying to get his body under control. The mere sight of her instantly aroused him and he was going to have to do a lot of concentrating to regroup.

He opened the car door for her and said, "Reece, you look stunning."

"Thank you," she said as she climbed inside the car. "You look handsome and stage ready yourself."

"Yeah, right," he answered unenthusiastically when he got into the car. He was dressed in grey slacks and a white silk shirt.

"Don't be nervous, Ky. This is going to be fun."

Ten minutes later they pulled up to the karaoke bar. Once inside, Reece signed them up. The bar was full and Ky even saw a few people in the crowd that he knew, which made him more nervous about performing. The only thing keeping him onboard was that Reece was looking so sexy. He had consumed a couple of glasses of Crown Royal and she was caressing his hand to keep him calm. Reece, on the other hand, was cool as a cucumber and had only consumed one apple martini. She was excited about performing with him and couldn't look more beautiful. After watching several performances, the time came when Reece's and Ky's names were called. Ky took one last sip of his drink before following Reece up on stage. As soon as they got on stage, he started sweating.

Reece hugged his neck, handed him a microphone, and whispered, "Calm down. You got this."

Reece then turned to the crowd and told everyone to go easy on them because this was Ky's first time. They responded with a thunderous applause as the music started for "Ain't No Mountain High Enough" by Marvin Gaye and Tammi Terrell. Reece immediately began a sexy dance around Ky to try to relax him. It took a minute, but he finally calmed down and got into the groove of the song since it was one of his favorites. He started dancing alongside his beautiful partner and began to sing when his part came up on the screen.

Reece was surprised that Ky actually had a very nice singing voice, and once the song was over, they were awarded with a huge round of applause. Ky was relieved it was over, but he wasn't sure if the applause was for their performance or for his gorgeous date. In any case, he was happy to get back to their table where he immediately ordered another drink.

Reece hugged his neck and gave him a kiss on the cheek. "Ky, you were wonderful! You have a great voice. I told you that you would love it. Now wasn't that fun?"

He laughed. "You better be glad I like you. Seriously, it was cool. I can see why you like it. You're a natural performer. You looked great up there."

She danced in her seat. "I've been doing it since college. It's a great stress reliever."

He took a sip of his drink. "You can sing too. For people like me it's a challenge."

Reece caressed his back. "Oh, stop it. You sounded great, and you've got moves too."

Ky had never dreamed he would do something like karaoke. He was a man's man and while he had never been to a karaoke bar, it wasn't as corny as he thought it would be. In fact, he was surprised to find out that they won first place and a one-hundred-dollar cash prize. About that time Ky's acquaintances came over to the table and shook his hand to congratulate them. They told him how much they enjoyed their performance, and then he introduced them to Reece.

When they left, Reece leaned over to him and said, "I told you, you were great. Now we have prize money to prove it."

Ky was shocked. He didn't even know he was in a competition, and to win was unbelievable. They watched a few more performances where some were good and others just plain funny. The main thing was that the performers enjoyed themselves and the crowd was very supportive.

Reece looked at her handsome date who had finally loosened up. "Are you ready to get out of here?" she asked softly.

"Yes," he said as he stood and held her chair for her.

Outside Reece said, "I haven't laughed or had this much fun in a long time. The fishing, karaoke, the great company—I couldn't ask for a better date."

He put his arm around her waist. "Thank you, and I'm glad you're enjoying yourself."

She kissed his cheek. "I'm really impressed with you, Ky Parker."

He looked into her eyes, wanting to give her a real kiss, but he held back. He didn't want to move too fast. She had kissed him twice on the cheek, each time getting closer to his lips. For now he would let her lead until she gave him a hint that she wanted a little more intimacy.

He pointed down the street. "Do you want to grab some coffee?"

"Sure," she said as she started dancing around him singing, "We're number one! We're number one!"

Ky laughed and admired her before she finally linked her arm with his and they walked a block down the street to the coffee shop.

The couple spent another hour talking and enjoying each other's company before calling it a night. Back at the hotel, Ky walked her inside to the elevator where Reece embraced him and gave him a quick peck on the lips. Ky didn't want to release her, but he did since she had taken a step forward and allowed him a quick sample of her luscious lips.

Over the course of the next two weeks, Reece and Ky went out at least four times. They were becoming extremely comfortable with each other and it had been torture for Ky to be so close to her without being able to kiss her like he really wanted to. Savoy's game was coming up this weekend, and he wanted Reece to go with him so his sister could meet her. Today he had taken her to an early dinner because she had a lot of work to do to prepare for an early morning breakfast meeting.

As they stood inside the hotel lobby, Reece said, "I'm sorry we have to end our night so early. If you're available this weekend, maybe we can drive up to this winery I read about."

"Unfortunately, I'm not. I have to drive upstate to my sister's college to see her perform with the band. She's on the dance team."

She took a few steps toward the elevator and said, "It's OK. I understand. We can do something next week. Have a great night, Ky."

Ky stopped her by taking her hand into his. He pulled her a little closer and said, "I don't want to scare you off, and I hope I'm not moving too fast, but I would love for you to go with me. It will be fun and you'll get to meet her."

Reece looked into his sincere eyes with amazement. She was starting to feel a closeness to him that she didn't expect, especially so soon.

"It's sweet of you to offer, but I don't want to interfere with your family visit."

He pulled her even closer and stared at her as he held her against his body.

"I don't know about you, but I feel like I've known you forever. You could never be an interference, and in fact it would make the trip that much more enjoyable."

She looked into his piercing green eyes. "Is it OK if I let you know by Friday?" she asked softly.

"Sure," he answered as he slowly kissed her on the cheek before releasing her.

"I guess I'd better get upstairs so I can get to work. I don't want to be up all night."

He took a step back. "Well, if you get bored or need to take a break, feel free to give me a call."

"I will," she replied. "Drive safely."

"Always," he stated as he turned to leave. "Sweet dreams."

"Every night," she answered with a smile.

The next morning was a rainy one, but Reece hoped her day would be better than the weather. As she got dressed for work she kept checking the time so she wouldn't be late for her breakfast meeting. While she sipped on her coffee she caught up on the morning news, which most mornings consisted of more sad stories than pleasant ones, but unfortunately that was the nature of society. Checking the time, she quickly grabbed her belongings and hurried out the door.

Traffic was heavy most mornings, but today it was even heavier due to the rain. Her commute should have been only ten minutes, but today it was taking a little longer. Instead of stressing about it, she decided to settle into the ride and listen to the local radio morning show. Then her cell phone rang. She recognized the area code as D.C., but she wasn't familiar with the number.

"Hello?"

"Reece Miller?"

"This is she," she answered.

"My name is Randall Vassar from the Washington D.C. District Attorney's office. I was calling to inform you that Cecil Thomas is scheduled to have an emergency parole hearing on Monday. We don't anticipate it will be granted, but it would mean a lot to the family if you were there to speak against it, being that you were Mr. Matthews's fiancée at the time of his death."

This bit of information rattled Reece. She didn't expect to have to deal with this so soon after the sentencing, and it was disheartening to even hear that horrible man's name again. He had been sentenced to eight to twenty-five years; however, only five years had passed.

"Why is he getting a parole hearing so soon?" she asked.

"It's because of good behavior and the fact that he's sick," the attorney revealed.

"Excuse my language, but that's some bullshit! Geno was gunned down like a dog. Just because he's sick and has been behaving in jail is no reason for the parole board to be lenient on him."

"I agree, and that is the kind of passion the parole board needs to hear on Monday. The hearing starts at ten AM. Can we count on you?"

"Of course! I'm living out of state right now, but I'll make arrangements to fly back for the hearing."

"Thank you, Miss Miller. I have the details if you're able to take them down."

She sighed. "I'm actually driving right now. Can I call you back when I get to my office?"

"Sure. I'll wait to hear back from you."

Reece ended the call and gripped the steering wheel. She wasn't looking forward to facing that horrible man again, but she would do it in a heartbeat to protect her fiancé's memory.

After parking her car, she hurried into her office. She exchanged a few pleasantries with her staff before entering her office and closing the door. After a short prayer she sat down and called Mr. Vassar back and got the details of the hearing. Before hanging up she thanked him for contacting her. She then immediately dialed Ky's number.

He answered on the second ring with a cheerful, "Good Morning, Reece."

"Good Morning. I hope I'm not catching you at a bad time," she replied.

"No, I'm actually just going over some paperwork. What's wrong? You sound a little stressed."

She let out a breath. "I'm OK. I was calling to let you know I won't be able to go with you this weekend. I have to fly back to D.C. Friday to take care of some personal business."

Ky leaned back in his chair and listened to the stress in Reece's voice. He wasn't going to pry into her personal business, but he could tell whatever was going on had her rattled.

"It's OK. There will be other games. Just let me know if you need help with anything."

"I will, and again, I'm sorry I can't go."

He chuckled. "Stop apologizing. Maybe we can do something when you get back."

"I would like that," she answered. "I should be back in town by Monday evening."

"OK. Have a safe trip and give me a call when you get back."

"I will, and I'll talk to you before I leave town."

"Sounds good. Try to have a great day, Reece."

"You do the same."

Reece hung up and put her hands over her face. She wasn't looking forward to the hearing, but it was something she had to do no matter how hard it would be. To take her mind off things she grabbed her presentation and headed to her meeting. Her morning flew by as she buried herself in work. Right before lunch she had a conference call with the school superintendent and the principals of the area schools to get an update on the new initiatives she had put in place. Most of the feedback was positive, but there was still some resistance. Reece explained the reasons behind the new guidelines to help the principals in justifying the new methods to their staff and students.

"Listen, I'll be happy to come to your schools and have a face to face with the staff or the entire student body if necessary. I can assure you if we can get these guidelines in place and running smoothly, you'll see a positive difference in not only academics but also in morale."

"I agree with Miss Miller," the superintendent said. "Our way has proven ineffective; therefore, we need to embrace these guidelines for the better of the students and the district. If any of you would like Miss Miller to make an onsite appearance, please reach out to her and make an appointment—the sooner the better. Our school year is just getting started, and I would like to see some improvement by January. With that said, I know it's lunch time, so if no one else has anything to add, we can end the meeting and not have to meet again until next month. Miss Miller, do you have any last remarks?"

"Yes, Superintendent Humphries. I just want to say I appreciate everyone's time and efforts. Please reach out to me with any questions, input, or concerns."

"On that note, meeting dismissed," the Superintendent replied. "Have a great afternoon."

Reece disconnected from the conference call and checked her watch. The meeting ran over thirty minutes and it was past her normal lunch time. She didn't feel like going out and she needed to purchase her plane tickets for her trip home. She walked out of her office and over to her assistant's desk. After a brief update on other appointments, Reece asked her assistant if she would mind picking up lunch for her, which she happily accepted.

Reece made her way back into her office so she could purchase her airline tickets. It was normally expensive purchasing airline tickets on short notice. Lucky for her, she was able to find a reasonable round-trip ticket on a travel Web site. As she sat and waited for lunch she gazed out the window at the skyline and her thoughts went to Geno and how much she still missed him. Sometimes she could still hear his voice, feel his touch, and smell his scent. He was her world, and since he was taken away from her, her world had stopped. She hadn't had the heart to move his clothes and other belongings that were still in their house. In some small way it allowed her to be close to him. She realized at some point she would have to let go. Unfortunately, she hadn't reached that point yet.

While she waited for lunch she decided to give her brother a call.

"Alston Miller. How may I help you?"

"Alston, it's Reece. Can you talk?"

"Sure, any time for you. What's up? You OK?"

"Not really," she revealed. I got a call from the district attorney's office today about that guy that killed Geno. He has an emergency parole hearing Monday, and the DA said it would be good if I spoke to the parole board."

"Already? That's crazy!" he replied angrily. "Are you going to do it?"

"I have to. I can't let that animal get out of jail."

"I agree. When are you coming home so I can pick you up from the airport?

Reece gave Alston her flight information and chatted with him a little while longer until a knock on her door interrupted them.

"Come in," Reece yelled out, and then waved her assistant into the room. "Alston, let me call you later tonight. My assistant just came back with my lunch."

"OK," he answered. "Hang in there, sis. You can do it. I'm proud of you and I'll go with you if you want me to."

With a smile on her face she said, "I would like that. I love you. Give Gabriella my love too."

"I will, and I love you too. See you soon."

She hung up the telephone and said, "That was fast."

"I didn't mean to interrupt your telephone call," Leah apologized as she set the bag on the desk.

Reece stood. "It's OK. I was finishing up anyway. What do you have?"

Leah opened the bag. "I hope you like it. I tried not to go too heavy or too light."

"I'm sure whatever it is will be delicious. It smells wonderful." Reece opened her container and inhaled the amazing aroma of shrimp and grits. "Oh my, this looks delicious."

Leah reached into the bag. "I also got a small side salad with a vinaigrette dressing too. I hope you like my selection."

"It's perfect, Leah, thank you. What did you get?"

She opened her container to reveal crab cakes with mixed sautéed vegetables and a twice-baked potato.

"That looks yummy as well. Leah, I appreciate you picking up lunch for me."

"You're welcome," Leah replied as she held out the change for the food purchase. "Oh! There's a tall, good looking man that just walked in to see you. Do you want me to send him in?" Leah asked.

Reece smiled. "Does he have green eyes?"

Leah fanned herself. "Yes, among some other very nice features."

Reece giggled. "Thank you, Leah. He's a close friend of mine. You can go ahead and send him in."

Leah smiled as she walked toward the door. "I wish I had friends that looked like yours."

"You're funny and you can keep the change for payment for your meal. I appreciate you running out to get lunch."

"Are you sure?" she asked as she called Reece's guest into her office.

"Yes, I'm sure," Reece replied.

Ky entered Reece's office, looked at Leah, and said, "Thank you."

Leah fanned herself as she closed the door behind her.

He walked over and gave Reece a kiss on the cheek. "I hope I'm not interrupting anything."

"No, you're fine. I was just sitting down to lunch. What brings you down here?"

"I wanted to see you," he admitted. "After your telephone call I was a little concerned."

Reece opened her food container. "Have a seat."

He sat down and stared at her with those intense green eyes. Today they showed genuine concern. She offered him some of her lunch, but he let her know he had already eaten.

"I appreciate you coming down to check on me, but I'm fine," she revealed. "Are you sure you don't want any of this food? It's really good."

"I'm sure," he responded as he stood. "Go ahead and enjoy your lunch. Look, I'll get out of your way. I couldn't let you leave town without me looking you in the eyes to make sure you were really OK."

She put down her fork, came around her desk, and gave him a warm hug and kiss on the cheek. She wiped her lipstick off his cheek and said, "That's really sweet of you. Thank you, but you don't have to rush off."

Holding onto her waist he kissed her forehead. "I have to get back to work. I wanted to wish you a safe trip. Make sure you call me when you get back into town."

Reece walked him to the door. "I will."

She watched him walk out of her office and down the hallway. Leah was right, Ky had some great features. He was really wearing those jeans and everything else he had on. He was a fine man that had a charm and confidence about him that was sexy, yet humble. Then there were those eyes. His eyes were so mesmerizing and possessed an allure that made her weak in her knees. She knew a dangerously sexy man like Ky Parker could take a woman like her to heights unknown. The question was if she would let him.

CHAPTER 6

Ky was glad the weekend had finally arrived. It had been a long week, so like most Fridays, he closed the business at noon to give his crew an early start to their weekend. This was one of the many perks for having a great crew who meet and exceeded his expectations each and every week. Ky used the first part of his afternoon to play a pickup game of basketball at the local YMCA. He had a few friends that often took their lunch breaks at the Y to work out.

Ky played a few games and toward the end of the last one, he noticed Yale walking into the gym. She took a seat alongside some other people who were watching the game. She was dressed in some form fitting yoga pants, and the men in the gym definitely took notice of her incredible body. Once they finished playing basketball Ky chatted with his friends for a brief moment before gathering his bag and heading toward the exit. The last thing he wanted was another altercation with her, so he decided to politely acknowledge her presence.

"Hello, Yale," he said as he walked past her.

"Can we talk?" she asked as she followed him out of the gym and down the hallway.

He stopped walking, turned to her, and sighed. "What?"

She put her hand on his arm. "Can we grab a cup of coffee or something and talk?"

"We have nothing left to talk about."

With tears in her eyes she said, "Everyone deserves a second chance."

He set down his gym bag and looked her right in the eyes. "You've had second, third, and fourth chances. I'm not doing it anymore."

"You can't mean that," she replied. "We are too good together."

"We were good at one time, but that ship sailed a long time ago. Please stop doing this to yourself," he pleaded with her. "There's a gym full of great guys in there, and any one of them would love to be that man for you, but I'm not that guy."

"Is it because of that woman I saw you with?" she asked curiously.

"It has nothing to do with her, and you know it. We were done long before I ever met her, so don't try to blame her for this."

Yale wiped away some stray tears. "I can't turn off my heart like you want me to. This hurts."

He picked up his bag. "I'm sorry, but that's something you're going to have to work on. I have to go. I'll see you around."

With a heavy heart Yale watched him exit the building and disappear out of her sight. That's when she pulled out her cellphone and tweeted a meme related to being betrayed. She knew he would see it and if he was no longer following her, someone close to him would.

After leaving the YMCA, Ky used the rest of his afternoon to run some errands and chill a while before heading over to his parents' house for dinner.

Ky ran home after his errands, showered, and then made his way over to his parents' house. When he pulled into the driveway a feeling of warmth filled his body. He had great memories growing up there, and he hoped to have a similar home with his own family one day soon.

"I'm home!" Ky announced as he entered the house. The aroma coming from the kitchen was familiar and welcoming, and his stomach immediately responded with a growl.

"There's my baby," his mother said lovingly as she met him in the hallway with a huge hug and kiss.

Ky kissed his mother on the cheek. "Hi, Momma. You look beautiful as always. I brought your favorite merlot and Daddy's caramel cake."

She took the bottle and cake out of his hand. "Thank you, baby. I'm sure your father will love it. Dinner's almost ready. Your father and grandmother are in the family room."

When Ky entered the family room he found his dad sitting in his recliner and his grandmother on the sofa working on a crossword puzzle.

"Hey, Daddy. Hi, Gigi!"

His father climbed out of his chair and gave his son a huge hug.

"Get over here, Bishop. I've been waiting on you."

He walked over to his grandmother, whom he called Gigi, although her real name was Geneva. He pulled a small bag out of his pocket as he sat down next to her. After giving her a hug and kiss, he set the bag in her lap.

"How have you been feeling?" he asked.

She opened the bag and pulled out the small bottle of Honey Jack Daniels. "I'm feeling just fine now that you're here with my treat. Thank you, baby."

Ky's father settled back in his recliner. "Ky, you need to stop bringing Momma liquor every time you come over."

"Hush, Gerald," she said with an elevated tone. "Correct me if I'm wrong, but I'm *your* mother. It's not the other way around. I'm grown, son."

Ky laughed and his father gave him that fatherly glare fathers give their children when they're not pleased with them. His grandmother was feisty and full of fun and he loved her personality. At seventy-seven-years-old, she looked like the actress Ruby Dee. She was classy, beautiful, and stylish, and her appearance was closer to someone in their early sixties. She stayed fit and was in a senior fitness group that walked every morning in one of the local malls. He loved his grandmother and would never do anything he thought would harm her health.

"Pop, a little Jack is not going to hurt Gigi. She's old school. She can handle it."

She poured a little of the brown liquor in a small glass and then took a sip. She held her glass in the air. "What is it you young people say? You better recognize."

Ky and his grandmother laughed together and she gave him a high five. His father squirmed in his recliner, clearly agitated with their antics. Ky knew his father disapproved of his mother drinking. Ky saw it as harmless, but decided to calm her down a little to not make matters worse.

"Now you go easy on that bottle and behave yourself if you expect me to bring you anymore," he said.

She poured a little more into her glass and drank it. After standing, she said, "I got this, son. I'm going into the kitchen to help Sinclair before she burns dinner."

Once she was gone, Ky said, "Pop, don't get so upset with Gigi about her drinking. She's in good health with a sound mind and in better health than most people her age."

"I still don't like it."

"Her and Granddad used to drink Jack together all the time before he passed," Ky reminded his father. "Maybe drinking it helps her feel close to him."

His father changed the channel on the TV before replying. "Maybe so, but she needs to ease up a little bit."

"OK, but you know she's not getting any younger. Let her enjoy herself."

At that moment, Ky's cell phone vibrated. He looked down at the screen and noticed a message from his cousin, Ja'el. When he opened it he saw a screenshot of Yale's meme with a warning from his cousin to watch his back. Ky sent a reply back to his cousin before tucking the cell phone back into his pocket just as his mother announced that dinner was served. Ky and his father made their way into the dining room to settle in for a delicious, home cooked meal.

After Pastor Parker blessed the food, he asked his son how the business was going.

"It's good. We're almost finished with a couple of projects, and I have a waiting list that will keep us busy for several years. I always send Uncle Rob and Uncle Eli quarterly statements so they know I'm keeping the business profitable."

Ky's uncles lived a carefree lifestyle. Ky knew he'd inherited that quality from them, and he embraced it. At the moment, his uncles were enjoying their retirement by traveling and enjoying life with their children and grandchildren.

"Bishop, when are you going to give me some grandbabies? I'm trying to be patient with you, but you're not cooperating," Gigi said suddenly.

Ky nearly choked on his food while his mom and dad stared at him and waited for his answer. It was clear they were in total agreement with his grandmother.

"Geneva," Sinclair called out to her. "Don't you think that's a bit much?"

"He's moving too slow for me."

Ky shook his head in disbelief. "I have to find the right woman first," he responded.

"Just make sure you pick someone who loves you and not your money," his grandmother answered. "And whenever you do marry, make sure you get a pre-nuptial agreement too."

"Momma, Ky's smart enough to know how to protect himself."

"I'm curious. Is it that hard to find a good girl, or are you being picky like your father? He almost let Sinclair get away," she admitted. "If I hadn't given him a swift kick in the butt, you and Savoy wouldn't be here."

"Tell the truth, Momma. You almost ran Sinclair away."

"I am telling the truth. You were trying to be all shy and reserved and you almost let that smooth talking funeral director take your woman. What was his name, Sinclair?"

Sinclair took a sip of wine. "Derrick," she answered.

"Yes! That's it! Gerald almost let Derrick steal her away. You know they make a lot of money in the funeral home business."

Ky's mother interrupted her. "Geneva, I've never been swayed to a man because of money. I'm a romantic and Gerald had the most sincere and loving eyes. He was a gentleman and a God fearing man. It was love at first sight."

"If that was the case, why did you keep going out with Derrick while you were dating Gerald?" Geneva asked.

Sinclair smiled at her husband. "I was only trying to make him jealous so he would propose. I knew Gerald was the only man for me and I guess you could say my plan worked."

Ky's father shook his head. "I couldn't stand her dating that greasy head funeral director another day."

Ky laughed. "How long were you dating before you proposed?"

"Four months," his father revealed as he put more fried chicken on his plate.

"We got married eight months later in a beautiful ceremony," Sinclair added. "You've seen the pictures."

Ky smiled. "Yes, it was beautiful, Momma."

"OK, back to you, Bishop," Geneva interrupted. "How much longer are we going to have to wait? Are you at least dating anyone? You know every time I run into a nice girl, I interview her to see if she would be suited for you."

"Gigi, why are you all up in my business?" he asked with a smile. "Thank you, but I don't need you quizzing women on my behalf."

"Boy! You are my business," she replied with a chuckle. "Well, whenever you do meet someone, make sure you bring her by so I can check her out. If she's not right, I'll let you know."

"I'm sure you will," he answered.

"Son, don't rush into any relationship because of pressure from your grandmother. God will send you your Ruth when he's good and ready," his father said, referring to the biblical love story of Ruth and Boaz.

"I know, Daddy, and thanks. Now can we please talk about something else? I'm going up to see Savoy perform tomorrow if anybody wants to go."

"Sorry, son, I can't, because I have choir practice. But I have some of her winter clothes she's been wanting somebody to bring to her," his mother said. "Gerald can't go either because he has that men's seminar at the church. I told Savoy we'll get to one of her games soon."

Ky turned to his grandmother. "What about you, Gigi? You want to roll with me?"

She wiped her mouth with a napkin before replying. "I can't because I have a date," she said softly.

"A date?" his father asked. "With whom?"

"Calm down, Gerald. It's just Walter Stone from the senior center. We're going to dinner and a movie."

Gerald stood to remove his plate. "Make sure you behave yourself, Momma. Mr. Stone is a few years younger than you, isn't he?"

Geneva frowned. "Mind your business, pastor. I told you I was grown, and age is nothing but a number. We're consenting adults, and if we want to—"

"Momma!" Gerald yelled, stopping his mother from saying anything that could possibly be inappropriate.

The family continued to enjoy the rest of their dinner and then they all shared the caramel cake Ky had brought for his father. Afterward, Ky volunteered to clean up the kitchen while his parents and grandmother retired to the family room. Once he rejoined them he thought it was the perfect time to give them their anniversary present.

"Momma, Daddy, your thirty-fifth anniversary is coming up in February, and I asked you both to clear your calendars for a reason. Savoy, Gigi, and I want to send you on a two-week trip to Europe. Momma, I know you've been wanting to go to Venice for a long time. Now you can, as well as a few other spots over there. And don't worry, we're covering all your expenses."

Tears immediately filled Sinclair's and Gerald's eyes. They hugged their son with love and appreciation and then walked over and hugged Geneva as well.

"This is the trip of a lifetime, and we love you all so much. Thank you," Sinclair said.

"Yes, thank you," Gerald added. "I haven't had a real vacation in a while. This is long overdue."

"My point exactly, Daddy. You and Momma are always there for us and your congregation. You never take time for yourselves. You need to do stuff like this more often so you can enjoy time together," Ky said.

Across town Yale tried to recover from her conversation with Ky earlier at the YMCA. She was also scanning through the responses to her earlier tweet. Some were supportive and one in particular caught her eye. Dani tweeted a response to the affect that some scorned women don't know how to move on with their lives, instead they love feeding off drama and chaos. She knew Ky's friends and family would know who she was talking about. In fact she hoped her tweet would spark a response from Ky. Her heart ached more and more each time saw him with the anger on his face. She stared at her phone and decided to dial his number to see if he would answer but as expected his voicemail picked up so she decided to leave a message. "Ky, I'm sorry. I'm sorry I disappointed you, hurt you, and let you down. Please give me a chance to show you I'm a better person. I love you."

She hung up her cell, burst into tears and prayed Ky would return her call.

Ky checked his messages before pulling out of his parent's driveway and the last one he listened to was Yale's message. He rubbed his temple in frustration. Even the sound of her voice was starting to irritate him. Instead of calling her back, he decided to text her in all caps to hopefully get his point across once and for all. WE ARE DONE YALE! MOVE ON WITH YOUR LIFE!

Yale's heart skipped a beat upon hearing her cellphone beep, alerting her to a text message, but once she read Ky's response she threw her cellphone across the room and pour herself a shot of tequila.

CHAPTER 7

Reece was happy to be back in D.C., but she wished her visit was due to different circumstances. A part of her was already beginning to miss Ky. He was starting to grow on her, but she didn't want to move too fast. Having someone to go out to dinner and other social events with in a new city was welcome, and she was definitely happy their paths had crossed, but she was still hesitant about relationships because of her past ones.

As she made her way through the busy airport and down the escalator to baggage claim, she was also anxious to see her brother. He always had a way of calming her when she was feeling overwhelmed. As she made her way downstairs she could see her brother standing at the bottom holding a sign with the words LITTLE SISTER on it like limo drivers held. She burst out laughing, then walked over to Alston and gave him a big hug.

"You are so silly," she joked.

He kissed her on the cheek. "I couldn't resist."

She looked around. "Is Gabriella here?"

"No, she's waiting for us at the house. Let's get your luggage and get out of here."

They chatted about their parents and work as the turnstile started rotating luggage through the small door.

"How many bags do you have?" Alston asked.

"Just one," she replied, and within minutes she pointed it out so he could grab it.

"I hope you're hungry. Gabriella cooked a lot of food for you."

"I can't wait. She knows I like to eat."

"I also have a new wine I want you to try," he revealed.

Reece loved Gabriella's cooking, especially when she cooked her native Caribbean dishes. Alston was a great cook as well, and at one point thought about going to culinary school. That changed after he got a taste working for the government when he obtained an internship with the Department of Defense the summer of his junior year in college. While he still enjoyed cooking, something he and Gabriella had in common, working for the government was what made him happiest.

"What did she cook?" Reece asked as they made their way out of the airport and to his car parked in the short term parking lot.

"You know how she cooks—a little bit of this and a little bit of that. I think you'll like it."

Minutes later they reached Alston's car, and once Reece's luggage was secure, they made their way to his house.

Alston earned a lucrative salary; however, he was very careful with how he spent his money. Right after he and Gabriella met, he'd purchased a fixer upper in an older, established neighborhood. The house was nearly fifty-years-old, and it needed a lot of work. He loved the character and sturdy construction of the older homes located a short drive outside the city, so he took on the challenge of a complete renovation. He eventually found the perfect home, but he didn't want to put an offer on it until he knew whether Gabriella loved it. In his heart he already knew he was going to marry her, and this would be their forever home where they raised their family. The house he purchased for three hundred thousand dollars had large, mature trees in the backyard and a huge front porch perfect for enjoying a hot cup of coffee or glass of wine. He invested an additional two hundred thousand dollars into the renovation to get everything up to codes and get all the design aspects he wanted in a home.

Once renovations were complete, he ended up with four bedrooms, three full bathrooms, and two half bathrooms. The house had an open kitchen concept, finished basement, two office spaces, and so much more. It was a dream home for anyone, and to purchase a new house with a similar design would cost well into the millions. Presently the home appraised for a little over eight hundred thousand dollars and was steadily climbing.

Gabriella knew Alston was the man for her early in their relationship and fell head over heels in love with him. While the renovations were taking place, she insisted Alston stay at her apartment close to downtown against her traditional parents' wishes. It took nearly eight months to complete the renovations inside and out of the house, mostly because of numerous delays due to weather. Alston moved into the home, and a few months later he proposed to Gabriella. She immediately gave up her apartment and moved into the home with her future husband. She had been in the home with him for several months now, and with their nuptials taking place in the spring, there were still a few details to finalize.

On the drive to his house, Reece called her parents to let them know what was going on. She made a promise to visit them over the weekend before leaving town. During the drive, Reece talked more about her job and how the city was growing on her. Alston assured her that he would visit her soon if he could finish up several complex projects for work. This excited Reece, because being away from her home and family had been difficult, and she also wanted to see what Alston thought about Ky.

"Home sweet home," Alston announced as he pulled into the garage.

Reece unbuckled her seatbelt and made her way into his spacious kitchen. Almost immediately, the aroma of dinner welcomed her. While Alston left the room to put Reece's luggage in a spare bedroom, Gabriella made her way into the kitchen to greet her future sister in law.

"Reece!" Gabriella yelled in her Trinidadian accent. She ran over to her and gave her a big hug. "I'm so glad you're home. I hope you're hungry."

"I am," she replied. "Everything looks so delicious. You know I love your cooking."

"Fabulous," Gabriella replied as she put the finished dishes on the table. "I have some corn soup, jerk and baked chicken with rice and salad."

"Everything smells great. Can I help you with anything?" Reece asked.

"No, it's ready. As soon as Alston comes back with the wine, we can eat."

"In that case, let me go freshen up."

Reece met Alston in the hallway as he was returning from the basement where he housed his wine collection.

"I put your luggage in the downstairs bedroom," he announced.

"Thanks. I'm going to wash my hands. I'll be right back."

Once Reece returned to the table, Alton blessed the dinner and they dug into the delicious meal Gabriella had prepared. Over dinner they discussed the upcoming wedding and honeymoon and whether Alston and Gabriella should get a dog. Gabriella was all for it, but Alston was a little reluctant knowing how much work it was to train a puppy. Their busy schedules didn't allow that much extra time.

Once they finished dinner, Reece cleaned the kitchen and then joined her loved ones on the patio around the gas fire pit with some peach cobbler and wine.

"This is so good, Gabriella. Did you make it yourself?"

"Yes. That's the only way I cook if at all possible," she admitted.

"So, sis, how did your date go with that guy that changed your tire?" Alston asked.

Reece was caught off guard by Alston's question and nearly spilled her wine. Little did her brother know, she had already been on several dates with Ky.

"It was nice until we ran into his ex. It was obvious she's not over him," Reece revealed.

Alston shook his head. "Be careful, Reece. Ex's can be very dangerous. Did he handle the situation?"

"He did, and he reiterated to her that their relationship has been over for months and he told her she needed to move on with her life. She had a friend with her that seemed embarrassed by the whole thing. She was trying to get that girl to leave us alone. It was crazy and unexpected."

"A woman scorned is a dangerous thing, Reece," Gabriella added. "Is your gut telling you he was being truthful to you about her?"

Reece tucked her legs under her body. "I believe him. There were a lot of people around at the time witnessing the whole mess. Ky kept his cool and tried to explain to that girl as clearly and calmly as possible where they stood. She started crying after that. It was a hot mess."

"Are you going to see him again?" Gabriella asked.

"I already have," she admitted. "We actually spend a lot of time together. I like him. He has a calm nature about him that I like. I was supposed to go to a football game with him this weekend to see his sister perform as a dancer with her college band, but I had to decline."

Alston took a sip of wine. "Have you told him about Geno?"

Just hearing Geno's name caused her to break out in chills. She gathered herself and said softly, "No, not yet. If he asks me, I'll tell him, but it's not something I want to volunteer right now."

"Is he good looking?" Gabriella asked with a sneaky grin on her face.

Reece took a sip of her wine and nodded. "That's an understatement. He's so good looking it's hard for me to look him in the eyes. He has these emerald eyes and a smile . . . well, let's just say it affects me."

Gabriella stood, walked over to her future sister-in-law, and gave her a hug. "Sis, if you really like this man, and I'm getting a vibe that you do, embrace it. You're a beautiful young woman, and if you don't find love with him, love will find its way back to you in due time. Just take it slow and keep your heart open, OK?"

Reece nodded and let Gabriella's words sink in.

Gabriella turned to Alston. "Babe, I'm a little tired. I'm getting ready to go up to bed."

Alston gave his fiancée a kiss. "OK, sweetheart. I'll be up shortly. I want to hang out with Reece for a second."

"OK. Goodnight, Reece."

"Goodnight," she replied.

Once Gabriella had disappeared upstairs Alston turned his attention back to his sister, whom he could see was clearly still emotional from the mention of Geno. He sat down next to her and put his arm around her shoulders.

"Reece, I know you still haven't gotten over losing Geno. I also know that you have made an effort to move on. I just don't want you to feel like you have to force yourself into a relationship. Gabriella's right, though. Love will find its way back to you eventually."

She laid her head on her brother's chest and hugged him tightly. "Thank you so much. I don't know if I would've been able to move on had you not been there for me."

"You know I'll always be here for you. You're going to be just fine. I want to meet this guy when I come for a visit, especially since you're spending time with him. I want you to be extra careful, though, since he has a bitter ex running around. Watch your back," he said with a kiss to her forehead. "I love you."

"I love you too," she replied softly.

"You coming in?" he asked as he stood and gathered up their saucers and wine glasses.

"No, I'm going to hang out here a little longer."

He walked toward the french doors and said, "Don't forget to turn off the pit and set the alarm when you come in.

"OK. Goodnight."

"Goodnight."

Reece sat alone on the patio and stared into the flickering flames. She thought about everything that Gabriella and Alton had said to her. Yes, she was still in a lot of pain over the loss of Geno, but she was also open to the possibility that a person could find their soul mate more than once in a lifetime. The men she had dated since Geno were decent men, she just didn't feel any spark or connection to them. They were either too serious and unemotional, or too immature and sex crazed. The one guy who had real potential turned out to be a liar. She wasn't going to rush into any relationship, but just having a male friend was at least one step in the right direction.

Deep in her thoughts, she almost missed her cell phone chiming. She looked down at the screen and noticed a text from Ky. Without even realizing it, a huge smile covered her face as she opened the message.

Just checking to make sure you made it home safe and sound. Enjoy your visit and don't forget to call when you get back. Miss you.

Instead of texting back she dialed his number so she could hear his soothing voice.

"What a nice surprise. I didn't expect to hear back from you tonight since it's so late," Ky admitted.

She let out a breath. "I know, but it's so sweet of you to check on me. I meant to text you once I landed, but I got distracted by my brother and his fiancée."

"I know all about distractions," he admitted.

"So, you miss me already?" she asked curiously.

He chuckled. "You caught that part, huh?"

With a smile on her face she said, "You can't get much by me, Ky Parker."

"I see that," he answered. "I do miss you, though."

"I'll have to admit, I miss you too."

They were quiet for a few seconds, and then she broke the silence. "So what did you do today?"

"I had dinner with my parents and grandmother and it was amusing as usual."

"Well, I hope it was a good visit."

"It was. Do you know what time you're coming back?" he asked, not wanting to appear too anxious to see her.

Reece took one last sip of her wine and told him the time she was returning.

"Did you leave your car at the airport?" he asked curiously.

"No, my assistant dropped me off. I left my car at the office so I wouldn't have to pay for parking," she admitted. "I'm going to catch an Uber back to my office."

Ky was trying to restrain himself as much as possible, but it was difficult. He couldn't wait to see her again.

"If it's OK with you, I would love to pick you up."

There was another awkward silence for a few seconds. Reece could tell that Ky was attracted to her. In fact, she was attracted to him just as much and was anxious to see him too.

"Reece?"

"I'm here, Ky. I'm sorry. Sure, that would be nice, but I don't want to put you out of your way."

"It's not out of my way, and I'm offering. Besides it'll give me a chance to maybe take you out for dinner or drinks or something if you're not too tired."

"That actually sounds nice. I'll text you my flight information and we can figure out what to do once I land. Is that a plan?"

"Yes, that's a plan," he answered with a huge smile on his face. "I look forward to seeing you. Have a safe flight back."

"Thanks, Ky. I look forward to seeing you too. Goodnight."

"Goodnight, Reece."

Reece hung up the telephone, not sure what the future had in store for her. For now she had to concentrate on her past with Geno and fighting for justice for him. She had no doubt that he would do the same for her and not allow her killer to walk free. Monday couldn't come soon enough. For now, she would make the most of her visit with her family and friends and then get back to work on whatever God had planned for her.

CHAPTER 8

The five-hour drive to Savoy's college passed quickly. A couple of Ky's first cousins decided to ride with him. During the ride to the university, they discussed Yale's tweets and her behavior since the breakup. His cousin, Ja`el, was twenty-six-years-old and had been working as a paramedic for three years. He always had a fascination with helping others and he had a calming nature similar to Ky's. Being a paramedic enabled him to help people and the job had just enough excitement for him since he was somewhat of an adrenalin junkie. He worked some long shifts, but it was very rewarding for him.

Ja`el's sister, Dani, short for Danielle, was twenty-four-years-old. After finishing beauty college she purchased her own salon. Growing up, she was always styling the hair on her dolls, so her destiny was determined at a young age.

Savoy was the only one out of the first cousins whose career choice was unpredictable. While she loved being a dancer with the band, she was a pre-med major. She said she wanted to be a pediatrician. As the baby in the family, she was spoiled and would get jealous anytime a younger child was around. She always wanted to be the center of attention as a child, and if she felt threatened in any way, she would react by either hitting or pushing the younger child. So her family found it hard to believe that Savoy wanted to care for other children as her profession.

When they arrived at Savoy's college, they immediately made their way to the football stadium since the game would start soon.

"Y'all want something to eat before we sit down?" Ky asked as he pulled the football tickets out of his pocket.

"I'm getting nachos and cheese," Dani announced.

Ky and Ja`el settled on hot dogs and soda before making their way to the seats. The band was already in the stands playing various songs to get the crowd riled up. Before making their way to their seats they made sure they walked past the band so Savoy would know they were there. When she spotted them she waved and blew them a kiss. Ky smiled seeing how beautiful she looked in her gold sequined dancer ensemble with the matching headband. They took their seats and finished their food and drinks before the starting kickoff.

"What's Patrick's number?" Dani asked.

"He's number eighty-five. He's a receiver."

"I should know that by now after all the games we've come to," Dani replied. "Come on, guys, let's take a picture."

Dani pulled out her phone and the cousins posed for a selfie so Dani could Instagram it. She took a few more pictures of herself before turning her attention back to the game.

The game was exciting from the very beginning. It wasn't long before it was halftime and time for Savoy to perform. She was as spectacular as expected. It warmed Ky's heart to see his sister do something that made her so happy. Her dance moves were provocative and sexy, yet skillful, and Savoy and the other dancers made it look easy. He was having a good time until he heard a couple of college guys yell out some explicit comments about Savoy and some of the other majorettes.

"Watch your mouth, bro. Savoy is my sister," Ky said as he turned around to look at the guy.

The second guy snickered and responded to Ky. "Don't pay him any attention. He's drunk."

The original guy who made the comment said, "I don't give a fuck who you are. She's a fine piece of ass, and I'm not going to stop saying it until I tap that."

Quicker than lightning, Ky stood and punched the guy in the mouth, knocking him over in his seat. Ja'el stood as well just in case the other guy decided to jump in.

"Bro, you really don't want to do this," Ja'el said. "You need to learn how to respect women. Savoy is this man's sister and my cousin. We don't play that."

People around the incident, especially the men who had heard what was said agreed with Ky and Ja'el and immediately stood in solidarity with them. Another man, who they later found out was one of the college's deans, motioned for campus policemen to intervene. When they came over they questioned Ky and witnesses to the incident. That's when the dean asked campus policemen to escort the troublemakers out of the bleachers and away from the area. As they were leaving, the fans in their section started applauding Ky and Ja`el for their chivalry and the dean's quick response.

Dani, who was sitting between Ky and Ja`el, said, "Damn, Ky. I thought you were going to kill that fool."

"I would do the same for you," he admitted as he calmly directed his attention back to the halftime show. "We're family and we stick together."

Ja'el laughed and said, "I thought you was having a flashback for a second. You use to get in a fight every other day either when we were in middle and high school either over Savoy or because someone was bullying you and calling you a half breed."

"Whatever, Ja'el," Ky replied as he took a bite of his food. "I'm not like that anymore."

"It's still in you though. I'll have to admit, it made you tough as hell and you put the fear of God in people," Ja'el pointed out and then laughed.

Once the game was over, Ky and his cousins were able to talk briefly with Patrick before he went to the locker room while Savoy and the band continued to perform in the stands. They watched for a while and knew that she wouldn't be able to join them until after she marched back to the music building and was dismissed.

"Let's go," Ky told his cousins. "We'll wait for her at the music building like we always do."

They waved to Savoy as they walked past the band and she nodded to let them know she understood. Fifteen minutes passed before the band finally made their way back to the music building. Once the band director dismissed them, Savoy ran full speed over to her family. She jumped into Ky's arms, hugged him, and then hugged her cousins.

"I didn't know you guys were coming," she said happily to her cousins. "Let's go get something to eat."

"Sure," Ky said with a huge smile on his face. "Text Patrick and see if he wants to come too."

"OK. Let me change and get my purse. I'll be right back. Dani, come with me. There are some people I want you to meet."

Dani followed Savoy into the building while Ja`el and Ky leaned against the car. As they waited, several females walked past them and made admiring comments.

Ja`el laughed. "I can't take you anywhere."

"Please! You're the one. You're closer to their age than I am."

He raised his arms and flexed his biceps. "They know fineness when they see it."

Ky laughed. "They're jail bait."

"Not all of them," Ja`el said before laughing.

The cousins were still laughing when Savoy and Dani returned. Savoy had put her university jogging suit on over her revealing uniform. Ja`el opened the car door for the young women and closed the door.

"Did you get in touch with Patrick?" Ky asked as he climbed in behind the steering wheel.

"Yes. He said he will meet us as soon as we decide where we're going."

"OK, where do you want to go?" Ky asked as he started the car.

"Uhhh, there's a place called Blaze a couple of miles from here. It's eclectic and has a variety of entrees. I think you'll like it."

"Sounds good. Let Patrick know."

Savoy sent a text to her boyfriend and it wasn't long before he joined them at the table to enjoy a delicious meal.

Toward the end of the meal Savoy asked, "Are you guys staying the night? There's a big party on campus tonight."

"Sorry, sis. We didn't come prepared for an overnight stay. Ja`el and Dani came with me last minute."

"All you have to do is go to the mall and pick up a change of clothes. You can stay and hang out with us."

Dani and Ja`el looked at Ky to make the final decision.

"Savoy, you know I'm not going to a college party. I don't want to ruin the trip for the rest of you if you want to go, so if you want to party, we can stay."

Savoy screamed with excitement and jumped out of her seat so she could hug her brother's neck.

"I love you, Ky. You know I don't get to see my family as much as I want to, so any time I can get you in town, I'm going to make the most of it. And because you guys are staying, we don't have to go party. How about we go do something fun like bowling?"

Patrick pumped his fist and said, "Yes! I would love to whip y'all's asses at bowling. I'm the bowling champ."

"I would like to see that," Ky joked with Patrick.

"Don't forget about me," Ja`el replied. "I'm better than all of y'all."

Ky motioned for the waitress to bring their check and then said, "Let us run to the mall and get a hotel room first. This will give you a chance to go back to campus and change."

Patrick stood. "I'll take her back to the dorm. How about we meet y'all at the bowling alley in a couple of hours?"

"Great! Savoy, bring an overnight bag if you want to stay at the hotel with Dani."

She nodded as she stood and took one last sip of her drink. Then gave them the name of the bowling alley.

"OK, I'll see you in a few," she said before walking out with Patrick.

Ja`el put cash on the table for the tip. "Ky I'll pay for my and Dani's hotel room."

"We can share rooms if you want," Ky replied.

Ja`el stood. "I'm sure you like your privacy just like I do. Besides, I might get lucky tonight."

"You wish!" Dani jokingly said to her brother.

Ky gave the waitress cash for their meals. "It's OK. I plan to put the rooms on my card anyway. I'm just happy you guys could come with me. I got everything this time. You can get it next time if you want."

Ja`el gave his cousin a brotherly handshake. "Thanks, bro, and, yes, I'll take care of everything next time."

The three cousins left together and headed out the door to begin their night of fun.

By the time everyone met up again, Patrick and Savoy had invited three more friends so they could play against each other as teams. They spent hours competing against each other. Everyone claimed to be the best bowler. The group had a great time and took a lot of pictures to document the night of fun. In the end, Patrick and one of his teammates were crowned the winners with Ky and Dani coming in second place. Savoy couldn't believe she lost. Growing up, she used to go bowling with her family and friends all the time. They were extremely competitive with each other, and Savoy always won, so she was taking this loss hard, but in a playful way.

Patrick looked at the time. "It's getting late, and we have a team meeting early in the morning. Ky, it was great seeing you again. I appreciate you guys coming to the game."

Ky gave Patrick a brotherly hug and then pulled him to the side. "Listen, Patrick, I appreciate you looking out for Savoy. All I'm going to ask is that you continue to respect her and not break her heart."

Patrick patted Ky on the shoulders. "I love Savoy. I could never hurt her. That you will never have to worry about."

"What are your plans for after graduation?" Ky asked.

"I hope to go right into a corporate position with the company I intern with if I don't get drafted."

"Well, whatever you do, make sure it's your passion and you love doing it. There's nothing better than making money doing what you love to do. I'm speaking from experience."

Patrick shook Ky's hand and hugged him. "I appreciate the advice. I guess I'll get out of here."

"OK, drive safely, and we'll see you next time."

"For sure," Patrick replied as he walked back over to the group.

Ky rejoined the group as well so they could return their bowling shoes and head back to the hotel. Ky watched his sister as she walked Patrick to the door. She gave him a loving hug and sensual kiss since she was going to be spending the night at the hotel with her family.

When she returned to the group, Dani looked at her. "Damn, Savoy. You kissed Patrick like you're grown."

"I am grown," Savoy replied as she sat down and removed her bowling shoes.

Ja'el laughed. "Neither one of you is grown, and you both better be taking care of yourselves. I don't want to see any babies until you're married."

"Whatever, Ja'el!" Dani replied with a laugh as she headed to the desk to return her shoes. The rest of the crew followed her so they could return their shoes, and then they climbed into Ky's car and headed to the hotel.

Back at the hotel they made their way to the hotel's bar where they ordered appetizers and drinks to cap off the night. After a couple of drinks Ky noticed Savoy was starting to get a little emotional.

"What's wrong with you?" he asked with concern.

With tears running down her face, she said, "Having you guys here is making me homesick. I don't want you to leave."

Dani looked over at Savoy and laughed.

"Ignore Savoy. She's drunk. She's just having a moment."

Ja'el started laughing as he took another sip of his beer. "Y'all funny as hell."

Ky hated to see his sister cry. He wasn't sure if it was the alcohol affecting her mood or if she was seriously having an emotional family moment.

"What's really going on with you, Savoy?"

With a frown on her face she said, "Can't I be emotional over my family? I love you guys and I am going to miss you when you leave."

Ky knew then that the alcohol was playing a huge role in his sister's emotional state.

"Sis, you need to ease up on the alcohol."

"I'm fine, big brother. Let me enjoy myself tonight," she said with an irritated tone. "I wish Patrick were here. He understands me."

Dani picked up a nacho chip, dipped it into some spinach dip, and said, "Here we go. First she's drunk and now she's horny."

"You can keep that thought to yourself," Ky said, who was starting to feel a little buzzed himself. "I don't want to sit here and think about Savoy and Patrick getting down or you either, Dani."

Savoy got out of her chair and twerked a little bit and said, "Yessss, baby."

Ja'el was laughing so hard he had to get up and go to the bathroom. Seeing Ky's reaction made Dani and Savoy laugh as well.

"Savoy!" Ky yelled. "Sit your ass down."

Dani and Savoy laughed and gave each other a high five.

"Ky, you're going to have to get over it. Savoy is screwing and from what she tells me, Patrick is putting it down correctly," Dani revealed.

"Y'all crazy," Ky said as he quickly got up and went over to the bar to get another drink.

The girls loved making their brothers uncomfortable when it came to their relationships and the last thing a brother wants to think about is his sister having sex.

Ja`el joined Ky at the bar. "You getting another drink?" he asked.

"Yeah, you want one?"

Ja`el nodded and gave the bartender his order. "Why are you looking so mad?"

"Savoy and Dani are still talking about their sex lives."

Ja`el laughed. "You're going to have to stop letting them know it gets to you. I hope you don't think they're virgins."

They got their drinks and Ky took a sip. "No, but damn! I don't want to hear about it."

"Me either, but the way I put a stop to Dani doing it is to ignore her. Speaking of getting some, have you had any tail since you and Yale broke up? You look like a man that could use some right about now."

Ky took another sip of his drink. "Don't you start. You know I don't talk about my sex life."

"I know, but you seem a little tense. Maybe you need a little something, something to take the edge off," Ja`el suggested.

They started walking back to the table. Ky took another sip. "I'm fine, cuz. Thanks anyway."

"If you say so," Ja`el replied as they sat back down with their sisters.

"What are you thanking Ja`el for?" Savoy asked.

"For riding up here," he lied. "Do you or Dani want anything else to eat or drink?"

"I'll take another margarita," Dani said. "Can we order another platter of spinach dip, chicken tenders, and cheese sticks?"

"Yeah," Ky answered as he motioned for the waitress. "What about you, sis?"

"I'll take another margarita too."

The young cousins spent another hour in the hotel bar laughing and talking before retiring to their rooms for the night. Ky entered his room and scanned through the pictures he had taken on his cell phone. He couldn't help but wish Reece had been able to make the trip with him. He believed she would've enjoyed herself and that Savoy and his cousins would love her. It was late and he thought about texting Reece, but the time was an hour later in D.C. She was constantly on his mind and he hoped the liquor in his system and a nice hot shower would help him finally go to sleep.

CHAPTER 9

Reece's visit with her parents was enjoyable. She attended church with them and then sat down to a fantastic dinner prepared by her mother. Gabriella and Alston joined them as well and after several hours of laughter and fun, Reece found it necessary to make the short drive to Baltimore to visit Geno's grave. This was something she wanted to do alone, but Alston insisted on accompanying her. He knew how devastated she was after his murder, and driving back to D.C. in an emotional state wasn't a chance he wanted her to take.

Before they hit the road, Reece and Alston stopped by her brownstone to check on it. Alston and their father often checked on Reece's place while she was out of town. When they arrived everything was just as she had left it, but it lacked that warmth she was used to.

"Is there anything you need to take back with you?" Alston asked.

She checked her closet. "No, I can't think of anything. You ready to go?"

Alston checked his watch. "Yeah, we better get going so we can get back before dark."

Reece looked over at a picture of her and Geno on her nightstand. "I miss him so much."

Alston hugged his sister. "I know you do. One day at a time. Remember?"

She nodded. "You would think this would've gotten easier by now."

He led her toward the door. "Don't force it, sis. It'll happen in its own time."

Reece set the alarm, locked her door, and climbed in the car next to her brother so they could hit the road. The ride to the cemetery was faster than normal. As they neared the location, Reece could hear her heart beating loudly in her chest. She clutched the flowers they'd picked up along the way. Once Alston parked, the pair walked through a few rows of tombstones until they came upon Geno's grave site. Reece froze. Seeing Geno's name engraved on the stone triggered a wave of emotion in her and it hit her extremely hard. Reece dropped to her knees and burst into tears as she called out Geno's name.

Alston's heart broke seeing his sister in such a raw, emotional state, but he knew it would happen. That was why he'd insisted on driving her. He wanted to give her a few minutes to release all the emotions she had built up inside before he approached her. Seeing her in this state was a prelude to what was to come at the parole hearing tomorrow. He just prayed she would be able to get through it. Reece placed the fresh flowers in the marble vase in front of the tombstone and then kissed it.

Before getting up she whispered, "I love you, Geno, and I miss you so much. I'm going to fight for you tomorrow. God give me strength."

Alston helped her to her feet and gave her a hug. He kissed her on the forehead and handed her some Kleenex.

"You did great, sis. I have no doubt that Geno is looking down on you smiling. He loved you, Reece, and he's going to be even more proud of you tomorrow."

She wiped the tears from her eyes. "Thanks. Can we go now?"

"Yeah, let's go. We have a big day ahead of us."

The brother and sister pulled out of the cemetery and hit the interstate back to D.C.

The room where the parole hearing was being held was cold like the proceedings were going to be. It was going to be nauseating to hear that murderer and his family plea for his release. She knew as a Christian it was wrong for not forgiving him or allowing him a second chance, but to be honest she didn't care that he was sick. In fact, she didn't care if he died behind bars. Geno didn't have a chance for life, so why should he? She was glad that man wasn't going to be in the same room and would only appear on closed circuit.

Accompanied by the prosecutor, Geno's parents entered the room and took their seats next to Alston and Reece. She found herself starting to get anxious. Alston could hear the changes in her breathing so he gave her hand a gentle squeeze hopefully to calm her down. Once the parole board was seated, the proceeding began. Reece hoped it wouldn't take long so she could get out of town and back to work. Working and her family had been her saving grace since losing Geno. As long as she was busy, she was able to cope with the loss, At that moment the prisoner's face appeared on the screen as one of the board members called the hearing into session.

After the hearing, Reece rushed out toward a garbage can and threw up. She had given the board a powerful speech on love, loss, and why Cecil Thomas did not deserve early parole. Prisons had medical care, and allowing him parole was insulting to her and Geno's entire family. Geno's parents also appealed to the parole board not to release him early. They spoke of Geno's bright future and pleaded that enough time had not passed for the murderer to be punished.

After their emotional pleas, the parole board had a brief discussion and then announced that the parole request was denied. Reece hugged Geno's parents before leaving the room. She didn't want to make eye contact with the prisoner's family members who had tried several times in the past to reach out to her. Each time she had ignored them.

As Reece leaned over the garbage can, Alston handed her his handkerchief. "Your speech was touching, sis. Geno would be proud. Are you OK?"

She wiped her mouth. "Not really, but I have no choice. I'm so glad they denied him parole. I pray the Lord has mercy on his sorry ass soul. Get me to the airport, Alston. I need to get out of here."

"Are you sure you're well enough to fly?"

"Yes. Just let me freshen up a minute before we leave. I can't be on the plane with stank breath."

Alston laughed. "That's my girl. Now I feel better about putting you on the plane. I'm going to miss you."

She hugged him. "I'm going to miss you too. Walk with me to the ladies' room if you don't mind."

Alston watched as Reece pulled a travel size bottle of mouthwash out of her purse and headed to the restroom. Two hours later, Reece was taking off down the runway heading back to the Gulf Coast.

Dozing off on a plane was normal for Reece. It had been an exhausting day and she was physically and emotionally drained. She woke up when the captain announced for passengers to put their tray tables up and make sure their seatbelts were fastened. As they were landing, Reece realized she had forgotten to text Ky to let him know she was boarding her flight. She couldn't worry about it now. If he weren't there she would catch an Uber like she'd originally planned. While she enjoyed seeing her family, the reason for the trip had her feeling a need to decompress.

It didn't take long for the plane to taxi around the runway and up to the terminal. She quickly exited the plane and made her way down the gateway toward the escalators. She only had one bag and she prayed hers would be one of the first to come around the turnstile. Her mind was thinking about a million things, but all of that ceased when she spotted a friendly face at the bottom of the escalator. Ky was standing there in a New York Mets baseball cap, orange polo shirt, and jean shorts. He waited for Reece to make her way over to him and when she did, he was shocked by what she did next. Without saying a word, or without any hesitation, she wrapped her arms around his waist, laid her head on his chest, and burst into tears.

Startled by her unexpected emotions, Ky slowly put his arms around her and asked, "Are you OK?"

"No," she said through her tears. "I feel like I'm about to lose it."

Not wanting to pry, he hugged her tightly and comforted her enough until she was able to calm down a little. He took her by the hand and said, "Let's get your luggage so I can get you out of here. OK?"

Reece nodded and did her best to wipe away her tears. She was embarrassed that she had caused a scene. As Ky stood in silence next to her he continued to hold her hand. She was absolutely gorgeous in her navy pantsuit, white blouse and matching navy heels. Her hair was pulled up, besides a few strands of wavy hair cascading around her face. A couple of minutes later her suitcase made its way around the turnstile and she pointed it out for Ky to grab.

"Ready?" he asked, still shaken by her tears.

"Yes," she whispered as she dabbed her eyes with a tissue she'd found in her purse.

The young couple quickly made it out to his truck where he opened the door for her and placed her suitcase on the back seat of the extended cab.

Once inside, Ky turned to Reece to see if he could get to the root of her tears.

"What's wrong, Reece? Did someone touch you or something on the plane, because if they did, point him out and I'll punch him in the damn throat," he said angrily.

She shook her head without speaking as tears started to form again in her eyes.

"Is your family OK?"

Without making eye contact with him she said, "My family is fine, and no one did anything to me on the plane. I'm just . . . I'm just . . ."

Ky could see she was struggling with whatever was troubling her, so he stepped up to try to make it more comfortable for her.

"I don't want to pressure you about it. Let's forget it for now and you can talk to me when you're ready. Are you hungry?"

"I don't know what I am right now. What I do know is that I don't want to be alone. Can you take me somewhere peaceful? I need to clear my head."

Ky took the tissue out of her hands and wiped the stream of tears off her face. He then turned on the ignition. "Sure. Buckle up."

He had no idea what was going on with Reece or what had happened in D.C., but whatever it was, it was serious, and she needed a friend. He was ready and willing to be whatever she needed him to be.

"Thank you," she whispered as he made his way out of the airport and onto the expressway. There were a few places he knew that he could take her to give her the peace she requested, but he decided to take her to his number one place for peace and quiet and it would only take him thirty minutes to get there. Reece was mostly quiet on the trip and stared out the passenger side window at the scenery. When she did speak, it was in a soft tone as she seemed to be getting her emotions under control.

"What's over there?" she asked as she pointed out the window at a large metal frame building sitting close to the water.

"That's a seafood company. The fishermen bring in their catch and sell it to the factory to be processed. Most restaurants around here get their seafood fresh from places like that. It's all USDA inspected of course."

"I would hope so," she replied.

"The food is safe. A lot of people who were raised on the water and in some of these bayous have always lived off the land and they live to be one-hundred-years-old or more. The problem with food comes with all the chemicals, pesticides and steroids, etcetera. Fresh and natural is the way to go."

"I agree."

Minutes later Ky turned into a long driveway that led up to a beautiful two-story Victorian house with a wraparound front porch. He pulled up to the front of the house and put the truck in park.

As Reece admired the home and the beautiful lake view, she asked, "Is this some type of bed and breakfast inn?"

He opened his door and climbed out. "No, it's my house."

"Your house?" she asked in amazement.

Ky pulled her suitcase off the backseat of his truck and walked around to open the door for her.

She took his hand as she slid out of the truck.

"Are you serious? This is your house?"

He closed the door. "Yes. Is it that hard to believe?"

"No. I just didn't expect a guy like you to live somewhere like this." she answered as they walked down the sidewalk and up the stairs to the porch.

He set down her suitcase before asking, "What kind of guy am I?"

She folded her arms. "I'm not trying to insult you, Ky. I just picture you living in a townhouse or a small house that would be low maintenance. This looks like a mansion."

He smiled as he stuck the key in the door. "I guess that's a compliment. I like nice things and I like to live comfortable with a lot of space. Now before I open this door, are you OK with dogs?"

"Why? Do you have a pack of dogs behind the door?"

"Just one very playful black lab named Samson. He's very friendly and highly trained. He's going to want to check you out. Are you going to be cool with that?"

"I think so," she replied in a slightly nervous tone.

Ky was anxious to see how Samson responded to Reece since he had hated Yale. He turned the key and said, "You two are going to love each other. Just relax. OK?"

She gently touched his arm and said, "I trust you. Go ahead."

Ky opened the door and found Samson standing in the entryway wagging his tail. He sat Reece's luggage down and began to pat his dog's head.

"Hey, boy, I have someone for you to meet. Now be on your best behavior because she's a very special friend of mine."

Reece smiled as Ky gave his beloved pet particular instructions. She walked over to the pair and said, "It's nice to meet you, Samson."

Samson turned his attention to Reece and raised his paw as if he was trying to shake her hand. She giggled and took his paw into her hand.

Ky took a step back and said, "He likes you."

She continued to pat him. "You're right. He's very well mannered."

"He has to be to live with me," he replied. "So, what would you like to do first? If you're hungry I can get dinner started."

"Can I please get something to drink first? I really need something to calm my nerves."

"Sure," he answered as he motioned for her to follow him.

As she followed him through the house she admired the décor, character, and beauty of his home.

"Ky, your house is stunning and this kitchen is to die for. Did you design it yourself?"

He opened his wine cooler. "Pretty much. It's a renovation. I fell in love with it the first time I saw it. I had to have it. The family who lived in it before me lived here fifty years and it was in their family for even longer. It's a well-built home."

Reece noticed Ky with the wine bottle. "Do you have something stronger than wine? I need a real drink."

"I'm scared of you," Ky joked as he put the wine back into the wine cooler. He turned back to her and asked, "What's your poison of choice? I have just about anything."

She sat in one of the chairs at the huge island and said, "Do you know how to mix drinks?"

"I do OK," he admitted. "If it's something I don't know, I can Google it."

"In that case I would like a Long Island Iced Tea if you don't mind," she requested.

He stared at her for a moment and then said, "You do know that a Long Island iced tea has five different liquors in it including gin and vodka?"

She stared right back at him and said, "Yes, and hurry up before I ask you to make it a double."

He laughed and shook his head in disbelief.

"Yes, ma'am. Coming right up!" he said as he washed his hands and exited the room.

Ky never met a woman who could drink that drink without it hitting them pretty hard. He realized then that he was in for an eventful evening. Hopefully the liquor would allow him to find out what had her in tears at the airport, but he would wait until she was relaxed and feeling the effects of the drink before bringing it up again.

He made his way downstairs into his game room where he had a fully stocked wet bar. He pulled a glass out of the cabinet and after mixing the alcohol, he poured the shaken mix into it. He took the drink back up to the kitchen and said, "Enjoy."

Reece immediately took a sip and said, "Perfect. Thank you, Ky. You're a great bartender. Where did you go to make it?"

He sat down across from her and said, "I have a bar in my entertainment room downstairs."

"You have an entertainment room?" she asked.

"It's just a place I hang out with friends and family," he revealed.

Samson was sitting next to Reece's chair and barked to get her attention.

She looked down at him. "You not getting enough attention, pretty boy?"

Ky threw the dishtowel over his shoulders and said, "If it's OK with you, I should probably go ahead and get dinner started. I'm going to grill a couple of steaks and corn on the cob, toss a salad, and make some baked potatoes. Is that all right?"

She stared at him with a smile on her face. "Who are you, Ky Parker?"

He laughed. "I'll tell you after your second drink."

She giggled and then took another sip of her drink. "Can I help you with anything, Chef Parker?"

He pulled the vegetables for the salad out of the refrigerator and said, "You sure can if you're up to it."

"I feel much better now. I don't mind helping."

Ky smiled. "In that case, you can make the salad and prep the corn and potatoes while I season the meat and get the grill set up."

She looked down at her clothes. "Is there somewhere I can change? I feel like I'm a little overdressed for the assignment."

"Sure," he said as he led her upstairs to a spare bedroom with Samson following close behind.

"Ky, I can't get over how beautiful your house is and that view of the lake is breathtaking. When I asked to go somewhere peaceful, I never expected it to be somewhere so beautiful."

"Thank you. I love it here. It's a nice place to come home to after a long day at work."

He placed her luggage next to the bed. "Make yourself at home. There's a bathroom right there and towels in the linen closet. If you need anything, just holler."

Ky walked toward the door and instructed Samson to come with him, but he lay down on the floor instead.

"Samson, come."

She laughed and took a sip of her drink. "It's OK. He can stay. It'll give us a chance to get to know each other."

"OK, see you downstairs in a second."

Reece quickly freshened up and changed into a pair of white shorts and a green, short-sleeved blouse. She swapped out her heels for some comfortable sandals. Before leaving the room she washed her face and reapplied her makeup since she had wrecked it earlier crying.

She then picked up her drink. "Samson, you ready to go?"

He stood and wagged his tail happily, and followed Reece out the door and back downstairs. When they returned to the kitchen, Ky was outside on the back patio preparing the grill.

Reece stepped onto the patio. "Oh my God, Ky! I had no idea you had all this in your backyard."

He took a sip of his beer. "Just another piece of my little heaven."

Reece gazed over the backyard at the in ground pool, hot tub, eating area, and full outdoor kitchen area. She also noticed a relaxing sitting area with a fireplace and an outdoor TV over the fireplace. The yard was huge and backed up to the lake. It had a boat dock and she noticed his boat in the boat lift.

She pointed towards the dock and said, "I see your boat."

"Yes, I take it to work sometimes when I don't feel like dealing with traffic. It takes less time than when I drive to work," he said as he glanced over at her empty glass. "I see you're ready for another drink."

She nodded. "Yes, but I want to get started on the side dishes first."

"I brought everything out here to make it more convenient. It shouldn't take long for everything to be ready. How do you like your steak?"

"Medium well," she answered as she rinsed the vegetables under the cool water.

He looked down at her curvy hips and athletic legs. "By the way, you look nice."

Reece began to cut the vegetables. "Thank you."

Ky could see that his houseguest was starting to loosen up a little. She was handling the Long Island iced tea very well, but by the time she finished her second drink, he would probably be able to ask her anything, and he knew she would answer. At that moment his phone rang. Reece watched as he glanced at the screen and hit ignore. Almost immediately it rang again.

"Maybe you should answer it," she suggested. "It might be important."

He frowned and said, "It's not. It's Yale. I don't know what it's going to take to make her understand it's over."

"I'm sorry, Ky. Maybe it would be best if I…"

He looked over at her and said, "Don't even go there. I'm not going to allow Yale to ruin our day."

Ky's phone rang again. He took a deep breath and said, "I'm sorry Reece but I need to handle this. Excuse me for a second."

"It's fine," she replied softly as she gathered some of the cookware and took it back inside the house to give Ky some privacy.

Ky answered his phone and walked further out into his yard towards the lake to put some distance between him and Reece because he knew he was about to go in on Yale for blowing up his phone.

"What in the hell do you want, Yale?"

"Stop ignoring me, Ky. Why wasn't you answering the fucking phone?" she asked angrily. "Are you with that bitch?"

"No. I broke up with that bitch over six months ago. Now, for the last time, stop calling me. Don't text me or show up at my job or house. If you keep this up, Yale, you're really going to get your feelings hurt."

"I hate you!" Yale yelled.

"Then stop calling me because the feeling is mutual. Good-bye," he replied before hanging up the phone.

Now he had to do some damage control and hope this fiasco didn't ruin his evening with Reece.

CHAPTER 10

Dinner was a big hit and Reece couldn't help but praise Ky on his culinary skills.

"These steaks are super tender and delicious, Ky. I don't know what you seasoned or marinated them in, but they're fabulous."

He stood, removed their empty plates, and took them into the kitchen. He returned to the table and said, "Family secret. I might reveal it if I can get you to smile more."

At that moment she gave him what he wanted and smiled. "I'll think about it."

Ky also smiled, showing off his sexy dimples again.

"OK, what would you like to do now? We can't go get your car because you've been drinking."

She leaned back in her chair and rubbed her stomach. "I'm not worried about getting my car. I'm so full. I don't even know if I can walk, but I would love a tour of this gorgeous house."

Ky held his hand out to her. "OK. The best way to get rid of that full feeling is to walk it off."

Reece put her hand into his. "Lead the way."

The couple walked together in silence for few seconds and then Reece asked, "Is everything OK with you? You seem different after that phone call."

Ky turned to her in the foyer and said, "I want to apologize to you for that. I honestly don't know what else to do to get my point across to her."

Reece could see that the phone call was causing her companion a lot of grief, now it was her turn to offer him some comfort.

She took his hand into hers and said, "Love is a powerful emotion, Ky. It's going to take her time."

"She's had plenty of time to get over it. Listen, I don't want to talk about Yale any more. Cool?"

Reece smiled and said, "Cool."

Ky started the tour in the foyer where he showed her his home office. Across from the home office was a formal dining area with a large dining table with seating for ten guests. The table was beautifully set and decorated in ivory and gold colors, which went well with his choice of place settings and stemware.

"What's down there?" Reece asked as she noticed a spiral staircase leading downstairs.

"Let's go check it out," he suggested proudly.

Downstairs Reece was in awe as they stepped into what looked like Ky's main area for entertaining. He revealed that it was one of the most expensive parts of the renovation because there wasn't anything originally down there but a dirt floor and rock walls, which was a typical basement for an older house like his. Now it was furnished with a full bar, pool table, poker table and large seating area with a gas fireplace and huge flat screen over the fireplace. There was also a half bath off the game room and a door leading outside and back up to the patio and pool area.

The couple made their way back upstairs where they ventured down the hallway toward the back of the house to Ky's bedroom. It had French doors leading out to a small balcony with a gulf view. It was perfect for sitting outside with a hot cup of coffee or evening cocktail. His bedroom and en suite was a combination of gray, white, and black with accents of teal and brushed silver fixtures. It had a large jetted soaker tub, double sinks, vanity area and a huge shower with rainforest showerheads and side jets. His gigantic walk in closet area was off the bedroom.

After viewing a small exercise room in the sunroom, they headed upstairs to tour the other bedrooms. One bedroom belonged to Savoy when she was home. She loved staying with Ky instead of at home because their father was overly protective. Ky wasn't a pushover. He could be hard on Savoy like a dad, but he understood her and their parents, so he was sort of a happy medium between the two.

"Your sister's bedroom is beautiful. I love the green with the subtle pink accents," she
stated. There were several stuffed frogs on the bed, which was covered with a beautiful pink comforter. She walked over to the dresser where several strands of white pearls hung off the mirror. Reece noticed a few pictures of Savoy in various sorority attire.

She picked up one to view it closer and started laughing. "Your sister is my soror."

"Is that right?" Ky asked as he watched Reece's face light up.

She turned to him. "Are you Greek too?"

He raised his shirt sleeve to reveal a rather elaborate Omega Psi Phi tattoo on his bicep.

Reece rolled her eyes playfully. "I would've thought you would've been a Nupe."

He walked closer to her and asked, "Why? Because I'm light skinned?"

She giggled. "That stereotype played out years ago."

He laughed as well. "I'll have to let Savoy know you guys are sorority sisters."

As they exited Savoy's room she asked, "What about your mom? Is she part of the pearls and ivy too?"

He nodded. "Yes, and so is my grandmother."

"Wow! That's a nice legacy. What about your dad?" she asked as they exited Savoy's room.

"Well, he's an Alpha man."

"Wow, y'all have a little bit of everything in your family."

"You could say that. What about your family? You have a brother, right?"

"Yes, he's a Kappa man like my dad, and my mother wears the pink and green too. Both my grandmothers pledged Delta and wore the crimson and cream though."

"That's cool," he replied.

They viewed two other beautifully decorated guest bedrooms and a nice sitting area for relaxing upstairs. Lastly they made their way back into the kitchen with the open concept overlooking the family room.

"I'm speechless, Ky. This is a dream home. My brother did the same thing with an older home in D.C. He renovated it and now it's valued at nearly three times what he paid for it," she revealed.

"The way I see it, that's the way to go. These older homes are better built than newer homes and they have so much more character. This house has handled all the major storms and floods. That was one of the priorities for me buying it so I had to make sure the shore elevation and storm wall were able to prevent a storm surge. I put a lot of money in it because I want it to be my forever home."

"Well, you did a great job. I'm really impressed. You refinished the original hardwood floors, there's crown molding, and so much more."

"I appreciate it," he replied. "Now, can I get you anything else?"

"You know, I think I would like a glass of wine now."

As he poured her a glass of wine, he said, "There's one more place I would like to show you if you're up for a short boat ride."

She raised her glass to him. "You're the tour guide. You lead and I will follow."

"OK, but I would feel better if you wore a life jacket," he announced.

"I have no problem wearing one, especially since I've had a couple of drinks."

Ky laughed. "A couple? Come on, let's go."

He set the alarm and locked the door, and then led her outside so he could check to make sure the gas grill was turned off. Samson followed the couple across the yard and onto the boat dock where he jumped in first. You could tell that he was used to taking boat rides with his owner. Ky helped Reece into the boat and into the lifejacket, and made sure she was seated before putting on his sunglasses and pulling the boat away from the dock. Once out on the water, he slowly increased the speed of the boat, but kept it to a comfortable speed for his guest. Fifteen minutes later, Ky pulled the boat into an inlet area with a boat dock. He helped Reece out of the boat and then pulled out a couple of chairs.

"Where are we?" she asked curiously.

Ky set up the chairs on the beach. "This is one of my favorite spots to come to and relax. I bring Samson here a lot and we take a swim and watch the fishermen and boaters. It takes me back to my childhood. A friend of mine owns this land. He lives on the other side of those trees. Sometimes we sit out here, make a fire in the pit, and just chill and drink a beer or two."

She sat in the chair. "Well it's definitely tranquil and beautiful with all the beautiful flowers and trees. Are there gators and snakes out here?"

"I've never seen any, but it is the gulf, so you can expect water snakes to possibly be around. The gators stick close to the canals and bayou area."

Samson barked, wanting Ky's attention to play catch. He found a stick and threw it down the beach. Samson took off after it and brought it back so he could throw it again.

Reece closed her eyes and laid her head back on the chair. "This breeze feels heavenly."

"Yes, it's always a nice breeze blowing through here. I hope I've been able to give you the peace you asked for today."

She reached over and placed her hand on his arm. "Yes, you have, and it couldn't have been more perfect. I guess I owe you some type of explanation for my psychotic outburst earlier at the airport."

"No, it's not necessary. I don't want you to feel pressured to divulge anything personal, but it hurt me to see you so upset. You don't have to talk about it if you don't want to, but I'm here for you if you want."

Reece took off her sandals, buried her feet in the cool sand, took a deep breath, and said, "I know, and I appreciate your friendship, but it might help me to talk about it. It's just so hard."

Ky became concerned and afraid that someone had taken advantage of her in the past, but he held his composure.

"I can see it in your eyes, Reece, and hear it in your voice. Just follow your heart and do what you're comfortable doing. Purging your heart and mind over it might help you feel better."

Reece took another deep breath. "Maybe you're right. I'm holding so much emotion inside and that's probably why I can't seem to let go and be happy, and I want to be happy so bad."

Ky put his hand on top of hers. "At some point you're going to have to release whatever it is so you can come to terms with it and start healing."

Tears fell out of her eyes and she whispered, "You're so right. I can't keep going on like this."

Ky sat silently while waiting for her to open up. She began by telling him she was engaged. Hearing those words completely blew him out of the water. Reece saw the shock on Ky's face and quickly corrected her statement.

She waved him off. "No, wait a second. I didn't say that right. I was engaged about six years ago. A few weeks before our wedding, my fiancée was shot and killed in a case of mistaken identity. I had to go back to D.C. this weekend because that bastard who murdered him was up for parole. I went home to fight for justice for Geno and to honor his memory. He was a good man with a bright future ahead of him, and I loved him with all my heart."

"Wow, that's horrible," Ky said. "I'm so sorry."

"That's why I was so upset when I got off the plane. I was emotionally drained."

"I'm sure you were. That would affect anybody that way."

"So, since that horrible day, it's been hard for me to get close to anyone because I can't go through that kind of pain again."

Ky stood and pulled Reece out of the chair and into a warm embrace.

"It's hard getting over a tragedy. Losing someone you love so suddenly is devastating, so it's normal for you to be cautious. Sometimes it takes a long time to move on with your life. I want you to know that I'm here for you if or when you need someone to talk to. I really like you . . . a lot, and I have to admit that I am also very attracted to you. Over the past few weeks, it has taken every restraint I own not to kiss you."

Without responding she reached up, cupped his face, and gave him a sweet and tender kiss on the lips. After releasing him she whispered, "Thank you. I needed to hear everything you've said to me today. I like you a lot too, but I don't want to come off weak or vulnerable."

He held Reece's hands in his and kissed them.

"I don't see you as anything but a beautiful, loving, friendly, intelligent, and amazing woman. Let's take this one day at a time and don't give it another thought. I appreciate you sharing something so personal and painful with me. I hope in some way I have made dealing with it a little easier."

She hugged his neck. "More than you know. Thank you."

He kissed her forehead. "You're welcome. Let's get the chairs and head back. We can watch the sunset from the patio unless you want me to take you back to your hotel. You're more than welcome to stay the night in the spare bedroom upstairs. I would love the company."

"I really don't feel like being alone tonight," she said as they walked across the beach together. "I would love to stay. Thanks for inviting me."

"Great," he replied as he climbed into the boat and then helped her climb in beside him. He whistled for Samson to jump into the boat so he could get everyone situated before he pulled off.

Once they were seated, he asked, "Ready?"

Reece buckled her life jacket and held onto Samson. "We're ready."

Once back at the house, Reece helped Ky secure the boat and they made their way back to the patio where Ky turned on the gas fireplace, poured two more glasses of wine, and each settled into their individual chaise. With Samson by their side, they relaxed and watched the orange and yellow glow of the sun set over the gulf while listening to the sound of one of Ky's soothing vinyl records. It wasn't long before he noticed Reece had dozed off. Her drinks and the long day had finally caught up with her. He turned off the fireplace and gently woke her so she could go to bed. She apologized for falling asleep on him and offered to help him clean up the kitchen.

"No, I got it. You're my house guest. You've had a long day. Go on up and get ready for bed. I'll check in on you before I turn in."

She kissed him lovingly on the cheek. "Thank you so much."

"You're welcome."

As Reece started toward the stairs, Samson followed right behind her. Ky called for him to come back. He didn't want his dog to be a nuisance to her, even though they were getting along very well.

Halfway up the stairs, she said, "It's OK. He can come. I'm going to soak in that huge claw foot tub and if I go under, he can save me."

With a worried expression on his face, he said, "Now you have me worried about you. Seriously, be careful."

She giggled. "I'm just joking. I promise I won't drown."

"You better not."

Ky was actually happy that Samson was going to be with her, because if something did happen, the dog was smart enough to come get Ky.

Fifteen minutes later, Ky had finished cleaning up the kitchen and then decided to make his way upstairs to check on his gorgeous house guest. He knocked on the bedroom door and waited for her to answer.

"Come in," she yelled from the bathroom.

When he opened the bedroom door, Samson was the one who greeted him.

"Is everything OK in here?" he asked as he rubbed his dog's head.

"Yes, I'm fine, and before I forget, I wanted to let you know I had a wonderful time today. It changed what started out as a somber day."

He smiled as he stood in the middle of the bedroom to make sure he didn't invade her privacy. He could only imagine what she looked like with her smooth, brown skin surrounded by all the suds, and the thought slightly aroused him.

"What time do you have to get up for work?" he asked.

"I called and told them I needed an extra day to finish up some family business, so I'm actually free tomorrow. You can drop me off at my hotel on your way in if it's not inconvenient."

Ky decided to go out on a limb and do something he normally wouldn't do. There was something about Reece that made him open up a part of his life he often kept guarded.

"No, it wouldn't be inconvenient. Listen, Reece, I'm sure your hotel is comfortable on a temporary basis, but I have plenty of room here. You're welcome to stay as long as you're in town if you're cool with it. I know your Realtor hasn't found you a place yet, and I would love the company, and so would Samson."

Ky's words rolled off his tongue and out of his mouth as if he had no control over his thoughts. Seconds later, Reece appeared in the doorway barely wrapped in a towel with suds running down her legs. Now he was completely aroused.

"Jesus give me strength," he mumbled under his breath.

Her expression was unreadable as she stared at Ky as if she were searching for his sincerity. As she looked at him she gazed at his sexy lips, unbelievable body, and intense green eyes, and smiled.

"It's a generous offer, but I would never impose on you like that. I'm sure my Realtor will come up with something soon."

He took a couple of steps toward her. "It's been weeks, and your Realtor hasn't found anything yet. The real estate market is tough right now. I'm inviting you, so there's no imposition to consider. I promise, I'll be a perfect gentleman. Let me make your stay comfortable while you're in town."

She took a deep breath. "It's a really sweet offer. Can I sleep on it?"

Staring into her beautiful, brown eyes, he said, "Sure you can. No pressure, remember?"

"No pressure," she repeated with a smile. "Now get out of here so I can finish my bath."

He chuckled. "Do you want me to take Samson out with me?"

As she walked toward him, she answered, "No, he can stay if he wants to stay. I'll call you when or if I want him to leave. He's so adorable and we're having a nice conversation."

He turned to walk out of the room. "Looks like you've won Samson's heart."

"And he's won mine," she replied. "You can leave the door cracked.

Ky politely left the door cracked, feeling very good about his conversation with Reece. He was a little shaken seeing her wrapped only in a towel, and now he needed to get his body under control. He would be lying if he didn't wish her towel had accidentally fallen on the floor. It didn't take much imagination to know what was underneath. He just prayed she would take him up on his offer so he could help her find happiness. As he made his way downstairs to his bedroom he knew his dreams would consist of her and the tender kiss they'd shared on the beach a few hours earlier.

CHAPTER 11

Reece lay in bed and stared at the ceiling, overwhelmed by the events of the day. To hear the voice of the man who had killed her fiancé sickened her, and it took her back to a time when she had a hard time functioning on a daily basis. She was emotionally drained by the time she saw Ky, but she was thankful to have the day softened by his kind words and gestures.

Now she had a dilemma on her hands. Ky's offer to stay with him was very kind, but he was still somewhat of a stranger to her. If she accepted his offer, she had a good idea what her brother would say about it. Maybe this would be the perfect time for Alston to fly down to meet Ky and help her make a reasonable decision. She looked at the clock and realized it was too late to call him, but it would be her first call in the morning.

The next morning, Ky woke up to a wonderful aroma coming from the kitchen. He showered, got dressed, and when he entered the kitchen he found Reece sitting at the island reading the newspaper with Samson by her side.

"Good morning." She greeted him as she put down her coffee cup.

"Good morning," he replied as he poured himself a cup of coffee. "You're up early."

"I couldn't help it. I'm an early bird. I hope you don't mind that I went ahead and raided your fridge to cook a little breakfast?"

He stirred his coffee and was surprised to see that she had cut fresh fruit and made pancakes, scrambled eggs, and turkey sausage links.

"No, it's fine. I want you to make yourself at home. Everything looks delicious," he said as he picked up a plate and started scooping the food onto it.

"I appreciate that. You have a lot of healthy and fresh food in your fridge."

He sat across from her, and after blessing his food he said, "I try to eat healthy most of the time. Are you feeling better today?"

"Somewhat. I still have a lot on my mind, but this too shall pass," she said as she put more fruit on her plate.

He nodded. "So have you made a decision about my offer?"

She stuck her fork into a piece of cantaloupe. "It's not an easy decision. I'm actually still thinking about it. I want to see if I can find my own place first. If I'm unsuccessful, I might have to consider it."

"I understand. Take your time. Just know that my door is open."

She smiled. "Thanks. Well I guess I'd better go get my things together. I don't want to hold you up from work."

"Take your time. I'm the boss, remember?"

She giggled and made her way upstairs to get her belongings while Ky finished his breakfast, cleaned up the kitchen, and prepared for work.

The ride into town was pleasant. After Ky dropped off Reece at her office parking garage to get her car, she decided to drive around town to see if she could find her own place to rent. Ky's offer was tempting, but she needed her own space to keep her mind clear and focused. Two hours in, she found a small, gated house on the edge of town in the garden district that had mature trees, beautiful flowers, and a porch perfect for sipping iced tea in the evenings. She nearly overlooked the FOR RENT sign behind the foliage on the gate. Her first impression was that it was warm and she could see that whoever lived there took great care of it. It wasn't far from her office, which was an added bonus. Reece climbed out of her car and saw an older lady sitting out on the manicured lawn with a small white poodle at her feet. The dog immediately began barking.

"Excuse me, ma'am. I noticed you have a for rent sign on your gate. Are you renting individual rooms or the entire house?"

The elderly lady looked at Reece over her glasses. "I'm renting the house, child. Are you interested? I just put up the sign yesterday."

Reece entered the gate and admired the well-kept exterior of the white cottage style house with coral trim. "Yes, I'm very interested. My name is Reece Miller and I love the exterior of your home. Is it possible that I could get a tour of the inside?"

The heavy set lady used her cane to help her climb out of her chair. She seemed to be having issues with her hips or knees and experiencing some slight discomfort.

"Sure. By the way, I'm Elsie Doucet."

Reece shook her hand as she followed her up the stairs to the front porch. After a short tour, Reece knew the house was perfect for her stay and after a brief discussion, the ladies finally agreed upon a figure.

Excited, Reece shook Ms. Doucet's hand. "Thank you so much. I will take real good care of your home."

"I know you will. Now how soon do you need to move in? I'm not leaving for California until next week. Does that give you enough time?"

"Yes, ma'am," Reece replied as she stood. "I really appreciate it."

"I'll have my attorney draw up a simple lease agreement and we'll go from there," Ms. Doucet said as she stood. "Give my assistant, Lyla your telephone number and make sure she gives you mine. We'll contact you when the papers are ready and I can give you the key."

Reece held out her hand. "Thank you again, Ms. Doucet."

She shook Reece's hand and said, "No, thank you, and good luck with your work here."

Lyla walked in and handed Reece Ms. Doucet's business card. Reece pulled out her business card and handed it to Lyla.

"Have a great afternoon," Reece said as Lyla walked her to the door.

Inside the car, Reece clapped her hands with excitement. She picked up her cell phone and sent Ky a text to let him know she had found a place to rent. Even though Ky had offered her a place to stay, she realized she needed a neutral space to which she could retreat. Being around a man as sexy as he was on a regular basis might become too much for her and cause her not to think clearly.

She started her car, but before she pulled off Ky texted back congratulating her. He also told her he was having game night at his house Friday night with some friends and family, and she was invited. He wrote that he would call her when he got off work with the details. Reece sent him a smiley face emoticon and then headed back to the hotel so she could relax for the rest of the afternoon. Just when Reece didn't think her day could get any better, she received a telephone call that Cecil Thomas wouldn't be able to have another parole hearing for another six years, if he lived that long. That news removed a huge weight off her shoulders and allowed her to actually breathe again.

Yale's desk was covered in paperwork. She had buried herself in her work since her altercation with Ky. She still couldn't believe that he didn't want anything else to do with her after all the good times they'd had. She was still madly in love with him, and she just didn't know how she was going to be able to move on. He was a good man, and while she finally admitted to herself that she'd crossed some boundaries in their relationship, Ky had to know her intentions came from love and nothing else. Women often called her a gold digger, and while Ky was a wealthy man, she wasn't with him because of his money. Well, at least not entirely. She was a woman who loved the finer things in life, and while her salary was sufficient, it was nothing compared to Ky's net worth. While they were together, he didn't live an extravagant lifestyle, but he liked nice things, and often shared those things with her. She missed him terribly, and while getting a man had never been a problem for her, she wanted Ky. None of the men she had dated since their breakup had measured up to Ky, and never would.

As she twirled around in her chair, a light bulb finally went off. First thing she had to do was size up the competition, and then eliminate her. That part should be easy if she could track her down. Now was the time when she could put her investigative reporting skills to work. She needed that woman's name and place of employment to put her plan in motion. Unfortunately, Ky was the only person she could get that information from, and there was no way he would release that type of information about the new woman in his life. The good thing was that she knew his schedule, habits, and routines, which would make it easy for her to follow him.

Yale's devious thoughts were interrupted when a coworker came over to her desk and requested some information. She quickly turned to her computer, put the finishing touches on her assignment, and printed it. She eagerly anticipated getting off work so she could change into some casual clothes to put her plan in motion and even though Anniston thought she should forget about Ky, she knew she would be down for whatever. But getting back in Ky's life was her priority, no matter what.

By the time Ky got home from work, he was exhausted. He had worked most of the day in the warehouse with his crew. The Lanbeaus' yacht was close to completion and he should be able to take it out for a test drive in a week or two. Tonight he barely had enough energy to heat up the chicken casserole his grandmother had made for him. Her casseroles came in handy on nights when he was too tired to cook. She often made dishes for him and placed them in his refrigerator because she knew he worked long, hard hours. She had a key to his house and often dropped by to leave a cake, cookies, or some type of treat, but she knew to always call first. It was a humid night and what he really wanted to do was go for a swim but tonight he might have to pass. As he sat at the island eating his dinner and watching ESPN, his phone rang.

"Hello?"

"Ky, it's Reece. Are you busy?"

He smiled. "No, just eating a little dinner. I just got in from work."

"Oh, I'm sorry. I know you're probably tired. I won't hold you."

"I'm OK. In fact I was getting ready to go for a swim to unwind. You're welcome to come join me if you like," he said in a sultry tone of voice.

The seductive tone in Ky's voice gave her goose bumps. She knew if she went over to his house there was no telling what would happen, and she didn't know if she was ready. Being in close proximity to him made her feel susceptible to his strong sex appeal. Not that it was a bad thing.

"It sounds nice, but can I have a rain check? It's getting late and we both have to work in the morning."

"I know it's getting late, but I never let that stop me from having a little fun."

"I know, but I would be up late doing my hair."

He chuckled. "I understand. What about Saturday then? I don't have plans, and since we're having game night Friday, you can just stay over. We can hang out and I would love for you to go to church with me Sunday morning."

She bit down on her lower lip and realized life was too short and asked "Are you asking me to stay the whole weekend?"

"I am, but you don't have to if you don't want to."

"I would love to stay, Ky."

She had realized that since losing Geno. If she was going to allow herself to ever be happy again, she had to establish friendships first, and Ky was turning out to be a wonderful friend.

"So who's going to be at this game night?" she asked curiously.

"Just a few friends and family. It'll probably be about twenty to thirty people. We do this at least once a month. My cousins will be there, some friends I grew up with, and a couple of frat brothers. That's all. My game nights are infamous. You'll see."

She smiled. "OK, it sounds like a lot of fun. What do I need to bring?"

"Nothing. You're exempt this time since this is your first time. You'll be there as my guest."

"In that case, count me in," she answered happily. "What time should I arrive?"

"We usually get started around six, but if you want to come early, you can. Just don't forget to bring enough clothes for the weekend, and a swimsuit. You're going to have fun. The people at game nights are pretty competitive, so bring your A game."

"What types of games do you all play?"

"Spades, dominos, pool, darts, poker—you name it and we play it."

"Wow, you do go all out. Get some rest, Ky, and I guess I'll see you Friday."

"I can't wait, and I would like to see your new place if you don't mind."

"I'm sure Ms. Doucet wouldn't mind. I'll call her ahead of time to make sure it's OK."

"Wait. Are you talking about Ms. Elsie who lives at the edge of downtown?"

"Yes."

Ky laughed. "That's one of my grandmother's best friends. She's a feisty old lady, isn't she?"

"That she is. She was nice, but about business though."

"Reece, Ms. Elsie is a millionaire a few times over. She and her husband made millions from the real estate market, and she's a legendary attorney."

"Wow! I could tell she was educated and very refined," Reece revealed. "I'll give her a call in a few days."

"Sounds good. Well have a good night, Reece, and I'll see you Friday."

"You too. Good night."

Ky hung up the telephone and felt in his heart that this weekend was going to define their relationship. It was his prayer that he could make her his woman once and for all.

CHAPTER 12

Over the next couple of days Reece was extremely busy with meetings and conference calls with her D.C. office. She was so busy she barely had time for lunch. When Friday arrived, she was anxious to get her weekend started. Just as she was about to leave the office, her cell phone rang, stopping her in her tracks.

"Hello?" she answered.

"Reece Miller, this is Elsie Doucet calling you regarding the lease agreement on my house."

"Yes, Ms. Doucet. It's so nice to hear from you."

"Likewise, young lady. Listen, my attorney has drawn up the lease agreement and I was calling to see when you would like to come by to go over it?"

"Well, I have plans tonight, but if tomorrow is convenient, I can come by then."

"I usually don't conduct business on the weekend, but I can make an exception since I called you so late."

"Ms. Doucet, I don't want to disturb you on the weekend, so if Monday works better for you, I can come by on my lunch break or when I get off work," Reece offered.

"No, tomorrow is fine. Will one o'clock work for you?"

"Yes, ma'am. Also, do you mind if I bring a friend along? He wants to see where I'm going to be staying."

"I guess it's OK. I'll see you tomorrow at one o'clock. Have a nice evening, Reece."

"And you do the same."

Reece hung up the telephone, told her staff to have a nice weekend, and headed out to her car.

It took Reece about twenty minutes to get to Ky's house. She pulled up to the garage, and to her surprise, the door started opening. Ky was dressed in one of his purple and gold fraternity T-shirts and khaki cargo shorts. He walked out of the garage with Samson right behind him. He made his way over to her car with a huge smile on his face.

She rolled down the window. "Hey, Que Dog. Am I too early?"

He stared at her with those mesmerizing green eyes and laughed. "No, you're right on time. I opened the garage so you could pull your car inside since you're going to be here for the weekend."

"OK, thanks," she said as she slowly pulled into the three car garage next to his two vehicles.

Ky met her at her vehicle. "What can I take in for you?"

She popped the hatch on her vehicle and said, "I have a suitcase and garment bag in the back."

She got out of the vehicle and Samson went wild jumping and barking with excitement. He was anxious for her to play with him.

Reece patted him on the head. "Let me get out of these heels first, pretty boy." She wore a red suit with a short skirt, exposing her muscular legs, and Ky couldn't help but stare at them. He couldn't let his imagination get too far away from him because it would cause him to get aroused.

Ky closed the hatch on her vehicle. "You have spoiled my dog."

She giggled. "I can't help it."

They walked toward the door to the kitchen and pushed the switch to close the garage. In the kitchen Reece set a bottle of wine on the counter. She noticed that Ky had a lot going on and several food items already prepped.

"Oh wow! You've been busy. Let me change so I can help. Do you want me to stay in the same room I stayed in last time?"

He wanted to tell her to put her belongings in his bedroom, but he would have to control his urges for now.

He opened the wine cooler to put up the bottle of wine and said, "Sure, that's fine. We have about an hour or so before people get here."

"I'm a little nervous about meeting your friends," she said before turning to walk out of the kitchen.

Ky took the suitcase out of her hand and they headed toward the stairs. He admired the sexy view as she walked up the stairs ahead of him.

"They're going to love you. You have nothing to worry about. Believe me when I say they're going to treat you like they have known you for years."

Walking into the bedroom upstairs she said, "If you say so. I trust you."

He set down her suitcase and said, "I'm starting to like the sound of that."

"What?" she asked curiously as she took off her blazer.

With a serious expression on his face he revealed, "This is the second time you've told me you trusted me. I'm glad you feel that way, because it's true. You can trust me."

"Wow!" she responded. "You must really pay attention to what I say, because I don't remember saying it."

"I pay attention to everything about you," he said before walking toward the doorway. He stopped and then turned back. "Before I go, is there anything you need me to unzip or unbutton?"

Reece giggled. "You're such a flirt."

"I know," he said before winking at her and closing the door behind him.

He returned to the kitchen and put on one of his favorite Earth, Wind and Fire albums. Upstairs, Reece quickly showered and changed into a teal maxi skirt with a matching crop top. She loved the way her outfit showcased her toned abs and curvy backside.

When she walked into the kitchen, Ky looked over at her and yelled, "Damn!"

His outburst startled her and made her freeze in her tracks.

"What's wrong?" she asked curiously, not realizing he was directing his excitement toward her.

He set down the spatula, wiped his hands on the kitchen towel, and said, "Nothing's wrong. I didn't mean to startle you. You look amazing. God's going to have to give me the strength to behave tonight."

She blushed. "If you think it's too much, I can change."

His gaze moved slowly over her beautiful body. "You don't need to change a thing. I just hope I don't have to punch anyone in the mouth for staring at you too hard. You look absolutely stunning."

"Thank you," she replied softly, blushing as she looked up into his sultry emerald eyes. She realized she needed to change the subject because she felt herself getting lost in his eyes.

"I love the music. They're one of my favorite groups."

"Mine too," he answered.

He felt himself losing the battle to keep his hands off her and he couldn't take it anymore, so he decided to go ahead and act on his urges. He walked over to her, pulled her into his arms, and kissed her firmly on the lips. Reece melted in his arms and savored his hot, sultry kiss. He held her tighter against his body and deepened the kiss as their tongues intertwined. Reece felt her lower body starting to throb. Being in Ky's arms felt heavenly, and it wasn't until Samson barked that they finally broke apart.

"I guess Samson doesn't like me kissing you," he pointed out. He kissed her on the curve of her neck and whispered, "I've been wanting to do that ever since the first day I met you, and it was everything I thought it would be and more."

Reece was shaken and somewhat out of breath when she stepped out of his embrace.

"It's not our first kiss. I kissed you on the beach, remember?"

He picked up the spatula and scooped the rest of the shrimp out of the skillet. "I remember. It was sweet, but I wanted to kiss you my way. Now that I have, I guess you can say I'm still a little thirsty. I'll try to restrain myself, but I can't wait to do it again."

She blushed. "I'm flattered and I enjoyed it as well, but I still want to take baby steps."

He handed her an apron. "I can respect that, but at some point you have to love past the moment."

She tied her apron and let his words sink in. *Love past the moment.* She'd never thought about it that way. Maybe he was right. Maybe instead of being so cautious she should throw caution to the wind and let life happen.

"That's an interesting sentiment," she pointed out.

"I think it's fitting under the circumstances," he replied.

She stared at Ky and realized he wasn't the typical man. Yes, he was handsome and fine, but he was also intelligent, patient, respectful, loving, and God fearing.

Ky hoped Reece would take heed to his advice. He wanted to tell her that he would do everything within his power to help her get past her tragedy. He decided to let his actions speak louder than words. He couldn't wait for another chance to chip away at her protective wall.

Once her apron was on, she asked, "So what do you need me to do? Everything already smells so delicious."

He pointed at the long loaves of French bread on the counter and said, "I'm making mini size shrimp po' boy sandwiches, so if you can put the sauce on the bread, and then the lettuce and tomatoes, I would appreciate it."

Reece got busy on the sandwiches while Ky switched gears and started working on a spicy artichoke and seafood dip to go with crackers. He'd already finished making a platter of honey BBQ wings, potato salad, and a vegetable platter. Last on his list was making fried pickles with a dipping sauce and placing a couple of pecan pies in the oven that his grandmother had made for him.

Once Reece had the lettuce and tomatoes on the bread, she asked, "What's next, chef?"

He inspected her work with a smile. "Just start piling on the shrimp."

"I had no idea you were this good in the kitchen. Where did you learn to cook like this?"

He washed his hands before replying. "My grandmother showed me most of the cooking. My mom was always so busy with church activities. I actually enjoy it."

"That's great."

At that moment, the doorbell rang. Ky wiped his hands. "That's probably my cousin, Ja`el. I'll be right back."

Seconds later, Ja`el and Ky returned to the kitchen. Ja`el set two large bags on the island.

He walked over to Reece and held out his hand. "Cuz, who is this gorgeous lady?"

Ky started pulling the beer, sodas, and liquor bottles out of the bags and said, "Reece, this is my cousin, Ja`el. Ja`el, this is a very special friend of mine, Reece Miller."

Ja`el shook Reece's hand and said, "It's so nice to meet you."

"It's nice to meet you too."

Ja`el stared at Reece. "I've never seen you around town. Are you new to the area?"

She nodded. "Yes, I'm in town for a few months on business."

Ja`el leaned against the island where Reece was working on the sandwiches. "Great. So are you seeing anyone? You are absolutely beautiful."

"Thank you," Reece responded as she blushed.

Ky intervened with a frown on his face. "Back the hell up, Ja`el. She's *my* guest."

His cousin put his hands up in surrender and laughed.

"My bad, cuz. I was just asking."

Ky pointed to hallway. "Well ask your ass downstairs to the rec room and make sure everything is set up."

Reece was amused at Ky's response to his cousin. While she knew he was somewhat joking with him, she felt he was also letting him know she was hands off.

Before leaving the room Ja`el leaned in closer. "I'm bartending tonight, so let me know what your favorite drink is and I'll hook it up."

With a smile on her face she answered, "Well, I like several, but I'm partial to margaritas."

"I thought Long Island teas were your favorite," Ky said.

"It's my go to drink when I'm stressed. I like apple martinis too."

Ja`el put all the liquors back in the bag and said, "Don't worry. I got you. In fact I'll make you a margarita right now."

"That sounds wonderful. It'll help calm my nerves."

"Why are you nervous?" Ja`el asked curiously as he picked up the bags.

She hesitated and then said, "I'm a little nervous about meeting all of Ky's friends."

With a huge smile on his face, he said, "You have no reason to be nervous. I like you and we just met. Relax, and I'll go make your drink."

With Ja`el out of the room she turned to Ky and said, "He's nice."

"Yeah, we're very close. We're first cousins. Our fathers are brothers. I'm sorry about him questioning you like that."

"It was no big deal. I get asked if I'm dating someone a lot. He didn't mean anything by it. Now, how do you like my sandwich?"

Ky looked at the sandwich and said, "Perfect. Now make about three more and we'll be set." He pulled a large square platter from under the cabinet and placed it on the countertop. "Go ahead and cut them in about four inch squares and place them on the platter. There should be enough to fill up the platter."

Reece cut the sandwich into the small sections and then started making more. They had all the food prepared and staged just as the doorbell rang again, signaling more guests had arrived.

Game night was a big hit as usual, and Ky was right about his friends and family. They did make her feel like they had known her for years, especially his cousin Danielle, who brought her boyfriend, Isaac. There was a good mix of both women and men, and Ky made sure Reece got the chance to meet everyone.

After sitting and talking for several minutes, Reece found out that Danielle, whom they called Dani, was a hair stylist and owned her own salon. The salon was her business that she'd started with the help of her father and former owner of the yacht building company. Dani had established a successful beauty salon business and clientele at a very young age. She asked Reece to let her be her stylist while she was in town. She also found out that Dani was Ja'el's sister, and Ja'el was a paramedic. They were extremely close to Ky and his sister Savoy, whom she still hadn't had the chance to meet. She would be meeting his parents and grandmother at church on Sunday. She was more nervous about that meeting than anything else.

Dani excused herself from Reece to get another drink. When she walked over to the bar area, she motioned for her brother to come over.

"Ja'el, do you know anything about Ky's friend, Reece?" she asked.

He poured his sister another drink. "I just met her tonight. He said they were friends, but I don't know how they met or how long he's known her."

"She's pretty," Dani said as she looked at Reece from across the room. "She seems nice too. A lot nicer than that other thang he was wasting his time with."

Ja'el laughed. "Her name is Yale."

"Whatever!" Dani said in an agitated tone. "I came close to bitch smacking her several times. I'm so glad he kicked her to the curb."

Ja`el glanced over in Reece's direction. "Well, I can tell he really likes this one. He got a little agitated with me earlier when I was flirting with her."

Before walking away, Dani said, "I guess we'll get the scoop eventually, but I'm going to see if I can get the info out of her. You know Ky's so secretive when it comes to his relationships. Thanks for the drink."

Just as Dani made her way back over to Reece and sat down, she asked, "So how did you and Ky meet?"

Reece took a sip of her second margarita, but before she could answer, one of Ky's frat brothers interrupted them for a dance. He took Reece by the hand and pulled her out of her seat. She set down her drink and followed the young man out onto the floor to dance alongside a few other guests. Dani also joined them as Ky and a few others guests watched. Ky could see that Reece was having a great time by the way she was laughing. By the time the song ended the dancers were winded. Reece fanned herself as she made her way back over to her drink.

Ky approached her, took her by the hand, and said, "Come take a walk with me. You look like you could use some fresh air."

"Yes, I could," she answered breathlessly.

He held her hand as they walked out the back door and up to the pool deck.

"That was fun," Reece said as they walked across the yard and down toward the lake.

"I'm glad you're having a good time. I told you that you would."

The couple came to a stop several yards from the water's edge and gazed out onto the water where the moon was shining off the surface. Reece felt very relaxed from the drinks she had consumed. There was a slight breeze in the air and it cooled the sweat she had produced dancing.

Ky wrapped his muscular arms around her and hugged her waist. Reece caressed his arms. "I love it here," she said.

He saw how relaxed and content she was in his arms and it made his heart thump hard in his chest. Having her body against his felt wonderful and natural. He kissed her shoulder and then her neck in a spot that caused her to let out a soft moan. The sensations rushing through her body felt incredible. She turned around in his arms, and when she looked up into his eyes he slowly leaned down and kissed her on her soft lips. Reece held on to him and pressed her lips firmly against Ky's as they deepened their kiss. She broke the kiss, laid her head against his chest, and listened to the fast rhythm of his heart.

"I couldn't stand not kissing you any longer," he revealed.

She looked up into his eyes and whispered, "You're killing me."

He tilted her chin and kissed her again, lingering even longer. This time he broke the kiss and whispered, "You taste so damn good."

Reece felt her lower region awaken once again upon hearing his sensual observation.

He gave her one last kiss and then said, "We better get back inside before they send out a search party for us."

"I guess you're right." As they walked back toward the house, Reece said, "I'm really glad you invited me over tonight. I'm having a great time with all your friends."

"Oh, sweetheart, the best is yet to come."

Hearing that statement sent shivers over Reece's body. She wasn't completely sure what Ky meant, but it let her imagination run wild and that both excited and scared her.

Back inside the house, Ja'el asked, "Where have you two been?"

Ky playfully punched his cousin in the arm. "Mind your business. I'm a grown man."

Ja'el laughed and then made his way over to the card table where he and Isaac challenged two other guests to a round of spades. After screams of victory and groans of defeat, it wasn't long before the evening came to a close. Ky thanked all his friends for coming and making game night fun and successful. He told them he would text them next month with information on the next game night. Once the guests left, Ja'el, Dani and her boyfriend, Isaac, stayed to help Ky and Reece clean up before leaving. With everything cleaned and put away, Reece sat down on the sofa and closed her eyes.

"I am exhausted."

Ky sat down beside her and put his arm on the back of the sofa.

"I am too, but it's always worth it when everyone leaves happy. I'm glad you were able to be a part of it."

As they sat there for a moment in silence listening to an Isley Brothers album, Reece looked up at Ky and noticed that he had his eyes closed and his head was moving to the rhythm of the song.

She smiled. "Is this one of your favorites?"

He nodded without speaking. Ky had an innocent way of making her feel special, and he was making it easier for her to slowly open her heart again.

Once the song ended, Reece said, "It's late. I guess I'd better go to bed."

Ky opened his eyes and looked over at Reece with a yearning she hadn't seen before, and it caused her to tremble. Then before she could speak or move he covered her body with his and began to shower her with a flurry of searing kisses on her neck and lips. Reece held on to him tightly, pulling him even closer. Ky went to that sensual spot on her neck again and when he kissed it, it electrified her body. It was then that he took things to a higher level and eased his hand under her skirt and into her satin and lace undergarments. As soon as he began to caress her, Reece let out a series of soft whimpers and her breathing increased in rhythm. Ky searched her face for any signs of her wanting him to stop, but there weren't any, so he continued to pleasure her with his gentle touch and kisses.

Seeing the way she was responding to him gave him a thrill beyond his wildest imagination, but he knew she was capable of even more, much more. He caressed her a few more seconds until she finally climaxed with a loud, long moan, which echoed throughout the house. She immediately covered her face with her hands and burst into tears.

Ky pulled her up into his arms and whispered, "I'm sorry if I pushed you too far. Please don't cry."

It hurt his heart to see her so distraught, but what Ky didn't realize was that he had broken through Reece's protective wall. He rocked her tenderly in his arms to comfort her. She held on to him as she continued to sob because what she had experienced was extremely overwhelming and long overdue. A few minutes later she eventually cried herself out.

"I'm so sorry, Reece," he whispered as he caressed her back. "Please forgive me."

She wiped her eyes. "I'm not angry, Ky, I'm embarrassed."

He wiped a few tears off her cheeks and said, "Sweetheart, you have nothing to be embarrassed about. You reacted naturally to what your body was feeling."

"It's still embarrassing."

"Well it shouldn't be," he said to assure her as he pushed curls of hair out of her eyes. "I was so worried that I had hurt you."

She reached for a tissue out of the Kleenex box on his coffee table and wiped her eyes. "No, it was actually amazing."

"All I wanted to do was make you feel good," he admitted as he held her tighter in his arms.

"Well, you succeeded," she shyly revealed.

He held on to her waist. "Reece, you are a beautiful and extremely sexy woman. I enjoy every second I spend with you, but it's been an emotional night. Go to bed and get some rest."

Reece started walking out of the room and when he didn't follow her, she turned and asked, "Are you turning in too?"

He shook his head and shoved his hands into his pockets. "I won't be able to sleep after what just happened between us. I'm a little worked up if you know what I mean, so I'm going for a swim to try to cool off."

"I can relate," she replied as she stared at him.

"So, are we cool?" he asked to make sure he hadn't damaged their relationship.

She bit down on her bottom lip and smiled. "We're more than cool. Goodnight, Ky."

"Goodnight, Reece."

Ky gave Reece enough time to make it upstairs to her room before he stripped out of his clothes and dived into the cool water of his pool. He swam several laps to try and put out the fire burning in his body, ignited by Reece's sultry moans.

CHAPTER 13

Nearly an hour had passed since Reece had her sexual encounter with Ky. Now she lay in bed staring at the ceiling fan, unable to sleep. She could still feel his hands and lips on her body and her mind was racing a mile a minute. She didn't hear any movement or sound in the house, so she decided to go downstairs to see if she could find some chamomile tea or something to help her sleep.

Reece tiptoed out of her room and down the stairs, but when she turned the corner toward the kitchen she was startled to see Ky walking toward her dressed in only a towel. She assumed he had just gotten out of the pool, but she wasn't sure. Just the sight of him with the tattoos on his chest and arms and extremely fit abs caused her body to immediately react. She had almost forgotten how sexy a man could look with a bare chest and Ky was the sexiest man she had seen in a long time. As he approached her, she folded her arms over her breasts to cover her stiff nipples straining against the satin fabric of her nightie.

He towered over her. "Where are you going so late? I thought you were asleep."

Stuttering, she pointed toward the kitchen and said, "I-I was going into the kitchen to see if I could find something to help me sleep."

He stared at her with a curious expression on his face. He was standing so close that she could feel the heat radiating from his muscular body.

"I don't have anything in the kitchen to help you sleep, but if you want to follow me back into my bedroom, I guarantee I'll have you asleep within the hour," he announced in a serious but sensual tone of voice.

Reece felt like her legs were going to give out from under her because of his remark. His sex appeal was off the charts, and being in such close proximity to him was making her light-headed, so she took a step back. Ky's invitation caught her off guard, and she couldn't tell if he was joking, so she let out a nervous giggle and headed back toward the stairs to return to her room.

He adjusted the towel around his waist and said, "I'm being dead serious, Reece. If you just want to be held, I can do that too."

Holding on to the railing, she shook her head. "I'm scared."

He moved even closer to her. "Sweetheart, you have nothing to be afraid of. I won't do anything you don't want me to do. Just know that my offer stands for the entire weekend." As she slowly ascended the stairs without responding, Ky said, "If you change your mind, my door will be open. He turned around and disappeared down the hallway, leaving his door cracked just in case.

Nearly forty-five minutes later, Ky found himself finally drifting off to sleep, but he could still smell the scent of Reece's heavenly perfume, making it difficult for him to get her out of his thoughts. Seconds later he was surprised by the silhouette of an angel standing in his doorway.

He sat up in bed and softly whispered, "You can come in."

Reece slowly approached him and stood on the side of the bed, clearly nervous.

"Does your offer still stand to hold me if I just want to be held?"

"Of course it does," he answered softly as he pulled the comforter back on the bed so she could climb in beside him.

She slowly climbed into the bed, knowing she was entering dangerous territory, but she felt somewhat ready to take the risk.

"I appreciate you letting me take baby steps with you. I don't want you to think that I'm easy or anything."

He pulled her into his strong arms, gave her a tender kiss on the shoulder and then said, "I'm not going to lie to you. This is hard as hell, but I respect you and I would never think you were easy. I promise I'll be a good boy tonight."

Reece let out a breath. "Thank you."

Ky pulled Reece firmly against his chest and they lay in the spoon position. He rested his hand on her thigh and Reece could feel her body trembling, especially when she felt his manhood pressing against her hips. She was beginning to think she had made a big mistake climbing into bed with Ky. He had a tenderness about him that made her want to get closer to him intimately, but she was still afraid—afraid that she was losing control of her emotions and moving too fast. She felt drawn to Ky, but she didn't want to get hurt so before trying to go to sleep she closed her eyes and prayed. Prayed for strength, guidance and favor that she would give love a second chance if it came her way again. For now, she savored the warmth, affection, and security Ky was giving her, and it felt wonderful.

Feeling the softness of Reece's hips against his groin was sheer torture. He knew he wouldn't be able to control his body. His desire for her was too strong and all he wanted to do was ravish her beautiful curves and make love to her, but he knew he couldn't if he wanted a chance with her. This was the first time he had ever lain in bed with a gorgeous woman with whom he hadn't already had sex. He knew in his heart that Reece was worth the struggle, and he would eventually be rewarded for his self control.

Before closing his eyes, he hugged her even tighter and whispered, "Goodnight, Reece."

Goose bumps covered Reece's body as she felt his warm breath against her ear. She blew out another deep breath to calm her rapidly beating heart. "Goodnight, Ky."

Sometime later they both fell sound asleep.

The next morning, Reece woke up to the smell of bacon and realized she had survived the night. She didn't know how long Ky had been awake, but it must've been awhile. She slept so soundly, she didn't even feel him get out of bed. She felt rested and was thankful that he had honored her request and just held her through the night. As she eased out of bed, she decided to quietly make her way upstairs to brush her teeth and wash her face before facing her handsome host. She fluffed her curls and then put on her robe before making her way back downstairs. When she entered the kitchen she found crispy bacon, sausage, toast and scrambled eggs, but Ky was nowhere to be found. As she searched for him, she was met in the hallway by Samson who appeared out of nowhere.

She rubbed him on the head and asked, "Where's your daddy?"

Wagging his tail, he ran toward the sunroom. When she entered, she found him on the treadmill dressed in some black gym shorts getting in his cardio. Seeing his sexy body drenched in sweat with ripped abs and those tattoos on his chest and arms instantly excited her. She could feel the urge to make love to him growing stronger each time she was anywhere near him. His eyes lit up when he saw her and a huge smile appeared on his face.

He turned off the machine and grabbed a towel to wipe the sweat off his body. "Good morning. Did you sleep OK?"

"It wasn't easy getting to sleep, but surprisingly I did," she admitted. "Thank you for making last night special."

"You're the one who made it special."

They stared at each other for a second and then Reece blushed. "I didn't mean to interrupt your workout."

Walking toward her, he said, "I was done anyway." He gave her a kiss on the lips and asked, "You hungry?"

She looked up into his sultry green eyes. "Starving."

He released her and while holding onto the towel hanging around his neck he said, "So am I."

Reece broke eye contact with her sexy house host and walked around the room inspecting the various exercise machines. She turned back to him and asked, "Do you always work out before you eat?"

"Not always. I needed it this morning to get my metabolism going because we're going to be eating some rich food today. I don't want to pay for it later."

"I see," she replied. "So what are we going to do today?"

He put on a T-shirt, took her by the hand, and led her toward the kitchen. "I want to show you around town a little more and introduce you to some more great food."

"I can't wait," she answered.

Once in the kitchen he said, "Let me take a quick shower before we eat."

"Oh, no, you don't. I haven't showered either. Besides, you're fine. It's not like you smell or anything."

Ky was amazed. Yale wouldn't let him anywhere near her if he were sweaty.

"Are you sure? I mean it will only take a second."

Reece walked up to Ky and wrapped her arms around his waist to reassure him. "Yes, I'm sure. Now let's eat. My stomach is growling."

He smiled. "OK, but I need to warm up everything a little bit. Have a seat and I'll pour you a cup of orange juice unless you want coffee."

Reece sat down and watched him move comfortably around the kitchen and appreciated just how sexy he looked from behind. "I'll take both."

Ky warmed their breakfast in the microwave and then poured her drinks. As he took their food out of the microwave he asked, "Don't you have to go by Ms. Elsie's house today?"

Reece took a sip of coffee. "Oh, yes, I need to sign the lease to her house."

"You know my offer still stands. I would love to have you stay here."

Reece poured a little more cream in her coffee. "I know, and I appreciate it, but I have family that will be coming to visit me while I'm here. I need to have my own space to accommodate them."

Ky sat down across from her and took her hand into his. "Understood. Now let me bless the food so we can eat."

Reece closed her eyes, bowed her head, and listened to a beautiful blessing. It was obvious he was a Christian man who had been raised in the church, but he was also the sexiest man she'd ever met.

Yale woke up furious. She had staked out Ky's house for hours last night and saw everything she needed to see. She knew that woman spent the night because she saw her standing on the porch with Ky as all his guests left. This meant their relationship was serious, and she felt angrier than ever. She still had to find out who this woman was and where she came from. The best place to start would be with Ky's cousin, Danielle. She was Yale's hair stylist, so Yale knew exactly where to find her on a Saturday morning. After a quick shower and a cream cheese bagel, she was out the door.

Dani had just finished doing a weave when Yale walked in the door and past the receptionist. She walked over to Dani as she was flat ironing her client's hair and asked, "How serious is Ky with that bitch he's fucking?"

Dani frowned, pointed the flat iron at her, and angrily said, "Yale, you need to get the hell out of my salon talking like that in front of my customers."

Yale folded her arms. "I'm not going anywhere until you tell me about Ky and that woman!"

Dani apologized to her customer and then yanked Yale to the side. She pointed her finger in Yale's face. "Yale, I swear to God if you don't leave right now, I'm going to beat your ass and then call the police. If you want to know the nature of Ky's relationship with whoever he's seeing, why don't you ask him?"

"He won't talk to me."

"And you wonder why?" Dani asked as she made her way back over to her client and continued to use the flat iron.

"Come on, Danielle," Yale pleaded. "Help a sista out."

"Look, I can't help you. Just leave Ky alone. You had your chance. Now get out of here unless you have an appointment."

Frustrated, Yale turned around and marched out of the salon, defeated. As soon as Yale left, Dani made a mental note to give Ky a call once she finished with her client.

Ky and Reece finished breakfast, got dressed, and then made their way into town. Reece didn't know what Ky had planned for them today, but whatever it was she knew it would be fun. Their first stop was by Dani's hair salon. Reece knew that if she was going to go swimming with Ky later that day she would need her hair styled for church. When they walked into the salon, Dani's receptionist greeted them with a smile. She knew Ky because he got his hair cut there but she didn't know Reece.

"Good Morning, Ky. Are you here for a cut?"

He leaned on the counter. "No, my friend is here for a consultation with Dani."

Dani looked up and saw her cousin standing at the front of the salon, so she made her way up to greet him. She gave Ky a hug. "What are you doing here?"

He smiled. "I brought Reece over to see you."

Dani gave Reece a hug. "Hello, Reece. I love your outfit."

Reece thanked her and complimented Dani on her attire as well as her salon. Dani revealed that she hoped to move into a larger facility in the near future.

"I'm glad you came by because I was going to call you." Dani said, turning to face Ky.

"Really? What's up?" he asked.

"I'll get to that in a second." She turned to Reece. "First, I want to know what I can do for you."

"Well, Ky wants me to go swimming with him later, and we have church in the morning, so I was wondering if you could do my hair this evening?"

Dani ran her hands through Reece's hair. "Girl, you have beautiful hair. Is your hair naturally thick and curly like this?"

"Yes, it is. I don't use any chemicals in it. Because it's so thick when I wear it natural it takes a lot of work and it is more than I can handle myself. Other times I flat iron it and wear it straight."

"Girl, your hair is beautiful with these big, soft, natural curls. Stop putting heat on it. Keep wearing it like this. These big curls are gorgeous on you. I wish my hair was this thick and naturally curly."

"You're so sweet, Dani. Thank you."

"Yes, I can do it. Do you want me to come by the house later? It'll take me no time to do it. What time should I get there?" Dani asked.

Ky looked at his watch. "Would five o'clock be too late? I know it's Saturday night and you probably have plans with your man."

"Shut up, Ky. Yes, five o'clock will be fine. Reece, can I borrow Ky for a second? I need to talk to him in my office about some business."

"Sure, go right ahead. I was going to make a call anyway."

Ky put his hand on the small of Reece's back, gave her a kiss on the cheek, and said, "Have a seat. This shouldn't take long."

"Take your time," Reece replied as she sat down, crossed her legs, and pulled out her cell phone.

Once they were gone, Reece quickly dialed her brother's number.

When he answered, she asked, "Alston, you have a second?"

"Sure, sis. How's it going?"

"Listen, I don't have much time because I'm in a hair salon and Ky stepped away for a few minutes. I need you to get down here ASAP and meet him. Things are moving fast and I want to make sure I'm not making a mistake."

"Hold on, Reece. What do you mean moving fast? What's going on?"

She let out a breath. "Let's just say we've gotten closer and I'm really falling for him. He's the sweetest, most understanding man I've ever met. I need a second opinion and I want to make sure I'm not being delusional and reacting from being by myself for so long."

Alston laughed. "Sis, it's been a while since you've been in a serious relationship. I think its past time for you to move forward, but you're the only one who can determine if you're ready."

She shook her head. "I know, but I still need you to meet him. I just need that reassurance that I'm not misjudging him."

He was silent on the telephone for a second. He could hear the urgency in his sister's voice and could tell she was struggling with her emotions, so he asked her a very important question.

"Have you had sex with him?"

"No, but we came close a couple times. He's not pressuring me at all, but to be honest, I want to. He's so comforting, fun, and so damn sexy."

"Does he know about Geno?"

With tears stinging her eyes, she said, "Yes, I told him."

"Then he knows you're somewhat sensitive to the whole relationship scenario. If he cares about you, and I mean really cares about you, he'll continue to be patient with you and allow you to let him know when you're ready for the next step."

"That's the vibe I'm getting."

"OK, and if you feel like you want to follow your heart and start a physical thang with him, do it! Just be careful."

"I will."

"When do you want me to come down?"

"As soon as you can. If you can come next weekend, that would be perfect."

"Let me check my schedule and see if I can get away. I love you, and I'll get back in touch with you later."

"Thank you so much. I really need you."

"I know," he replied. "I'll work it out, and trust yourself. You've always been a great judge of character. If he's everything you say he is, I'm sure he's a good dude."

"Thanks, Alston. I needed to hear that. I love you."

"I love you too," Alston said before hanging up.

After her talk with Alston, Reece felt somewhat relieved. She didn't know how much longer she could resist her urges with Ky, and knowing she had her brother's support in whatever decision she made eased some of her worries. Now she just had to wait for Alston to meet Ky.

Ky and Dani entered her office in the back of the salon and closed the door.

He sat down in the chair opposite her desk and reached for a peppermint in a glass dish on her desk.

"What's up, cuz?"

Dani sat down and let out a breath. "Your psycho ex came charging in here in front of my customers a little while ago trying to quiz me about Reece. She walked up on me and was like 'How serious is Ky with that bitch he's fucking?'"

Ky sat up abruptly. "Are you serious? What did you tell her?"

"I pointed my finger at her and told her she needed to ask you, and if she didn't get out of my salon, I was going to beat her ass and then call the cops. She's also still tweeting a lot of slick stuff on Twitter about exes and men overall. I just ignore her because I know she's talking about you and she's trying to get a reaction."

Ky stood and started pacing. "Yale has lost her mind. She can't get it through her thick head that we're done! I've moved on. I'm glad you're ignoring her."

"I told her to leave you alone but Savoy went in on her one time when she tweeted something about preacher's kids. You know Savoy has a temper like you do. This is a small town so most people already know she's talking about you. I'm just glad you ended your relationship with her because she's crazy."

"Dani, I swear to God if she messes things up between me and Reece I'm going to break her damn neck."

"How does she even know about Reece?" Dani asked.

"We ran into her one night downtown. She started causing a scene like she always does."

Dani stood. "Well you're going to have to handle her, because she's out of control. I don't allow ratchet people in my salon, and I can't have her coming in here cursing like that. If she does it again, I'm going to ban her from coming in here, and she'll have to find another stylist."

"I'm sorry, Dani. Yale is one of those women who won't take no for an answer, and it looks like she will try to do everything in her power to destroy my happiness."

"Speaking of Reece, how did you two meet anyway?" Dani asked, having never gotten the answer from Reece the night before.

"She was on the side of the road with a flat tire and I changed it for her."

Dani folded her arms and leaned against her desk. "A flat tire, huh?"

"Yes, but the bad thing is, she's only in town for four more months. She works for the Department of Education in D.C., and when her assignment is up, she'll be going back to D.C. I'm not looking forward to her leaving."

Dani stared at her cousin for a few seconds. "You've already fallen for her, haven't you?"

Surprised by her observation, he thought for a second before answering. "Something's happening. I mean, we've only known each other for a couple of months, but she's always on my mind when we're not together, and when we are together I feel so relaxed. She makes me happy."

"She is gorgeous, and that body . . . I would kill to have curves like hers," Dani admitted with admiration. "I can't believe she's single."

Ky walked over to the window and stared out at the city traffic. "She's not completely single emotionally."

"What does that mean?" Dani asked.

"It's complicated."

"What do you mean complicated?"

He turned to Dani. "You know how private I am, right?"

"Yes, we all do."

"Well, Reece is too, so don't say anything to anyone about it. She was engaged several years ago, but her fiancé was murdered in a case of mistaken identity. She hasn't gotten over it, and I think she's reluctant to get into another relationship."

Dani hugged Ky and said, "That's horrible, but I can understand why she would be a little nervous about getting into another relationship. My heart goes out to her, and if anyone can help her start over, you can. You're a cool guy, and I know you would love her the way she needs to be loved, even if you are a Que Dog."

They laughed together and then Ky told her he had better get back to his date. He told Dani that they were going to take in some sights and grab lunch before returning back to the house to relax in the pool.

As they walked out of her office, he put his arm around her shoulders. "Thanks for the info and I'll see you this evening. Call and let me know when you're on the way."

"Will do," she answered, waving at Reece. "Have fun, you guys, and be safe."

CHAPTER 14

Yale was livid again. She didn't know what she was going to do next since Dani wouldn't tell her any information about this new mystery woman in Ky's life. There had to be someone that could tell her something. It would help if she ran into the mystery woman again, but alone, so she could try to talk to her. When Ky was around he was quick to run interference, and Yale could tell he was obviously feeling something for the woman since he was acting so defensive. She decided her best bet was to stake out Ky's house again and follow the woman once she left. In the meantime, she would chill and wait for the perfect opportunity to strike.

It had been a wonderful day. Ky had shown Reece some beautiful parts of the city and now they were finishing up lunch at a waterfront restaurant before heading to Ms. Doucet's house to sign the lease.

"That was the best seafood I've ever had. I can't eat another bite," Reece announced. "I'm going to have to work out hard hanging around you."

Ky laughed as he caressed her soft hand. "Staying in shape is a pet peeve of mine too, but you have a fabulous body and I can't see a little seafood hurting you."

Reece blushed. "Thank you, but I work out very hard to stay fit."

He looked at his watch. "It's definitely a commitment. We'd better go if you have a one o'clock appointment with Ms. Doucet."

Reece pulled out her credit card. "You're right. She doesn't seem like the type of person who appreciates tardiness."

Ky picked up the check and then pulled some cash out of his pocket. "Put your card up. I got it."

"Ky, when are you going to let me pick up the tab on something?"

He pulled out her chair and said, "If you insist, next time lunch is on you."

"Great."

The couple left and headed to his car.

Twenty minutes later they pulled into Ms. Doucet's driveway where they found her sitting on the porch with her poodle by her side. As soon as Ky got out to open the car door for Reece, the poodle started barking.

Reece waved at Ms. Doucet. "Good afternoon, Ms. Doucet."

"Hello, Reece. You're right on time," she replied as she stood and met them on the front porch.

Reece shook Ms. Doucet's hand and said, "I brought my friend, Ky Parker, with me. I hope that's OK."

Ms. Doucet gave Ky a hug before he opened the door for her to walk through.

"If I had known Ky was the friend you were talking about, I would've had you come over for brunch. Ky, Geneva talks about you and the rest of her grandchildren nonstop. You know you're her pride and joy, and she's so proud of all of you."

Ky helped Ms. Doucet to her seat in the sitting room. "Well, she's special to me too."

Ms. Doucet pulled out a document that appeared to be the lease. "Now, let's get down to business. Reece, look this over and make sure you're fine with the terms. It's pretty standard. Here are your keys. You can move in next Saturday. Lyla will make sure you have everything you need. All the important telephone numbers are on the refrigerator."

"Yes, ma'am," Reece said as she scanned over the document.

Ky admired the character of Ms. Doucet's house. "I've always loved this house," he said. "I can remember coming here with my grandmother when I was younger. Everything was always bright and shiny. The architecture is beautiful and the detail of the columns and crown molding, as well as the décor is relaxing, yet elegant. You have great taste, Ms. Doucet."

"I'm glad you like it. My late husband had a lot to do with it too," she admitted.

Reece signed the lease. "I appreciate you putting the clause in there that I could leave early or stay later depending on my job responsibilities," Reece said.

"It's the least I could do. I understand why you're here and what you're up against with our education system."

Reece shook Ms. Doucet's hand. "Well, I appreciate your support."

Ms. Doucet stood with Ky's help and her cane and put the keys in Reece's hand.

"The day you move in, we'll get the alarm code changed and make sure you're settled before I catch my flight."

Reece gave Ms. Doucet an appreciative hug. "Thank you so much, and don't worry, I'll take care of your furnishings."

"I know you will," she said as she opened the front door for them. "Ky, it's nice to see you. Make sure you look out for Reece and check in on her to make sure she's OK."

He gave Ms. Doucet a kiss on the cheek. "It's nice to see you as well, and don't worry, I'll make sure Reece is more than taken care of."

"See you next weekend, Ms. Doucet," Reece said as she made her way down the stairs and to the car.

Ky climbed into the car beside her. "She's a cool old lady. Now that business is done, are you ready for some pleasure?"

"More than you know," she answered softly.

He loved the way she responded to his question. Hopefully it meant a lot more than just a dip in his backyard pool.

It didn't take the couple long to reach his house. It was an extremely hot and humid day and the pool was going to be a welcomed relief. Ky pulled into the garage and closed the garage door. They exited the vehicle and entered the house to find Samson wagging his tail and excited to see them. As Ky attended to his dog, he told Reece he would make them something cool to drink and would meet her poolside. She made her way upstairs to quickly change into her canary yellow bikini, flip flops, and sarong. By the time Reece arrived poolside, Ky was already in the pool splashing around.

Reece removed her sarong and put her hands on her hips. "I can't believe you started without me."

He looked up at her and said, "Daaaaamn!"

Her body was incredible, and it was even more fit than she originally appeared. Her curves were undeniable, and those thighs—whew! He knew he would have to struggle to keep his body under control since it was defying him already.

Ky's reaction to seeing her in her bikini made her blush. She pointed her finger at him. "Behave."

He laughed and held out his hand to her. "There's no way in hell I'm going to make that promise today. Come on in. The water feels great."

Ky held her hand and assisted her down the steps and into his awaiting arms. Her soft body felt heavenly against his and he instinctively ran his hands down her back, holding onto her.

"Oooo, it's definitely cool," she pointed out as Ky silently took her farther out into the pool and then pulled her body even closer. He looked into her eyes and then tenderly kissed her. Reece wrapped her arms around his neck as he deepened the kiss, taking her breath away. He wanted to palm her hips, but he decided to resist that urge for now because he didn't want to come on too strong.

Ky finally broke the kiss. "Mercy," he said softly.

With her arms still wrapped around his neck, she smiled. "You're a great kisser, Ky."

"Thanks, but you make it easy for me. If I had it my way, I would be kissing you twenty-four seven," he said as he scooped her up in his arms.

"You make it easy for me too."

He gave her another firm kiss on the lips, and then asked, "When was the last time you've been dunked in a pool?"

"When I was in college. Wait. Why do you want to know?" As her eyes widened, she said, "You wouldn't."

He winked at her and whispered, "I want to see what you look like completely wet."

Before she could resist, he fell backwards in the water with her in his arms, taking them both under water. When they re-surfaced Reece swam after him and splashed him. They continued to play in the water, swimming laps and then chilling while drinking a tropical flavored alcoholic mix. A few hours later they noticed their skin wrinkling. It was nearing the time for dinner and Dani would be over soon to style Reece's hair, so they called it a day and headed inside.

In the shower Reece was overcome with emotions and began to tear up. Ky was a wonderful man and a true Southern gentleman who knew how to be affectionate without being overbearing. She knew in her mind that it wouldn't take much for her to fall in love with him, but her heart was telling her she was already there. He had entered her life unexpectedly like a breath of fresh air, and he had become the best thing that had happened to her in a long time. She was thankful he had brought some light to the darkness she'd been experiencing, and she felt an immediate urge to thank him for all that he'd done.

Wiping away her tears, she exited the shower, wrapped the towel around her body, and made her way downstairs. She quietly tiptoed down the hallway to his bedroom door and peeped in. She pushed open his door and found Ky, also wrapped in a towel, staring out the french doors at the lake. He was so engrossed in his thoughts that he didn't realize she was in the room until she wrapped her arm around his waist, somewhat startling him.

He looked down into her beautiful brown eyes. "I didn't hear you come in. Is everything OK?" he asked.

She untucked her towel and let it fall to the floor, giving him an up close view of her curvaceous and naked body. Ky nearly swallowed his tongue. He was so stunned by her actions that he was unable to speak.

Reece kissed him firmly on the lips and whispered, "It will be."

Ky's body immediately reacted. He tried to swallow the lump in his throat. He was caught off guard by Reece's boldness and he knew whatever he said next would determine how their night was going to end.

He cupped her beautiful face. "Sweetheart, are you sure about this?"

She looked into his eyes and said, "It's been a long time since I've felt like this. You're important to me, Ky, and I can't deny how I feel about you any longer."

He caressed her cheek. "You're important to me too, and for the record, I fell for you the first day we met, so I'm going to ask you again. Are you sure about this?"

She removed his towel, allowing it to hit the floor, and answered, "We're standing here together, butt ass naked. Yes, I'm sure."

Ky felt like his entire body was pounding as he began to shower her face, lips, and neck with heated kisses. He slowly kissed her over to his large bed and gently lifted her into it. He covered her body with his and kissed every inch of her soft, brown body. Reece closed her eyes and let out soft moans as she welcomed the detailed attention he was giving her, but she craved more.

"Reece," he chanted over and over as he slowly kissed his way down from her ample breasts, to her stomach and then to her center where he settled in to indulge upon her sweetness.

She gasped, writhed, and moaned loudly as Ky flicked his tongue against her core and feasted on her. He was lost in heaven and couldn't wait to experience the grand prize. Reece gripped the sheets and held on for dear life, but she found herself losing total control of her body and her emotions. He had awakened sensations in her she thought were long gone, and her breathless moans took him to an elevated level of ecstasy. He paused briefly to open his nightstand, remove a condom, and quickly put it on.

Before continuing he looked at her with his emerald eyes full of raw emotion, kissed her hard on her lips, and whispered, "Last chance to back out."

"I couldn't want you more than I do right now. Bring it, babe," Reece softly replied as she pulled him tightly against her body and prepared herself for what she imagined was going to be nothing short of magnificent. And she was right! She gasped as he pushed himself into her moist body. Within seconds, the young couple was engrossed in an erotic and extremely sexual dance. Reece let out a series of moans with each thrust of his hips and Ky was engulfed with electrifying sensations running through his body as he devoured her stiff, brown nipples.

Ky was hitting spots that had lain dormant in her for years, and she was unable to control her emotions or her body. The pleasure he was giving her was so intense that she couldn't help but scream out her satisfaction as she wrapped her legs around his waist. Her groans and moans excited Ky even more, causing him to quicken his pace and let out a few moans of his own. Sensing she was nearing climax, he wanted to make sure their first encounter was memorable, so he leaned down to her ear, and with an even deeper thrust of his hips he whispered an unexpected commitment to her.

"Reece, I'm never letting you go."

Reece immediately let out a loud, long moan with Ky quickly following her. Breathless, he tenderly kissed her lips as well as the tears rolling out of her eyes. His heart was still pounding in his chest and he didn't want to move. Being inside her felt right and he never wanted this feeling to end.

"Babe, are you OK?" he asked as he continued to kiss her tenderly.

She nodded. "I'm fine. I'm just a little emotional right now."

He smiled. "Well, you're not alone. I'm a little emotional myself."

Reece nuzzled her face against his warm neck. "I want you to know that I don't sleep around with men I haven't known for very long."

Ky rolled over onto his back, pulling her onto his chest. He caressed her back and said, "That thought never crossed my mind. It's not something I do either."

Reece traced the lines of the tattoo on his chest before kissing it. "Thank you," she whispered.

He ran his hands through her curly hair. "You have no reason to thank me. I should be thanking you for trusting me. My prayers were finally answered, and I could stay like this forever."

They were silent for a few seconds. Reece thought back to what Ky had whispered to her and wondered if he had meant it or if he was just caught up in the moment. As she lay there, she contemplated bringing it up, but decided against it. She didn't want to put him on the spot or make him feel like he had to immediately define their relationship.

She finally broke the silence. "I should probably get dressed. Dani will be over soon to do my hair."

He looked at the clock on the nightstand and then ran his hand over her bare bottom. "We still have some time before she gets here. She's going to call anyway when she's on her way. Your hair looks fine, so if you cancel, we don't have to get dressed at all."

Reece giggled. "You're sweet, but I can't meet your parents if my hair is not styled like it should be." She eased out of his embrace, climbed out of bed, and wrapped her towel around her body.

Ky sat up in bed. "My parents are going to love you regardless."

"I hope so."

He climbed out of the bed and slowly walked over to her. With a body built like a mythical god he stood over her, tilted her chin upward, and ran his tongue across her lips before kissing her. He stared at her with his loving emerald eyes. "I can't wait to make love to you again."

His statement made her body tingle and she was beginning to feel somewhat out of her league, but she didn't want him to know it, so she put on a brave face.

"As soon as Dani finishes with my hair, you have me for the rest of the night."

"On that note, I'll start dinner. The sooner she finishes with your hair, the sooner we can get back to bed."

Reece nodded and slowly made her way out of his bedroom and back upstairs to shower again. Just as she finished dressing in some denim shorts and a T-shirt, Dani arrived. Ky put together dinner for them while his cousin got started on Reece's hair. It didn't take her long to have Reece's hair red carpet ready, so they all sat down to fellowship together over crispy crab cakes, risotto, and sautéed mixed vegetables. The trio had fun talking over dinner and Dani even let Reece in on a few hilarious incidents from their childhood, so Reece shared a few of her own. It wasn't long before Dani announced that she had to get going. She offered to help clean up the kitchen, but Ky and Reece assured her they would take care of it. Reece tried to give Dani cash for doing her hair, but Dani refused to take it.

"Reece, this one is on the house. I really like you, and I can tell my cousin does too. He's different in a good way," she revealed. "I just hope you will let me be your stylist while you're in town."

Reece hugged her. "You can count on it, and thank you. I don't feel right not paying you something, so how about I pay it forward and pay for someone else's hair? Maybe you know someone who could use a fresh style?"

Dani thought for a moment. "Now that you mention it, there is a high school girl who works next door to my shop as a waitress. She's an honor student who's helping her single mom raise her siblings. She always wears her hair in a ponytail and she's so pretty. I would love to bless her with this gift."

"Consider it done," Reece replied as she placed the money in Dani's hand.

Dani gave Reece another hug, and then she gave Ky a hug and kiss on the cheek. "Thanks for dinner, Ky."

He opened the door for her and said, "Any time. Drive safely and text me when you get where you're going."

"Don't worry, I will," she said as they watched her get in her car and drive off.

Ky closed the door and turned to Reece with a sly grin on his face. He had been staring at her the whole evening with those mesmerizing green eyes and knew Dani had probably picked up on the sexual tension between them.

She took a step back. "I guess we better get the kitchen cleaned up, huh?"

"Uh huh," he replied as he slowly walked closer to her. The T-shirt he had on displayed his huge biceps and broad chest, and his shorts showed off his toned and muscular legs.

"Do you want to wash or dry?" she asked as she continued to back away from him. The sensual look on his face with those piercing green eyes staring at her had nothing to do with cleaning the kitchen, and her body was starting to react. With her back against the wall and all his male sexiness towering over her, he sprinkled her lips and neck with tender kisses.

"You feel and taste so good," he whispered as he ran his hands slowly down her back, gripping her hips.

Shivers increased over Reece's body and she closed her eyes and breathlessly said, "Ky, please. Don't you think we need to get the kitchen cleaned up?"

He stopped kissing her and looked into her eyes.

"Sweetheart, cleaning the kitchen is the furthest thing from my mind right now, but I can see that I have you a little overwhelmed. Why are you so nervous? We already got the hardest part behind us," he pointed out as he took a step back from her and folded his arms.

"I don't think you realize how strong your personality is. You would overwhelm any woman with blood running through her veins. Maybe I'm not enough woman for you."

He took her by the hand and chuckled. "You're giving me way too much credit, and don't ever doubt yourself again. You're more than enough woman for me, and I love everything about you, especially that shy quality you have. I don't mean to come on so strong with you, but it's hard for me to keep my hands to myself. You are so sweet and sexy and I feel so blessed to have met you."

"Thank you, but it's been a long time since I let a man this close to me. Being with you feels amazing and scary all at the same time," she admitted as she walked into the kitchen with him.

"You're right. I wasn't thinking about it from your perspective," he admitted as he started filling the sink with hot, sudsy water. "Babe, if I'm coming on too strong, tell me and I'll back off."

Reece didn't want to hurt his feelings so she maneuvered herself between him and the sink and cupped his face in her hands. Looking directly in his eyes she said, "I can honestly say that you are the best thing that has happened to me in years. I love the way you show your affection, and I love how you make me feel. I would never want to diminish your passion, so please don't feel like you have to hold back or back off. I'm going to have some quirky moments off and on, but I'll be fine. OK?"

He smiled and kissed her lovingly on the lips. "I appreciate that, and believe me when I say I've *never* felt like this either. That's why I'm acting so greedy with you. I hope you can forgive me."

She wrapped her arms around his neck and gave him an electrifying kiss that lasted several seconds. She released him and breathlessly said, "You're forgiven."

He let out a loud breath. "You might want to slide over because you've started me up again, and if you're not careful I'm going to have you bent over this counter."

She saw the serious look in his eyes as she slowly stepped away from him. His warning caused her body to immediately get moist, especially when she envisioned herself bent over the counter making love to him.

"Oh my God! Are you serious?"

He closed his eyes and nodded as he braced himself against the sink, attempting to will his body back under control.

"Babe, honestly, all you have to do is be on my mind to set me off. It doesn't take much."

Reece rubbed his back to comfort him, but he had to stop her because having her hands caressing him was making matters worse.

"Maybe I need to leave for a while," she suggested.

"No way. Just give me a second," he said softly.

Amazed that she could affect him this way she said, "Now I know why your ex can't let you go."

Mentioning Yale instantly deflated him. Bringing her into their romantic evening was the last thing he wanted, but it did help him get his body under control. He figured Yale had been in the back of Reece's mind ever since their encounter on the pedestrian mall anyway.

"I'm OK now," he said as he scooped up Reece in his arms and sat her on the counter. He handed her the dishtowel so she could dry the dishes as he washed them. "Forget about her," he said as he washed a plate and handed it to her. "She's my problem. I don't want you pulled into her drama."

"I've seen scorned women before," Reece said as she dried the plate. "They can be crazy and unpredictable."

He handed her another plate. "I know, so if she ever approaches you, ignore her and let me know. Don't let her pull you into a confrontation."

"Did you love her?" Reece asked curiously.

"I was beginning to have stronger feelings for her. She was cool. She's beautiful, passionate, self-sufficient, and intelligent, but she started to change. I started seeing her arrogance, greediness, jealously, and insecurity. I can't be with a woman I can't trust."

Reece detected a touch of sadness in Ky's words. It was obvious he had possessed some feelings for his ex at one point, and she was glad he wasn't minimizing them. He seemed to be honest about it.

"I know all about trust and it's so important," she replied. "I was dating a guy a couple of years ago and he was great until I found out he was married, so thanks for not lying about her."

This bit of information peaked Ky's interest since he didn't know much about her dating history. He looked up at her and saw the disappointed look on her face. Now he fully understood why she was so cautious. And he wanted to know more.

"Were you in love with that married guy?"

"I was almost there," she answered without any hesitation. "I think God gave me a sixth sense. I always had a feeling there was something not quite right with him, but I never could put my finger on it. He was doing and saying all the right things. We took trips together, went out a lot, and spent time with each other. He definitely wasn't acting like a married man. He even had an apartment where I would spend the night with him sometimes."

"Are you serious?"

"Yes, it was his secret place I guess. I later found out he had a beautiful home in Virginia with his wife. His job required him to travel a lot, so most times I went with him. It all came to light one day when I ran into him with his wife and two small kids at an outdoor festival. When he saw me he looked like he had seen a ghost. He knew he was busted at that point."

"What did you do?"

She laughed. "I knew it was wrong, but I walked up to his wife and complimented her on a gorgeous necklace she was wearing. She told me her husband bought it for her. I looked him in the eyes and told him he had great taste and I walked off."

He handed her a skillet. "That was awkward. He should've felt like an asshole."

"Oh, you should've seen him. I'm sure he thought I was getting ready to put him on blast, but I wouldn't do that with his kids there. He found me in the crowd and tried to get me to meet up with him later so we could talk. He was telling me he loved me and he was sorry, blah, blah, blah. I told him to forget he ever met me because he had committed the ultimate betrayal, but he wasn't hearing it. When he grabbed me by the arm the male friend I was with had to snatch him up and make him leave me alone. It really hurt me."

"I'm sure that was crazy," Ky replied. "Well you don't have to worry about that with me. Number one, I don't lie about or in my relationships, past or present. Number two, I have no lingering feelings for Yale or any woman from my past. Number three, I'm a one-woman man. Always have been, and always will be."

"I appreciate you saying that, but I don't think your ex is going to go away quietly, regardless of how you feel about her," Reece said as she hopped down from the counter so she could put the dishes in the cabinet. "She's still in love with you."

Ky laughed. "If you say so. What about that guy? He was clearly acting like he was in love with you. Did he leave you alone after what happened in the park?"

"Not at first," she revealed. "He continued to call my phone from sun up to sundown so much that I had to change my number. Then he started showing up at my house and job and pretty much became a stalker until I told him if he didn't leave me alone, I would tell his wife everything. He didn't want that because he had a high paying job and position in government. With two kids, if she divorced him, his pocket would take a big hit. He finally backed off."

"I wish Yale would back off," Ky stated. "Have you seen him since you ended it?"

"A few times, but he knows to keep his distance. I was angry that he played with my emotions like that, especially after what I had been through, but I eventually got over him. It's going to take your ex some time too. You can still see the pain in her eyes and hear it in her voice."

Without responding he let the water out of the sink. He remembered how Yale had pulled a gun on him when he broke up with her. He just prayed she wouldn't try something like that with Reece, because the outcome could be totally different, and he didn't want Reece to get hurt.

"Just promise me that you won't get into a thing with her if you run into her."

"I'll try not to," Reece said as she hung the dishtowel on the stove handle, "but my response will depend on her approach. Hopefully we'll be able to avoid each other while I'm in town, but if she comes at me crazy, I will knock her out."

Ky laughed. "I hear you, Ali."

Reece laughed too. "Is there anything else that we need to do?"

"No, we're done. Thanks for your help. Do you want to go downstairs and watch a movie or something before turning in?"

"I'd rather chill and listen to some music from your great record collection. Is that OK?"

"Sounds good to me. I'll make us a couple drinks while you go pick out some music."

After they made their way downstairs to the entertainment room, Ky mixed them a couple of drinks—a margarita for her and a Crown Royal and Coke for him—while she scanned through his record collection. When he handed her a drink, she was holding a Johnnie Taylor album.

"This one brings back a lot of memories. He's one of my dad's favorites," she said.

Ky took it out of her hand. "My dad likes him too. He likes the song 'Just Because.'"

Reece then noticed he had a Marvin Gaye album. "What about this one?"

He took it out of her hands. "Perfect! It'll be a nice nightcap on the evening, especially if you dance with me."

She took a sip of her drink, opened her arms to him, and said, "Well let's get it on."

Ky laughed, noting that she was referencing one of Marvin Gaye's most famous songs.

The couple danced to the song, clearly enjoying being held in each other's arms. Ky was giving her warmth, affection, and security, while Reece gave him peace, stability, and love. He felt it without a doubt and loved having her soft body pressed against his as he showered her with kisses.

A couple of hours later they decided to call it a night since church service was going to be at eleven o'clock, and Ky didn't want to be late. She accompanied him back upstairs where he held her hand as he checked all the doors and set the alarm.

As they walked around, Reece said, "My brother might come down for a visit next weekend. I hope you don't mind."

"Why would I mind?" he asked as he checked the front door. "I know you miss your family. I think it will be good for you. I would love to meet your family."

She touched him lovingly on the arm. "I hope you don't have any plans."

He turned out the lights in the foyer. "I'm free and I think it will be cool for us to meet."

Reece smiled. "Great."

When they got to the staircase he pulled her into his arms and gave her another tender kiss on the lips. "Do you need anything before you turn in?"

"No, I'm good."

He caressed her body and said, "We need to leave the house by ten fifteen to get a seat at church, so set your clock accordingly."

She lay her head on his chest. "I was hoping to stay down here with you so you could wake me up in the morning."

"Sweetheart, you don't ever have to ask. You're welcome in my bed any time," he replied as he caressed her cheek. "I didn't want to assume it just because of what happened between us earlier."

She turned to go up the stairs. "You're such a gentleman. I'll be back down shortly."

"I'll wait up for you."

Reece trotted up the steps while Ky retired to his bedroom to get ready for bed. Having Reece in his bed was a welcomed pleasure and he couldn't wait to feel the warmth of her soft skin against him. It didn't take long for her to return dressed in a white lace and satin chemise. Ky was closing the drapes when she entered, and when he turned around he shook his head and realized it was going to be a long night. She was stunning.

"Lord have mercy," he mumbled.

"What was that?" she asked as she eagerly climbed into bed and waited for him to join her.

He slowly climbed into bed beside her. "Reece, you're making it hard on a brother."

She giggled. "Now you're giving me too much credit."

The couple kissed each other goodnight and he spooned his body against hers. "Lord knows I prayed hard for strength to give you a break tonight, but looks like the devil won."

"The devil won what?" she asked curiously before she felt it and said, "Oh!"

He kissed the back of her neck and whispered, "I'm sorry, baby, but I can't help myself."

She closed her eyes and pulled his arm tighter around her waist. "It's OK, you don't have to apologize. Follow your heart."

He kissed her cheek and neck and jokingly said, "My heart is not the body part I'm struggling with."

Reece turned to face him and gave him a tender kiss on the lips. "I want you too, babe."

He kissed her firmly on the mouth, ran his hand up her thigh, and began to stroke her. Reece closed her eyes and let out a series of loud breaths as he covered her nipples with his warm mouth. A few seconds later he protected them and gave her a sensual nightcap that filled the room with breathless moans and cries of satisfaction. They felt as if they were one with each other. After their bodies released the essence of their love and affection for one another, they gave each other one final kiss goodnight and fell into a deep, satisfying sleep.

CHAPTER 15

The next morning, Reece and Ky woke up to get ready for church. He was caught up in the fabulous night he'd had making love. After church they would be going over to his parents' house for dinner to give them a chance to meet Reece. When they returned to his house, he hoped to indulge himself again with her fabulous body. This time he wanted to be able to give her his undivided attention and take his time pleasing her. Ky checked his watch and realized they needed to leave in about ten minutes. He put on his dark gray suit with a light blue shirt and silver and blue tie. He made his way upstairs to check on Reece's progress. He tapped on the bedroom door before walking in. The smell of her perfume was in the air and he found her in the mirror putting on makeup.

"Hey, beautiful. You about ready?"

With her eyeliner in hand, she turned to him and said, "Yes, I'm ready."

"We need to go ahead and move your things downstairs. There's no reason for you to keep running up and down the stairs to get dressed."

She walked over to him, smiled, and then said, "Like you told me last night, I didn't want to assume."

He scanned Reece's body from head to toe. She was dressed in a beige suit with a red silk blouse and red high heels. She was stunning.

"We can take care of it when we get back from church."

"Great, and, babe you're wearing that suit. Your shoulders are so broad," she said as she put her makeup in her red purse.

"Thank you. I hope you're OK with an early dinner at my parents' house along with my grandmother. I want them to meet you."

Reece gave him a kiss on the cheek. "I'm a little nervous about it, but I'm looking forward to it."

"Good. You'll be fine. Let's go so we can get a seat."

Reece wiped her lipstick off his cheek. "I can't have you walking up in church with my lipstick on your face, showing everybody our business."

He laughed and took her hand into his. "You're right, but they'll know soon enough."

Reece was surprised by Ky's admission. While she wasn't sure whether they were a couple, Ky's heart and mind already seemed to be made up.

The church was already filling up when the couple arrived. Ky and his family usually sat in a particular section and he hoped to do the same today. Reece noticed several females staring at Ky and whispering. A couple of them even came over to greet Ky or give him a hug. Each time he made a point to introduce them to her, which she appreciated. Reece understood Ky was an eligible bachelor and a fine one at that, but she also knew there were messy women who didn't have respect for others. One woman proved that point when she came over and eased between them, acting as if Reece wasn't even there.

"Ky Parker, you get better looking every time I see you. When are you going to give me a ride on that big boat of yours?" the young woman asked as she looked down at his crotch. She looked like she had just left the club, and her dress was so short, if she sneezed her undergarments would be revealed.

Reece frowned. "That is so disrespectful," she whispered.

He laughed. "That will never happen, and you know it."

"You'll change your mind one day," she replied as she gave his biceps a squeeze.

"I don't think so," he replied. "By the way, this is my friend, Reece. Reece, this is Tara. We grew up together."

Tara looked Reece up and down and said, "Oh, hey." Before Reece could reply, she walked off and said, "I'll catch you next time, handsome."

Reece looked at Ky. "That woman is bold. What she said was disrespectful, and that dress is so short it's almost obscene.

He kissed her on the cheek. "I know. For a second I was kind of worried. I saw that look on your face. She's been trying to get with me since middle school. She always says something crazy when she sees me. I'm surprised she didn't say something even more inappropriate. She does it to get a reaction out of me, so I try not to react. My mother and some of the other women of the church had a meeting one time to talk to all the females about coming to church wearing provocative clothes. Some took offense and others agreed. It's better than it used to be."

Reece sighed. "Well it looks like she needs to call another meeting, because that woman's dress is so short it looks like a blouse."

Ky laughed. "You've got that right."

Reece made a mental note to be prepared for that woman if she ever said something inappropriate in her presence again, even though her relationship with Ky was new. They walked farther into the sanctuary together and Reece noticed even more women staring at them.

"I see a lot of women staring at you, Ky. What is going on?"

"Ignore it. I've been dealing with it since I was sixteen, and they're not staring at me. They're staring at you," he revealed.

"Why me?" she asked.

"They haven't seen me at church with a woman in a while, so I'm sure they're wondering who you are."

Just then a couple of little girls ran over calling out for Ky. One of them appeared to be about seven, and the other around four-years-old. Ky picked up the smaller one and gave her kiss on the cheek. The girls were some of Ky's cousins, and he was quite fond of them, and they of him. He introduced them to Reece and gave them some peppermints before watching them make their way back to where their parents were sitting. He explained that they sit with him and his grandmother sometimes. Reece could see that Ky was a man full of love and was well loved amongst the congregation where he'd grown up. When they finally made their way to their pew after greeting a few more church members, he found his grandmother wearing a big hat and standing in her normal spot.

Ky leaned down, kissed her on the cheek, and said, "Good morning, Gigi."

"Bishop! Good morning, baby. I was wondering if you were going to make it today," she said as she sat down and scooted over so he could sit next to her.

Before sitting he said, "Gigi, I want you to meet my friend, Reece Miller."

With a look of surprise on her face his grandmother stood back up and gave Reece a friendly hug.

"Friend?" she asked as she raised her eyebrows at her grandson. "OK. Reece, it's so nice to meet you. Come have a seat next to me."

Reece sat down between Ky and his grandmother. "It's nice to meet you as well."

His grandmother leaned out and looked at Ky. "I assume you will be bringing Reece by for dinner after church today?"

"Yes, ma'am."

Geneva glanced over and noticed Ky was holding Reece's hand. She smiled and couldn't wait to find out how this came about. Just then the music started and the choir began to sing. Ky pointed out his mother to Reece. She was a beautiful woman who looked exotic, but she couldn't tell what her ethnicity was. She definitely wasn't African American. His father, the pastor, was handsome, and she could easily see that Ky had inherited his fabulous genes from both parents. Ky was modest when he talked about his family, so Reece Googled them one night and found out that his father was a well-known pastor. He was somewhat of a spiritual leader to the mayor and was very active in community affairs. Pastor Parker also served as an advocate between the citizens and the police force to make sure that everyone's civil rights were protected, and that there was peace and trust between them.

Ky's mother was involved in most of the ministries in the church, but also found time to serve as an advocate for education and after school programs, since she was a former teacher. The things Reece found out about Ky's grandmother were really fascinating, including that she had performed with some legendary jazz musicians.

Service was going along great, and when it came to the part about visitors, Reece stood, but thankfully did not have to speak. The pastor thanked the visitors for attending church and when he did, he focused on Reece, seeing that she was sitting with his mother and son. The ushers passed out cards for the visitors to fill out and gave them a token of appreciation, which was a welcome booklet with Bible scriptures and peppermint candy.

In the back of the church Yale nearly fell off her pew when she saw Reece sitting next to Ky. She had hoped to get a chance to talk to him today, but that was out of the question now since he had that woman with him. At least she had a chance to find out more about who she was and where she came from. Yale thought for a moment, and then realized the best way to get the information was through the usher who handed out the visitor card. So as soon as the usher returned to her post in the back of the church, Yale discreetly exited her seat and motioned for the usher to meet her in the vestibule.

"Excuse me, sister, but do you know anything about the lady in the beige suit sitting next to Pastor Parker's mother?"

The usher peeped through the window of the door and said, "I'm not sure. I gave her a visitor's card to fill out. I'm sure she'll return it on her way out after service."

Yale thought for a second to come up with a lie on why she needed information from the visitor's card, and then a light bulb went off.

"I want to welcome her to our congregation and invite her to join some of our ministries. I can't stay until the end of service, otherwise I would introduce myself to her. Do you think you could pass her information on to me when you get it?"

The usher thought for a moment and didn't see any reason why she couldn't. Yale was active in church and involved with several ministries, so her request wasn't really out of the ordinary. This was a new usher, and she didn't know the connection between Yale and Ky. If she had known, red flags would've gone up alerting her to potential other motives behind Yale's request.

"I guess I can," the usher replied.

"Good," Yale said with appreciation as she gave the usher her business card. "When you retrieve her card, text me her information as soon as you get it. I'll introduce myself to her personally next Sunday."

The usher tucked Yale's business card into her pocket. "Will do. Sorry you can't stay."

Yale put on her sunglasses. "So am I. Have a blessed week, sister."

"You too," the usher replied.

The usher watched as Yale exited the church before returning to her post.

Reece enjoyed the church service and was glad that Ky wanted to share it with her. Once service was over, Ky made his way up to his mother so he could introduce her to Reece.

He gave his mother a big hug and kiss and then said, "Mom, you look beautiful. I want you to meet my friend, Reece Miller. She'll be coming over for dinner today."

Sinclair was just as surprised as her mother-in-law was to see her son with a woman he'd never mentioned. She tried to conceal her surprise as she greeted her son's new friend.

"It's so nice to meet you, Reece, and I'm glad you made it to our service today. You're very pretty."

Reece blushed. "Thank you, and it's nice to meet you too."

Sinclair turned and motioned for Ky's father to come over. When he finally made it over to them, Sinclair said, "Gerald, your son has someone he wants you to meet."

Pastor Parker hugged him and said, "It's good to see you, son. Who is this lovely young lady?"

"Daddy, this is my friend, Reece Miller. I'm bringing her over for dinner today."

He looked at Sinclair and then back at Ky before shaking Reece's hands.

"It's nice to meet you, Reece. Forgive me for my hesitation. We would love to have you join us for dinner. I hope you're hungry."

"Yes, sir," she replied.

Geneva walked over, wrapped her arms around her grandson's waist, and said, "I baked your favorite pie today."

With his arms around his grandmother's shoulders he said, "Thank you, Gigi."

"We'd better get going so I can warm up dinner. Honey, are you coming?" Sinclair asked her husband.

Gerald unzipped his pastoral robe and said, "I'll be there shortly. I have a few things to tie up here and I'll be leaving, but don't you two have a missionary meeting?"

"Oh, shoot! I forgot about that," Sinclair replied. "Come on, Geneva, let's get this meeting over with so we can get home."

Ky put his hand on the small of Reece's back and said, "We're going to head on over to the house. Don't worry about dinner. Reece and I can warm it up."

Sinclair gave her son another kiss on the cheek. "OK, thank you and drive safely. We'll be there as soon as we can."

The three of them watched Ky and Reece exit down the aisle. Once they were out of earshot Geneva asked, "Who is that?"

"I don't know," Sinclair answered. "She seems nice. She's definitely pretty."

"I wonder why he hasn't mentioned her to anybody." Gerald asked.

"Because he likes her more than he's putting on. Friend my butt," Geneva noted. "He looks at her the way a man looks at a woman when he's in love. I can't wait to hear the story behind this one."

"In love?" Sinclair asked. "He can't be in love with her. I'm sure he hasn't known her for very long."

"He's a Parker man," his father stated. "In case you've forgotten, we fall fast and hard."

"Bishop's always been particular with women," Geneva reminded them. "I'm telling you, there's something special about this one, but I need to check her out first before she gets her hooks into my grandson."

Sinclair linked her arm with her mother in law and said, "Don't start, Geneva. I'm sure we'll get to know her in due time, and don't pry too much into their business. Ky will tell us what he wants us to know."

"Sinclair, please! I will have to approve any woman he chooses just like I had to approve you."

Ky's father laughed. Before walking away he said, "Momma, behave yourself, and I'll see you guys at the house in a few."

Outside, Ky and Reece ran into Ja`el and Dani along with their parents and a few other members of Ky's extended family. Reece got to meet the uncles who owned the yacht building business before Ky bought it. Dani complimented Reece on her attire and Reece did the same. The two had a similar taste in style. Ja`el gave Ky a brotherly handshake and hug before pulling him to the side.

"Bro, you and Reece have gotten tight. What's up?"

Ky took off his jacket since they were standing out in the hot sun.

"Nothing's up. She's a cool person."

"Bro, it's me. Your boy. You know I know you. Come on, what's up? Have you hit that yet?"

Ky was used to Ja`el prying into his sex life. He put on his sunglasses and smiled without responding. He wasn't about to kiss and tell his business even if they were close cousins, especially not about Reece. She was special and he wouldn't dare risk ruining it.

"OK, I see how you're going to be. I would tell you," Ja`el stated.

"I know you would," Ky pointed out. "Look, cuz, Reece and I are good. We're having a great time getting to know each other."

Ja`el gave Ky another hug. "All right, I guess I have to accept that . . . for now."

The pair walked back over to the rest of the family. Ja`el gave Reece a hug and said, "Reece, it's good seeing you again. I can't wait until the next game night."

"Me too," she answered as Ky took her hand and led her toward his car. "I'll see you guys later."

Dani and her family waved and watched as Ky opened the car door for Reece and she climbed inside.

Dani turned to her brother and said, "Stick Ky with a fork because he's done. He's in love."

"I was thinking the same thing, sis, but I'm happy for him. What's funny is he doesn't think it shows, but it's all over him. They look good together and I like Reece."

"I like her too," Dani replied as she grabbed her brother by the arm. "Let's go. Momma said she cooked dinner and I'm hungry."

Back inside the church, the ushers cleared the pews of leftover church programs and litter. In a back office, the young usher Yale had spoken to gathered the visitor card she'd retrieved from Reece. She texted the information to Yale, who was already sipping on an alcoholic drink in a nearby restaurant with Anniston.

When Yale's phone signaled her to a text message she quickly opened it and yelled, "I got it! That bitch is going down!"

At the Parker house, Ky and Reece made themselves at home in the kitchen where they set the table and put the stove on warm so the food would be warm by the time his family arrived. He poured Reece a glass of iced tea and then gave her a tour of his childhood home. As they made their way upstairs, he showed her his room, which housed all his athletic trophies and certificates he'd earned over his lifetime. She got to see some of his photographs over the years as well.

"Wow, look at you," she said as she picked up one of his framed football pictures. "You played every sport, didn't you?"

"Pretty much. I tried to stay busy to keep myself out of trouble."

She set down the picture. "You haven't changed much over the years."

"If you say so," he replied as he adjusted a couple of pictures on a nearby shelf.

Reece turned to him. "Your mother is really beautiful. What ethnicity is she?"

He laughed. "I knew that would come up once you saw her. She's half Brazilian and half Canadian, but as you can see, she looks more Brazilian. My grandmother was from Brazil and my grandfather was from Canada. I'm surprised you haven't wondered about me."

She shook her head. "No, I just thought you were a light-skinned black man who'd been in the sun a lot."

He laughed. "I am. My dad's black."

She nodded. "Oh, because of the one drop rule. I hope you're not offended that I asked about her ethnicity."

"Of course I don't mind. I've been asked about my parents all my life. It's not a problem, is it?"

She put her arms around his neck before responding. "Of course not. So from whom do you get those handsome green eyes?"

"My grandfather," he revealed.

"Oh, I see. Your bronze skin tone is sexy too.

He set their iced tea on his dresser and pulled her closer as he sat down on the edge of the bed. He hugged her waist and laid his head against her stomach. Reece caressed his hair and shoulders and savored the tenderness between them. She wasn't sure what was happening with him, but she was enjoying the moment. The couple held each other for several minutes and then he ran his hands under her skirt and up her legs, massaging them. He caressed her backside and she closed her eyes and enjoyed the sensation of his hands on her body. Then, out of nowhere, Ky unexpectedly began to slowly ease her panties down until she tilted his head upwards and interrupted him.

"What do you think you're doing?" she nervously asked. "We just got out of church and your parents will be here any minute."

"I know, and don't worry, babe. We have time to do what I want to do. I promise," he whispered.

Reece was extremely nervous, but she trusted him and allowed him to finish removing her undergarments. He raised her skirt over her hips and then placed one of her legs over his shoulder and buried his face between her thighs. Reece immediately arched into him and tried her best not to scream as she held onto his broad shoulders. Ky meticulously kissed and ran his tongue over her center, devouring her flesh while gently caressing her bottom. She moaned and squirmed as shivers ran all over her body and as she struggled to balance herself on one leg. The thought of getting caught by his parents excited her and she knew she wasn't going to be able to stand much longer.

"Oh my God, Ky," she called out to him breathlessly as her body began to tremble.

That's when he flicked his tongue against the most sensitive part of her and she let out a satisfying loud moan.

He came up for air, kissed her, and said, "That was music to my ears. I love making you feel good."

With tears in her eyes she kissed him and said, "I don't know how I'm going to face your family after that."

He picked up her panties off the floor and shoved them in his pocket. "They're not going to know, and these are for me."

At that moment they heard his mother's car pull into the driveway. He pulled her into his arms and kissed her again as she tried to retrieve her panties. Ky playfully held her hand, preventing her from getting them as he heard his mother and grandmother come inside the house.

"Ky, you're going to get us in trouble."

"No, I'm not." He chuckled as he seductively kissed her neck and caressed her breasts.

"How do you know?"

"I know my people, and they know how I am. They're not going to come up here. For all they know we're up here having a private conversation, which we are."

Reece let out a deep breath. "If you say so. Now, hand over my panties. I need to freshen up."

He laughed. "OK, you can use the restroom across the hall."

The couple made their way across the hallway to the restroom where Ky opened his sister's cabinet and found all the toiletries Reece would need to freshen up.

She held out her hand for her panties and he reluctantly gave them to her.

"Do you need some help?" he asked mischievously.

With a smirk on her face, she answered, "No, but you can go downstairs and distract them before they come up here to see what's taking us so long."

He chuckled. "Relax, sweetheart, I promise they won't come up here."

"You better be right, Parker," she replied as Reece did her best to freshen up.

Needing to freshen up himself, Ky closed the bathroom door and quickly brushed his teeth and rinsed with mouthwash while Reece put her undergarments back on. Once they were presentable, they made their way out into the hallway.

"Ky, we're home! Where are you?" His mother finally yelled up the stairs for him.

"We'll be down in a second," he replied. "I'm talking to Reece."

"OK," she answered, seemingly not suspecting anything out of the ordinary was going on.

Reece turned to him. "How do I look? Do I look like I've been fooling around with you?"

He laughed. "No, you look great. Listen, babe, I've been thinking and I have another proposal for you."

She straightened his necktie and asked, "What kind of proposal?"

"Since this is your last week before moving into Ms. Elsie's house, I want you to stay with me until you do."

She looked into his eyes. "Are you serious?"

"Of course I am. Remember I tried to get you to stay with me instead of renting anyway," he reminded her. "I've gotten used to having you around, and I like it."

Reece thought for a moment and then decided to test him. "What if you wanted to have a date over or something? Wouldn't that be awkward?"

He backed her against the wall and kissed her seductively on the lips. "You're the only woman I'm interested in having in my house or my bed. I told you I am a one-woman man. Say you'll stay. We can go pick up the rest of your things from the hotel after dinner."

She had to admit that she loved being with Ky and making love to him was beyond amazing. The main reason she wanted her own place to live was so she would have a neutral place to retire when things got emotionally overwhelming. He was a remarkable man, so maybe he was worth the emotional risk.

"OK, I'll do it as long as it won't cause you any problems."

He pulled her hips against his body and whispered, "I can't wait to get you home."

After kissing once more, the couple made their way downstairs to join his mother and grandmother.

CHAPTER 16

When Reece and Ky reached the bottom of the stairs and walked into the dining room, Geneva asked, "What took you two so long to come downstairs?"

Ky kissed his grandmother on the cheek and said, "We were upstairs having sex."

Reece's eyes widened in sheer shock as she put her hand over her heart in disbelief and screamed, "Ky!"

"Boy! I know you didn't just say that!" his mother yelled as she hit him with her dish towel and then suspiciously glanced over at Reece.

He laughed and put his hands up in defense. "I'm just kidding, Momma!"

Geneva stared at her grandson and said, "That wasn't funny, Bishop."

He held Reece's chair out for her and continued to laugh. "Yes, it was. You should've seen your faces, and for the record, Reece didn't know I was going to do that."

"I can't believe you did that," Reece whispered to him, clearly embarrassed.

His mother set a bowl of cornbread on the table. "This is the first time you've brought Reece over here, and you do that to her? Reece, you should give him a good smack upside the head."

He laughed. "I'm sorry, sweetheart. I couldn't resist messing with them. As you can see, my grandmother is very nosey. I didn't mean to embarrass you with my joke. I have to do these women like that from time to time to keep them in check, because they like being all up in my business."

Reece didn't respond or look at him, and that was when he realized he had gone too far with his joke. He immediately took her by the hand, got up from the table, and said, "Excuse us for a second, ladies."

Ky led Reece out of the dining room and into the family room for some privacy and pulled her into his arms. He tilted her chin up and gave her a tender kiss on the lips. He looked at her with all kidding aside and then with genuine seriousness he said, "I wasn't thinking, sweetheart. I really didn't mean to embarrass you. I'm so excited for my family to meet you, I guess I was a little too anxious to pull a joke on them. I kid around with them a lot like that, and I forgot to take into account how shy you are, and how it would make you feel since it's your first visit. Can you please forgive me?"

Reece sighed. "Of course I forgive you. I just don't want them to think I'm some kind of slut or something."

"Impossible," he replied with another kiss. "Again, I'm so sorry. Are we cool?"

She playfully punched him in the arm. "Yes, we're cool. Don't do that again."

He rubbed his arm and said, "Yes, ma'am."

As the couple rejoined his mother and grandmother in the dining room, Ky's father finally made it home. Dinner started without a hitch; however, his grandmother didn't waste any time asking Reece a lot of questions. She wanted to know how she met her grandson and how long they'd known each other. His mother and father were impressed with Reece's credentials, especially Sinclair, since she was a champion for education too, but his grandmother wasn't completely sold.

The one thing that troubled Geneva was that Reece's visit was temporary, and if her grandson fell for her and she left, he could be heartbroken. It was obvious to her that Ky already had feelings for this young woman because he referred to her as babe and sweetheart. She also noticed the way he looked at her and how he seemed unable to keep his hands off her. Just how deep his feelings ran remained to be seen. Reece was a career woman from a large city with a lot of ambition and a huge responsibility—probably too much ambition for Ky's low key lifestyle.

"So, Reece, what are your plans when you finish your assignment here?" Geneva asked.

"Well, I plan to go back to my office in D.C. until I get my next assignment."

"I see," she answered. "Bishop, what do you think about that?"

"Momma," Gerald interrupted. "That's none of your business.

"It's a legitimate question, Gerald."

Ky knew exactly what his grandmother was up to, and he wasn't about to fall for her tactics.

"Why wouldn't she return to D.C.? She has a job to do, and I wouldn't expect her to do any less," Ky replied.

Reece could see something very profound was going on between Ky and his grandmother, and she didn't want to be the subject of any issues between them.

"Mrs. Parker, Ky and I are friends. In fact, since I've been here we've become great friends. While I do have to go back to D.C. at the end of my assignment, he's welcome to come visit me at any time. I know he's been a Godsend for me since I've been in town."

"That's sweet," Geneva replied. "We taught him to be a gentleman and assist people who need it."

Ky smiled with appreciation as he took a bite of chicken, especially since he'd just gotten an open invitation to D.C. from Reece.

Hoping that line of questioning was over, Reece turned to Sinclair. "Dinner is delicious, Mrs. Parker. I see where Ky gets his cooking talent from."

"Sweetheart, let me correct you just a little bit. Ky learned how to cook from me," Geneva announced proudly. "Sinclair was too busy to do much cooking. I'm surprised Gerald has any meat on his bones now."

Ky looked at his grandmother. "Are you OK? You're acting weird."

"I'm fine, Bishop. I'm just clearing up the facts."

"Wow," Ky's father said as he leaned back in his chair. "Momma, what are you doing? This is not a competition of who did what for Ky. Stop it now. Reece, please excuse my mother's behavior. She obviously didn't listen to my sermon today."

"It's OK, Mr. Parker," Reece said before taking a sip of tea.

"No, it's not OK," Ky said, clearly displeased with his grandmother's behavior. "Gigi, stop whatever you're trying to do right now. Reece is my guest."

"What am I doing?" she asked, widening her eyes and trying to play innocent.

Sinclair wanted to change the mood at the table because she could sense it going from bad to worse. She put more macaroni and cheese on her plate and asked, "So, Reece, where are you staying while you're here? I hope you found somewhere nice. We have beautiful townhouses and apartments close to downtown and some near the lake too."

Ky choked on his tea and started coughing. Reece patted and rubbed his back lovingly. "Are you OK?" she asked.

He nodded and prayed Reece would give the right answer to keep his family out of their business. Sensing Ky's nervousness she gave the perfect answer without telling a lie.

Reece turned to Sinclair and spoke. "Well, I've been staying at an extended stay hotel downtown, and next weekend I move into a house I'm renting from a friend of yours, Mrs. Parker. Her name is Elsie Doucet."

Geneva noticed the loving way Ky and Reece behaved with each other and knew in her heart they were a lot more than friends. He had never looked at any woman like he was looking at Reece, but there was no way she was going to let him fall for Reece until she made sure she wasn't a gold digger.

"Is that so?" Geneva asked after hearing a familiar name. "I knew Elsie was going to California to have her hip replaced. I didn't know she was going to rent out her house."

Gerald pointed his fork at his mother. "See, Momma, this proves you don't know everything about everybody, even though you think you do."

Sinclair laughed. "Ain't that the truth."

Geneva reached for a dinner roll, ignoring their comments. "So, Reece, is there a boyfriend or baby daddy back in D.C. that Ky needs to know about before he comes for a visit?"

Reece was stunned. Never had she been drilled so hard by a family member of someone she'd dated. She could clearly see that Ky was agitated and trying to restrain himself, but that question just sent him over the edge.

"Gigi, what the hell is wrong with you?" he asked angrily. "If there is a boyfriend or baby daddy in her life, it's none of your business. Listen, if you're trying to treat her like this because of what I said earlier when I was joking around, stop it. It was a joke. Reece is a perfect lady."

"Son, I don't know what happened before I got here, but take a breath," Gerald said to his son to calm him down.

"No, Daddy! This needs to happen. Come on, old lady. Is there something you want to know about Reece and me because we can get it all out on the table right now! What is it you really want to know?"

Geneva set down her fork, wiped her mouth, and said, "Well since you asked, yes, there is something I want to know, and it has nothing to do with that joke you played on us earlier. I want to know what Reece's intentions are with you. You're a very wealthy young man and we can't have just any woman with a pretty smile and a firm backside sizing you up for your bank account. You almost made that mistake with that other girl. I knew she was trouble from the beginning because all her people have issues, but did you listen to me? No! Now you show up out of the blue with a woman you haven't told any of us about and expect us not to be suspicious of her intentions? You know better than that."

"Geneva!" Sinclair yelled.

"I don't believe this," Ky said in anger as he scooted his chair back from the table.

"Momma, how dare you? Apologize to Reece and Ky right now!" Gerald yelled as he pointed his finger at her.

Ignoring her son and Sinclair, Geneva turned to Reece and said, "Reece, you're a very beautiful girl and I can see how my grandson could be mesmerized by your looks. It's nice that you have a reputable job and you seem to be self-sufficient, but if you're trying to trap Ky to get at his money, it won't work. We don't allow baby mamas or gold diggers in this family."

"Momma, that's enough!" Gerald yelled at his mother. "What the hell is wrong with you? Are you drunk?"

"No, I'm not drunk."

Ky shook his head in disbelief. He was beyond angry and Reece could see the vein in his neck starting to pulsate. It was a side of Ky she hadn't had to the opportunity of witnessing until now, and she hated that she was seeing him like this because of his grandmother.

Trying not to disrespect his grandmother, Ky gritted his teeth and said, "I love you with all my heart, but you are beyond out of line, and as far as my bank account, it's *my* bank account, which means I can share it with whomever I want. Lastly, whoever I'm dating or sleeping with is my choice and my choice only. It has nothing to do with you, and you need to stop being judgmental of Reece when you don't even know her."

With her elbows on the table and fingers linked together, she said, "It has everything to do with this family. You're a Parker and you have a legacy and name to uphold, and I won't have it tarnished by anyone, no matter how pretty she is."

Gerald stood. "This stops now!" he yelled. "Momma, you're supposed to be a Christian and you're sitting here acting like anything but one! Sinclair and I welcome any young lady Ky brings to us because we know him, and I thought you did too. Your treatment today of Reece and Ky is inexcusable. If you can't behave with some class, you need to leave the table."

Geneva sat quietly in her chair. She was used to being scolded by her son, but not like this. She realized she had angered all of them, but somebody had to be the one to screen potential mates for their children and grandchildren.

Gerald sat back down and turned to Reece. "Reece, I can't begin to tell you how sorry I am about this. My mother must be getting dementia or something because this is not who we are. You are a lovely young woman and we trust Ky and his decisions. You're welcome in our home any time. Please don't take this personally."

Before Reece could reply, Ky wiped his mouth with his napkin and said, "Well, Daddy, it's hard for us not to take it personally. Gigi's basically called Reece a gold digging whore and I can't sit here and let her insult her anymore."

Reece was overwhelmed. She knew she hadn't done anything to make Ky's grandmother think she wasn't anything but respectable. Why she was treating her this way was confusing, so she decided to see if she could fix things.

"Mrs. Parker, if I've said or done something to make you think I would hurt or take advantage of Ky in any way, I'm sorry. I don't know Ky's financial situation, and he doesn't know mine. Frankly, I couldn't care less about it because that's not the reason we're friends. I respect you as my elder and as his grandmother, but I'm not going to sit here and let you continue to verbally abuse me for no reason. All I can say is judge not, and ye shall not be judged; condemn not, and ye shall not be condemned; forgive and ye shall be forgiven, therefore I forgive you." She took Ky by the hand and looked him in the eyes. "I really, really care about you, but I can't stay here any longer. Take me home."

Ky smiled after watching Reece put his grandmother in her place. He gave her a loving kiss in front of all of them and with a smile said, "Baby, I couldn't agree with you more."

He stood and helped Reece out of her chair. Tears welled up in Sinclair's eyes as she watched her son and his date leave the table.

"Wait!" Sinclair said as she stood and walked over to the young couple and held Reece's hand.

"Reece, you don't owe Geneva an apology. My mother-in-law is being rude, insensitive, and out of order. Please stay and finish dinner."

"I appreciate your and Pastor Parker's kindness, but unfortunately I've lost my appetite," Reece answered.

Geneva continued to sit there in silence as she let Reece's words sink in. She had surprisingly been handled by Reece, and she knew she needed to redeem herself.

"Let's go, baby," Ky said as he led Reece out into the hallway where he got his jacket from the coat rack and handed Reece her purse.

Geneva joined them in the foyer. "Reece, I'm sorry if I came off like a bully. I can't help it that I'm protective of my grandchildren. I don't mean to be rude, but I do feel that I have a right to ask certain things. They may not be popular questions, but they need to be asked. The wrong woman could ruin Bishop, not only financially, but emotionally, and I can't let that happen. So if you have skeletons in your closet we have a right to know about them."

Gerald threw his hands in the air. "What the hell kind of apology is that? Momma, go home! You're being nasty and toxic today and I don't want it in my house."

"Never mind, Daddy, we're leaving," Ky said before looking at his grandmother. "Gigi, I brought Reece over for you guys to meet her because she's important to me, not to be interrogated and insulted. You have no idea how much I care about her, so your attack on her is an attack on me. Also, just so you know, Reece didn't target me for my money if that's what you think. I pursued her and I'm so glad I did, because I know how special she is."

"It's OK, Ky," Reece whispered as she linked her arm with his.

"No, Reece, it'll never be OK."

Reece lowered her head, feeling like her presence had broken up a happy home.

"Son, please don't leave." Sinclair touched his arm lovingly. "I promise you, Geneva will keep her mouth shut the rest of dinner."

"That's impossible for her to do, Momma," he replied before giving her a kiss on the cheek.

Geneva walked closer to Ky. "I'm just trying to protect you, Bishop."

He gave her a kiss on the forehead. "Call it whatever you like, Grandma, but I don't need your protection. I forgive you because I love you, but we have to go."

Hearing Ky call her Grandma broke her heart. He only called her that when he was angry with her. She returned to the dining room table, sat down, and took a sip of tea as tears filled her eyes. While she knew her tactics weren't popular, in her mind they were necessary to separate the strong from the weak. She was impressed that Reece had stood up to her and basically put her in her place. If her behavior ruined her relationship with her grandson, it would kill her because he was so precious to her.

Returning to the foyer, Geneva approached Reece again, and with tears in her eyes she said, "Reece, I really didn't mean to insult you or upset my grandson. It's obvious he has special feelings for you. I would love for you to come back so I can get to know you properly. I just hope you can find it in your heart to accept my apology."

Reece gave Geneva a hug. "Apology accepted." While her feelings were hurt, she knew as a Christian she needed to forgive, so she played nice.

"You had your chance to get to know Reece. There's no way in hell I would put her through this again." Ky took Reece by the hand and pulled her away from his grandmother. "Let's go. You don't owe her anything after the way she treated you."

Ky gave his parents a loving hug and kiss and said, "Thanks for dinner."

"You're welcome, son. Don't you want to take some to go plates with you?" Sinclair asked.

"No, we're fine, and if we get hungry, we'll put something together or we'll go out."

"I really appreciate your hospitality, Mr. and Mrs. Parker," Reece said as she also gave them a hug.

"Likewise, my dear," Sinclair replied. "Please come back and visit us soon."

"That would be nice," Reece replied.

Gerald gave Ky one last hug. "I love you, son, and don't worry about your grandmother. I'll handle her."

"I love you too, Daddy, and thanks, because I can't talk to her right now. I'll call you tomorrow."

"I look forward to it," he acknowledged before turning to Reece and pulling her into an embrace. "Reece, it was so nice to meet you, and if there's anything you need while you're here, you let us know."

"It was nice meeting you as well, and thank you for the open door invite," she responded.

As soon as Ky and Reece left, Sinclair lit into Geneva as she cleared the table.

"Geneva, I swear if you keep this up, we're never going to have any grandchildren. You're going to have to stop acting like this every time Ky or Savoy brings someone home. They're good kids, and they know how to take care of themselves. Stop being such a tyrant."

"I don't know what gets into me," Geneva admitted. "Ky is my first grandchild and I love him so much. I just want him to pick the right girl."

Gerald walked in on their conversation. "Momma, it's their choice, not yours or ours. God will send them the right mate when he's ready. In the meantime, you need to get ahold of yourself before our children stop coming around."

"I need a drink," Geneva announced as she threw her hands in the air and made her way toward the family room to get a drink and to reflect on her behavior.

"That's part of your problem," Gerald yelled out to her as she disappeared down the hallway.

Reece noticed that Ky was quiet when he got in the car and buckled his seatbelt. She touched him lovingly on the cheek and asked, "Are you going to be OK?"

He turned the ignition and said, "I will be fine as soon as we pick up your things at the hotel and get home."

It took Ky and Reece about an hour to get back to his house after packing all of her belongings and checking out of the hotel. Once at home, Ky unloaded Reece's luggage and put it in his large walk-in closet. She took off her blazer and sat down on the bench at the foot of the bed to remove her heels while Ky removed his tie and started unbuttoning his shirt.

She looked over at him. "I'm not used to you being this quiet."

He shook his head. "I don't mean to be. I'm just upset over the way my grandmother treated you today."

"Listen, Ky, about that. I can tell you are close to your family. I never want to be the reason you're fighting with them."

He put his hand up and said, "Stop it! You have no reason to apologize or feel like this is your fault. My grandmother was out of line and I called her on it."

"I know and I appreciate you defending me, but your grandmother loves you, Ky. While I don't agree with her methods, she only asked questions I expected to have to answer from your parents at some point."

"My parents are not psycho like my grandmother. Momma and Daddy would never talk to you like that."

Reece giggled. "Your grandmother is not psycho. She's old school, and while she did upset me, I understand why she did it. I'm sure your parents would've asked the same questions but in a different way. Your grandmother is kind of gangsta."

He removed his wallet and other items from his pockets in silence and set them on the dresser. It was obvious that he was still very upset over the way his grandmother behaved.

"Why does she call you Bishop?" Reece asked as she removed her nylons.

He took off his shirt. "I used to imitate my dad preaching when I was little, so she started calling me Bishop, and has been ever since. She hardly ever calls me by my name."

"That's sweet," she said before walking over to him.

Reece helped him out of his undershirt, then started unbuckling his belt in silence.

Ky looked into her eyes and with a smile he asked, "Oh! Is that what's up?"

She rubbed her body against his, gently bit his ear, and whispered, "Most definitely."

"After everything that happened at my parents' house?"

She nodded.

"I really am sorry about embarrassing you."

"I know, babe. I've already forgiven you for that. Now I'm ready to forget about what happened with your grandmother so I can concentrate solely on you."

Ky could see the sensual expression on Reece's face and it made him immediately turn all of his attention to her. He unzipped her skirt and allowed it to fall to the floor. He gripped her backside and said, "You don't have to ask me twice."

Reece held onto his strong arms as she stepped out of her skirt and allowed him to remove her blouse. Standing before him in her red lace bra and matching panties, she gave him a searing kiss on the lips and unzipped his pants. He stepped out of the pants and threw them on the bench at the foot of the bed. Ky could easily be a model with his muscle tone and chiseled facial features, along with those emerald eyes. Reece, standing at nearly five-feet-seven-inches tall was gorgeous in her own right with smooth brown skin and a body that would make any man weak in his knees.

She climbed onto his bed and said softly, "Let me give you a massage. You look a little tense."

Ky lay across the bed and Reece immediately straddled him and started to massage his tense muscles.

"That feels nice. You're good at this."

She massaged his shoulders and lower back. "I can't have you walking around tense with your muscles tight. I need you loose and agile."

Ky had had enough. Having her straddling his body with her hands all over him dressed in her sexy undergarments had him fully aroused. He rolled her off his back and covered her body with his. He showered her with heated kisses on her lips and neck before removing her bra. He immediately took her stiff nipples into his mouth and gently consumed them. Ky wanted to take his time, but

173

he wasn't able to resist her any longer, especially when she started letting out breathless moans. He momentarily ceased kissing her so he could apply protection. Reece took the packet out of his hand and kissed him hard on the lips before removing his briefs.

"Let me," she said as she opened the packet and removed the condom.

Ky lay on his back and closed his eyes, but what he got was more than he bargained for when she took him into her mouth. In shock, he quickly opened his eyes and stared down at her. He was in disbelief as he watched her give him oral gratification. He felt like he was going to explode as she ever so slowly worked him over.

With his voice strained, he called out to her. "Reece, babe. Daaaaamn!"

She finished pleasuring him and finally applied the condom. Ky didn't expect her to take control, but she did, and he loved every second of it as she mounted him without any hesitation. He felt like he had died and gone to heaven. She braced herself against his shoulders as she began to slowly gyrate her hips. As she rode him, she threw her head back and moaned even louder as his large manhood filled her. She nearly had him at his peak, but he didn't want to relinquish to her so soon. Now it was his turn to take charge.

He sat up, engulfed her breasts momentarily, and then whispered, "Turn over, baby."

Hearing the yearning in his voice excited her and she happily rolled over. She glanced at him over her shoulder and said softly, "I want all of you."

He swallowed the lump in his throat, positioned himself between her thighs, and went all in. When he entered her, she sucked in a breath and let out a loud whimper. Ky immediately thrust his hips into her, first slowly and then faster. The expression on her face was a combination of pleasure and pain, but she begged for more. Ky pounded his hips into hers for what seemed like an eternity until he felt his body nearing completion, but he wanted to take her there first. He rolled her over onto her back, placed her legs over his shoulders, and ground his hips deep into her several more times until she let out a scream. Her release ignited him and they climaxed hard.

Breathless, Ky kissed her and then collapsed on top of her. Unable to move, he whispered, "Oh my God. I feel like my heart is going to burst."

She giggled. "That was amazing."

"That's an understatement. You definitely surprised me."

Reece looked into his emerald eyes. "If your grandmother knew what I just did to you, she would really think I was a heathen."

Ky laughed and pulled her into his arms. He softly caressed her back. "Don't let my grandmother fool you. She's no saint. She's told me stories about some of the things she did when she was younger, especially when she was touring. She's a hypocrite."

"Everyone has a past. I just wish she didn't think I was some type of gold digger."

Feeling Reece's sadness, he gave her a tender kiss on the cheek. "I know you're not with me because of my bank account, so that's all that matters. You having that flat tire was God putting us together, and no one, not even my grandmother, could ever convince me otherwise. I'm so happy our paths crossed."

Reece nuzzled her face against his warm neck. "I agree. I never dreamed I would come here and meet someone as wonderful as you."

"I feel the same way, babe," he replied as he caressed her soft body.

Reece lay her head on his broad chest and after nearly fifteen minutes of silence, she found herself drifting off to sleep. That was when she heard Ky ever so softly whisper, "I love you, Reece."

Shocked by his admission, she quickly became more alert as she continued to lay still. She assumed he'd only said it because he thought she was asleep. Not wanting to make the moment awkward for him, she continued to pretend to be asleep until she finally drifted off into a happy slumber.

It was nearly six o'clock when Reece woke up from her nap, and she was still reeling from Ky's secret confession. He was still asleep so she quietly eased out of bed, gathered her toiletries, and entered his bathroom. She gently closed the door and started running a hot bath in his large soaker tub. Once it was full she eased into the sudsy hot water and closed her eyes.

She didn't realize how sore her muscles were from making love to Ky until she got out of bed. She realized she was going to have to step up her workout routine in order to keep up with him. It had been a magical afternoon in spite of what had happened at his parents' house, but the serenity of her bath allowed her to gather her thoughts. Her main thoughts surrounded Ky's confession that he loved her. It had changed her entire perspective on their relationship, and she realized they were no longer just friends.

She was enjoying the peace and quiet of the bath so much that at one point she felt herself starting to doze off again.

"You look so relaxed," Ky said softly, startling her.

Reece opened her eyes and quickly sat up in the tub. Ky was standing next to the tub, still nude and with a big smile on his face.

"I didn't mean to scare you," he said as he knelt down and gave her a kiss.

"It's OK," she answered as she played with the suds in the tub. "How long have you been standing there staring at me?"

He chuckled. "Just a couple seconds. Why didn't you wake me?"

"I didn't want to disturb you. You were sleeping so peacefully."

He laughed. "That's because you put my ass to sleep. I only woke up because I
felt you missing. Are you hungry?"

"A little bit. What about you?"

He rubbed his stomach. "Yeah, I guess we sort of burned what little dinner we had right off, huh?"

She giggled. "Probably."

"Well, I'll go put something together," he said, still smiling at her. She was glowing and her beautiful brown skin looked amazing surrounded by the suds, the ivory candles, and the silver fixtures. It was an image he hoped to see for many years to come.

"I hope you don't mind me taking a soak in your gigantic tub."

Without answering her he reached over into the hot water and started caressing her inner thigh, and then her center.

She closed her eyes and laid her head back on the tub. "Oh my God. That feels so good. You should join me."

With a sly grin on his face he stood. "No, you go ahead and enjoy yourself. If I get in there, dinner will never get cooked. I'll jump in the shower and head to the kitchen. Take your time and relax."

Reece watched Ky make his way over to the large shower and climb in. She could see the image of his masculine body through the patterned design glass and it warmed her heart. Several minutes later he exited the shower and wrapped the towel around his waist.

On his way out of the bathroom he winked at her and said, "See you shortly."

"OK. I won't be long."

When he opened the bathroom door, Samson immediately ran in and went over to inspect Reece.

Ky whistled for him, but the dog totally ignored him.

"It's OK. He can stay and keep me company. You know this is kind of our thing. Just leave the door cracked in case he gets bored."

"OK," he answered as he left the bathroom door cracked, leaving her to enjoy her bath. Once Ky was gone, Samson lay down next to the tub as if he was on guard. They had a great relationship and Ky could already see how protective Samson was of her.

Once Ky was dressed he made his way into the kitchen and started cooking. His cell phone rang, interrupting him. He looked at his phone and smiled.

"Hello, sis," he answered as he poured the alfredo sauce onto the sautéed chicken.

"Ky Gerald Parker. I can't believe you didn't tell me you had a new bae," Savoy said, playfully scolding her brother. "I hear she's gorgeous and really nice. What's up? Why have you been holding out on me?"

Ky laughed. "Who told you?"

"Dani told me. Now who is she and why haven't you told me about her?"

"Calm down," he said softly as he poured the pasta in the strainer. "I wasn't hiding her from you. In fact, I had planned to bring her to your game the last time we were there, but she had to go out of town unexpectedly. Dani's right. She is gorgeous, but she's also sweet and sexy. I'm really into her."

"Why are you whispering?" she asked. "She's with you, isn't she?"

Ky walked over to the hallway and looked in the direction of his bedroom to make sure Reece wasn't nearby.

"She's here in the house with me, but not in the same room. You'll get to meet her soon."

Savoy was silent for a few seconds and then said, "You sound different, but in a good way. Yeah, there's something going on that you're not telling me, but it's cool. I think I know what it is, but I'll get to the bottom of it when I can look you in the eyes."

"You're tripping," he said before laughing.

"You can laugh all you want. I know you, remember?"

"If you say so."

"We have a bye week so I'm coming home Thursday," she announced. "I can't wait to see this woman that has you acting so mysterious."

"You're silly. Have you told Momma and Daddy that you're coming home?"

"No, and don't tell them. I want it to be a surprise."

"You flying or driving?"

"I'm going to fly so I can spend more time at home, so I'm going to need you to pick me up at the airport."

He stirred the alfredo, chicken, and pasta together and said, "I can do that. Text me your flight information so I can put it on my calendar."

"I will. Look, I'd better go. I have an exam to study for and I want to get something to eat before I start studying."

He turned off the stove. "OK. Is everything good on your end? You need anything before you come home?"

"No, I'm fine."

"Listen, before I let you go, remind me to tell you about your grandmother and how she acted when I took Reece over to the house for dinner today."

"Her name is Reece? At least she has a cool name."

"She's the full package, sis," he answered softly. "I can't wait for you to meet her."

Savoy could hear the emotion in her brother's voice and she could tell he was in love, but she decided not to put him on blast just yet.

"Full package, huh? Well, hell, I might come Wednesday instead."

They laughed together and then Savoy said, "Ky, don't let Gigi get under your skin. You know she can be extra, and you are

178

her favorite, so she's going to act like that with any chick you bring around."

"Well she was more than extra. She actually insulted Reece asking her all sorts of crazy questions and was insinuating that she was with me for my money. I'm really pissed off at her right now, and so are Momma and Daddy," he revealed.

"Well, I hope you stood up to her."

"Oh, I did, and so did Reece. I think that caught the old lady off guard," he said with a chuckle. "Listen, sis, enough about Gigi. Go study and don't forget to text me your flight info. I love you."

"I love you too. See you Thursday."

"Later, sis."

Several minutes later, Reece finished her bath, dried off, and put on some of her fragrant lotion. When she entered the bedroom she saw Ky's dress shirt from church on the bench and decided to put it on instead of her robe. His cologne was still on it. As she sniffed the sleeve, she made her way into the kitchen. When she walked in, Ky was finishing up dinner. He was dressed in Under Armour shorts and a T-shirt, and he looked extremely sexy at the stove.

"It smells great in here," she said as she hugged his waist. "You need any help?"

"Yes. Can you get the garlic bread out of the oven?" he asked as he spooned their entrée onto two plates.

Reece put on oven mitts, removed the steaming garlic bread, and placed it on their plates.

She sat at the kitchen island and said, "I love your cooking."

"Thank you," he answered as he poured them a couple glasses of wine.

"You don't mind me wearing your shirt, do you?"

He sat down across from her. "Of course not. You look a lot sexier in it than I do."

"I disagree. There's nothing sexier than a man who can pull off looking fine in a suit and in casual wear too."

He held her hand and tenderly stroked the back of it. "And there's nothing sexier than a woman wearing a man's dress shirt. Now come on and let me bless the food so we can eat."

Ky blessed the food and they began to enjoy the delicious dinner and wine.

After dinner Reece cleaned the kitchen and then joined him on the sofa in the family room where he was watching a football game.

"Thanks for doing the dishes," he said as he took a sip of wine and rested his hand on her thigh.

"I can't have you doing all the cooking and cleaning. I want to do my part while I'm here," she said as she grabbed a sofa pillow and laid her head in his lap.

"I appreciate that and please make yourself at home. You don't have to ask if you can use something or do anything around here. What's mine is yours."

She looked up at him. "That's so generous of you. Thank you."

He smiled. "You're welcome. By the way, Savoy's coming home Thursday afternoon. I have to pick her up from the airport. She's really anxious to meet you."

Reece sat up and asked, "Do you think it's a good idea for me to be here?"

"This is my house," he reminded her. "Savoy's not running anything around here. Besides, she's cool. She knows how our family is, which means she knows how to be discreet, and she's going to love you."

"I hope so," she answered before lying back down across his lap.

They watched the game for a little while longer before turning in for the night.

CHAPTER 17

Now that Yale knew Reece's name, she spent the majority of Monday morning researching Reece's background rather than preparing for the special segment that was due to air next week. She discovered that Reece was highly educated and held a prestigious position in Washington.

"Let me see if I can find out where you're working while you're here, Miss Thang," Yale said to herself as she read Reece's professional profile on Linked In.

She spent the next hour searching the Internet and making telephone calls to see what else she could find out about Reece. Now she had to figure out how to proceed with getting Reece out of Ky's life without throwing suspicion on herself. If there was any chance for Ky to forgive her, she would have to make sure nothing she was doing could come back to her. What she wanted was some dirt on Reece that would turn Ky against her. It was impossible that Reece was truly as innocent as all the information Yale found seemed to say she was. There has to be some skeletons in her closet, and Yale was determined to find them.

"Yale," her coworker Jeremy said. "I think I found something." Yale had enlisted Jeremy's help in researching Reece without telling him it was a personal matter.

She walked over to his desk and asked, "What is it?"

"I found a news report about a murder in D.C. several years ago where an investment banker named Geno Matthews was shot and killed outside a bar by someone named Cecil Thomas. It goes on to say that Matthews was engaged to be married to Reece Miller, a senior at Howard University and intern for the Department of Education. Could it be your girl?"

"Are there any pictures?" she asked.

Jeremy clicked on a link on the news report and found a video attached to the story that showed pictures of the shooter and an engagement picture of Reece and Geno Matthews.

"That's her!" Yale said as she pointed at the computer screen. "Oh my God! That's tragic, but I'll be damned if I let her come here and take what's mine."

Jeremy swung around in his chair. "Oooo, I smell a cat fight coming on."

"Shut up, Jeremy," she said as she sat down at her desk. "Since she works for the Department of Education, she's probably working at the local office downtown. That's my next telephone call."

"So, is there a real story on this chick, or is this one of your fake witch hunts?" he asked. "You know we have a deadline on that story about grandmothers raising grandchildren, and we're not even halfway ready."

With her hands on her hips she asked, "Have we ever missed a deadline?"

"No," he replied. "But I don't like scrambling around at the last minute. What's your interest in this woman?"

She looked over her shoulder to make sure her boss wasn't around, and then leaned forward and whispered, "She's trying to steal my man."

Jeremy laughed and said, "I thought you and that guy broke up a long time ago?"

She gathered some folders on her desk. "Yes, he broke up with me, but it was all a huge misunderstanding. I know he still loves me. How can any man resist all of this?"

Jeremy, who was a young, Caucasian man fresh out of graduate school said, "I agree. You are a beautiful woman with a huge personality. I don't know why you won't go out with me."

"Because you're a horny college boy and I don't have time for any foolishness. I need a real man, Jeremy."

He leaned over her so he could whisper in her ear. "I'm not in college anymore. I'm a real man, Yale, and if you give me a chance, I'll show you just how much."

"Sit down, Jeremy," she said with a giggle as she looked him up and down. "You're cute and fine for a white boy, but my heart belongs to someone else."

He sat down. "It sounds like he's moved on if you ask me, and this woman is beautiful, intelligent, and seems to be excelling in her career."

"She has nothing on me," Yale said, snapping back at him.

"True, you have similar assets, but you have to admit, you have a quick temper and sometimes come off insecure."

"What are you talking about?" she asked as she printed some information from her laptop.

"Well from what you told me about him, he hates a nosey ass woman, and that was your downfall. No man wants a woman who's always going through his phone or emails. Why do y'all do that anyway?"

"You wouldn't understand," she answered as she typed on her laptop.

"Enlighten me. I really want to know."

She stopped typing. "OK, I'll tell you why. Men are dogs! They're never satisfied with one woman, so when a woman finds that one special man she'll protect the relationship by any means necessary. Men can't be honest and admit they don't want to be in a committed relationship. They want to have their cake and eat it too. Checking a man's phone is a way of making sure he's not screwing around behind a woman's back, and if he is, it will be dealt with."

"That's crazy," Jeremy replied. "You and all your sister girl friends like you are psycho. All men are not dogs, and there are some men who can commit to one woman. You have trust issues. That's why you can't keep a man."

"Go to hell, Jeremy."

"So what are you going to do with the information on your competition?" he asked curiously. "Because we have a segment that we have to get done pronto. You're not going to get me fired over your ex-boyfriend obsession."

"Calm down," she replied as she sat there in deep thought. "I don't know how I'm going to play this out yet. I want to get her alone so I can talk to her and see what kind of vibe I get off her. Then I'll be able to get a better read on her and find out if she's fucking my man."

"You said she spent the night at his house and was at church with him," Jeremy reminded her. "They're fucking."

Yale put her hands over her ears. "Don't say that! It drives me crazy to think about him screwing another woman."

"You might as well face the fact that he is. I've seen him and he's a good looking guy. A man like that has no problem getting women, and I'm sure he hasn't been abstinent since he kicked you to the curb."

Yale grabbed a Kleenex and dabbed a few tears in the corner of her eyes.

Jeremy massaged her shoulders and said, "I'm sorry, baby. I didn't mean to upset you, but at some point you're going to have to face the fact that he's moved on. Yale, give me a chance. One night. I can make you forget all about him."

Yale pushed his hands off her shoulders and stood.

"I don't want to talk about it anymore. Do you want to grab some lunch with me? I need to think."

"Sure," he answered. "My treat, and let's forget about her and him for now. OK?"

Yale grabbed her purse and answered, "OK."

The two of them headed out of the office for lunch, but her mind was full of thoughts on how to handle the situation. It was going to be a huge risk, but she realized she might have to ask for a little assistance to remind Ky that she was the right woman for him.

Ky and his crew had worked hard all morning on the Lanbeaus' yacht. It was almost finished and he would hopefully get a chance to take it out for a test drive soon. The interior decorator and her team would need a few days to put the finishing touches on the interior décor before the Lanbeaus could come in and give their final inspection on the finished product.

Ky sat down at his desk and pulled out his cell phone. He was a little tired and it was only lunch time.

Trish walked into his office and said, "You look exhausted. Why don't you sit down somewhere and let the crew finish up the rest of the day?"

Without looking up from his cell phone, he said, "You know how I work, Trish."

She set a stack of invoices on his desk. "I need you to review these invoices and sign off on them so I can send them over to the accountant before the end of the day."

He typed a text message on his cell phone and then said, "OK."

She walked toward the door. "I'm headed out to lunch. Do you need anything before I leave or while I'm out?"

"No, I'm good. Thanks and enjoy your lunch."

Trish left the office and within seconds his cell phone rang.

"Hello, Ky," Reece said with a song in her voice.

He smiled. "Hello to you too. I was just checking in on you to see how your day was going. I've been working hard to finish this yacht. I'm beat now."

"Well I'll give you another one of my famous massages when you get home, and maybe that will make you feel better," she said in a seductive tone.

Ky chuckled. "That's a date. How's your day going?"

Reece twirled around in her chair. "Well, it's been hectic and I feel like I've been in nonstop meetings and on conference calls all morning."

"I'm sure that can be draining. Hang in there."

Reece's assistant came in and signaled to her that she had an appointment waiting.

"Ky, I have to go. I've been summoned to another meeting. Don't forget I'm cooking dinner tonight. I plan to get out of here by four thirty," she said as she looked at her watch. "What about you?"

"It'll probably be closer to five thirty or six for me. Do you remember how to work the alarm at the house?"

She stood, gathered her notebook, and slowly walked toward the door. "Yes, I remember. Once I get in the house I'll give you a call."

"OK, be safe."

"You, too. See you later,"

Reece joined her coworkers in the conference room while Ky decided to head out for lunch.

Later that evening, Reece put together a delicious dinner of lemon chicken, green beans, and red potatoes. While she waited for dinner to finish cooking, she changed into her workout attire and decided to work out in Ky's home gym. Once she worked up a good sweat on the elliptical and treadmill she checked on dinner before going out into the backyard. There she spent some time out on the dock with Samson watching boaters and fishermen pass by. Later they played a game of fetch. They played for a while and she enjoyed every minute of it. Reece and Samson had a great afternoon together, but it was time to take dinner out of the oven. On their way back to the house, Ky met them halfway.

"When did you get home?" she asked.

He gave her a quick kiss on the lips. "A few minutes ago. I was watching you play with Samson. He's crazy about you."

She patted the Labrador on the head and said, "I love him too. He's so sweet."

Reece was hoping that Ky would confess his love to her face to face so she would know it wasn't just a spontaneous utterance after sex, but so far he hadn't. She realized she might have to come to terms with the fact that she may never hear those words again.

Samson turned his attention to his owner. He jumped up in Ky's arms to greet him. Ky patted his dog and then told him to sit.

Reece started walking toward the house. "I have to take dinner out of the oven."

He grabbed her hand and pulled her into his arms. "I've already taken care of it. It looks delicious."

She wrapped her arms around his neck and stroked his hair. "Thank you."

Ky ran his hands over her round bottom and let out a loud breath.

"Babe, I'm loving you in these yoga shorts. You have some dangerous curves, woman," he announced as he admired her in the short, tight fitting apparel. She was looking so sexy she had instantly aroused him.

"I'm glad you like," she answered as she twirled around. "Your gym is convenient, but you don't make it easy to keep in shape with all the good cooking you've been doing."

He laughed and wrapped his arm around her waist.

"I know, but I try to cook as healthy as possible. Do I have time to shower before dinner?"

"Of course you do," she said as they walked into the house. "I need to shower too. After my workout and playing outside with Samson, I'm a little tart."

"In that case you might as well join me," he said with a sly grin on his face.

"Just a shower, right?" she asked as she removed her shoes.

"Sure," he answered with a wink.

He took her by the hand and led her into the bathroom where they undressed and climbed into the large shower. The shyness she used to have around him was long gone and she loved every second she spent with him. The couple lathered each other's bodies and talked about the stresses of their day. Reece couldn't help but run her hands over his muscular arms, shoulders, and abs. She gently traced the tattoo of a cross on his chest with her soapy fingers and the ones on his arms too. Ky tried to restrain himself as he enjoyed rubbing lather on her backside and voluptuous breasts. He wanted her more than anything, but he didn't want her to think he was a sex starved maniac, so he played it cool, even though she wasn't making it easy for him.

She touched him on his private area and looked into his eyes as if she was daring him to react. The first time he was able to let it slide, but the second time he caved. He pushed her back against the wall of the massive shower, kissed her hard on the lips, and picked her up in his arms. He entered her with one solid thrust. She let out a loud whimper as she wrapped her legs around his body and held on to his broad shoulders. He followed with several more deep thrusts, causing her moans to echo throughout the room. She was driving him crazy, so crazy that he broke his most important cardinal rule as he vigorously made love to her. Ky quickly came back to his senses and froze, but he wanted nothing more than to finish what he'd started.

"Reece, we have to end this little game right now, because I'm not wearing a condom."

She looked into his dreamy eyes without responding and gently kissed his neck, and then ran her tongue along his lips before kissing him. Ky cursed and ground his hips into her several more times before finding the strength to plead with her again. She was driving him insane, and being inside her felt heavenly.

"Reece," he called out to her with his voice strained as he struggled not to move.

She finally looked into his eyes. "I know, I know, but I wish we didn't have to stop."

Breathing heavily, Ky said, "We have to. Baby, please don't move or it'll be all over."

Ky knew he had already gone farther than he ever had with any woman, and if he didn't hold his composure, they could be faced with some serious consequences.

Reece nodded as Ky slowly pulled out and sat down on the shower seat, visibly shaken. With his head in his hands he mumbled, "That was close."

Reece sat down next to him and lovingly wrapped her arms around his shoulders. She kissed him on the cheek. "I'm sorry. It's all my fault."

"We're both at fault," he replied softly as the water continued to rain down on their bodies from the large overhead raindrop showerhead.

"I guess you're right," she answered. "Let's get out of here."

He stood. "You go ahead. I'm going to need a few seconds to calm down."

She nodded and stepped out of the shower. As she grabbed a towel she was worried that he was pissed off at her. She watched him as he adjusted the water and turned on additional shower heads so that he was showered from various angles.

She opened the glass door, interrupting him, and said, "I want you to know that it wasn't a game. You make it hard for me to keep my hands to myself."

He stared at her as the water ran over his manly physique.

"Reece, it's not easy for me either, but we have to be careful."

"You're right, especially since we're *just friends*," she emphasized as she closed the door to the shower and made her way over to the vanity where she sat down and continued to dry off. Reece realized she had lashed out at Ky for making her feel some type of way, but she quickly came back to her senses once she really thought about what could've been the ramifications of their actions.

Ky turned off the water and stepped out of the shower, sensing that she was upset. He grabbed a towel and slowly made his way to his sink where he dried off in silence. The truth was that he was madly in love with her and only had the courage to admit it out loud when she was asleep. Unbeknownst to him, she'd actually heard his confession. It was his prayer to tell her face-to-face real soon, and while he didn't want to have children out of wedlock, having a child with Reece would make him more than happy.

Reece finished drying off. While putting on her lotion she said, "I can understand if you're pissed because I'm not on birth control, but don't worry, I'll get some ASAP."

Ky nodded without responding. He wasn't pissed. He was extremely emotional. No woman had ever made him feel this way or go to these lengths sexually or emotionally. He was afraid that if he started talking right now he might say something that could be misinterpreted and cause him to lose her. He didn't want to risk that for sure, so he remained quiet until he could get his thoughts and emotions in check.

Reece, on the other hand, was trying to get a read on Ky's mood. She couldn't tell if he was angry. What she did know was that she was head over heels in love with him. He was everything she'd ever wanted and more, but she wasn't sure if she should tell him since she would be returning to D.C. in a few months.

"Do you want me to finish getting dinner set up?" Ky finally asked as he stared at her with his intense green eyes through the mirror's reflection.

"No, I'll take care of it. Just give me five minutes."

He leaned down and gave her a tender kiss on the shoulder. "Will do."

He disappeared into the bedroom where he put on some sweats and a T-shirt and made his way back into the family room. Reece wasn't far behind after dressing in some lounge pants and a tank top. She set up dinner at the island where they ate their meals while Ky quietly watched TV on the sofa. As she watched him from the kitchen, she still couldn't tell if he was angry over what had happened in the shower. He did give her a kiss on the shoulder before leaving the bathroom, but that could've been just to ease the awkwardness. Now his continued silence was making her nervous.

"I have everything ready. What would you like to drink?" she asked.

He turned off the TV and joined her in the kitchen. After sitting down at the island he said, "Lemonade is fine. This smells great."

"Thanks," she said as she poured his drink and then sat down across from him.

Unable to take it any longer, she had to get rid of the elephant in the room. She set the pitcher of lemonade on the counter and asked, "Are you upset with me over what I did in the shower?"

He reached across the table and held her hand tightly. "No, sweetheart. I'm pissed at myself. I'm not sixteen-years-old, so I know better. There's no excuse for me to put you at risk like that, so I want to apologize to you for doing it."

Reece couldn't believe her ears. Ky was a real man to take responsibility for his actions, even though she was the obvious instigator.

She caressed his hand. "Don't be so hard on yourself. It was all my fault. I should've stopped when you asked me the first time."

He smiled. "I know from experience it's not easy to do, so it's cool. We survived."

Reece bit down on her bottom lip. "Ky, I'm sure you have to know that I'm extremely attracted to you, both physically and emotionally. So any time I'm near you, it's hard for me not to want you. The last thing I want to do is ruin your life by getting pregnant, so I'm serious about getting birth control right away."

Ky looked at her in disbelief. He couldn't believe she thought that having his child would ruin his life. Yes, it would put them in an awkward situation, but not ruin his life. It was not the way he wanted to start his family, and he was pretty sure she felt the same way.

He kissed her hand. "Babe, you having my child would not ruin my life, but it would put us in a situation that wouldn't be ideal for either one of us. I have strong feelings for you too. That's why it happened. But can we both agree to be more careful moving forward?"

"Pinky swear," Reece said, clearly relieved as she held out her pinky finger.

Ky linked his pinky finger with hers, gave her a tender kiss and said, "Pinky swear. Now let's eat."

Reece blessed their dinner and they began to eat her delicious meal. Ky was right, they weren't prepared for something like that to happen between them and she had to do a better job keeping her emotions in check.

Later that evening, with the shower incident behind them, the young couple played a friendly game of poker downstairs, complete with poker chips. Reece hadn't played in a long time, but it didn't take long for her skills to come back to her.

"You have a good poker face," Ky acknowledged after losing a hand. "I need to take you to Vegas."

Reece slid the winning poker chips over to her side and said, "Sounds like fun. I've never been. I would love to go."

He took a sip of beer. "Are you serious? You would go with me?"

"Of course I would," she said as she stacked her chips. "I haven't had any excitement like that in a long, long time."

Reece immediately got solemn after her statement and Ky quickly picked up on it. He knew she was thinking back to her past relationship and what she had been missing out on since her fiancé's death.

Ky put down his cards. "Reece, I know you've been to hell and back, but I'm here to help you through it any way I can."

"I'm sorry. I didn't mean to bring the mood down when we're having such a good time."

He stood and pulled her out of her chair, and into his arms.

"Babe, there is light at the end of the tunnel, whether you believe it or not. I know it's hard to imagine because you're still mourning, but I want you to know that I'm crazy in love with you. All I want to do is love you and make you happy."

Reece was happy that he'd finally repeated his confession out loud to her. She stared into his emerald eyes and asked, "Really?"

He smiled and caressed her cheek lovingly. "Yes, without a doubt. I've known for a while, but after our shower incident it left no doubt in my mind. I would never do anything like that with someone I wasn't truly in love with. I wanted to tell you then, but I didn't want us to be in a sexual situation the first time I said it."

Reece swallowed the lump that had formed in her throat as tears fell out of her eyes. She was in love with him as well and couldn't be happier as she laid her head on his chest.

"Hearing you say that is such a relief. You've made it so easy for me to fall in love with you. I've known for a long time as well, but I've been afraid to say anything because of my temporary situation here. Besides, I wasn't sure if you felt the same way. You always made it a point to tell your friends and family we were friends, so I thought that was all you wanted to be."

"I do that to keep them out of our business. They'll know what we mean to each other in due time. Do you remember the first time we made love and I told you I was never letting you go?"

She nodded. "Yes, I remember."

He kissed her softly. "I meant it."

Surprised by his admission, she said, "I thought you only said it because you were caught up in the moment."

He kissed the back of her hand. "Baby, you are my moment. You're in my system now, Reece Miller, and I love the way it feels, and I love you."

"I love you too," she answered with tear filled eyes.

He took her by the hand and they slowly made their way upstairs to the bedroom. When they got to the foyer he said, "We'll work this thing out one way or another, because I can't see myself being separated from you."

Reece's heart thumped in her chest. She couldn't see herself living without him either. Just being separated from him during the day was difficult, so to try to carry on a long distance relationship would kill her.

They climbed into bed, and as Reece curled up in his arms, she said, "What are we going to do, Ky?"

He pulled her tighter against his body. "Don't you worry about a thing. What I do know is you're not staying at Ms. Doucet's house. I want you here with me."

She looked into his eyes. "Money's changed hands and I signed on the dotted line. Ms. Doucet doesn't seem like the type of person you cancel on, and she's an attorney."

He kissed her hard on the lips and then started removing her clothing.

"I can handle Mrs. Elsie, and if I have to pay for the four months myself, I will in a heartbeat, because I don't want to spend a night away from you. OK?"

"You don't have to do that, Ky," she whispered. "I'll give her a call tomorrow to see what I can work out. Her concern is not the money. She wants someone in her house while she's out of town."

He kissed her cheek. "OK, but if she doesn't go for it, let me know. I can get you out of it. Just know that this is the bed you're sleeping in every night." He ran his hands all over her body. "Now, how about we finish what we started in the shower?"

"Bring it," she whispered before nibbling on his earlobe.

She wrapped her legs around his waist so they could seal their affirmation of love by making some hot, steamy love before going   to   sleep.

CHAPTER 18

The following morning, Reece went into her office early so she could call Ms. Doucet. She was feeling a little anxious, but knew it was necessary. She dialed Ms. Doucet's number and within seconds there was an answer.

"Doucet residence. Lyla speaking. How may I help you?"

"Hello, Lyla. This is Reece Miller. Is Ms. Doucet in?"

"One moment please."

Reece became more nervous as she waited. Ms. Doucet had a strong and authoritative personality.

"Hello, Reece. How can I help you?"

"Good morning, Ms. Doucet. I'm so sorry to call you so early, but there's been a change in my housing situation. I was calling to see if it was possible to cancel my plan to move into your home?"

Ms. Doucet was silent for a few seconds and then asked, "Do you have to return to Washington earlier than expected?"

Reece took a breath. "No, ma'am. I got an offer to stay somewhere else free of charge. I would totally understand if you can't change the plans, and I'm more than prepared to pay you for the lease agreement considering my short notice."

Ms. Elsie laughed. "Reece, your timing couldn't be better. My family in California decided to come here to stay with me for my surgery. They feel like I would recover faster in my own environment. I had planned to call you sometime today to discuss the change of plans. I was worried that it was going to put you in a bind, so I was prepared to offer you an alternative place to stay at a friend's house."

"That's wonderful news for you, Ms. Doucet. I'm sure you would feel better in your own bed anyway. I wish you a speedy recovery and I really appreciate your kindness and consideration."

"It was my pleasure. I'll send you documentation to void the lease agreement and return your payment. Give me your address and I can have a courier send it over later today."

"Yes, ma'am," Reece replied before giving her the address to her office.

After hanging up the telephone, Reece called Ky and updated him on the situation, which made him extremely happy. The other good news for the day was that Alston was going to be flying in Friday afternoon to meet Ky. Reece was excited about the upcoming weekend. She would get the opportunity to meet Savoy, and Ky would be meeting Alston. What more could she ask for? She was starting to get a new outlook on life, and she loved the way it was looking.

The week passed quickly, and on Wednesday Ky was excited to finally have the Lanbeaus' yacht ready for a test drive, pending a few minor tweaks. He was just about to leave his office and return to the shipyard for final preparation when his grandmother walked through the door. She looked elegant as ever dressed in a pale green pantsuit, pearls, and heels.

He looked up from his computer screen. "Where are you going so dressed up?" he asked.

With her purse on her wrist, she answered, "I was hoping that I could get my grandson to take me to brunch so we could talk."

He walked around his desk. "It's not a good time, Gigi. You should've called. I have a lot of work to do."

Geneva grabbed him by the arm and said, "Please, Bishop. I've been sick about everything that happened on Sunday. Give me thirty minutes."

Ky hadn't spoken to his grandmother since the infamous Sunday dinner fiasco. He was still upset with her over her behavior and wasn't expecting to have to deal with her today. He sighed and then looked at his watch. Luckily there was a cafe around the corner from his office.

He pulled out his keys and said, "You have thirty minutes."

Geneva smiled. "Thank you. I brought you some of my chess squares that you love."

He took the container out of her hand, set it on his desk, and said, "Thanks." On the way out the door, he told Trish he was stepping out for a second, but to call him if she needed him.

At the cafe, Geneva ordered a ham, spinach and mushroom omelet and coffee and Ky ordered egg whites, hash browns, turkey sausage, and orange juice.

Geneva took a sip of coffee before speaking. "I know you don't have much time, so I'm going to get to it. I want to apologize for how I behaved on Sunday. Reece seems like a wonderful young woman and I had no right to treat her that way, or accuse her of being a gold digger. It's obvious you're in love with her, and because of that fact alone, I shouldn't have talked to her the way I did."

"What makes you think I'm in love with her?" he asked curiously.

"Because you're my grandson and I know you. You have a lot of me and your grandfather in you. I can tell by the way you carry yourself around her, and it's written all over your face. You look and talk to her like a man in love. We're Parkers, and we love hard. Anyway, you were right when you said it's none of my business who you date. I was only trying to be protective of you because the last thing I want to see is you being taken advantage of or hurt. I love you, and you mean the world to me, so if you give me the chance, I would like to make it up to you and Reece by inviting you both over for dinner so I can try to make amends with her."

He looked his grandmother in the eyes and said, "Even though you treated her like crap, she already forgave you because she's cool like that. Chill with the invite right now because it's too fresh. Give it some time."

Geneva could clearly see that her grandson was still unhappy with her behavior, and understandably so. The waitress interrupted them when she returned with their order. They blessed their food and started eating. Between bites Geneva continued to work on mending her relationship with her beloved grandson.

"I don't want Reece to think I don't like her. You deserve to be happy with whomever you choose, and I love and support you all the way. I'll keep my mouth shut from here on out."

Ky knew he couldn't stay angry at his grandmother for too long, but he wanted to keep her on the hook a little while longer because of how out of line she was. While she said she would keep her mouth shut from here on out, he knew better, so he decided to have a little fun with her.

He took a bite of sausage and then said, "I'm glad you said you support me all the way because there's something I need to tell you, but you can't tell Momma or Daddy."

195

She looked up at him. "You can tell me anything. What is it?"

He leaned back in his seat and said, "Reece is pregnant."

Geneva's eyes widened and she tried to restrain her true emotions upon hearing the news. Ky, on the other hand, could see that she was about to burst a blood vessel.

She cleared her throat. "You know you were taught better than to let something like that happen. What were you thinking?"

"We got caught up," he replied as he took a sip of his orange juice. "We only did it once."

"Well, that's all it takes, Bishop," she said as she started squirming in her seat. "Jesus Christ!"

"You OK?" he asked as he tried to keep from smiling. "Are you mad? You've been nagging me about giving you grandchildren."

She pulled a napkin out of the napkin holder and patted her forehead and cheeks. "No, I'm not mad, but I'm not OK either. I want grandchildren, but I didn't expect to get them like this. What are you going to do?"

"We don't know yet," he answered. "But there's something else you need to know."

Geneva began to fan herself as she prepared herself for what he had to tell her.

"What is it?" she asked curiously.

Ky leaned closer to her and whispered, "It's twins."

Geneva nearly swallowed her tongue. "You have got to be kidding me! Boy! What the hell are you going to do with one unplanned child, let alone twins? How far along is she?"

"Just a couple of months," he revealed calmly.

Ky could see that his grandmother was starting to hyperventilate. He smiled and finally decided to let her off the hook before he gave her a stroke.

He took her hand into his and said, "Calm down, Gigi. I was just kidding. Reece is not pregnant. I made the whole thing up to mess with you."

Geneva balled up her napkin and threw it across the table at him.

"Damn it, Bishop! Why would you do something like that?"

He laughed. "I couldn't resist, and I deserve to give you a little payback after what you did on Sunday. I love you, old lady, and I forgive you, but you really did hurt Reece, and you pissed me off too. She means a lot to me, so make sure you don't do anything like that again. Comprende?"

"Comprende," she replied as she fanned herself to try to cool off because Ky's little joke had made her blood pressure go up a few notches. "I love you too, and thank you for forgiving me."

He stood, pulled his grandmother into his arms, gave her a huge hug and said, "You're welcome, Gigi."

Geneva looked up into her grandson's eyes and proudly said, "Bishop, if Reese was pregnant, I have no doubt that you would be a great dad."

Ky kissed his grandmother on the cheek and with a smile answered, "I appreciate your confidence in me."

"Always, Bishop. Come on, so you can get back to work before I whip your ass."

Ky laughed as he paid their bill and they exited the café.

Inside the car she said, "The church's scholarship gala is coming up in a few months. If you plan to bring Reece, let her know because women need time to find an evening gown."

He put the keys in the ignition and said, "I'll tell her. Thanks for the reminder."

"No problem," she answered after popping a piece of peppermint in her mouth and offering him a piece as well, which he accepted.

Once his grandmother left, and before he returned to the warehouse floor, he called a florist and ordered a dozen long stemmed red roses to be delivered to Reece's office. For the card, all he wanted it to say was: JUST BECAUSE, LOVE, KY. He smiled with satisfaction because he knew the flowers would brighten up Reece's day and her office.

On the way home Reece stopped at the open market to look for something exciting for dinner. She also sampled food cooked onsite at some of the market restaurants. As she walked amongst the stalls, she thought about her conversation earlier with her Ob-Gyn in D.C. Her doctor was able to recommend a local doctor so Reece could get an IUD inserted for her birth control. She didn't want Ky to feel like their birth control was his sole obligation, so now that her IUD was inserted, they could stop using condoms when Ky was ready.

She was enjoying sampling the various food items and thinking about her night with Ky and the flowers he had delivered until she was approached by Ky's ex-girlfriend.

"Excuse me. Aren't you Ky's friend, Reece?" she asked.

"You know who I am," Reece said as she set down the bag of nectarines she was thinking of purchasing.

Yale smiled. "I was hoping I would get a chance to see you again. I'm sorry about what happened the last time we saw each other."

Reece nodded. "OK," she said and stepped around Yale to continue looking at the fruit, completely ignoring her. She remembered what Ky said to do if she ever ran into Yale, but she hoped to leave the market without any altercation.

Yale turned to follow her. "So, I saw you at church with Ky last Sunday. Things must be getting serious between you guys, huh?"

Reece rolled her eyes. "I'm not going to have that type of conversation with you. It's really none of your business."

Yale grabbed Reece by the arm to keep her from walking away. "I'm not finished talking to you."

Reece frowned, looked down at the grip Yale had on her arm, and then up at her. "You must have me confused with someone else, because if you don't take your hand off me, you're going to be sorry."

Yale slowly removed her hand when she saw that Reece wasn't the pushover type. She folded her arms and announced, "Ky is mine. He always has been and always will be. We have something special that no one can touch, so you're wasting your time."

Reece got in Yale's face. "Sweetheart, Ky is a grown ass man, so if he wanted you, he would be with you. Oh, and before I go, if you ever put your hands on me again, I will knock your ass out."

"Look, I'm just trying to let you know what's up."

Reece stepped even closer to Yale. Through gritted teeth she said, "I don't give a damn about anything you're saying. OK? Now let me tell you what's up. Ky is free to do whatever he wants to. I'm not holding him against his will. Believe it or not, he's very happy where he is."

"Bitch," Yale mumbled.

Reece laughed. While backing away she said, "It takes one to know one, and if I have to bring Ky in to really clear up your bullshit, I will."

"You may have won the battle, but not the war," Yale said as she flipped her hair over her shoulder and turned to walk away. "Oh, and before I go, I just want to say that I hope you don't let anything happen to Ky like what happened to your other man."

Reece's head jerked around upon hearing Yale's comment. How could she know about Geno? The only person who knew was Ky, and there was no way he would share something so private with his ex. She knew Yale had mentioned Geno just to get a reaction out of her, but it worked.

Yale's face split into a sneaky grin after seeing how her comment affected Reece.

Just then Yale's cousin Andre` walked over. "What's up, cuz?" he asked.

"Hey, Dre`. What are you doing down here?"

He pulled up his sagging pants and said, "I had to get some green peppers for Momma. Who was that chick you were talking to? She looks familiar."

Yale frowned. "That's Ky's new bitch."

"Yeah? You guys must be really done this time, huh?"

"Not if I have anything to do with it. I found out she works for the Department of Education so I think she works at the downtown office. She has another thing coming if she thinks I'm going to let her waltz in here and take what's mine. I just wish I could make her disappear."

"Really?" he asked. "Wow, that's cold." Andre` laughed. "You know Ky has a temper, and if he's really into that chick, you'll piss him off if you start tripping."

"Whatever!" she replied. "By the way, he said you need to get yourself together. Did he catch you doing some licks?"

"Man, Ky don't know what he's talking about. I hustle a little, but I haven't hurt nobody. He saw me one day trying to get at a woman that looked something like that chick you was talking to."

"It probably was her," Yale replied as she opened her purse. "You're going to have to chill with that life. It's not cool. You wouldn't want anyone doing that to me, your sister, or your mother, would you?"

He frowned. "If they do, they're dead."

She pointed at him. "Exactly! Look, you're family, and I love you. I don't want to see you locked up or dead over some stupid shit. Here, take this money. If you need some more come to me. I'm sure I can help you find a job too if you act right."

He took the money out of her hand, tucked it in his pocket, and said, "Thanks, cuz, and you let me know if you need me to do anything for you. We're blood, so I got you."

"I got you too, but please try to stay out of trouble," she requested. "Now get home without doing anything illegal and tell your momma I said hello."

"Later, and forget about Ky. There's other dudes around here you could kick it with."

She smiled without responding and watched him exit the market.

Reece was so angry she was trembling. She had to gather herself before she drove away from the market. When she pulled into the garage she turned off the car and sat there for a second. She didn't remember much about driving home. She couldn't remember whether the traffic lights were red or green. Luckily she hadn't caused an accident. She finally climbed out of the car and made her way inside. When she walked into the kitchen Samson greeted her lovingly like he always did. She quietly took her market purchases into the kitchen and then made her way down the hallway to the sunroom where she could hear Ky working out in the gym.

"Hey, babe," he said as he ran full speed on the treadmill.

She leaned against the door frame solemnly.

"You're a little later than normal. I was starting to worry," he said.

"I stopped at the open market to get a few things," she revealed. "I'm sorry I didn't call."

Ky lowered the speed on the treadmill, brought it down to a walking pace, and said, "It's not like you have to check in with me."

"I know, but I could've called to see if you needed me to pick up something for you."

"Don't sweat it. I would've called if I needed anything."

Reece stood there in silence not making eye contact with him. He studied her body language and noticed something wasn't quite right. There was no life in her voice or eyes. She seemed distracted, so he decided to end his workout early. With his body glistening with sweat, he turned off the machine and picked up a towel. He wiped the sweat off his face and neck before walking over to her, but she still wouldn't look up at him.

"You OK?"

"Not really," she answered as she finally looked up at him.

He kissed her tenderly on the lips and then asked, "What's wrong?"

She sighed. "I ran into your ex at the Market, and she had a lot to say about you."

"Damn! I'm sorry, babe," he said to comfort her. "I know you didn't sign up for this type of craziness."

"I'll be fine," she answered softly.

He took her by the hand and led her into the bedroom where she sat down in the chair to take off her heels.

"You say you'll be fine, but I don't like it. What did she say?" he asked as he kicked off his sneakers.

"First she tried to find out how serious our relationship was, and then she told me that you were and always will be her man. Then she called me a bitch and before she walked off she told me not to let anything happen to you like I did my last man. How could she know about Geno?"

"I don't know," he replied angrily, "but I assure you I'm going to find out.

She sighed. "Leave it alone, Ky. She's trying to provoke me into something physical, and she almost got her wish today. I told her if she ever put her hands on me again she won't like what happens."

Ky briefly put his hands over his eyes. "Wait a second! She put her hands on you?"

She shook her head. "I'm fine. She just grabbed me by my arm to keep me from walking away from her."

He hugged her. "This is ridiculous. I don't know why she keeps trying to blame you for everything. The only person I told about your past was Dani, and I know she wouldn't say anything to anyone about it."

"It's no big deal I'm sure if you Google it, you can find some type of article about it. It's not like it's a secret. I'm just private with my personal business."

"So am I," he replied as he took off his sweat drenched T-shirt. "Please don't let it ruin your day. She's messy like that, and that's another quality I hate about her."

Reece stood. "Just so you know, if she puts her hands on me again I will crack her skull, so get your bail money ready."

He saw the seriousness in her eyes and he knew he would have to do something before Reece and Yale got into a real fight.

"No, babe, I don't want you putting yourself at risk like that. I'll take care of her."

"And I don't want you getting into a big thing with her. That's what she wants, Ky."

"She's gone too far," he said as he removed the fitness monitor from his wrist. "I'm sorry, but I have to do something. I wouldn't be a man or your man if I didn't."

Reece decided not to argue with him about it. He knew Yale better than she did, and he knew how to handle her, so she backed off and changed the subject.

"I understand," she replied. "By the way, thanks for the roses you sent to my office. They're beautiful."

He smiled. "I'm glad you like them. I'm sorry I haven't done it before now."

"They really did make my day. I stared at them all day and they made my office smell so good."

He hugged her tightly. "You make my day."

"And you make mine," she replied before giving him a sultry kiss. She stepped out of his embrace and said, "After I finish with dinner, I'm going to take a long soak in the tub to clear my head."

"Let's go out. I need to run some paperwork by my uncle's house anyway," he said as he walked into the bathroom.

"I'm really not up to it, Ky. I don't think I'll be good company," she said as she followed him.

He removed his shorts and threw them in the hamper with his T-shirt. He turned on the water for the shower and patted her lovingly on her backside. "I'm sure you feel that way right now. Let's go have a little fun. I won't keep you out late. I promise."

She smiled and looked down at his chiseled, naked body which made her forget all about Yale.

Ky noticed the sensual look on her face. "Reece, if you're thinking what I think you're thinking, let me suit up first. You know what happened last time."

"We can revisit what I have on my mind when we get back home," she announced.

He opened the shower door and said, "That's a date."

"Where are you taking me anyway? I need to know how to dress."

"A friend of mine has a little club uptown," he revealed as he stepped into the huge shower. "I think you'll like it."

"OK. Do you mind sharing the shower?" she asked. "I promise I'll behave."

He laughed. "Come on in."

Reece stripped out of her clothes and joined Ky in the shower. It was difficult for them to stay focused as they lathered up, but they were able to maintain their composure and get through their shower quickly.

Within the hour they were dressed and ready to go. Ky looked extremely handsome in his starched white shirt, black slacks and matching jacket. Reece chose a body hugging short, black, one shoulder dress which showcased not only her long, shapely legs, but her voluptuous body as well. She looked flawless, and Ky couldn't be more proud to have her on his arm.

"You look beautiful," Ky told her.

She put on her three-inch, black sandals with silver embellishments and said, "Thank you. You look handsome yourself."

He picked up his cell phone and said, "Thanks, babe. You ready?"

"As ready as I'm going to be."

"Great! Let's go."

CHAPTER 19

Once in the car, Ky texted his friend to let him know he was coming by the club.

His friend quickly responded, acknowledging he had his table set up and ready. When Ky pulled up at the club, he opted for valet parking so Reece wouldn't have to walk far in her heels. There were a lot of excited people filing into the club and Reece was starting to get excited about being out. She hadn't been dancing in a long time, and this was going to be another welcomed change in her life. There was a long line of people waiting to get in, but Ky was able to bypass the line. When they stepped in the door he pulled out a card for the attendant to scan.

Curious, Reece asked, "What kind of card was that?"

He took her hand into his. "I have VIP status. I paid a lump sum, which gives me access to all the shows and to the club whenever I come. I grew up with the club's owner."

"Wow," Reece replied. "So are you like an investor in the club?"

"I guess that's a way of looking at it. I'm just glad he's finally doing something legit. He used to be in the streets if you know what I mean."

About that time Pepto walked up to the couple and gave Ky a brotherly hug. Ky quickly introduced him to Reece and then they followed him upstairs to their VIP seating area. Once there, Pepto quickly told his hostess to bring them a bottle of his best champagne and a platter of finger food. Ky thanked him. Pepto was happy to have his friend in his club tonight and was especially happy to see him with Reece.

"I think you guys are going to like the show tonight. We have a very funny comedian to open up and then we have a great band that specializes in R&B music. I found them on YouTube, and as you will see, they are worth every penny," Pepto bragged.

Ky took a sip of his drink. "Where are they from?" he asked.

"Atlanta. They're young, but they're true musicians and have old souls. They have a great female lead singer. They have a male singer that is da bomb too."

With a smile, Ky said, "I can't wait to hear them."

Pepto turned to Reece. "Reece, it was a pleasure to meet you. I hope you enjoy yourself, and if you guys need anything else, just let your hostess know. Enjoy the show."

"Thank you, and it was nice meeting you as well," Reece said, shaking Pepto's hand.

"I need to go check on my staff and the entertainment. I'll swing through later to check on you guys. If you need refills on the champagne and food, your hostess will take care of you."

Once he was gone, Reece looked around the club and noticed a familiar face.

"Ky, there's Dani."

He scanned the crowd. "Yeah, looks like she's with Isaac. I'll text her and let her know we're up here."

Ky texted his cousin and within seconds she looked up and waved at them sitting in the balcony area. Minutes later, Pepto came to the stage and introduced the comedian to the crowd. He was hilarious and had the entire room in tears with laughter. His jokes were clean but hysterical. His humor was similar to the style of Sinbad. After about an hour, he left the stage to thundering applause. Between the acts, the DJ played a couple of songs that the crowd could dance to until the band finished setting up. As soon as Pepto introduced the band, they electrified the crowd with dance tunes that had them on their feet for several minutes before they slowed it down.

Ky stood and held out his hand to Reece. "Come on, babe, let's dance."

Reece took Ky's hand and followed him out to the dance floor and into his arms. It felt wonderful to be in his arms dancing to the band's rendition of Mint Condition's song "If You Love Me." Reece closed her eyes and melted into Ky's body. Once that song ended the band went into another slow song, "Wait For Love" by Luther Vandross. Both songs were fitting for their relationship and they paid close attention to the lyrics as they looked into each other's eyes. Ky couldn't resist any longer, so he leaned down and kissed her tenderly on the lips.

They stayed out on the floor for a couple more dance songs before they decided to head back to their seats. On the way, they stopped briefly to talk to Dani and Isaac, and then Reece made a pit stop into the ladies' room. While washing her hands, Reece was surprised to look in the mirror and see Yale and her friend walk over to her at the sink.

"Hey, Reece," Yale greeted her as she leaned against the counter.

Reece rolled her eyes without replying and then grabbed a handful of paper towels to dry her hands. Running into Yale twice in one day was more than enough for Reece.

"Enjoy Ky while you can, bitch," Yale said and then laughed.

Reece opened the door to walk out, but then she changed her mind. She turned around and came back into the restroom.

Reece walked right up to Yale and said, "It's funny you said that, because Ky and I have been enjoying the hell out of each other every chance we get. In fact, I'm going to enjoy the hell out of him as soon as we leave, and I don't give a damn what you say to try to piss me off. Sweetheart, let me enlighten you on something so you'll stop wasting your time. You might think you can come between me and Ky, but you can't, and as far as that shade you threw at me regarding my ex, you should be ashamed of yourself because he was murdered. I thank God every day that I have Ky in my life after losing someone I loved. Furthermore, if there's anything else you want to know about me, here's your chance to ask. Otherwise, stay the hell away from me and keep my name out of your mouth. Ky has made his choice, so get over it."

Yale's friend Anniston stood by quietly while Reece handled Yale. She was shocked to see the surprised look on Yale's face. She could be a bully at times, but the table had turned completely and unexpectedly on her friend.

Yale pointed her finger at Reece. "We'll see."

Reece pointed her finger back at Yale and said, "I guess we will."

Reece turned and walked out of the restroom, leaving Yale furious. She had never had anyone step to her like Reece. This only fueled her anger and made her more determined to split them up.

Anniston put on her lip gloss. "That was interesting," she said.

"That bitch don't know who she's messing with," Yale replied. "She needs the fear of God put in her so she'll know I mean business."

"I don't think you want to mess with her anymore. She's not scared of you," Anniston pointed out.

"She will be," Yale replied with a sly grin on her face. "And Ky's in for a rude awakening too."

"Are you sure you want to keep doing this?" Anniston asked. "It's not a good look for you. There are too many fine men around here for you to keep wasting all of your energy on Ky."

Yale waved off Anniston. "There aren't any men around here with Ky's pedigree. I've got something that will make him change his mind."

"What?"

"I might tell you later. Let's get out of here."

The two women exited the bathroom and joined other patrons out in the club. As they made their way across the room, Yale was stopped by a guy.

"Yale Spencer. It's so nice to see you again."

Confused, Yale asked, "Do I know you?"

He laughed and pulled out his cell phone. "No. Well somewhat. You took a selfie with me in the pedestrian mall a while back. See, here it is."

Yale looked at the picture and then remembered this was the guy with the ashy hands. She looked at his hands tonight and they looked fine. She also looked at him a little closer and realized he wasn't a bad looking guy.

She smiled. "Oh, now I remember. I'm sorry I didn't recognize you."

He tucked his phone back into his pocket. "It's OK. You're so beautiful. I'm sure you meet a lot of guys. May I buy you a drink?"

"Sure you can," she said before walking over to the bar with the stranger.

Reece made her way back to her seat, and when she sat down, she leaned over to Ky and whispered, "Your girl's here."

He frowned and set his drink on the table.

Reece took a sip of her drink. "We had a little conversation in the restroom."

"You didn't knock her out, did you?"

She giggled. "No, but I wanted to."

"Are you cool?"

She kissed him on the lips. "Everything's fine, babe. Don't you worry about Yale. I think I handled her once and for all."

"If you say so," he answered, seeing that Reece didn't seem to be worried about his ex anymore.

But Ky was worried, because he knew Yale could act irrational sometimes, and she did carry a gun. He didn't want anything to happen to his new love, although he didn't want to scare her unnecessarily either. His mind was made up. He would have to pay Yale a visit, but he needed to know what happened in the restroom to gauge Yale's demeanor. He decided to wait until they got home before bringing it up to Reece again. For now, he wanted her to enjoy the evening, so they danced and visited with friends for another hour until Ky noticed his date yawning.

"You ready to go? It's getting late," Ky said.

"Yes, I am getting a little tired," Reece answered. "I had a great time. Thanks for bringing me out for some fun."

He stood. "Any time. We'll come back again soon."

Ky said his goodbyes to several people on their way out. Downstairs, he ran into a few friends and then made his way over to Dani and Isaac where they briefly chatted before heading to the exit. At the door they said goodbye to Pepto and headed outside to wait for the valet to bring the car. As they waited, Ky held Reece close with his arm around her waist.

Yale walked over to them and asked, "You two leaving so soon?"

Ky shook his head in disbelief, and then calmly said, "Go on about your business, Yale."

She put her hands on her hips and asked, "So I can't even talk to you anymore?"

"We don't have anything left to talk about, and you know it, so I would appreciate it if you would leave us alone."

Yale looked over at Reece and then back at Ky. With tears forming in her eyes she asked, "What makes her so damn special?"

The valet pulled up to the curb with Ky's car and jumped out, handing him the keys. He tipped the valet and then opened the door for Reece to get inside.

"Have a seat, baby. Let me handle this for a second."

Worried, Reece said, "Let's just go, Ky."

He kissed her. "In a second."

Ky closed the car door and turned to his ex with an angry expression on his face. He calmly walked over to her and grabbed her tightly by the arm. Then with his mouth inches from her ear he whispered, "Get your ass together. If you come near Reece again talking some bullshit about me and you, you won't like my response. This is the last time I'm going to remind you. We are done! Do you understand?"

She yanked her arm out of his grasp. "Go to hell, Ky!"

Ky watched as she angrily walked back toward the entrance of the club.

About that time Yale's admirer from the club started walking toward Ky and asked Yale, "Is that man bothering you?"

With a sly grin on her face, she lied and said, "Yes, he is. I don't know what makes him think he can grab me like that."

"Don't worry, I'll take care of him."

Ky saw the man walking in his direction, so he pointed at him and said, "Bro, don't let Yale get you hurt."

Reece saw what was happening and fear gripped her heart. She didn't want anything to happen to Ky, and she started to have flashbacks of how she'd lost Geno to violence. There was no way she could go through that pain again.

The man stopped walking when he saw the look in Ky's eyes. Yale's cousin, Andre`, and some friends got out of a car parked nearby and walked over to see what was going on.

"Yo, cuz! What's going on?" Andre` asked Yale. "Is that your boy, Ky?"

"Yes, that's him," she replied angrily.

"What's going on?" he asked.

She sighed. "He got pissed at me and grabbed my arm because I had a few words with his bitch in the restroom."

Andre` pulled up his sagging pants. "Hold on, I got this. Yo, Ky! Why are you putting your hands on my cousin?"

Ky now had two people to worry about. He had his eyes on the stranger and now he had to deal with Andre`.

"Dre`, I know you're not going to step to me. I don't know what Yale told you, but she's no saint. Do you really want to do this?"

Andre` stopped walking when he also saw the look in Ky's eyes. Yale saw it too and realized things were about to get completely out of hand. She ran over to the two men defending her and grabbed them each by the arm.

"Don't worry about him. I'm fine. It's not worth either one of you getting into trouble."

She turned to her male friend and thanked him for coming to her defense. She then asked him to wait for her inside, which he happily agreed to do. Andre` could see the pain in his cousin's eyes and it angered him. He didn't know the whole story, but nobody put their hands on the females in his family regardless of the circumstances.

"Cuz, forget about Ky. He's with that other chick now."

"I know," she replied. "I don't know what makes her so damn special."

He put his arm around her shoulders. "Who cares? That guy you were just with stepped up, which I like. Maybe you need to give him a chance, because if I ever see Ky put his hands on you again, you won't be able to stop me from kicking his ass."

"That's sweet, but I don't want you getting into a thing with Ky. I am hurt that he's treating me like he never had any feelings for me."

Andre` hugged her. "He's a fool. Fuck him."

Ky noticed that the stranger had returned to the club and he stared at Yale and Andre` until he was sure they were no longer a threat.

When he got behind the wheel of his car, Reece looked at him and said, "That was crazy. I was so scared. Who were those guys?"

Ky pulled away from the curb and said, "I don't know who that man was, but the other one is Yale's cousin, Andre` who was one of the teens at your car that day you had the flat."

"Small world," she replied. "I didn't know what was going to happen. I was worried about you."

"You don't have to do that. I can handle them and take care of myself. That girl has issues, and I don't want anyone to get hurt, especially you. Yale has a gun permit and her cousin is reckless too. While I don't think either of them would try to come at you, I don't want you to be vulnerable. Do you own a gun?"

"No, but I know how to use one. I used to go to the gun range with my dad," she revealed. "Do you think I need to get a restraining order against her?"

"No, but I would feel better if you were armed when you're out alone. I have a .38 you can keep with you if you're cool with it. Dani carries a firearm for protection of not only herself, but for her business since it deals with a lot of cash. Savoy has one too, but she's had to keep it on the down low while she's at school because weapons are not allowed on campus, and it could get her kicked out of school."

Reece looked out the window and thought about it. In this day and time most women were armed and needed to be to stay safe.

"If you feel better with me having it, sure, I'll take it," she replied.

He reached over and rubbed her thigh lovingly, and then rested his hand there.

"I hate drama and I never expected you to be harassed like this. Yale is really delusional."

Reece covered his hand with hers. "She would be doing this to whomever you had in your life. I just hate to see any woman act like that, but especially one with a nice job and with her beauty. She would have no problem meeting someone new."

"Meeting someone has never been her issue. This is about rejection," he revealed. "I've known Yale for a long time, and as friends she was cool. Even when we started dating she was cool. She's spoiled and used to getting her way. I didn't see that in her until a few months into the relationship. I thought she would change, but she never did. I still hung in there with her longer than I should have because I cared about her. When I caught her going through my phone, that was the last straw."

"That's a shame. At least you tried."

He continued to rub her thigh as he drove out of downtown toward the house and softly said, "Yeah, but had it not happened, I wouldn't be with you. Everything happens for a reason."

She leaned over and gave him a kiss on the cheek. "I love you. Don't you ever scare me like that again."

"I love you too, and I'll try not to."

When they got home, Samson met them at the door. The ride had made Reece extremely sleepy. She kicked off her shoes, lay across the bed, and said, "I am so sleepy."

Ky laid his jacket on the bench at the foot of the bed and said, "Let me help you out of that dress."

He pulled her off the bed, unzipped her dress, and pulled it over her head.

"Are you hungry?" he asked softly. "We only had finger food at the club."

She sat back down on the bed in her panties and bra. "I'm starving, but it's too late to eat anything heavy."

He walked into the bathroom and put her dress in the dry clean only hamper along with his jacket, shirt, and slacks.

When he returned he said, "How about I make us some fruit smoothies? Will that hold you until morning?"

She stood and rubbed Samson on the head. "It's better than nothing. I'm getting ready to hit the shower."

"OK, but before you take your shower, what did Yale say to you in the restroom?"

Reece sighed. "She said, 'Enjoy Ky while you can, bitch.'"

"What did you say to her?"

Reece laughed. "I told her I was enjoying you every chance I got. She didn't like that at all."

He knew Reece's comment probably hit Yale hard, but he was glad she stood up to her and let her know she wasn't a pushover.

"Thanks for telling me. Again, I'm going to put a stop to it, but I'm glad you stood up to her. She can be a bully if you let her," he said before walking out of the bedroom. "I'll be back in a second."

Reece entered the bathroom to take a quick shower. Ky returned to the bedroom with her smoothie just as she was drying off.

He handed it to her, gave her a kiss on the cheek, and said, "Enjoy."

She took the drink out of his hand and thanked him. Ky entered the bathroom where he took his shower. Finally they turned in for the night, but he couldn't sleep. Yale's antics that night had made his patience run out. Once Reece fell into a deep sleep, he eased out of bed, got dressed, and made his way out to his car where he quietly drove away.

It was nearly two AM when he drove past Yale's house. He saw a light on downstairs and upstairs and he knew she was still awake. The problem was that he didn't know if she was alone. He didn't see any other cars in her driveway, but it was still possible she wasn't alone. He decided to take the chance anyway as he parked his car around the corner and walked back up the block to her house. He hoped the key he still had to her place worked as he eased it in the lock and turned it.

The door opened easily. When he walked in, he noticed there was one glass sitting next to a bottle of Tequila on the coffee table. He could hear the shower running and Yale singing as he made his way upstairs undetected. He wanted to catch her off guard because of her gun, so he had to be cautious because he still wasn't 100 percent sure she was alone.

When he got upstairs, he peeped into her room and didn't see any traces of anyone else, so he removed Yale's gun from her nightstand and placed it on top of her entertainment center. He had his own gun in his waistband just in case things got out of hand, but he prayed he wouldn't have to use it. He knew he was taking a huge risk being there, but he needed to do this to make Yale understand there was no chance of them ever getting back together. He'd made his choice with Reece.

Ky looked around the bedroom and noticed Yale's clothes and shoes thrown around on the floor. Just then he heard the shower turn off so he decided to sit in the chair in the corner of the room and wait. Seconds later, she entered the bedroom still humming, not realizing she wasn't alone. She sat on her bed with her back to him and starting putting on lotion.

"We need to talk," Ky said calmly.

Yale screamed and jumped off the bed in fear. She scrambled for her nightstand but when she reached inside she found that her gun was missing. She looked up to search for another weapon of choice and realized that her intruder was Ky.

She immediately calmed down. "What the hell are you doing here? You scared the shit out of me. And how did you get into my house?"

He stood and slid her house key across the dresser in her direction. "You really need to change your locks when your relationships end."

Yale had completely forgotten about the key Ky had to her house, but in all reality she had hoped he would come back to her, and now he had.

With a seductive expression on her face she walked over to him and opened her robe, exposing her curvy, naked body. "I knew you couldn't stay away."

He pushed her away from him. "I'm not here for sex or you."

Ignoring him she put her hands on her hips and asked, "Then why are you here? I hope you're not upset about what happened earlier. You know how I am when I've had too much to drink."

"You're not drunk and I can't believe you would get other people involved in your drama."

She laughed. "I don't know that guy that confronted you and as far as Andre`, well you know how he is."

Ky grabbed her by the chin, pointed his finger in her face, and said, "I don't give a damn about you, who you're screwing, or your thieving cousin, but let's get this cleared up once and for all. I am not your man. We are done! And if you ever put your hands on Reece again or get in her face talking a bunch of bullshit, I won't be responsible for my actions."

"Is that why you're here?" she asked as she giggled and pushed his hand from her face. "I should've known Miss Thang would run back and tell you about our little conversation."

"I'm serious, Yale. Leave her alone."

She got in his face and poked him in the forehead with her finger. "Please! Boy, I'm grown! You don't control me, and I will say what I want, to whom I want, whenever I get good and damn ready, especially to your precious little Reece."

Ky lost it. Before he realized it, he grabbed Yale and threw her on the bed. He straddled her body, sitting on her chest while pinning her arms over her head. As he sat on her chest it was hard for her to breathe.

He leaned down in her face. "Woman, it's taking every muscle in my body to keep from hurting you right now. My father taught me to respect women, but you are about to make me forget all about that. I could snap your neck right now over the way you've been harassing me and Reece. I can make your life a living hell, so stop pushing me, because you will lose, and you know it."

Yale continued to wiggle underneath him, pleading for him to get off her. "I can't breathe," she panted.

"After all you've done, do you think I care if you can breathe?" he asked as he yelled at her. "Stay away from Reece, and if you ever try to start a fight again between me and some guy you're screwing, you'll be sorry."

Yale had never seen Ky this angry, and he'd never gotten physical with her, even when she'd given him plenty of reasons to. He had a look in his eyes that scared her, and she realized she had pushed him too far. He really could hurt her or kill her and not give it a second thought.

"Get off me, Ky! You're hurting me!" she pleaded with him.

At that point Ky came back to his senses. He knew that if he hurt Yale, it would devastate Reece and his family, so he slowly climbed off her. She sat up and took deep breaths as she struggled to get air back into her lungs.

"Are you crazy?" she yelled as she got off the bed. "You could've killed me!"

He stared at her in silence with a cold and callous look on his face. Ky hoped he had finally gotten his point across to his ex and that she would move on with her life. He walked over to her, backing her against the wall.

He towered over her and calmly said, "I don't want to have this type of conversation with you ever again. Stay away from me and Reese. Are we clear?"

With tears in her eyes she said, "Yes! Just get the hell out of my house!"

"Get your life together, Yale," he said before he exited her bedroom and made his way downstairs and out the door. When he returned home he found Reece still sleeping peacefully. He quietly removed his clothes and eased back into bed. Reece let out a soft moan as she rolled over and put her arm around his waist. He pulled his woman closer and finally drifted off to sleep.

The next morning Ky gently woke Reece with soft kisses. She had slept so soundly the night before that she had no idea he had snuck out in the darkness. He just hoped Yale would stay true to her word and stay away from Reece. He felt comfortable that his late night excursion had finally put an end to Yale's crazy antics so he could concentrate solely on Reece. Ky knew Savoy would be coming home later today, so he wanted to make sure he was able to give Reece his undivided attention before his sister arrived.

He kissed her lovingly on the lips and whispered, "Good morning."

She smiled and caressed his cheek. "Good morning. You're the best alarm clock a girl could have."

He pulled her into his arms and said, "I love you, Reece. I never thought I would ever meet anyone that could make me open up like you have, but you're definitely that woman."

"I love you too, baby."

At that moment Ky lost it emotionally. He had never shown a woman his tears. Now he was 100 percent certain that Reece was the only woman for him, and he wanted her to know just how much she meant to him. Seeing how emotional he was made Reece get emotional too. She kissed him lovingly and gently wiped away his tears and hers.

"It's OK, Ky. I know exactly how you feel."

Ky kissed his woman and never wanted to stop. Reece breathlessly held onto him as he slowly moved lower to her breasts where he covered her brown nipples with his warm lips.

"Sweet Jesus," she whispered to him as her body heated up even more when he eased between her thighs.

"Reece, babe. I love you so much," he whispered as he entered her and slowly began to grind his hips into hers.

She held on to his broad shoulders and wrapped her toned legs around his waist to give him full access to her love. Ky greedily kissed her lips and neck and he thrust his hips harder into her, moaning with each thrust. Reece felt like her body was on fire as the love of her life drove deeper and harder into her feminine core. Ky grabbed her legs and held them securely in place so he could delve even deeper as he quickened his pace. Reece felt a familiar wave starting to overtake her body as Ky nibbled on her lips. Her moans became even louder and more frequent as he boldly confessed how good she felt and tasted. He continued to drill his body into her until he felt her body shudder beneath him and she let out a soft moan. Hearing her sensual moan caused him to increase his tempo once again, and within seconds he screamed out her name, pounded his fist on the upholstered headboard, and released his seed into her. He collapsed on top of her and buried his face against her warm neck.

Reece caressed his sweat-drenched body and softly said, "Mercy."

The young couple lay in each other's arms in silence for several minutes as they slowly regained their breath.

Reece continued to caress his body and then asked, "What are you thinking about?"

"You. Babe, I messed up," he softly admitted.

She looked into his eyes and asked, "Messed up how?"

"I probably just got you pregnant."

She smiled and gave him a tender kiss on the lips. "You don't have to worry about that. I'm on birth control now, so you can relax."

He looked into her eyes and asked, "Why didn't you tell me?"

"I was going to tell you, but I didn't want you to stop doing something you were comfortable doing until you were ready. It's not your sole responsibility anyway."

"I couldn't love you more," he proclaimed to her with a kiss.

Reece's mood instantly changed when she sat up in bed and said, "What's going to happen to us when it's time for me to go back to D.C.? I can't leave you."

He sat up as well and caressed her cheek. "None of that matters to me right now, because it will work out. Our relationship is solid and I know exactly where it's going."

She looked into his loving eyes and asked, "You do?"

Without answering, he climbed out of the bed and disappeared into his closet.

"What are you up to?"

"Close your eyes," he yelled from the walk-in closet.

"OK, they're closed," she yelled back as she closed her eyes.

Seconds later she could feel him back in the bed next to her where he reminded her to keep her eyes closed. He wrapped his arm around her shoulders and kissed her firmly on the lips and then softly asked, "Reece, are you happy here with me?"

With a smile on her face and her eyes still closed she answered, "I'm so happy when I'm with you that I feel like my heart is going to burst. I'm crazy in love with you, Ky Parker."

He took her hand into his and said, "I'm crazy in love with you too. That's why I decided to get you a little something as a token of my affection."

At that moment she felt something amazing and totally unexpected.

"Now you can open your eyes," he whispered with a voice full of love and commitment.

Reece opened her eyes and looked down at her hand. She saw a two-carat, double framed emerald cut diamond ring resting on her finger and tears immediately flowed out of her eyes.

With his voice barely above a whisper he asked, "Reece Miller, will you marry me?"

Sobbing, Reece nodded since she was unable to speak. Overjoyed, he pulled her into his arms where they held each other. He lovingly caressed her back and tenderly kissed her until she eventually stopped crying.

He wiped away her tears and said, "I hope that nod means yes."

She finally found the strength to answer him with a loud, "Yes, Yes, Ky. I'll marry you."

He laughed and said, "Whew! You had me sweating there for a minute. I take it you like your ring?"

"Oh my God, it's stunning. Thank you."

"Just so you know, I had a feeling I was going to marry you after our first date. After our second date and seeing you fishing, I was sold. I bought the ring the next day. I've wanted to propose to you for a while but I've been waiting for the right moment. Today just seemed right."

"I'm in shock, but what are we going to do about our living situation?"

"We have time to work all of that out. For now, I'm just happy to know that you want to be my wife."

Still staring at her ring, she asked, "Have you told anyone about this?"

"No, but we're going to have to let everyone know because they're not going to be able to miss that ring on your finger. We can tell Savoy tonight and then tell your brother when he gets in town tomorrow. I was thinking we could invite the whole family over for a family dinner and say we're doing it for Savoy and your brother being in town. That way they won't be suspicious of why we invited everyone over."

"I'm OK with that. Alston's the only brother I have and Savoy's the only sister you have. We're very close and there's no way I could hide it from him anyway. I have to be honest with you. The whole reason for Alston's visit was to check you out."

Ky laughed. "For real? That's cool, though. I hope I pass."

She kissed him tenderly. "I have no doubt you will. Besides, I'm sure Savoy is anxious to check me out as well."

"True, but I know she'll love you too, so I'm not worried."

With her fingers crossed she said, "I hope so. So the deal is we only tell Savoy and Alston and everyone else will find out Saturday night. Agreed?"

"Agreed," Ky replied.

"For now, I'll only wear the ring around the house," she said with a huge smile on her face as she held out her hand to admire her ring again.

"Whatever you want to do, sweetheart. I'll make some calls tomorrow to look into a caterer, because I'm not doing all that cooking."

She giggled. "I guess you could use a break from the kitchen."

He climbed out of bed and said, "True. We had better get up before we're late to work. You want breakfast, Mrs. Parker?"

"Wow, I like the sound of that," she answered as she looked at the clock. "Don't worry about me. I'll grab something on the way in."

"You're right, we are getting a late start. I can do the same."

"Do I need to do anything before Savoy comes in tonight?" she asked as she walked into the bathroom.

He followed her into the shower and said, "If you can stop at the bakery and pick up a half dozen red velvet cupcakes I would appreciate it. She's addicted to them. I'm going to grill tonight, so other than that, we're good."

"Consider it done," she said before turning on the hot water and lathering up her fiancé.

Yale woke up to a terrible hangover and sore ribs. After her altercation with Ky she had been angry and needed to do whatever she could to get him off her mind. The tequila shots had helped, but they also made her lose control of her senses, so she'd decided to spend the rest of the night with the man she'd run into at the club, inviting him over after Ky left. It wasn't bad that she'd invited him over. It was what she did after he'd arrived. Now she sat up in bed and looked over at the stranger beside her and shook her head. When she tried to ease out of bed he pulled her into his arms and rolled on top of her.

"Where do you think you're going?" he asked as he started kissing her neck and breasts.

She squirmed beneath him. "I have to go to work, and you need to leave."

He palmed one of her breasts and took the other into his mouth. Yale arched her back and massaged his shoulders as he consumed her rigid nipples. She let out soft whimpers as he greedily moved from one to the other, causing her body to react.

"This is really nice, but duty calls," she reminded him again.

He started kissing down her body and said, "OK, OK, but first let me get another taste."

Before she could respond, he was already between her thighs greedily savoring her sweetness. Yale wasn't one to turn down this kind of loving, and to be honest, he was somewhat masterful in that area. So masterful that it didn't take long for him to have her moaning loudly as he buried his face into her flesh.

He was lost and in heaven and had the one woman he had desired for a long time in his grasp. He wanted to prove his worthiness to her. Yale closed her eyes and made hissing sounds as she grabbed the sheets. He kissed and consumed her for what seemed like an eternity. He devoured her body and flicked his tongue against her swollen nub until her body shuddered hard and she let out a loud moan.

He kissed her and whispered, "I could do that all day, every day. You taste as sweet as you look."

"That was da bomb, uh, uh. What's your name again?"

"I can't believe you forgot my name the way you were screaming it out last night. It's Quincy, babe," he answered before covering her breasts again with his warm lips.

"That's right. Quincy. Sorry about that."

Yale could feel the hardness of his body and knew that he wasn't finished with her yet. In fact, she kind of wanted to sample a little more of what he had to offer, so she grabbed a condom off the nightstand and said, "Well, Quincy, if you can make this quick, count me in, but you have to go right afterwards."

He ripped open the packet, hurriedly rolled on the condom, rolled her over onto her stomach, and plowed into her voluptuous body. She grimaced as he vigorously made love to her. She listened to him grunt and moan as he gripped her hips and drove his body deep into hers.

Yale urged him on, which excited him even more as he pounded his body against her round hips. Yale was happy Quincy was able to satisfy her sexually. He had some big shoes to fill, and so far, he was doing a great job. She realized she could probably get him to do just about anything if she asked. Minutes later, he let out one loud, long grunt and collapsed on top of her.

Breathless, he rolled off her and said, "Damn! You're going to give me a heart attack."

"You're going to give yourself a heart attack," she said, sitting up on the side of the bed. "Now get up and get dressed because you have to go."

"Let me catch my breath first and I'll go," he said as he pulled her up into his arms and kissed her. "I'll let you kick me out now, but, girl, I'm addicted to you, and I can't wait to see you again."

She eased out of his embrace and said, "Slow down a little bit. I can tell you're a cool guy and we had fun last night. I don't want you to get ahead of yourself. You were there for me when I really needed a friend, and I appreciate it. Let's just take things slowly, OK?"

He nodded, started getting dressed and said, "I can get with that. If you ever need a friend again, you know how to reach me, and if you have any more trouble out of your ex, just let me know. I'm glad your cousin stepped in when he did, because I was a second away from kicking his ass when I saw him grab you."

Yale looked at Quincy and smiled. Quincy was not as handsome as Ky, but he was handsome and he was fine. Her night with him was a physical and emotional relief, but she didn't want her new friend to think they were a couple, even though they clicked sexually.

She gave him a hug. "I can handle my ex, but I appreciate you wanting to come to my defense last night."

"A beautiful woman like you? Any time, sweetheart," he replied as he followed her out of the bedroom.

Yale walked him downstairs to the door and opened it. She didn't tell him what Ky did to her last night, and decided to keep that tidbit to herself.

He gave her one last kiss on the lips and said, "Have a nice day at work, and don't forget to call me if you need another fix."

She smiled. "Don't worry, I'll be in touch."

"Promise?" he asked as he caressed her cheek.

"Promise."

She closed the door behind him, looked at the clock, and hurried back upstairs and into the shower.

At work, Yale entered her office singing a Nicki Minaj song.

Jeremy turned to her and said, "Somebody's happy this morning. You must've had a good night."

She put her purse inside her desk drawer and said, "I did, and I had a good morning too."

He studied her body language. "Well, you look great, and you are wearing that dress."

Yale walked over to Jeremy and gave him a kiss on the lips. "Thank you."

Shocked by her actions he whispered, "Whoa! Where did that come from? Did you get laid or something, because I haven't seen you this happy in months."

She twirled around in her chair and said, "As a matter of fact, I did, and it was amazing."

"Did you hook up with your ex, because you've never talked about anybody but him."

"No, I didn't," she answered as she turned on her laptop.

Jeremy frowned. "You mean to tell me you let somebody else hit that, and you won't even give me a chance?"

She giggled. "Jeremy, I told you, I don't mess around with horny college boys."

"I'm out of college, and you don't know what you're missing," he replied before turning his back to her. "It's your loss."

Yale could see that her friend and co-worker's feelings were hurt. She liked Jeremy and he was a good-looking white guy, but she wasn't going to have sex with him just because he wanted her to. She hugged his neck and gave him a kiss on the cheek.

"Come on, Jeremy. Don't be upset with me," she said as she wiped her lipstick off his cheek and sat back down. "You're the best friend I have here. Don't let something like this come between us. I'm sure you're a wonderful lover, but I want us to stay friends. I'm sure the right girl is out there for you, but I'm not that girl. We're friends, OK?"

He shook his head and said, "I guess."

Yale smiled. "Let's get to work. I want to finish that piece today so we can air it Monday. Is your head clear? Are we cool?"

"Yeah, we're cool," he replied before turning back around in his chair.

When she looked back over at him he had a smile on his face. Without making eye contact with her he asked, "So are you going to tell me who you screwed last night?"

She laughed and then waded up a piece of paper, threw it at him, and said, "Get to work."

CHAPTER 19

Savoy stepped off the plane looking like a fashion model in her skinny jeans, three inch heels and fuchsia blazer. When she saw her brother she ran and jumped in his arms.

Ky gave her a kiss on the forehead and said, "Welcome home, sis."

"You don't know how happy I am to be home. I missed you guys," she said as they walked over to the luggage turnstile. "Where's your new bae?"

He laughed. "She's at work. You're going to love her, Savoy."

"I'm sure I will," Savoy replied as she stared at her brother. She could see an obvious change in him. He was more relaxed than normal and he had never talked about a woman like this before.

"Is that your suitcase?" he asked as a suitcase with her sorority's crest came around the turnstile.

She nodded and popped a piece of gum in her mouth, then offered him some gum as he pulled her suitcase off the turnstile.

"Let's go. You hungry?"

Walking with him she said, "I'm always hungry. What are you cooking?"

He laughed. "What do you want?"

She climbed into his car and said, "It doesn't matter. You know me, I'll eat whatever."

"Good, because I have everything ready to go on the grill."

Ky had steaks and chicken marinating for the grill. Reece was going to put together a seven-layer salad and the rest of the menu would include roasted steak fries, grilled corn on the cob, and sautéed asparagus.

"So what's she like?" Savoy asked as they pulled out of the airport.

"Who, Reece?"

With a smirk on her face she asked, "Who else could I be talking about? Yes, Reece. What is she like?"

He pulled out onto the expressway and said, "She's beautiful, smart, sexy, but she has a shyness about her, and I love to see her blush. It's one of her most attractive features."

Ky went on to tell his sister how he met Reece, what she did for a living, and he revealed that they were living together at his house unbeknownst to their parents and family members.

Savoy laughed. "I knew it."

With a huge grin on his face he asked, "You knew what?"

"Big brother, you're in love, and it looks good on you too. I've never seen you like this, so I can't wait to meet this woman."

"You're funny," he answered without admitting anything to his sister as he sped toward his house. When he pulled into the garage he noticed that Reece's car was there.

"Reece must've gotten off early."

They entered the house and Samson met them at the door. Savoy started rubbing him and talking to him in an excited tone of voice. When they got into the kitchen Ky found Reece had already changed into jeans and a T-shirt and she was prepping the rest of the food for dinner.

Ky walked over to her, gave her kiss, and said, "I didn't expect you home early."

She wiped her hands on the dishtowel and said, "I know. I wanted to get off so I could help with dinner."

"Reece, this is my sister, Savoy. Savoy this is Reece."

Reece gave Savoy a hug. She noticed that Savoy had features similar to Ky's mother. She had the body of an African American woman with curves in all the right places. She had long, auburn hair with blond and reddish highlights, but her skin tone was Brazilian bronze like Ky's. The only difference between her and their mother were those green eyes.

"It's so nice to finally meet you, Savoy," Reece said. "I hope you had a nice flight."

"I did," Savoy answered as she opened the refrigerator and pulled out a bottle of wine. "It's nice to finally meet you too, and you're even prettier than my brother said you were."

Reece looked over at Ky. "Is that right? Thank you. You're pretty as well, and your brother talks about you nonstop. He's a great guy."

"Thank you and he's all right," she joked as she poured herself a glass of wine and then offered Reece some.

They laughed while Ky checked the container holding his marinated meat. He turned to his sister and said, "Why don't you get out of those heels and come back down and help finish getting dinner ready?"

"Ooooh, is that what I think it is?" Savoy asked as she noticed a box with the name of her favorite bakery on top. She opened the container of red velvet cupcakes and started dancing.

Ky playfully slapped her hand as she reached for one.

"That's for later. Now get."

Savoy laughed and made her way upstairs with her glass of wine and Samson following close behind.

"Savoy is nice and she's gorgeous just like your mom."

Ky washed his hands. "Thanks, and I told you she was cool."

"Yes, you did," she replied. "I have everything prepped and ready to go on the grill. The only other thing I need to finish is the asparagus and iced tea."

Ky thanked Reece before heading to the grill with the marinated meat and corn. Once everything was ready, the three of them gathered at the table where Reece and Savoy got to know each other better.

By the end of the night, Savoy could see why Ky was crazy about Reece, even though he hadn't confirmed his true feelings for her yet. Savoy did notice how he looked at Reece when he spoke to her and how affectionate he was with her. He was always kissing her and couldn't seem to keep his hands to himself. Savoy had never seen her brother act like this with any woman, so she wasn't surprised when they revealed to her that they were engaged.

"I knew it!" Savoy screamed as she gave her brother a big hug. "I'm so happy for you guys."

Reece showed Savoy her ring and asked, "Isn't it beautiful?"

Savoy gave Reece a hug. "Yes, it's beautiful. He has good taste. I wouldn't expect any less. You did good, bro, on both."

"Thanks," he answered proudly. "But you can't tell anybody, not even Dani. We're having the whole family over Saturday night to tell them, and Reece's brother is coming into town tomorrow. We're going to tell him then, but that's it. OK?"

"Can I tell Patrick, please?" she begged.

"Yes, but tell him not to put anything on social media," Ky instructed her as he gathered their empty plates from the table.

Savoy took them out of his hands and said, "I got it. I'll clean the kitchen so you lovebirds can relax since you did all the cooking. Reece, your seven layer salad was da bomb!"

"Thank you," Reece replied as she got up from the table. "I'm glad you enjoyed it."

Reece and Ky made their way over to the sofa to watch TV. As Savoy worked in the kitchen she watched the couple. Reece lay on the sofa with her legs across Ky's lap and he was massaging and caressing them.

"Hey, guys, the kitchen is clean, so I'm going up to my room. Dinner was great and I appreciate these cupcakes," she said as she pulled one out of the container.

"You're welcome," Reece answered. "And thanks for cleaning up the kitchen."

"Any time," she replied. "Can I get you anything before I head upstairs?"

"No, we're good," Ky replied. "Goodnight."

"Goodnight," Savoy said as she exited the kitchen.

Once she was gone, Ky pulled Reece into his lap and started kissing her.

"I told you Savoy would love you," he whispered as he ran his hands all over her body.

Fearful that Savoy would walk in on them she said, "Ky, don't forget your sister is here."

Seeing her uneasiness, he turned off the TV and said, "OK, let's take this to the bedroom where you won't be so shy."

Reece followed him into the bedroom where Ky turned on the gas fireplace and threw several pillows on the plush rug in front of it. He also grabbed a thick comforter from the closet before picking up where he left off on the sofa. He began to kiss her as he removed her clothes.

She caught her breath and asked, "How thin are your walls?"

He thought for a second as he removed his own clothes. "It depends on how loud you plan to be. Just so you know, I'm not holding back."

Reece's eyes widened and she whispered, "Oh my God."

He pulled her down on the floor and into his arms in front of the warm fire. He chuckled. "It's your fault for being so damn beautiful and sexy."

"Ky, please don't make me embarrass myself," she replied knowing just how intense he could be when making love to her. There was no way she would be able to keep Savoy from hearing them.

Ky nibbled on her neck and lips. "I'm just teasing you, sweetheart. I won't do anything to embarrass you."

"I'm worried about embarrassing myself," she answered as she caressed his huge biceps.

He gave her another kiss and said, "In that case, I won't do anything that will make you uncomfortable. Deal?"

"Deal," she replied before giving him a tender kiss on the neck.

Ky held Reece in his arms and they talked about their future while admiring the flickering flame from the fireplace. He pulled her tighter against his chest and ran his hands over her soft body.

"Reece, I don't know if I can wait to marry you," he said softly in her ear.

She looked him in his eyes and asked, "What are you saying?"

He traced the outline of her lips with his finger and said, "I'm saying I don't want a long engagement. I'm ready now."

She cupped his face. "I'm ready to be married too, but I want to do it right. I want a church wedding and I know you do too."

"You're right, I do. We'll get it together. You can't blame me for being anxious."

She snuggled her body against his. "I'm anxious too, and if we can get everything planned quickly, count me in."

He laughed. "I guarantee you that people at church will think it's a shotgun wedding."

"Really?" she asked. "Why?"

"Because I'm a preacher's kid, and the fact that we haven't dated for very long. Also because they haven't seen me with a woman in a long time."

"Are you worried about it?"

He kissed her. "No. I've never concerned myself with what people thought. I've lived my life as a normal twenty-something-year-old would. True, I've made mistakes and gotten in my share of trouble, but who hasn't? People are so quick to judge others before looking at their own faults. I'm going to be me regardless, and I appreciate that my parents have never tried to make me and Savoy change our personalities."

A huge smile appeared on his face as the couple lay there silently for several minutes while Reece caressed Ky's muscular arms surrounding her. She loved his spirit and conviction, and couldn't be happier. Without speaking a word, she began to kiss his chest. Ky instinctively ran his hands over her round bottom and pulled her tighter against his body.

He kissed her and then whispered, "You do know it's about to go down, don't you?"

She nodded and continued to kiss and hold on to her man.

He stared at her sexy body illuminated by the light from the fireplace and asked, "Do you have any idea how incredibly beautiful you are?"

She blushed. "I don't look at myself that way."

He nibbled on her lips. "That's cool, because I'm here to tell you that you are, but I know there's much more to you than your beauty."

"You're so sweet," she said before burying her face against his warm neck.

He towered over her and whispered, "You're welcome. Now hold tight, baby."

Reece held on to her man as he pushed his body into hers several times, causing Reece to utter, "Oh my God," over and over again. She had to stifle her moans because she didn't want Savoy to know what they were doing, however she was with the man she loved, and nothing else mattered. Ky was torturing her with no mercy, and after several minutes of making love, she came to a point where she couldn't contain her emotions any longer. She felt the wave starting to build in her body and Ky noticed her legs trembling. Reece knew she was on the threshold of a magnificent feeling, so she grabbed a pillow and covered her face. Seconds later her entire body spasmed and she screamed at the top of her lungs into the pillow.

Ky laughed and removed the pillow from her face and asked, "Are you OK? I don't want you to smother yourself."

She hit him with the pillow playfully and said, "You knew I was going to do that. Thank God I had that pillow."

He laughed again and said, "I know you don't want Savoy to know our business, but believe me, she would never say anything to you to embarrass you or let you know she heard us even if she did. She might tease me about it, but she knows we're in love, which means she would expect us to be down here making love."

"I guess you're right, but I still can't help but feel weird about it since she's right upstairs."

"I guarantee you she probably has her earbuds in listening to music or video chatting on the phone with Patrick."

She blushed. "I hope so."

He rolled off her and onto his back. "This floor is killing my back. You ready to get into bed, or do you want to go again?"

Reece looked at him in awe. "Are you serious?"

"I would never joke about that," he replied as he sat up.

She smiled and sat up as well, "I would never deny you, Ky. I love you."

Ky felt his heart thump hard against his chest, and while he would love to make love to her every chance he could, he didn't want to come across as if that was all he wanted from her. He was in love with her, and he knew he could express his love in other ways too. He helped her off the floor and she helped him gather the linens. After putting the pillows on the bed and the comforter back in place, they climbed in and held on to each other.

He stroked her hair, gave her a kiss, and whispered, "I love you."

"I love you too."

"Goodnight, sweetheart."

Reece hugged him tightly and said softly, "Goodnight, babe."

The next day Ky had a big surprise for his future wife, and he hoped she would love it. Since he wanted to express his love to her outside of the bedroom, he enlisted Savoy's help in picking out office furniture so he could create a workspace just for her inside his office. The office was large enough to share with her, and he wanted her space to be functional, yet feminine. He took a few hours off work and asked Savoy to ride with him to the local office furniture store to pick out a desk along with all the necessary accessories. He knew they would be able to share the printer and fax machine, but this space would be just for her. Savoy picked out a mahogany desk with brushed silver hardware along with a matching three-drawer file cabinet. She also found a brushed silver lamp with an ivory lampshade trimmed in lime green. Before leaving, Savoy noticed a lime green upholstered slipper chair that was comfortable, yet feminine. She thought Reece would love it, so she added that to the purchases.

After paying, Ky asked for the items to be delivered and set up before five o'clock. The only other thing he had to do was hook up a telephone for her desk, but he could do that himself with the right accessories.

Savoy was in charge of directing the setup once everything arrived at the house, and coordinating accessories. She was able to find a couple small paintings that matched the color scheme. Once the room was completed, Savoy tied a large pink bow around the chair

That afternoon when Reece got in from work, Ky asked her to retrieve a book for him in his office. When Reece entered the room they heard her scream with excitement. When they joined her she immediately jumped into Ky's arms and gave him a kiss.

With tears in her eyes she said, "Oh my God! This is beautiful. Thank you so much."

"You're welcome, sweetheart. Savoy was a big help. She picked out some things she thought you would like."

Reece pulled her future sister-in-law into her arms, gave her a big kiss on the cheek, and said, "Thank you, Savoy."

"You're welcome," Savoy replied before asking Reece to let her take a picture of her beside her new work area.

"Make sure you don't post the picture," Ky reminded her. He didn't want anything to spoil their surprise for Saturday night.

"I won't," Savoy replied before walking out of the office.

"You like it?" Ky asked softly.

"I love it," she replied. "You didn't have to do this."

He hugged her waist. "I know, but I wanted you to have your own space to work."

Still in shock she sat down in the chair to get a feel for it. She admired the lamp and other items suited for a work space. Ky's surprise went better than he could have ever imagined, and her reaction was priceless.

After dinner Savoy and Reece spent time together outside on the patio talking about their sorority sisterhood, Savoy's plans for after graduation, and so much more. Savoy had no doubt that Reece was perfect for her brother. The fact that Samson loved her was another indication. It was almost like having an older sister, something she'd always wanted.

The next day when Alston arrived in town, Reece finally felt completely content. Ky's entire family had been notified about dinner, and so far everyone had acknowledged they were coming. Ky was able to find a caterer to provide a menu of ribs, baked chicken, and pulled pork with sides that included jalapeno mac 'n cheese, slaw, potato salad, baked beans and corn muffins. Ky had a huge family and was expecting no less than seventy-five people, so he had rented a tent and tables and chairs.

It was the night before the big dinner and Reece, Savoy, Alston, and Ky had just finished eating a dinner prepared by the ladies. The men decided to play pool while the ladies left for Dani's salon to get their hair styled. With Reece out of the house, Alston had a lot of questions for Ky. He wanted to get to the root of Ky's intentions and affection for his sister. Alston knew Reece was still fragile from losing Geno and the drama she went through with the married man, so he wanted to make sure Ky was not playing games with her heart.

"So, Ky, now that the ladies are out of the house, we have a chance to talk," Alston pointed out.

"Of course," Ky replied as he took his turn on the pool table. "Ask me anything."

"Since you know that my sister has been through hell, I have to make sure your feelings for her are genuine. She can't take another heartbreak."

Ky sighed and looked Alston in the eyes and said, "I don't know how else to convince you that Reece is important to me. She is the missing piece in my life and I can't imagine dating anyone else. I honestly believe that God made our paths cross for a reason."

232

"That's cool and all but she's heard that before," Alston revealed.

Ky put his hand up in defense and said, "She told me all about that married man and how he deceived her. I hope you tried to knock his damn head off. I know I would have."

Alston smiled and said, "Oh he felt my wrath. I got him good."

"What did you do?" Ky asked.

"Let's just say the punk ass bastard had an expensive dental bill," Alston replied as he laughed. "His mouth had to be wired shut for a few weeks."

Ky took a sip of his beer and said, "Good for you. How did Reece feel about that?"

Alston took another pool shot and said, "She doesn't know and I want to keep it that way."

"You don't have to worry about me telling her. I'm sure dude will think twice before he tries to run that game again."

Alston took another shot and then looked up at Ky and with seriousness said, "I like you Ky, but if you hurt Reece I'm going to mess you up."

Ky held his hand out to Alston and said, "That will never happen so I'm not worried."

"Then you have my blessings," Alston replied as he shook Ky's hand. "Reece was in a dark place for a long time after Geno died. We didn't know if she was ever going get over it, but I see how she looks at you and how you look at her. I can see there's something real going on between you guys."

"I'm glad you approve," Ky replied before reminding Alston it was his turn on the pool table.

Ky was very forthcoming with Alston and a couple of times he almost let it slip that he was in love with her. What he told Alston was that he had strong feelings for Reece and that she was the best thing that had ever happened to him. The thing that impressed Alston the most was that Ky didn't hesitate with his answers and he made sure to look Alston in the eyes when he answered his serious questions. Alston couldn't find any deception in Ky's body language or answers to his questions, and he had drilled him as hard as a brother could. Ky was different than the men his sister usually dated. Reece normally went for the overly ambitious, corporate type. While

Ky owned his own extremely successful business, he was humble and appreciated a simple life. Satisfied, he shook Ky's hand and gave him a brotherly hug. They played another game of pool before settling down to watch a football game. About that time Reece and Savoy returned and joined the men downstairs. Reece wasn't sure what had gone on between the two favorite men in her life, but she hoped Alston had gotten the chance to see how wonderful Ky was. Now she felt it was time for them to let him in on their huge secret. Reece sat down and asked Savoy to pour her a glass of wine. Savoy stopped texting long enough to pour Reece and herself the wine and rejoined them on the sectional.

Reece took a sip of wine and asked, "Did you guys have a good time getting to know each other?"

Alston took a sip of beer and looked over at Ky. "Yes, we did. He's a really good pool player and he seems to be a cool guy. I believe he really cares about you."

"I'm glad you feel that way, because there's something we need to talk to you about," Reece said anxiously.

Savoy sat quietly next to the couple, already knowing where the conversation was headed.

"Alston, I know I asked you to come down here to meet Ky and to make sure I wasn't falling for him for all the wrong reasons, but there's something we need to tell you."

Alston sat up quickly. "What's wrong? You're not pregnant, are you?"

She smiled. "Nothing's wrong, and, no, I'm not pregnant."

Savoy couldn't help but laugh.

Ky took over the conversation. "What Reece is trying to tell you is that I took it upon myself to show your sister just how much she means to me. To be honest, Alston, I'm in love with her, and I have been for some time now."

This got Alston's attention even more. He looked at the couple closely. "Is that so?"

"Yes," Ky said as he lovingly held Reece's hand.

"What are you trying to tell me?" Alston asked curiously.

Reece held up her hand and finally revealed the large diamond on her finger. "We're engaged and we're getting married."

"No shit!" he yelled. "Married?"

"Alston, I love Ky. He has made me so happy and I can't see myself living without him."

"And I can't live without her either," Ky added. "I just hope you're OK with it. I know it's pretty much been a whirlwind romance, but Reece is the real deal for me. We're having dinner here tomorrow to tell the whole family, but we wanted you and Savoy to be the first to know. We wanted to get your blessings because you and Savoy are the closest to us."

Alston was stunned, but when he looked at the ring on his sister's finger he knew Ky meant business. He could also see the love between Ky and his sister, and there was nothing he wanted more for her than for her to be happy, especially after losing Geno. It seemed like love had blindsided her in an unlikely way and with a genuine guy that really loved her.

He hugged his sister and said, "I'm shocked, but I'm happy for you guys. I know Momma and Daddy are going to be shocked too. Wait! How are y'all going to do this? You live in D.C."

"We haven't worked out all the logistics yet," Ky revealed. "But if I have to move to D.C., I will to be with my baby."

Surprised by Ky's admission, she caressed his arm and said, "We might as well discuss it now. Alston, you know I love my job, but I love Ky more. D.C. has been good to me, and it's where I have my roots, but ever since Geno died, I can't be there without thinking about it. It makes me sad. I would have no problem living here permanently."

Savoy stopped texting on her cell phone and asked, "Who's Geno?"

Reece sighed and took a moment to tell Savoy about the tragedy of her former fiancé.

Savoy hugged Reece. "I'm so sorry that happened to you, but I'm glad you met my brother."

"Me too," she replied as she wiped away a stray tear running down her cheek.

"Babe, are you serious?" Ky asked after waiting for Reece to finish telling Savoy about Geno. "You know you don't have to decide anything right now."

"I know and, yes, I'm serious."

"I can understand that," Savoy added. "I will go wherever Patrick ends up. If he gets drafted into the NFL, that would be awesome, but if he doesn't, that's cool too. While we haven't talked about marriage, we love each other, and we'll do whatever we have to in order to stay together after graduation."

"We'll talk about that another day. I don't have the strength to do it today," Ky said. Savoy pointed her finger at him.

"Maybe not today, but we will talk about it, big brother."

Getting back to Ky and Reece, Alston asked, "But what about your job? You've been there for a while and you have a bright future there, not to mention the big salary they're paying you."

"I'll work all that out. Ky already has a successful business established, and I wouldn't want him to give all that up. It's been in his family too long. Besides, it's so beautiful and peaceful down here on the water. Since I've been here I've been less stressed, so I really don't care about the salary as long as I'm happy."

"I'll give you that," Alston replied. "It is beautiful, and this house is amazing. I can tell you put your heart and soul into it."

"I appreciate what both of you said, and I'm willing to do whatever I have to so we're together," Ky answered.

"So when are you guys thinking about tying the knot?" Alston asked.

Reece looked at Ky and they started laughing.

"What's so funny?" Savoy asked.

"Well, the other night, Ky was talking about doing it right away."

"What do you mean right away?" Alston asked.

"Like next week," Reece replied with a smile.

Savoy stopped texting. "Y'all can't do that!"

Alston shook his head. "I agree with Savoy, so you might as well get that out of your head because the family will want you to have a proper wedding."

Ky put up his hands. "We know. I was having a moment, but I'm back to my senses now."

"Alston, whenever we do it, we don't want it to interfere with your wedding this spring, nor Savoy's graduation in May."

"Do you want a big wedding?" Savoy asked.

"It doesn't matter to me. I just want it to be beautiful. The only problem I see is that we will probably need to have two ceremonies since we have friends and family in two different states. I wouldn't want anyone to feel left out."

"I agree," Ky replied as he caressed Reece's thigh and gave her a kiss. "I can't wait for you to be my wife."

"Get a room, you two," Savoy joked, which caused everyone to laugh. "Ky, I'm tripping off you because I have never seen you act like this with any female. Never!"

"Well it took the right one to make me feel like this."

"I totally understand where you're coming from, Ky. Until I met Gabriella, I felt like I was spinning my wheels in sand," Alston admitted.

Savoy snapped her fingers. "I have an idea. Why don't you have a destination wedding somewhere tropical with just immediate family and close friends, and then have two receptions?"

Reece looked at Ky. "That's another option. We'll just have to see what can be worked out as far as venue, caterer, my wedding gown, and other things before we can make a decision. Is that fair?"

Ky held her hand. "Whatever you want, babe."

"Cool, just keep me posted," Alston requested.

"Me too," Savoy said as she took a couple of selfies. "I hope you pick out some sexy bridesmaid dresses."

Alston held out his hand to Ky. "Welcome to the family, bro. Hopefully the wedding planning won't overwhelm you like it did me."

Ky hugged Alston. "Thanks. Welcome to my family as well."

Savoy looked at them and said, "Me and Reece have already hugged."

They all laughed together as they settled in to watch the rest of the football game before turning in for the night.

The next afternoon Yale drove by Ky's house and saw a huge white tent set up in his backyard. Her heart sank because she knew it was the type of tent used for most outdoor wedding receptions, so she feared the worse. There was no one close to Ky that she could get information from either. Everyone close to him knew their history and that he did not deal with her anymore. She pulled over on the side of the road to gather her thoughts, and then she decided to see if she could get Ky to answer his phone. Surprisingly he did.

"What do you want?" Ky asked in an unenthusiastic tone of voice.

"I just wanted to call to tell you I'm sorry about everything. I never meant to push you or make you so crazy. I let my emotions get the best of me. This is hard for me."

Ky was silent on the other end of the phone. This was typical Yale. She would act a fool and then she would apologize, only to repeat the cycle.

"Ky, are you there?"

He sighed. "I'm over it, Yale, so there's nothing left to say."

"Well, anyway, I wanted to tell you I'm sorry. We were too close for us to be like this with each other and regardless of what's going on, I'll always love you."

"That's something you're going to have to work through. I forgive you because I'm a Christian and I have to. I wish you well, but please don't call me again with this foolishness."

"This is not easy," she admitted as her voice began to crack. "Can't you please find it in your heart to give me another chance?"

"Yale!" he yelled. "No! I'm with someone else!"

A lump formed in her throat. "You don't have to keep reminding me."

"Obviously I do," he pointed out. "Goodbye."

Ky hung up the telephone, which still left Yale to wonder what type of event he was having at his house. She threw her phone on the floor of her car, gripped the steering wheel, and started screaming at the top of her lungs. This went on for at least a minute until she finally pulled herself together. She picked up her phone and dialed Quincy's number.

"Hey, babe. I was hoping I would hear from you. What's up?" he asked.

She wiped the tears off her face and said, "Can you meet me at my house in about fifteen minutes?"

"Sure. Is everything OK?"

"I'm having a really bad day and I need some company."

"I'm sorry to hear that, sweetheart. Don't you worry about a thing, because I got you," he assured her. "I'll pick up something to eat and drink and meet you at your place in about thirty minutes. Is that cool?"

She smiled. "Sounds good. Thanks, Quincy."

"Anything for you, sexy. I'll see you shortly."

Yale hung up the telephone and headed home. She hoped Quincy would be able to distract her and help get her mind off Ky and what could possibly be happening at his house. Her heart was broken and she didn't know if she would ever get over Ky.

By the time Quincy made it to Yale's house she had showered, thrown on some shorts and a T-shirt, and straightened up around the house. He arrived with vodka and other ingredients to make them some drinks and he had a bag full of delicious food for them to snack on. She opened the door, welcomed him into her house, and directed him to the kitchen.

He looked in her eyes and asked, "Have you been crying?"

She pulled the items out of the bag. "I don't want to talk about it right now. OK?"

He wrapped his arms around her waist and gave her a kiss. "That's cool. Let me fix you a drink."

"Thanks. I really appreciate you coming over."

Quincy combined a mixture of vodka, rum, lemonade, peach schnapps, pineapple juice and blue curacao. He handed her the glass and said, "Taste this."

She took a sip. "Whoa! This is good and potent."

"I knew you would like it," he said as he took a sip of his own drink.

They settled in her living room where he opened several food containers. One had a variety of spinach and queso dip with chips. Another had mozzarella cheese sticks and honey BBQ wings. They started to get to know each other as they talked about themselves and their careers. They continued to enjoy their drinks and snacks.

Quincy told Yale that he was a Coast Guard officer. Yale had a hard time believing him until he showed her his ID and a picture of him in uniform standing on his ship with some of his shipmates. Yale was really feeling the buzz from her second drink when their conversation finally turned sexual and they started getting physical. While Quincy was caressing her thighs, Yale started rubbing her hands over his toned abs.

"Girl, you keep that up and you're going to be in trouble."

Her hand went from his stomach down to his crotch as she ran her tongue across his lips and whispered, "I thought you could tell I was a troublemaker."

Quincy grabbed her, pulling her into his lap where she straddled him and kissed him greedily. He removed her T-shirt and bra and covered her breasts with his mouth. Yale closed her eyes and moaned as he ran his tongue over her perky breasts.

"Let's go upstairs," she suggested.

He kissed her lips and neck. "No, baby, I want you right here on the floor."

This excited Yale even more as she stood and allowed him to remove her shorts and thong.

"Damn, girl," he whispered as she dropped to her knees, unzipped his pants, and buried her head in his lap. Quincy cursed and gripped the back of her hair as he guided her over his shaft. His groin was on fire and Yale was very skilled in the way she was pleasuring him. When she had him exactly how she wanted him, she helped him out of his pants and shirt. Quincy moved her coffee table out of the way and quickly pulled a condom out of his pocket and applied it.

He kissed Yale. "Lie down, baby."

She followed his instructions and lay back on the rug, waiting for him to join her. He stared at her and admired her unbelievable beauty. He kissed her hard on the lips and then kissed his way down until he settled between her thighs and began to consume her sweet nectar. Yale writhed and moaned as his tongue danced against her core. Her moans got louder and louder and he knew she was close to releasing, but it was too soon. He stopped his oral assault, placed her legs over his shoulders, and eased his body into her. The warmth and moisture from her center sent shivers over his body as he begin to slowly move in and out of her.

Yale's moans turned into pleas for him to make love to her harder and he was happy to oblige. Quincy was like the Energizer bunny. He pummeled her body for several minutes. Yale was beginning to think she had taken on more than she could handle. He was able to delay his orgasm as he covered her breasts with his mouth once more.

He kissed her and then leaned down to her ear and whispered, "Give it to me, baby."

The sensual tone of his voice caused Yale to let out a loud scream as her body shuddered hard beneath him. He thrust his hips a few more times into her and let out his own loud groan, completely satisfied.

Quincy kissed her neck and yelled," Goddammit!"

She hugged his neck. "You like?"

"You damn right I like," he said as he helped her off the floor. "You good?"

She picked up a blanket she had on the sofa, wrapped it around her body, and said, "Yes, I'm good, but I'll be even better if you make me another one of those drinks."

He slid back into his briefs. "You've already had two. One more might put you out for the night, and I'm not ready for you to go to sleep. I was hoping to have another go at you first."

She giggled and opened the blanket to give him another view of her sexy body. "Baby, if you make me another drink, you can have me as much as you want, but I want to take it upstairs. You almost broke my back."

"I didn't hurt you, did I?" he asked as he walked over to the kitchen and started mixing her drink.

"I'm bruised, but not broken."

"I'm sorry. You turn me on so much it's hard for me not to go all in on you," he admitted when he sat down next to her and handed her the drink.

"I appreciate you coming over today. I was really feeling down."

He caressed her cheek. "What's got you so messed up today? Work?"

She took a deep breath. "I had an argument with my ex."

"The guy from the club the other night?"

She nodded. "Yeah. We had a bad breakup and I haven't gotten over it yet."

"You still love him?" he asked as he sipped his drink.

Yale looked into his eyes. "Would you be upset if I said yes?"

He sighed. "I don't like it, but I understand. Listen, Yale, I can help you forget all about that dude if you let me. He was with another chick, so it seems like he's moved on. Maybe it's time for you to do the same, because I'm going to tell you now, I don't share."

Yale gave him a sultry kiss on the lips. "You're right, but it's a process. Are you able to put up with me while I work through my feelings?"

He massaged her thigh. "I'll do my best, but it's going to be hard knowing you have feelings for a guy that doesn't seem to give a damn about you. It makes me wonder if you were thinking about him when you were making love to me."

"That's not the case. I wouldn't do that to you. You've been nothing but sweet and nice to me."

He stood. "Cool. I'm going to warm up the food."

She held up her glass and said, "Thanks."

Yale and Quincy were able to lighten the mood before retiring to her bedroom where they made love again. Yale was beginning to feel a closeness to Quincy who was sympathetic to her situation, and he treated her with tender loving care, but he still wasn't Ky. She eased out of bed and made her way into the shower while Quincy slept. He seemed to be a decent guy, but she'd lied to him. She was imagining she was making love to Ky when she was having sex with him. It was the only thing keeping her sane, but how long her sanity would last was unknown. It was still frustrating to her that she couldn't figure out why Ky had a tent in his backyard and she wouldn't be able to rest until she found out.

CHAPTER 20

Ky's house buzzed with activity as family and friends gathered while the caterers set up the food for dinner. Seeing the large crowd started to make Reece nervous—so nervous that she had to steal a moment away from the activity. She headed to the bedroom, and then out to the patio, which is where Ky found her.

"What are you doing out here, babe? Everyone's asking about you."

She took a deep breath before answering. "I'm sorry. I had to step out for minute. I started feeling a little overwhelmed about doing this in front of your whole family. You have a huge family. I don't know if I can do it."

He pulled her into his arms. "Listen, if this is going to be too much for you, we don't have to tell them tonight. I want you to feel comfortable whenever we do it."

She caressed his shoulders. "Thanks, but I can tell you're excited. I just need a moment to get myself together and we can do it."

Ky kissed her. "Take all the time you need, and I must say you look stunning in that dress."

Reece blushed. Her royal blue dress with quarter length sleeves fit to her curves and showed off her long, shapely legs.

"You don't look so bad yourself," she replied. Ky wore jeans and a starched yellow button down shirt. "I feel a little overdressed, though."

He gave her another kiss. "No, you look perfect. You got the ring?"

She held out her hand, showing him she had the ring turned so no one could see the large diamond. Ky knew that some of the women in his family were very observant and it wouldn't take them long to spot the ring on her left hand, so as long as Reece was on board, he would make the announcement right away before dinner was served.

"OK, I'm getting ready to go back out there. I'll cover for you until you're ready. When you come out, let me know what you want me to do."

She nodded. "I'll be out in a second."

Ky left Reece on the patio with her thoughts. She closed her eyes and said a short prayer before finally making her way back out to the family room. Alston spotted her and excused himself from one of Ky's aunts so he could talk to his sister.

He pulled her to the side. "You look like you could use a drink."

Reece laughed. "You know me so well. I'm so nervous. I told Ky I don't know if I can go through with the announcement tonight in front of his entire family. He said we didn't have to do it tonight, but I know he's excited about it."

Alston took her by the hand and they made their way downstairs to the bar where they found Ja`el mixing drinks.

"Hey, Reece, you want me to make you a margarita?"

"No, pour me a tequila shot."

He stared at her, then asked, "Are you sure?"

Alston laughed. "Your whole family is here. She's a little nervous, that's all."

Ja`el poured the shot of tequila and said, "Reece, you worry too much. My family's cool people."

Reece downed the shot of tequila. "Give me one more and I think I'll be fine."

Ja`el looked at Reece and asked, "Are you sure? It's pretty strong."

Reece nodded.

Alston said, "She can handle it."

After she downed the second one, Alston reached into his pocket and gave her a couple of breath mints. He massaged her shoulders and said, "You should be good to go now. How do you feel?"

"Besides my throat burning, I'm starting to feel a little relaxed. My whole body feels warm and tingly. Thanks."

While Ky patiently waited for Reece to decide if she was up to making the announcement, he played with some of his young cousins in the foyer. That's when his excitement was diminished by Yale boldly walking through his front door. She was clearly intoxicated and her curiosity had gotten the best of her. Once Quincy fell asleep at her house she decided to make her way back over to

Ky's house to see if she could find out what event Ky was having at his house.

She walked towards him and angrily yelled out, "I know you bet not be having a wedding up in here. What's with the tent in the backyard, Ky?"

Ky quickly told his cousins to go play and he hurriedly met Yale before she could get to far into the house.

He grabbed her firmly by the arm and said, "You're trespassing and you need to leave."

"I'm not going anywhere until you tell me what's going on!" She yelled as she pulled her arm away from him and drawing the attention of Savoy and Dani.

When Ky saw Savoy quickly walking over he motioned for her to stop, knowing that Savoy wouldn't hesitate punching Yale in the throat. He was trying to do everything in his power to get Yale out of his house so she wouldn't ruin their evening.

"What I do is none of your damn business! Now, if you don't leave, I'm going to call the police."

Yale folded her arms and arrogantly said, "I'm not going anywhere until you tell me what's going on?"

"It's a family affair and you're not family so goooo!" Ky yelled in anger.

"Where's your little bitch girlfriend? She's not family. Why do she get to be here?"

Just as Ky took a step towards her Ky's father approached asked, "Lower your voices. What's going on?"

Ky shook his head and said, "Daddy, Yale came here uninvited and she needs to go before I make her."

Pastor Parker could clearly see that his son was on the brink of losing his temper so he intervened and got between them.

"Yale, this is a family event and since you weren't invited, you need to leave like Ky asked you to. You're embarrassing yourself. I can tell you've been drinking and this is not a good look for you. My office is always open if you want to talk, but you're going to have to come to the realization that your relationship with Ky is over."

She looked at Pastor Parker and said, "No disrespect, Pastor, but Ky owes me."

"I don't owe you a goddamn thing!" Ky yelled.

"Son, calm down."

"No, Daddy! I want her gone!" Ky yelled as he pointed at Yale. "She's not going to mess this up for me."

"Yale, please leave. I would hate to see you taken off in handcuffs," Pastor Parker said, pleading with her.

"This is some bullshit!" She yelled as she turned and walked out the door.

Pastor and Ky watched as she sped off, squealing her tires in the process he said a prayer that she would make it home safe without hurting herself or others. He turned to his son and said, "That young woman needs some psychological help. I didn't know she was so distressed over your breakup."

Ky looked at his father and before walking off he said, "She's crazy and I don't want her anywhere near me or Reece."

At that moment, Alston and Reece met Ky upstairs in the hallway. When Reece looked at him he seemed agitated.

"I'll give you two some privacy," Alston said before walking away from the couple.

"Babe, are you OK?" She asked as she lovingly cupped his face.

"I'm fine," he answered as he kissed her hands. "What do you want to do, sweetheart? We don't have to make the announcement tonight if you're not up to it. Just tell me what you want to do."

Reece thought for a moment and felt the tequila taking its calming effect over her body and mind. She smiled and gave his hand a gentle squeeze. "I'm ready."

"Let's get everyone together so we can get it done now. You sure you're good?"

"Yes, I'm sure."

He kissed her on the lips. "I love you."

"I love you more."

With that said, Ky asked Reece to wait for him in the family room while he went downstairs and had everyone come upstairs. After his encounter with Yale, he needed these few minutes to calm down as he called for everyone on the second floor as well as those outside to join them. It took several minutes to gather all their family and friends together, but once they were in the room, Ky immediately went into his speech.

While holding Reece's hand he said, "I want to thank everyone for accepting our invitation to dinner on such short notice. I know you're hungry and can smell the food, so I'll make this quick. With the holidays around the corner I know it's hard for us to get together as one big family. I thought this was a good opportunity to come together as one, especially since Savoy is able to be here, which was a nice surprise for Momma and Daddy. I know you might be wondering who this beautiful woman is standing next to me. Some of you have already met her, but for those who haven't, this is Reece Miller from D.C. She works for the government and she's in town to help our school system improve. Reece's brother Alston is also here visiting her this weekend. Alston, wave your hand so everyone will know who you are."

Alston waved his hand to greet Ky's family. Ky could feel Reece trembling and he gave her hand a squeeze and continued with his speech.

"On a more personal note, not only did I want all of you here for us to fellowship together as a family, but also so you can hear me admit to something I've never admitted before. Since Reece has been in town we have become close. Very close. So close that I can't see myself living without her. She means the world to me and we're standing up here to let you all know that we're very much in love and we're engaged!"

There were immediate screams, gasps, tears, and applause from the group.

Ky held up Reece's left hand, revealing her large diamond ring. "This is the real reason we wanted all of you over for dinner tonight."

Ky's mother and father ran over to the couple and embraced the two of them. With tears flowing out of his mother's eyes, she cupped Reece's face and gave her a loving kiss on the cheek. Ky's father embraced him and gave him a kiss on the cheek as well, and then he gave Reece a loving kiss. Savoy recorded the entire speech on her phone and Alston secretly FaceTimed their parents, unbeknownst to Reece, so they could be a part of the announcement as well. Seeing their daughter so happy made them extremely emotional because of what she went through losing Geno. The room was loud and chaotic as family members and close friends swarmed the couple to congratulate them.

Ja`el walked over to Ky and gave him a huge hug. "Congratulations, bro. I'm kind of shocked, but then again I saw it coming. I'm happy for you guys. May I kiss your beautiful fiancée?"

"Sure you can, and thanks, cuz," Ky replied.

Ja`el gave Reece a kiss on the cheek and then hugged her. Dani had tears in her eyes when she approached the couple. She hugged both of them and told them how much she cared about them. After several minutes of chaos, Ky's father interrupted the celebration.

While choking back his own tears he said, "It's always good to spend time with family and friends. Tonight was even more blessed as we add to our family and welcome Reece and her entire family into our loving embrace. Now let us join hands everyone so I can bless the food."

The family members did what they were told and joined hands. The pastor's blessing was more than a blessing. It was a prayer of thanks and love. Afterward most of the guests made their way into the tent where they started settling down for dinner.

Geneva walked up to Ky and Reece. "I want you two to know that I see the love between you, so I know without a doubt that it's real. I couldn't be happier for you and you have my blessings and support. Reece, welcome to our family."

Reece hugged Geneva. "Thank you, Ms. Parker. I really appreciate you saying that."

She gave her a kiss on the cheek and said, "No more of that Ms. Parker stuff. You're family now. You're my granddaughter so you're welcome to call me Gigi."

Geneva turned to her grandson with tears in her eyes and gave him a hug that only a grandmother could give. She kissed him and said, "Bishop, I couldn't be more proud of you. I love you so much and I know your grandfather is smiling down on you. You and Reece are perfect for each other."

He hugged his grandmother. "Thanks, Gigi. I love you too."

Alston walked up to the group around Ky and Reece. "Excuse me, Ky. I need to borrow my sister for a minute."

Alston pulled his sister to the side so Reece could have a private moment over the telephone with their parents. Reece excused herself to the office where she was able to talk to her parents. She expected them to scold her for keeping her relationship with Ky from them, but they did the opposite and showered her with love and support. As expected, it was an emotional conversation, and before hanging up, Ky joined her so he could meet them via FaceTime. He assured her parents that he loved Reece and would take care of her forever. They told Ky they couldn't wait to meet him in person and thanked him for loving their daughter. When she hung up from her parents, she immediately contacted her future sister-in-law, Gabriella. Through FaceTime she was able to introduce her to Ky as well and show her the ring. As expected Gabriella was emotional and couldn't wait to meet Ky. Reece hung up the telephone and laid her head on his chest.

"I'm glad that's behind us. I didn't know Alston had my parents on the phone so they could witness the announcement. I'm glad he thought about it. I wouldn't want to leave them out of something so important."

He caressed her back. "I'm glad he thought about it too. Your family is my family and vice versa. I can't wait to meet your side of the family."

Reece kissed her fiancé. The kiss got hotter as neither of them was willing to pull away. They only stopped when Alston came back for his cell phone.

He knocked on the door to the office before opening it and asked, "Are you finished with my phone?"

Reece handed her brother his phone and embraced him.

"Yes, we're done. Thanks for making sure Momma and Daddy got to be a part of this."

He tucked his phone in his pocket. "You're more than welcome, sis."

"I talked to Gabriella too. She got to meet Ky," Reece revealed.

Ky gave Alston a hug. "I'm so glad you were here for this."

"Me too. I'm starving, though. Let's eat!"

They made their way into the tent to join the rest of the family so they could finally sit down and enjoy some of the delicious food. Savoy took several pictures of their family gathering to post on Instagram. One picture in particular she loved was of her and Reece with their hands together in their sorority hand sign. Savoy's caption read: SO HAPPY TO GET A FABULOUS SOROR AS MY NEW SISTER-IN-LAW. LOVE YOU REECE!

As the night went on older family members gradually left and most of the younger family members stayed to enjoy themselves downstairs playing cards, pool, and just hanging out. Ky loved having his family around, but he couldn't wait for some alone time with Reece. He was happy his cousins were having a good time while he relaxed on the sectional with Reece curled up next to him.

Ja`el sat down across from the couple and asked, "So when is the big day?"

"We don't know yet, but you'll be one of the first to know," Ky answered.

Ja`el smiled. "Reece, I want to thank you because I've never seen my cousin this happy."

Reece linked her fingers with Ky's and said, "I've never been this happy either."

Ja`el could see the love between the couple and realized it was time for them to leave. With the caterers gone and the house cleaned up, he stood and said, "All right people! It's time for us to roll out!"

"Y'all don't have to leave," Ky said. "Savoy and Alston will be flying out tomorrow, so stay and enjoy yourselves. There's plenty of food and drinks leftover, so chill."

Ja`el looked at his watch. "Nah, you have a beautiful woman sitting next to you and you're in love. We've been here long enough."

Savoy stood. "Who wants to go to the club for a little while?"

Most of them accepted her invitation and Savoy asked Alston if he wanted to ride along as well. He agreed to go if they didn't keep him out too late. They all knew they were expected to be at church the next morning, so staying out too late was not an option. Ky and Reece stood and gave everyone a hug before walking them to the door.

"Take my car," Ky said as he handed Alston his keys.

"Thanks, bro. I'll be careful. Savoy, you ready to go?" Alston asked.

"Sure," she said as she followed him into the garage where they pulled out and disappeared down the street.

Ky closed the door, turned to Reece, and said, "Finally!"

Reece wrapped her arms around Ky's waist. "You up for a hot bath?"

He patted her on her backside. "You run the bath and I'll get the champagne."

Reece and Ky relaxed in his huge soaker tub and sipped on champagne to celebrate their engagement. They weren't sure how long Alston and Savoy would be out, but for now they had the house to themselves, and they were going to take advantage of it.

After a long soak in the tub in each other's arms and a few glasses of champagne, they retired to the bedroom. It had turned into a chilly night so Ky turned on the gas fireplace and climbed into bed next to her.

"I can't wait to make you my wife," he whispered while caressing her cheek.

"And I can't wait to make you my husband."

He looked into her loving eyes for a few seconds and decided to tell her about Yale. He didn't want any secrets between them and wanted her to be aware of what she did.

"Babe, I need to tell you that Yale barged in here tonight before we made the announcement and we got into a huge argument in the foyer. If it wasn't for my Dad, I don't know what I would've done to her."

Reece sat up in the bed in disbelief.

"You mean to tell me she just walked into your house?"

He pulled her back into is arms and said, "Our house and yes, but she didn't get far. It took every ounce of strength I had to keep from throwing her out the door on her face. Daddy finally talked her into leaving. You could tell she had been drinking."

"Why was she here?" Reece asked curiously.

"She was being nosey. She saw the tent in the backyard and thought we were having a wedding. Little does she know, we will be very soon."

Ky could tell that Reece was thinking hard about what he just told her and it worried him

"She's never going to leave us alone is she?" Reece solemnly asked.

He caressed her cheek and said, "Trust me, Sweetheart. She will be dealt with, OK? I don't want you worrying."

"It's hard not to when she's bold enough to walk up in our house like she did. She's reckless and unpredictable."

"Like I said, she will be dealt with," he repeated as he ran his hand through her hair.

Needing to change the subject, Reece asked, "OK. I trust you. So, have you thought about any dates for our wedding?"

He kissed her welcoming the change in their conversation. "To be honest, I would do it tomorrow, but I know there are some things to work out regarding your job and other personal business, and the fact that we both want a church wedding."

"We grew up in the church and it would seem wrong if we didn't. Call me old fashioned or traditional, but it's something I value, and I know you do too."

"I agree. I say we have the ceremony in D.C. the weekend after Thanksgiving. We can have a big reception here at my church the next weekend, which will satisfy everyone on my end."

"That's only a few weeks away," she pointed out. "Also, will it be a hardship for your family to travel to D.C.?"

"No, they'll be OK. Those that can make the trip, will. Those that can't will come to the reception here. I know we can make this work. What do you think?" he asked as he ran his hand seductively down her back and rested them on her hips.

She smiled. "Only if you're sure this will be OK with your family."

"It's really about what we want, but I appreciate you being considerate of my family," he said as he covered her body with his and started kissing her neck. "With that settled, how about we practice for the honeymoon?" he joked.

Reece giggled as his kisses went lower, causing her giggles to turn into a soft moan, which instantly aroused him as he moved even lower. Reece gasped and moaned as he made her body shiver and throb even harder. She begged for mercy as she gripped the sheets and called out to him, but he ignored her pleas. Not wanting to leave him unappreciated, with tears in her eyes she returned the favor and surrounded him with her soft, luscious lips.

Ky felt like his body was being jolted with electrical charges as Reece slowly and skillfully ran her lips and tongue over the length of him. He closed his eyes and hissed from the sheer ecstasy his body was experiencing. She was his mate in every sense of the word.

As he positioned himself between her legs and pushed deep inside her moist, warm body, he let out his own groan. They were inseparable as he seared her lips with hot kisses.

A few minutes later, Reece began to pant and moan even louder. Ky plunged his body deeper and deeper into her. Their erotic and rhythmic dance went on for several minutes until they reached satisfaction. Breathless, Reece caressed his back and held on to him, not wanting to move. She could feel his heart beating rapidly against hers and it put a smile on her face.

The couple slowly drifted off to sleep. Ky woke up only when he heard Alston and Savoy returning from their night out on the town. He slid into his jeans and met them in the hallway to make sure they had a good time. He then secured the alarm before going back to bed.

CHAPTER 21

At church the next morning Savoy and some of their cousins and friends yawned continuously from being out so late the night before. Word had spread around the sanctuary about Ky's engagement. Social media more than likely played a big part in the news getting out because Savoy and other family members had posted pictures from the night before on Instagram. And some of the older family members circulated the news by word of mouth, which often traveled faster than social media.

After service was over, a couple of church members approached the couple to congratulate them. There were a few nosey females who came over just to see Reece's ring. In the vestibule Yale noticed all the attention the couple was getting and then she spotted the large diamond on Reece's hand.

She nudged Anniston. "Look at that woman's left hand. Is that what I think it is?"

Anniston glanced over at the couple and said, "Oh my God! That is a big ass diamond on her finger. I heard Shauna and Janice talking about somebody being engaged. I guess they were talking about Ky."

Yale waved Shauna over to them and asked, "Have you heard anything about Ky being engaged?"

"Yes, I saw it on Savoy's Instagram last night."

Shauna pulled up Savoy's Instagram to show the two women and they saw pictures of Reece and Savoy. They also saw other pictures of Ky and Reece in a loving embrace and kissing each other, a few more with the parents, and one last one of all the younger cousins with raised glasses toasting the couple. She also showed them tweets from Savoy's Twitter account acknowledging Reece as her sorority sister and future sister-in-law.

Yale felt like she had been punched in the gut. "Now I know why he hustled me out of his house. I can't believe he would do this to me. He doesn't even know that woman. He's known me most of my life."

Anniston could see the pain in her best friend's eyes. Yale had told her about crashing the party at Ky's house the night before.

She thanked Shauna for showing them the pictures and then took Yale by the arm and led her outside.

"Let's get out of here. You have a new man anyway, and the last time I saw him he was looking really fine. You need to concentrate on him,"

Yale gave her a high five and said, "He is a cool guy, but I can't forget about Ky. I'm still in love with him."

"I still can't believe you walked up in the man's house like a boss."

Yale climbed into Anniston's car and started texting on her phone. "I knew something was up when I saw that big ass tent in his backyard. No wonder he was freaking out about me being there. Now we know."

"Well you're going to have to get over him because he's marrying that woman," Anniston pointed out.

"Maybe, maybe not," she said with a smirk on her face.

"What do you mean by that?" Anniston asked as she started her car.

Yale put on her seatbelt and said, "That woman doesn't deserve Ky. We have a history, and I know he still has feelings for me. We both have passionate personalities and Ky knows we have a love-hate relationship. That woman just got here and I'll be damned if I'm going to let her waltz into town and take him from me."

Anniston pulled out of the church parking lot. "What's done is done. Leave it alone and move on before you make things worse between you and Ky. He's still pissed off over the things you've already done. If you do anything else, who knows what he'll do."

Little did Anniston know that Ky had already warned Yale one last time and nearly killed her.

"I don't care," Yale said. "I can't let go. Not yet, probably never."

Anniston pulled into the soul food restaurant they usually went to after church and turned off the ignition. She turned to her friend. "Have you looked in the mirror lately?"

"Why?" Yale asked.

"There are a lot of women who wish they had your brains and beauty," Anniston said as she opened her car door. "You have a great job, a beautiful home, and you're using all your energy for evil instead of for good. You better change your ways and pay attention to what God is saying to you. He's sent Quincy to you, so you need to acknowledge him. If God meant for you and Ky to be together, you would be together."

Yale and Anniston walked into the restaurant and were immediately shown to a table. When they sat down, Yale said, "I hear you but this is hard for me. I thought by now I would be engaged to Ky or even pregnant with his child. That's what I really wanted."

"I understand, but it's not in the cards anymore, and you know Ky's not having any illegitimate kids. You're going to have to pray and try harder to get over him. God's sent you Quincy, which is the best ammunition to get back at Ky. He's not a bad looking guy. What does he do anyway?" Anniston asked as the waitress set two glasses of water on the table and handed them menus.

Yale scanned over her menu and said, "He's a Coast Guard officer. That's about all I know about him right now. We haven't been doing much talking if you know what I mean."

"Make sure he doesn't have a wife tucked away somewhere. If everything checks out on him, take advantage of it. Even if you don't get a love connection with him, he can be your snuggle buddy," Anniston suggested.

"That's true, but I still can't let go. I just can't believe Ky's in love with that woman."

"He's put a ring on it, so he must be," Anniston reminded her best friend. "He wouldn't have done that if he wasn't serious about marrying her. You know Ky doesn't play games in his relationships. You guys would still be together if you had just chilled and trusted him. He had a right to be angry with you for going through his phone. Hell, I would pissed if my man went through my phone."

The waitress returned to their table and took their order. When she walked off, Yale said, "I see how women look at Ky. He's so damn fine and handsome and every time you turn around there's always some woman in his face. I had to make sure he wasn't stepping out on me. Now it drives me crazy at the thought of him screwing that woman. He's definitely got it going on in that area, and for some other woman to be getting the benefits is messed up."

"Well, from what you've told me, Quincy's not bad either."

Yale laughed. "Girl, I thought he was going to break my back. I'll have to admit, the boy has some skills too."

"That's who you need to concentrate on," Anniston reminded her once again.

"I can't. At least not yet."

Anniston put her napkin in her lap and said, "I'm trying to help you, but you're so stubborn. Don't say I didn't warn you."

The waitress returned to their table with their meals. They blessed their food and dug in.

Across town, everyone met at Ky's parents' house for Sunday dinner. Sinclair and Geneva went all out and made some of Ky's and Savoy's favorite dishes. They had pot roast, chicken and dressing, turnip greens, macaroni and cheese, mashed potatoes, deviled eggs, broccoli cheese casserole, chess pie, vanilla pound cake, and cornbread. Ky's father blessed the food and then welcomed Alston to the family.

"Thanks, Rev. Parker. I appreciate you all making this fabulous dinner. I would be three hundred pounds eating all this good food on a regular basis."

Gerald laughed. "They try to cook as healthy as possible, but you know some food has to be prepared the original southern cook's way. We have to work out a lot to stay fit. Otherwise we all would be three hundred pounds."

Savoy handed Alston the broccoli casserole dish. "Momma, Alston invited us to his wedding this spring. He's going to add us to the guest list so we will get an invitation."

Sinclair took a sip of her lemonade and said, "Congratulations! I didn't know."

"Yes, ma'am," he replied. "My fiancée's name is Gabriella. She's from Trinidad."

"I'm sure it's going to be a lovely wedding and we would love to come and support you. It'll give us a chance to meet your parents and the rest of your family too. By the way, Reece, have you and Ky talked about a date for your wedding yet?" Sinclair asked.

Reece looked at Ky and then said, "Ky wants us to do the ceremony in D.C. the weekend after Thanksgiving."

"The weekend after Thanksgiving?" Geneva asked. "That's just around the corner."

Sinclair nearly spit out her iced tea upon hearing Reece's response.

"Will that give us enough time?" Reece asked.

Ky put up his hands and said, "Calm down, ladies. That's plenty of time for us to do what we want to do. This is the plan. We're having the wedding and a reception in D.C. the weekend after Thanksgiving, and then we want to have another reception here at the church the following weekend."

"Son, will that give you and Reece enough time to get a caterer, flowers, a dress, and invitations sent?" Sinclair asked.

Alston intervened. "Gabriella's already checking with our wedding planners to see if they can work their magic for Reece and Ky. They're going to call Reece tomorrow and let her know for sure. If they can pull everything off, they'll be good to go."

"The main thing I want to do is get the invitations out once we're able to confirm the church and obtain a caterer. I can always find a dress," Reece said.

"Why don't you get two dresses?" Savoy asked. "That's how the celebrities do it. We can go to a boutique in Atlanta or New York and find the dresses. I can't have you wearing the same dress at both receptions."

"Savoy, I'm not a celebrity. That could get kind of expensive," Reece pointed out.

"Babe, don't worry about the cost. I want you to get whatever you want. I'll pay for the dresses," Ky proudly announced.

Surprised, Reece said, "You don't have to do that. It's sweet of you to offer, but I can afford to buy my dresses. I just want to shop smart since you only wear them once. I'm sure there are some boutiques in D.C. or around here I can go to."

"Not here. Reece, let Ky pamper you," Savoy suggested. "You only get married once. Those boutiques in Atlanta and New York have beautiful dresses and they're affordable. We'll find you something sexy that will show off your incredible body."

Alston laughed. "I'm glad to see someone else going through what I'm going through."

Gerald, Sinclair, and Geneva sat back and listened to the colorful conversation between the young people.

"Ky, don't you want to see Reece coming down the aisle in something hot on your wedding day?" Savoy asked.

He smiled and looked over at his fiancée. "Babe, you'll look beautiful in any style, so get what makes you feel good, but if I had a preference it would be something fit to your sexy curves."

Savoy gave him a high five. "That's what I'm talking about. I'm team sexy!"

Reece laughed at Savoy and said, "Whatever I choose for the wedding, I want to make sure it's appropriate for a church ceremony and elegant. I don't want to show too much skin."

"We need to go soon because there's not enough time to order a dress," Sinclair said. "That usually takes months, so you'll probably have to get something off the rack. I'm sure between us and your mother, we can help you find something beautiful for both ceremonies."

"I'd like that," Reece replied. "My dad and grandmother would love to be there too."

"You guys need to hurry up and settle on a color scheme because you need to pick out bridesmaid dresses too," Savoy said.

"Ky and I are going to sit down tonight and make a list of everything we need so we can start making calls."

Geneva looked at her son and asked, "Gerald, is the fellowship hall available that weekend in December?"

"If it's not, I'll make it available. I'll have the secretary check the calendar tomorrow."

The family fellowshipped for another hour before Ky looked at his watch and said, "Hey, guys, we're going to have to hurry up. I have to take a yacht out for a test drive before I drive Alston and Savoy to the airport, and I want to get your opinion."

Alston wiped his mouth and said, "Sounds fun. I'm game."

Savoy looked at her parents. "I wish I could stay longer. I'll be back home soon for Thanksgiving."

Gerald winked at his daughter. "We understand, and while I know you like staying with your brother, it would be nice if you spent some time here while you're home next time."

"I will, Daddy. I promise."

Gerald turned to Alston. "Alston, it was so nice to meet you. We're family now and you and your wife and your parents are welcome to come for a visit anytime. Our doors are always open."

"I appreciate that, Rev. Parker. The same goes for us as well. I want to thank all of you for being so kind to Reece, and to you, Ky, for making her so happy."

"Reece made loving her easy, but you're welcome," Ky replied. "Are ya'll ready to head down to the marina?"

They all stood so they could say their goodbyes before heading out.

At the marina, Alston and Reece got the chance to see just how good Ky and his crew were in the yacht building business. The vessel was beautiful and had all the bells and whistles a luxury yacht should have. Before beginning the visible inspection, Ky made all the necessary introductions to his foreman and office manager, Trish. When he introduced Reece as his fiancée, Trish screamed. She knew they had been spending a lot of time together and Reece would come by to visit for lunch, but she never knew things were so serious. The couple was able to keep the real nature of their relationship under wraps until now.

"I told you she was special the first day she came into the office," Trish said to Ky as she hugged Reece. "You were trying to act cool, but I could tell you felt it too."

He nodded as he let Trish have her say.

"Thank you so much. I knew he was a nice guy when I first met him too," Reece said

"I'm so glad he didn't let you get away from him," Trish said as they entered the family room area of the yacht.

"Me too," Reece replied as she stepped into the family room behind Trish. "Oh my God! This is beautiful. What do these clients do for a living?"

With her clipboard in hand, Trish turned to Reece and said, "They have old money. This is the second yacht they've purchased from us."

Alston sat down on the sofa. "This is nice, and those windows will give your clients great views wherever they are."

The group continued down to the kitchen area and staff quarters where the foreman pointed out how he had he separated the sleeping quarters in case there were male and female staffers. Some crew members had to share, which limited the clients from hiring mixed sex crew members.

They finished up the visual tour and then it was time to take the yacht out on the water. Ky and the foreman started it up and slowly guided the yacht out onto the open water. Ky was in business mode and was making note of anything that felt out of order. They monitored vibrations, maneuverability of the steering, exterior cameras, and all of the electrical items on the panel that assisted the captain in steering the yacht. They were out on the water for about an hour and once they all signed off on the inspection, they headed back to the marina. Now the yacht was ready to be delivered to the Lanbeaus and Ky would have another perfect project under his belt.

Once they arrived back at the marina, Ky thanked his staff for coming out on a Sunday evening to complete the inspection and made a mental note to reward them for their loyalty. With this business behind him, it was time to get Alston and Savoy to the airport to catch their flights, which were supposed to leave within thirty minutes of each other. Once they arrived at the airport, everyone said their goodbyes curbside. Alston thanked Ky one last time for making his sister so happy and for his hospitality. Reece and Savoy took another picture together and so did Reece and Alston. Savoy put her arm around her brother's neck and took a picture with him. Then they took a group picture before saying goodbye one last time. It was a bittersweet send off, but they knew they would see each other again soon.

With Savoy and Alston on their way, Ky turned to his future bride and said, "Ready to head home?"

"More than you know," she answered as she climbed inside the car.

CHAPTER 22

Ky couldn't be happier as he drove into work on Monday. It had been a fabulous weekend and he had let his whole family know that Reece was the love of his life. He stopped by a cafe to grab breakfast for his crew. As he sat down at a table to wait, he decided to check his email on his cell phone.

Seconds later, Yale sat down in the chair across from him and said, "I can't believe you're marrying that woman!"

"Lower your voice," Ky demanded softly with a frown on his face. He put his phone back into his pocket and asked, "Why are you here? I'm getting tired of you popping up in my life."

"I want you to look me in the eyes and tell me what's going on. You can't be in love with her because you've only known her for a few months. Is she pregnant? Is that why you feel like you have to marry her?"

Ky looked into her eyes and saw the tears forming. He knew she was in pain, but it was past time for her to start working on moving on. She was a beautiful woman and she was dressed to perfection as always in a light blue pantsuit with a royal blue silk blouse. Her makeup enhanced her natural beauty and today she was wearing her hair curly. Despite her outer beauty, Yale had issues and he was exhausted from going around and around with her over their breakup. It was tiresome and he had no idea what it was going to take for her to finally accept once and for all that their relationship was over. So today he thought about trying to use kindness instead of anger to get his point across.

He reached across the table, took her hand into his, and said, "I care about you, Yale, and I hate to see you keep doing this to yourself. We had a great time together while it lasted, but we just didn't work out, and I'm pissed at a lot of the things you've done and forced me to do over the past few weeks. You know me. I don't do drama and that's all you've given me. I wish you would stop doing this to yourself."

"Tell that to my heart," she replied as tears ran down her face. "I'm in constant pain over what I did to lose you and I don't know what to do to make it stop. I promise I get it now. I know I can trust you and there's no reason for me to be jealous. Please don't marry that woman, Ky. I love you!"

At that moment the barista called out Ky's name to let him know his order was ready.

Even though Yale had pushed him to his limits and caused him to lose his temper, he was raised to forgive and give people second chances. In Yale's case, all he could offer was forgiveness.

He gave her a tender kiss on the cheek as he stood and said, "I'm sorry you keep doing this to yourself, but it's too late. I've moved on. Just pray and you'll be OK. I want us to be able to be cool around each other without all this animosity."

She pulled a napkin out of the napkin holder, wiped her eyes, and screamed at the top of her lungs, "I'll never be OK!"

Employees and patrons stared at them in disbelief. They weren't sure what was going on between the couple, but whatever it was, it wasn't good.

Ky shook his head. "See, it's that kind of bullshit I hate about you. Get yourself together and stop making a fool of yourself."

Yale wiped the tears from her cheeks and watched him as he picked up his order and walked out the door. She took her compact out of her purse, freshened her makeup, and mumbled, "Pull yourself together, Yale."

She put her compact back into her purse and exited the coffee shop.

The next couple of weeks seemed to fly by. Ky decided not to tell Reece about his conversation with Yale at the cafe. There was no need in upsetting her unnecessarily, and he recognized Yale still hadn't taken his advice and moved on like he had hoped. Ky realized this drastic situation called for drastic measures. He had given her every opportunity to come to terms with the demise of their relationship but she refuses to accept it. Now it was time for him to turn up the heat on her once and for all. When he got back to his office he called a frat brother on the police force and explained the situation to him and asked for assistance in putting the matter to rest once and for all. The officer assured Ky he would have a talk with Yale off the record but if that wasn't enough to diffuse the situation and she continued with her antics he should consider a restraining order. Ky agreed and thanked the officer for his help.

The couple was able to get a lot of their wedding planning out of the way, which took some of their stress away. The decision had been finalized. They would have the wedding and reception in D.C. with all the bells and whistles and a big reception in Ky's hometown. The couple had chosen purple and pink as their primary color scheme. The bridesmaid's dresses would be purple, one shouldered, tea length gowns and they would carry pink roses as their bouquets, while the groomsmen would wear black tuxedos with purple ties and handkerchiefs to match the bridesmaids' dresses. Their vision was for the reception to be decorated in pink, purple, and white flowers, accented with crystals to add sparkle to the venue. The place settings of crystal and platinum on white linen tablecloths. They were able to hire the same wedding planners that were doing Alston's and Gabriella's wedding, so everything was being handled by experts. All the bridal party had to do was show up.

Reece still had to find her wedding gown and pick the dresses for her bridesmaids, and Ky needed to select the tuxedos for his groomsmen. They had narrowed it down to their top two favorite choices and tonight they had to make their decision. After a long day at work, the couple settled down on the sectional in the entertainment room with their iPads to make their choices.

"OK, babe, tell me which one you like," Reece said to Ky.

He looked at the two bridesmaid dresses and pointed at his choice.

"I agree. I think that one will look best on anyone regardless of their body type. I want everyone to feel beautiful and be comfortable too."

Ky then showed her his two choices for tuxedos and they agreed on a classic black tuxedo with vests and neckties to match the bridesmaids' dresses. Ky's tuxedo would have a white jacket to match Reece's gown with a black bowtie.

"I can't wait to see you in your tux," Reece said. "I'm sure I'll have to struggle to keep from crying. I don't want to ruin my makeup before I get to the altar."

He smiled and then leaned over and kissed her. "Babe, that's sweet, but I already know I'm not going to be able to hold my composure when I see you, so you've been warned."

"Ky, seriously, you're going to have to be cool because if I look at you and see tears, I'm done."

He pulled her into his lap and said softly, "I can't promise you anything, but I'll try."

Reece stared into his mesmerizing green eyes while straddling his lap. "I can't believe it's really happening."

He caressed her hips and said, "Yes, it is, but there are some legal issues we have to take care of too. You and I both have assets and I have a business. We need to get with an attorney to make sure our family is taken care of if anything happens to either one of us."

Tears formed in her eyes and Ky knew exactly where her thoughts were going, but before he could say anything, she said, "The thought of anything happening to you terrifies me."

He caressed her thighs. "I feel the same way, but it's reality, sweetheart, and we need to be prepared regardless. Don't you agree?"

She climbed out of his lap and said, "You're right, and I'm going to eventually have to get past my fear."

"It will take time, but it'll happen."

Reece nodded and then picked up her iPad and said, "Do you already have an attorney?"

"I do, and if you're OK with it, I can set up something this week so we can get it out of the way."

"That's fine. Just let me know when and where. The only asset I have is my brownstone, which I'm selling as soon as possible. Oh! I also have an investment portfolio and an inheritance from my grandparents."

He looked over at her. "Inheritance?"

"Yeah, from my grandparents. My grandfather was a surgeon for over forty years and my grandmother was a pharmacist for about the same length of time. They did very well for themselves, but lived a humble lifestyle. I miss them so much. They were in their mid-eighties and died a couple of years apart from each other when I was in college."

"I'm sorry to hear that," Ky replied as he changed the station on the TV.

Samson put his head in Reece's lap so she could pat him. She happily accommodated the lab before casually revealing to Ky what her net worth was.

He laughed. "That was slick. I like how you eased that in on me."

Then without hesitating he revealed his net worth to her as well. "There's no other woman I would rather share my life or my assets with than you."

Reece smiled. "Babe, you and I both know we're not with each other because of our bank accounts. I would be with you regardless, because I fell in love with you."

"I couldn't say it any better," he replied before kissing her and turning off the TV. He stood and said, "Let's go to bed. I'm exhausted."

She looked at her watch and said, "It's only nine o'clock."

He took her by the hands and pulled her off the sofa. "I didn't say anything about going to sleep."

"Lord have mercy," she replied with a smile as goose bumps consumed her body.

After entering the bedroom Ky received a text message from the officer that he had contacted regarding Yale and he felt confident that it was successful. Ky said a short prayer that the officer was right.

Across town Yale slammed the door after the officer had a conversation with her and gave her a stern warning about staying away from Ky and Reese. He assured her that if he had to come back he would have a warrant for her arrest and would have no problem putting her in handcuffs.

Pacing the floor, she said to herself, "I see you have taken this to another level, Ky Parker. How dare you call the police on me? That's fine. Two can play at that game."

Reece felt like she was on cloud nine. All the details for their wedding had been set so she decided to take Ky home to D.C. to meet her friends and family and to find her wedding gown. She was low key and wanted to have this experience with the people closest to her, and allow her parents a chance to get to know their future son-in-law. Reece wanted Ky with her when she went dress shopping, but she also wanted to keep with tradition, so although he was there, he wasn't able to see her in any of the dresses. He made himself comfortable in the waiting room area where he chatted with Alston and played games on his phone. They kept each other company until Reece made her choice. That was when Alston was called to the runway area to see her in the dress and give his opinion.

For the ceremony, she chose a white, long sleeved, fit and flair gown with a sheer back and elaborate lace designs with a nude colored underlay. She chose a cathedral veil that contained similar beading. She had changed her mind about getting a different dress for the reception at Ky's church. She did purchase a second dress for the D.C. reception as a surprise to Ky. The dress she chose was a pale blush color in a mermaid style with a sweetheart neckline covered in crystal beading and a whimsical organza skirt. Once all the family had come to an agreement with Reece on the dresses, Alston rejoined Ky in the waiting room area and gave him a thumbs up.

He patted his future brother-in-law on the shoulders and said, "Bro, you're going to be blown away when you see my sister. I'll have to admit, I got a little choked up when I saw her. Everyone was in tears back there."

"I'm in trouble, huh?" he asked before laughing.

"Yes indeed," Alston said as he also laughed. "Seriously, she looks stunning."

"I have no doubt," Ky answered with pride.

Ky was getting even more anxious to marry Reece upon hearing how beautiful she looked. Their wedding day couldn't come any faster and then he would take her on the honeymoon of their dreams to the Four Seasons in the beautiful South Pacific, which would be his surprise to her.

It wasn't long before Reece and the family joined the two men in the lobby area of the salon.

He gave her a kiss and asked, "Did you get everything you needed?"

She hugged his waist and with a big smile on her face she said, "I did. Luckily I found a gown I don't have to order and I was able to get fitted. I'll do my final fitting when I come back Thanksgiving weekend to make sure it's perfect. I hope I didn't keep you waiting too long."

"Not at all," he replied. "Alston told me you looked stunning."

She looked at her brother. "Is that all you told Ky?"

"Yes," he said as he opened the door for the ladies. "Ya'll ready to grab something to eat?"

Reece's father said, "Yes, I'm starving."

Maxine Miller linked her arms with her husband and said, "James, you're always hungry."

As they all walked to their cars, he said, "It's been a great day, and my baby looked so beautiful. The best way to cap this day off is with a great meal."

"I agree, Poppy," Gabriella added. "Can we go to Georgia Brown's? I love that place."

The family agreed and climbed into their vehicles and headed for the restaurant.

While in D.C. Reece had several issues she had to deal with. First she had to meet with her director about the status of her job. She didn't want to quit and the agency didn't want to lose her as a valued employee. They discussed a few options and agreed that Reece could keep her position and work out of the Gulf Coast office she was working in now; however, she would have to return to D.C. several times a year for various conferences and meetings, and would still have to travel to other districts, but she would not have to endure the long assignments like the one she was on now. Reece couldn't ask for a better outcome, but she was prepared to look for a new job if it came down to it. It was going to be bittersweet leaving D.C. with so many memories there, especially those she had with Geno.

Also while in town Reece thought it was appropriate that she visited Geno's parents and tell them in person about her upcoming wedding, the selling of the brownstone, and her move to another state. They were very close and Reece hoped to remain that way even though she was starting a new chapter in her life. Her visit with Geno's family was emotional but also joyous. They wished her well on her new life. They had been encouraging her for a couple of years to move on with her life and they were happy she was finally taking their advice. She would always have a special place in their hearts and they accompanied her for one more walk through the brownstone before she signed the papers to put it on the market. They ended their visit with prayer, hugs, and kisses and an invite to the wedding.

Reece decided to leave her car in D.C. and let her first cousin, who was a freshman at Howard University, drive it so it wouldn't just be sitting. When they came home to visit, they would have transportation and wouldn't have to rely on family or rent a vehicle. While taking care of business, she was able to meet up with her two best friends for lunch. She was excited to see them and they were excited to be her bridesmaids. They were anxious to meet Ky and were able to meet him briefly before he left to go play basketball with Alston and some friends. Reece filled them in on everything that had gone on the past few months. She even told them about Yale and everything that had happened leading up to her engagement. They were proud of her and wished her well before leaving.

The weekend flew by and after attending the church they would be getting married in they returned to Alston's house where Gabriella insisted on cooking some of the traditional meals from Trinidad for the family. Ky really enjoyed the meal and even asked her for a couple of recipes so he could make them once he returned home.

The night before they were to return back to the Gulf so they relaxed around the fireplace with a few drinks.

Reece cuddled up to Ky and asked, "Have you enjoyed yourself this weekend?"

He took a sip of his beer and said, "Of course. Your parents are sweet and they make me feel like they've known me for years."

Alston sat down. "I'm glad you feel comfortable around everyone. I hate to see you guys leave."

Gabriella sat in Alston's lap and said, "Me too. I'm going to miss you, Reece."

"I'm going to miss you guys too," she replied as she took a sip of her wine.

"Ky, you make sure you take care of our girl," Gabriella said in her thick Trinidadian accent as she playfully pointed her finger at him.

"Don't worry, I will, and you guys are welcome to come down and visit us anytime."

"For sure," Gabriella said. "Alston told me how beautiful it is there."

Alston poured himself another drink and said, "We'll come visit, but not too soon after the wedding. We don't want to intrude on you newlyweds."

Reece looked at Ky and said, "We're going to be newlyweds regardless. Nobody can stop us from doing what we want to do when we want to do it."

"You're so nasty," Gabriella jokingly said before laughing.

Alston waved off his sister and said, "Now that's where I draw the line."

"Please!" Reece replied. "Like I haven't had to suffer through you guys being all over each other."

"Touché'" Gabriella said as she raised her wine glass.

Ky laughed. "Ya'll crack me up." He finished off his drink and then looked at his watch. "It's getting late. We'd better turn in if we're going to catch our flight in the morning."

"You're right," Reece answered as she stood and gave Gabriella a hug. "We'll see you guys in the morning."

Alston gave his sister a kiss and Ky a hug and said, "OK. Have a good night."

CHAPTER 23

Thanksgiving was less than a week away and Ky was looking forward to spending time with his family. Reece would be going home for the final fitting of her wedding gown, and while he would miss her, he knew she had to get it done. As he sat down to finish up paperwork before heading home, he got an unexpected text message from Reece.

Ky, I love you, but I can't marry you. I'm leaving town to try to get my head together. Don't try to find me. Go back to Yale. Goodbye.

"What the hell?" Ky mumbled to himself as he dialed Reece's cell. After two rings it went to voicemail, so Ky immediately left her a message.

"Reece, I just got a crazy text from you. I don't know if it's a joke or what, but it's not funny. Call me right away."

Ky hung up and read the text again as he waited for Reece to return his call. After five minutes had passed, he called again and this time her phone didn't ring. It went straight to voicemail as if it was turned off. Then he decided to send her a text message for her to call him right away.

After another fifteen minutes passed and there was no call or text response, Ky started to panic. This behavior wasn't like Reece, but it also wasn't out of the ordinary for someone who had been through the type of tragedy she had to second guess a new relationship.

Ky let another twenty minutes pass before he called her again, and once again it went straight to voicemail. He decided to reach out to Alston to get his opinion. After Ky forwarded the text to Alston, he called his future brother-in law. Alston was just as stunned as Ky.

"Ky, I don't know what to make of this. Reece never gave me any indication she was having second thoughts."

Alston could clearly hear the stress in Ky's voice and as a matter of fact, he was feeling a little stressed himself.

"It don't make sense Alston. Everything was fine this morning. She's been so excited about the wedding, living here and starting a life together."

"Well, if she was really having second thoughts, I know for a fact she would reach out to me to talk about it and I haven't spoken to her since day before yesterday."

Ky nervously said, "Something's wrong, bro, I can feel it. There's no way in hell Reece would be second guessing our life together. The crazy thing is the text suggests I get back with Yale. That's total bullshit and Reece would never do that. I'm going to call her office to see if they noticed anything about her demeanor."

"Call me back ASAP," Alston pleaded. "If she is having a second thoughts moment, I'm sure she will come around."

"I pray you're right. I'll call you in a second."

Once Ky hung up with Alston he dialed the number to Reece's office. Thankfully her assistant was still there and she told Ky that Reece had left the office nearly an hour before. She said she didn't notice anything unusual about Reece's demeanor and it seemed like a normal busy day. Ky thanked her without alerting her that something might be wrong.

Since he didn't seem to be getting anywhere in figuring out what was going on with Reece, Ky decided to head home. It was his prayer that when he got home, he would find Reece standing in the kitchen with a huge smile on her face, but something told him that wasn't going to be the case. On the entire drive home he continued to call her phone but it was still going to voicemail. He left a few more messages before reaching his driveway. When he pulled up to the house and raised the garage doors, Reece's car was not there, causing him even more anxiety. He entered the house, and as he made his way into the kitchen he could tell that Reece had not been there, so he decided to check to see if she had packed any of her clothes or personal belongings. When he looked in the bedroom closet he saw that nothing had been touched since they left the house that morning. He knew there was no way Reece would leave him without packing some clothes. Something was very wrong.

He pulled out his phone again and whispered, "Come on, baby, answer the damn telephone." The call went straight to voicemail once again. "Shit!" he yelled. He decided to call his friend, Officer Wayman, since he wasn't sure what else to do.

"Officer Wayman, it's Ky Parker," he said when the officer answered. "I need your help. My fiancée is missing and she's not answering her phone. I'm worried that something's happened to her."

He went on to explain that his fiancée was the woman he came to the aid of months earlier when he was changing her flat tire. Officer Wayman remembered her well and congratulated him on his engagement before getting back to business. Ky explained everything to the officer, because although he knew he couldn't file an official missing person's report for twenty-four hours, he desperately needed help.

Ky gave him the description of Reece's car and what she was wearing. He also told Officer Wayman what time Reece had left the office and that her coworker didn't think there wasn't anything strange about Reece's behavior that day. Officer Wayman could hear the stress in Ky's voice and assured him he would do everything possible to locate Reece. When Ky told him about Yale and how she could be involved it was concerning to the officer. Ky also revealed that he asked his frat brother on the police force to have a talk with Yale. Hearing this information elevated a sense of urgency with Officer Wayman.

While Officer Wayman did what he could to locate Reece, Ky decided to drive around town in hopes of finding her or a clue. He called Alston again to update him and let him know he had the police helping. Alston still hadn't heard from his sister and she wasn't answering his calls either, so now he was extremely concerned. He decided to catch the next flight out to come help Ky in the search. He didn't want to worry their parents if Reece really had just run off, so for now he would keep the information to himself. Luckily he was able to fly out right away on a friend's private jet, which would put him in town sooner than taking a commercial flight.

After hanging up with Alston, Ky quickly hit the streets to search for Reece. He drove down every street, back alley, and dirt road searching for her. It was as if she had vanished into thin air. Officer Wayman called Ky and told him he'd reviewed the security tapes at Reece's office. She was seen walking to her car, but the camera didn't have a view of the driver's side of the vehicle. There was approximately a three-minute gap where there was no visual of

Reece before the car backed out of the parking space and pulled out of the parking garage. Unfortunately, the camera couldn't pick up the image of the driver.

It was going to be getting dark soon, which was going to make the search for Reece that much harder and more desperate. Ky just prayed that she wasn't so distraught that she had taken a wrong turn somewhere and ended up in harm's way or crashed into one of the many canals in the area. He tried not the think the worst and he prayed she would call him to let him know she was just having a moment. But what really puzzled him about the mysterious text was why she would suggest he go back to Yale. Even if she was having second thoughts about getting married, he didn't believe she would ever suggest he get back together with Yale, not after all the drama she'd put them through.

An hour or so later, after picking up Alston from the airport, Ky stopped at the gas station to fill up his truck. While he pumped the gas, Alston continued to try to call his sister, but to no avail. Then Ky got a call from Officer Wayman to let him know they had found Reece's car. After the officer told Ky where to meet him, Ky quickly jumped in his truck and sped across town to the location.

When they arrived and saw the ambulance, Ky's heart sank. He prayed she wasn't hurt. He barely got his truck in park before jumping out and running toward the ambulance.

"Is Reece OK?" he asked. "Where is she?"

Officer Wayman blocked his path and put up his hands. "We have a problem."

"What kind of problem?" Alston asked as they tried to push past the officer.

"Miss Miller is still missing."

"What do you mean she's still missing?" Ky yelled. "That's her car, so where is she?"

"I'm sorry, but we don't know. We found someone you know driving her car. He has a gunshot wound in the arm and he's being treated in the ambulance, but he's not talking."

Ky could not believe what he was hearing. He pushed past the officer and looked in the ambulance where he found his cousin Ja`el working on Andre`.

Ky turned back to Officer Wayman. "You have got to be kidding me!"

Before Officer Wayman could respond, Ky jumped in the back of the medical van and pulled out his gun. He aimed it at Andre` and asked, "Where the hell is Reece?"

"Reece?" Ja`el asked as he put an IV in André's hand. "Why are you asking him about Reece?"

"Reece is missing and that's her car the police found him driving," Ky revealed.

There was no way the police could make him talk without violating André's rights, but Ky could even if he had to pull the trigger to do it. Ky was beyond enraged and would do whatever it took to find Reece, even if it meant going to jail.

"Ky, put that gun away before you kill somebody," Ja`el pleaded.

Officer Wayman also pleaded with Ky to put away his gun. Ignoring both of them, Ky pointed the gun at André's foot and said, "I'm going to count to three, you son of a bitch, and if you don't tell me where she is, I'm going to blow off your damn foot."

Officer Wayman climbed into in the back of the ambulance and said, "Ky, I'm going to ask you again to put that gun away before you do something you'll regret. I don't want to have to arrest you."

"You can arrest me after we find Reece," Ky replied without looking at him. "He's going to talk if I have to start with his foot and work my way up to his damn head. I have no problem going to jail tonight if I have to shot him but he's going to tell me where Reece is one way or another."

"Ky, please," Officer Wayman said.

Ja`el saw the redness in Ky's eyes and tried to restrain his cousin. He had seen him angry before, but never like this. "Cuz! Chill with that gun!"

Ky pushed Ja`el away, held Andre`'s leg down by the ankle, and pointed the gun at his foot. "I'm not going to ask you again, boy! Where is Reece?" he yelled.

"Officer! Are you going to get him or what?" Andre` yelled as his eyes widened in fear.

"He can't save you from me," Ky announced. "Your sorry ass better pray Reece is not hurt, and if you laid one finger on her, you'll be dead before you ever see a jail cell."

"He's not lying, and if he don't kill you first, I will," Alston added.

Ja`el looked at Andre` and said, "Kid, you better tell Ky what he wants to know. You're about three seconds from losing your foot or your life."

Andre` squirmed on the gurney and yelled, "Yo, officer, get this fool out of here before he kills me."

With his hand on his Taser, Officer Wayman pleaded again. "Ky, please don't do this. I can't stand here and let you shoot my suspect."

The situation had just gone from bad to worse. Ja`el held up his hand and said, "Wait! Wait! Wait! Everyone needs to calm down. Officer Wayman, please don't taser Ky. He's just upset, and understandably so."

Ignoring Ja`el the officer pulled out his Taser. "Ky, please put away your gun. I don't want to hurt you."

Ky reluctantly lowered his gun and turned to the officer. "You better get him to talk, because if you don't, I will."

The officer leaned down to the teen. "If you know what's good for you, you'll tell me where Miss Miller is located. This is not a man you want to play with."

"I thought I had the right to remain silent?" Andre` asked.

"You do," Officer Wayman replied. "I just know you're in a bad spot right now and need to do the right thing."

Andre` looked at the officer and then back at Ky who still had the gun in his trembling hand. He could see he was staring at him with a glare that could kill.

"Ok! Ok! I'll take you to her, but you have to give me something for this pain first since that bitch shot me."

Without hesitation, Ky punched Andre` dead in the mouth and said, "You're lucky she didn't blow your ass away. Now where is she?"

Nearly hyperventilating, Andre` yelled, "I'm hurting. I need something for my pain if you expect me to tell you anything."

"You'll get something for the pain once we have Reece," Ja`el calmly explained, knowing it was against his code of ethics not to fully treat a patient. "For now, I'll give you something just to take the edge off."

Andre` looked at the officer. "Officer, can you please get him away from me and help me with this charge?"

"That depends on how everything turns out tonight and what you have to tell me to convince me you deserve it," Officer Wayman answered. "Right now, your best bet is to tell me where Miss Miller is located and fast."

"OK, OK, but we need a boat," Andre` finally revealed.

"A boat?" Ky asked. "What the hell did you do with her?"

As Ja`el administered the medicine in the IV to ease some of Andre's pain he said, "She's in a fishing camp out in the bayou."

"You left her alone in the swamp?" Ky yelled in disbelief.

"Hell yeah!" he yelled. "That's what you get for what you did to my cousin."

"I didn't do a damn thing to Yale," he replied in anger. "You need to get your facts straight, kid, and pray to God Reece is not hurt, because if she has one scratch on her, I will kill you."

"Kiss my black ass, Ky! You treated my cousin like shit! You need to hurt just like she's hurting. It don't feel so good, does it?"

Ky could feel himself losing control of his emotions. He wanted nothing more than to shoot Andre`, but he needed to find Reece first. He looked at Ja'el and said, "I need you, cuz. You know what can happen to her out there. There're all sorts of things out there that could hurt or kill her."

Ky climbed out of the ambulance and told Alston they needed to move fast. They drove to the nearest boat ramp where two police boats picked them up and headed out into the dark bayou. On the ride Ky and Alston prayed that Reece was OK and that no harm had come to her. Ky knew how to survive in this type of wilderness, but Reece didn't, and he knew she had to be scared to death.

Ky turned to Andre` and said, "You need to get the facts straight about Yale. I didn't do anything to her but end our relationship because she was so goddamn controlling, jealous, and paranoid. So while you think you're showing loyalty to her by getting back at me, you're only making life harder for yourself. Your cousin has some serious issues that she needs to deal with. She wasn't the woman for me. Now tell me how you got Reece's car?"

"Hold up, Ky," Officer Wayman suggested. "The kid should be interrogated by law enforcement and he has rights."

"Rights? He don't deserve any rights," Ky told Officer Wayman. He turned back to Andre` and said "Once we find my girl, if I find out that you've put your hands on her or violated her in any way, you're a dead son of a bitch."

"Ky, you can't say things like that in front of me," the officer reminded him.

"I know you have to do what you have to do, Officer Wayman, but I have to do what I have to do too," Ky replied.

"He's right," Alston added. "My sister is my world and I can assure you that you will be a dead man by one of our hands if she's hurt in any way. Ky showed some restraint in the back of that ambulance. I WON'T."

Andre` could see the anger in Ky's and Alston's eyes and knew they were not bluffing. He had no doubt that Ky would kill him. Now to have the chick's brother on board too made going to jail sound a lot safer for him. So after the officer read him his rights, he admitted to approaching Reece in her parking garage. He said she put up a fight and shot him before he used a stun gun on her. He told them he did it because Yale was hurting over her breakup with Ky and he wanted to do something to make her feel better."

"Did Miss Spencer put you up to this?" Officer Wayman asked.

"I don't want to talk anymore," Andre` replied as he rubbed his bruised jaw where Ky punched him earlier.

"Yale has to be involved, Officer Wayman. How else would he know where Reece worked in order to kidnap her?" Ky pointed out to the officer.

Officer Wayman told Ky he was definitely going to bring Yale in for questioning, but without any direct evidence she was involved, there was nothing he could do to formally charge her.

"What about the damn text messages?" he asked. "Reece didn't send those."

"There's a lot we have to investigate so we can't jump to conclusions," the officer said in response.

At that moment Andre` pointed down a canal to a small floating house used by fisherman. When the police pulled the boats up to the dock, Ky, Alston, and the officers quickly exited. The police entered cautiously and found Reece blindfolded and tied up on a dirty cot in the middle of the room.

"Reece!" Ky yelled as he quickly removed the blindfold and duct tape off her mouth while the police officer cut the grip ties off her hands and ankles.

"You OK, sis?" Alston asked softly as he tried not to cry at seeing his sister so frightened and in distress.

She was eerily quiet and would not respond to either Ky nor Alston.

"Ja`el! Get in here!" Ky yelled frantically.

"What's wrong with her?" Alston asked with a trembling voice.

"I don't know," Ky replied as he frantically inspected her body for injuries. That was when he noticed an obvious insect bite on her leg.

"Damn it! She's been bitten by something," he told Alston.

Ja`el came in with his medical case and asked, "How is she?"

"I think she's in shock. She's not talking and she has some type of bite on her leg. What does it look like to you?"

Ja`el inspected the area and then her pupils and said, "Looks like a spider bite. She has a mark on her chest where he probably hit her with the stun gun. I think she's in shock too."

Ky and Alston were trying to stay calm, but seeing Reece so traumatized didn't make it easy.

"Reece, talk to me, babe," Ky said as he caressed her face. "You're going to be OK. Ja`el's going to take care of you and then get you to the hospital."

She looked at Ky with tears in her eyes, but she was still speechless.

Ja`el checked her vital signs and then said, "She has a fever, her breathing is shallow, and she has a rapid heartbeat. We need to get her to the hospital right away."

"Help me remove her clothes so I can see if she has any other injuries," Ja`el said as he reached for the buttons on Reece's blouse.

Ky grabbed Ja`el's wrist faster than lightning and said, "The hell you are! You're not taking off her clothes with all these men around."

Ja`el smiled and said, "Cuz, it's not like that. I have to examine her."

Ky shook his head. "I can't let you do that, bro. That's my lady."

Alston put his hand on Ky's shoulder and said, "Ky, I understand how you feel. I'm sure Ja`el is keeping it professional. He's your cousin, for God's sake. It's for her own good. Officer Wayman, can you and your men give us a little privacy so Ja`el can examine her?"

Officer Wayman shook his head and said, "I can send the others outside, but I have to be here to document everything for my report."

"Understood," Alston replied. "Ky, the sooner we get this done, the sooner it'll be over."

Ky thought for a few seconds as he looked into Reece's eyes, knowing how shy and private she was. It was a hard decision and while his heart was telling him no, his mind knew his actions could cause her more harm. So he sucked up his pride and convinced himself that the men were not going to see any more than they would if she had on a bikini.

Ja`el hugged his cousin and said, "Our only concern is with helping Reece. Trust me because if something bit her it could still be inside her clothing. I would never disrespect you or Reece. Let me do my job, Ky."

Ky finally nodded. He kissed Reece and whispered, "I got you, baby. I'm going to remove some of your clothes so Ja`el can examine you. OK?"

Reece was still verbally unresponsive as Ky removed her clothes down to her undergarments. Alston waited to cover her with a blanket and they all noticed she was trembling. Ja`el found another bite on her torso as well as scrapes and bruises on her arms and legs. When Ky shook out her clothes a large spider fell to the floor.

"There it is," Ja`el said as he stepped on the spider and then scooped it up in a specimen jar. "I'll take it back with me so we can determine what treatment she needs. For now, I need to get this IV in her and we need to get moving. I don't like the way she's breathing and her blood pressures is dropping."

Alston wrapped the blanket around his sister so Ky could carry her to the boat. While Ja`el stabilized Reece in one boat, the other paramedic attended to Andre` in the other boat. There was no way Ky was going to let Reece anywhere near Andre`. Once they made it back to the boat ramp there was a second ambulance waiting to transport Andre`. Ja`el wanted to stay with Reece. By the time they made it to the emergency room, Reece was starting to come around. She wasn't talking but she was squeezing Ky's hand and was able to form a weak smile at Alston.

When Ja`el wheeled Reece into the ER and turned her over to the hospital staff, he patted Ky on the shoulders and said, "You did good, cuz. Don't worry, Reece will be OK. She's in good hands."

Ja`el assured Ky and Alston that the best doctors were working on Reece. Ky thanked him before he returned to duty. Ja`el called his sister Dani to come sit with Ky before leaving the hospital and told Ky and Alston he would check back on them shortly.

While they waited for word on Reece, Ky contacted his parents and Savoy while Alston called his parents. They were all upset and wanted to get to the hospital as soon as possible. Alston was able to get his family booked on a flight that left within an hour. Ky's parents and grandmother arrived at the hospital within minutes of his call and they immediately gathered together as a family to pray for Reece's full recovery.

It was taking every fiber in Ky's body not to explode, but he knew he had to be cool until he knew Reece was OK. While he waited for word on her condition he thought about how powerful Yale's influence was over her cousin to make him act on her wishes. He couldn't hate Yale more than he did.

Ky's grandmother saw Ky's distress and walked across the room to sit next to him. She patted him on the leg and asked, "Are you OK, Bishop?"

"No, and I won't be until I know Reece is going to be OK and that bitch is behind bars."

"Baby, I know you're angry, scared, and hurting right now, but don't use that kind of language around me," she said in a firm tone.

"I'm sorry, Gigi," he softly apologized.

"This is the time for you to hold on to your faith and trust that God will take care of Reece and get justice for her. Yale will get what she deserves one way or the other if she's involved in this. You just let the police handle it."

"I can't promise you anything right now," he replied.

Geneva could see the wheels turning in her grandson's head and she realized he was putting things together. She had seen that look on his grandfather's face many times and it usually ended up with the release of his explosive temper. Ky had a lot of his grandfather's personality and it concerned her.

She stood, gave him a kiss on forehead, and said, "I know that look on your face. You remind me of your grandfather right now. Don't do anything stupid because I can only handle one crisis at a time."

Ky watched his grandmother rejoin the rest of the family. At that moment the doctor came out to update the family on Reece's condition. She was stable but was in ICU. The doctor explained that if they hadn't found Reece when they did, she would be in worse shape. For now they were working to keep the swelling down and prevent the venom from the spider bites from causing organ damage. They had her vitals stabilized and were monitoring them.

"Can I see her?" Ky asked.

"Yes, but she's sedated. Try to keep your visits short and no more than two people at a time. Hopefully we can get her moved to a regular room before morning."

The family let out a sigh of relief and gathered for a prayer of thanks before Ky went in to see her. Before entering the ICU, Ky motioned for Alston to join him at Reece's bedside, but he told him to go ahead so he could update their parents first. The status on Reece's condition eased their minds before they boarded their flight, but they were still anxious to get to their daughter's bedside.

Inside the ICU, Ky made his way over to Reece's bedside where he found her hooked up to all sorts of IVs and machines. He could tell that the color in her face was paler than normal but he hoped the medicine they were giving her would improve her appearance and health.

He leaned down close to her ear and whispered, "I love you, Reece."

She slowly opened her eyes and tears spilled out of them. He caressed her face, wiped away her tears, and said softly, "It's OK. You're safe and you're going to be just fine."

"I'm sorry," she whispered.

Happy that she was finally talking again he kissed her and said, "Babe, you have nothing to be sorry about. I'm sorry I wasn't there for you, but you handled yourself great. All I want you to do now is concentrate on getting well because I have a date with you at the altar in a couple of weeks."

She smiled and although her voice was weak and she could barely keep her eyes open, she said, "I'll be there."

Ky gave her another tender kiss on the lips. "Alston will be in here in a second and I'll be back to see you shortly. I have to pick up your parents at the airport as soon as they land. Everyone's here and praying for you."

She nodded and whispered, "I love you."

He caressed her cheek. "I love you too. Get some rest."

Alston walked in and Ky embraced him before giving him some privacy with his sister. He needed to decompress because he felt like he had been holding his breath the whole time. He needed to release his emotions, but he didn't want to do it in front of his family, so he made his way out to his truck where he broke down in tears. Ky was thankful Reece was going to recover from her injuries. Now all he wanted to do was stay by her side and make her feel safe.

After several minutes, he finally gathered himself together so he could return to her bedside. She was sleeping soundly, but it didn't stop him from holding her hand. As he sat there Ky's father came in to check on his son and to pray over Reece. Each one of Ky's family members came in to see Reece, and after about an hour, Ky rejoined them in the waiting room. He asked them to stay at the hospital with Alston until he picked up Reece's parents from the airport. He told them once he returned they could all go home.

Pastor Parker told Alston that they would be honored to have his parents stay with them while they were in town. Ky told Alston and Gabriella that they could stay at his house, but he wasn't leaving Reece's side unless it was extremely urgent.

At that moment, one of the detectives assigned to the case came into the waiting room and asked to speak to Ky.

"Mr. Parker, I'm happy your fiancée is going to be OK. Is it possible that I can have a few moments of your time so I can interview her?"

Ky shook the detective's hand and said, "It's too soon. She's still somewhat sedated. Tomorrow might be a better day."

The detective put his notepad into his jacket pocket and said, "It can wait until tomorrow. I also want you to know that Andre` had been treated and released from the hospital and he's been charged with kidnapping, assault, false imprisonment and aggravated assault. He's facing some serious time, especially with his juvenile record."

"What about his cousin, Yale Spencer? Have you talked to her yet?" Ky asked.

"No, but we're trying to gather as much evidence we can before we bring her in for questioning."

Ky sighed. "I know she put it in his head to do it even if she wasn't directly involved."

The detective patted Ky on the shoulders. "We're working the case as hard as we can. I'll keep you posted."

"What about her phone or purse? Have you found either one of them?" Ky asked.

"Unfortunately we haven't, but we're still looking and trying to get the kid to talk more, but he has a lawyer now."

Ky didn't like anything the detective told him and there was no way in hell he could be patient while Yale was walking around. He was trying his best to concentrate on being there for Reece, but he wanted justice for her as well.

The detective gave Ky his business card and told him to call if he needed anything or if Reece said anything about her ordeal before he was able to question her. Ky tucked the card into his pocket and then went to visit with Reece once more before leaving to pick up her parents. He found her sleeping peacefully, so he quietly left the room and headed to the airport.

By the time Ky returned with Reece's parents, she was awake again.

"How are you feeling, Sweetheart?" Reece's Dad asked and he kissed her forehead.

"Hey Momma and Daddy. I'm getting there. I'm just a little tired and sore."

Ky walked in and said, "The nurse said your condition is stable so they're going to be moving you to a room shortly."

"That's wonderful," her mother replied. "Reece, we don't want to overwhelm you. The doctors said it's best we tag team our visits with you until you get your strength back."

"This medicine makes me so drowsy. All I feel like doing is sleeping anyway. There's no need for you to be here," Reece replied.

"Well, I'm not leaving," Ky announced. "I'm sure you guys are tired so you can go rest."

Mr. Miller walked over to Ky and gave him a huge hug and said, "Ky, I want to thank you for saving our daughter's life. I couldn't ask for a better son-in-law. I know you want to be here with Reece but you look like hell. You need to get some rest."

"I'm fine," he replied. "I'm not leaving her."

"No you're not fine. I can see you're exhausted," Reece intervened. "Babe, please go lay down. Seriously, I'm OK."

Ky no longer had the strength to resist sleep, so he finally agreed to go home and get some rest. The Parkers took the Millers' luggage back to their house with them. Before leaving, Ky told her parents he would be back in a few hours to relieve them so they could get some sleep too since it was so late. Alston took Ky's keys from him so he could drive. He knew Ky was too exhausted to go any farther, so he trailed Dani back to Ky's house where they could get some sleep. When they got home, Ky asked Dani to make sure Alston and Gabriella got settled before she locked up. He took a quick shower and collapsed onto his bed. Before going to sleep he set his alarm to wake up in few hours so he could return to the hospital to be with Reece.

It was nearly three AM when Ky's alarm woke him. As he got dressed, his heart ached knowing how terrified Reece must've been being left alone in the swamp. The more he thought about it, the angrier he got. He was still angry that Yale wasn't behind bars already. He knew in his gut that she was behind this. The police were moving too slow in his opinion and he had no idea what Yale would do next to try to get Reece out of his life. The more he thought about it, the easier it was for him to decide that there was no way he was going to give her a chance to do something worse to Reece. He was going to end this once and for all.

CHAPTER 24

Yale couldn't wait to get off work to have some fun out on the town with Anniston, and to hopefully run into Ky. She was still angry that he sent the police to her house but she still wanted to see him to hopefully convince him not to marry that woman. First she wanted to get home, shower, and change so she would be refreshed for her night out. In spite of what she thought were strong feelings that Quincy had for her, she still wanted Ky, and felt like a new beginning was on the horizon for them.

When Yale walked into the bar, she found her friend Anniston and a couple of other girlfriends sitting at a table with their first round of drinks taking selfies. "Sorry I'm late," she said when she joined the group.

"You're always late, but you look great," Anniston said.

Yale wore a low cut, red, curve hugging, short bandage dress, leaving little to the imagination. She had a great body and she loved to flaunt it.

She sat down and waved for the waitress to bring her a drink. By the time she finished her first one, she was surprised by a kiss on the side of her neck.

"Hey, baby."

Yale was shocked to find Quincy and a couple of his friends standing behind her. Anniston and the other ladies smiled as they admired Quincy and his fine friends.

"Yale, why don't you ask your friends to join us?" one of her girlfriends suggested.

Quincy put up his hands and said, "No, you ladies go ahead and enjoy your girls' night out. We can hang out another night when it's planned."

Yale smiled. "Thank you, Quincy."

He leaned down, gave her a kiss, and whispered, "Girl, you are wearing that dress. I'll text you in a second."

She nodded. "OK."

Yale turned back to her friends and found all of them staring at her. One of them immediately wanted to know why she had been hiding Quincy from them. She waved them off and told them she and Quincy were just friends with benefits. Anniston told them she was hoping that Yale and Quincy could be more because he seemed to be a nice guy.

Ignoring them, Yale pulled out her cell phone and looked at the text Quincy had sent.

I missed you and you look sexy as hell. I hope we can get together once you're finished hanging with your girls. You're long overdue for some of my special treatment.

Yale knew exactly what he wanted, but tonight she was hoping to show her new dress to Ky. She quickly texted back.

I missed you too. I'll let you know shortly about your offer. I didn't expect to run into you tonight and I had promised my friends we would all hang out.

Quincy texted Yale back and just told her to let him know. What she was really hoping was to hook up with Ky and hopefully maneuver the evening in her favor with the help of a little Ecstasy pill, which would allow him to end up in her bed for the night. To see what she could set up, she sent Ky a text to see if he would respond.

Ky, I hope all is well. Just checking to see if you were free tonight to come over so I can apologize for all the stress I've caused you. I'm embarrassed and ready to make amends. We definitely need to talk. It's really important.

Now all she had to do was wait and hopefully he would reply. It would be hard for any man to resist her looking this good, even Ky. Thirty minutes later there was still no reply from Ky and it dashed her hopes. She took another sip of her drink and decided to take advantage of Quincy's offer instead. She texted Quincy back and told him she was anxious to spend time with him and would meet him at her house shortly.

It had been over twenty hours since Reece's terrible ordeal had begun. At the hospital, Reece's room was filled with both sets of parents, Alston, Gabriella, Ky, and Geneva. Reece was feeling much better and her pain was minimal, but she was feeling overwhelmed with so many people surrounding her. It seemed like the room was closing in on her, making it hard to breathe. As Ky held her hand her grip got tighter and tighter and the conversations in the room turned into noise, quickly irritating her. He stood, leaned over, and gave her a loving kiss.

"I feel like I'm about to have an anxiety attack," she whispered to him.

Ky could see the stressed look in her eyes so he caressed her cheek and said, "Take some deep breaths, baby. Hold on. I'll take care of it."

She nodded and took several deep breaths to keep an anxiety attack from coming.

Ky motioned for everyone to exit the room where they gathered in the hallway.

"Hey guys, Reece is getting a little overwhelmed with everyone here at one time. You know she loves all of you and appreciates everyone's concern, but if we can keep doing the tag team instead of everyone being here at one time it would be better. I'm staying regardless so if one or two other people want to stay I think it'll be OK. We can switch up in a few hours. Agreed?"

"Agreed," Reece's father said. "I can see how having all of us in her room could be overwhelming. I'm just thankful she's feeling better."

"Why don't we go get some dinner and decide who wants to come back and sit with her?" Sinclair suggested.

Ky gave his mother a kiss on the cheek. "Great idea." He walked them to the elevator, but before returning to Reece's bedside he looked down at his cellphone and noticed a text from Yale. He read it, shook his head in disbelief, and ignored it. He knew she was trying to create more drama and he was over it and her. He had no idea if she knew Andre` had been arrested or that Reece was found and now in the hospital, but he didn't care.

Back inside the room, he sat down next to Reece's bed and held her hand once again while watching TV.

"Thanks for clearing the room."

He smiled. "You know I'll do anything for you."

"Are they angry you kicked them out?"

He laughed. "No, they're cool. They realized they were overwhelming you. How are you feeling?"

"I'm not as sore as I was yesterday. I'm so ready to get out of here and go home. I miss laying in your arms."

He stared at her for a few seconds and then said, "I can fix half of that right now."

Ky climbed into bed with her so she could snuggle up to him and lay her head on his chest. She closed her eyes and savored the warmth of his body and the manly scent of his cologne as well as the rhythm of his heartbeat. She couldn't see herself sleeping any other way or with any other man, and she'd fight by any means necessary to keep it this way.

"Reece?" Ky softly called out to her.

"Uh huh?" she answered.

"Do you want to talk about what happened?"

She sighed. "I told the detective everything. I really don't want to talk about it again."

He tilted her chin so he could look into her eyes. He could see she was still hurting, but there were things he needed to know that were troubling him.

"Babe, I have to know some things, otherwise my mind will think all kinds of thoughts and I don't want to do that unnecessarily. Did he hurt you in any way?"

She buried her face against his chest and said, "If you're asking me if I was raped, the answer is no. Everything happened so fast, Ky. I got in the car and I didn't immediately lock my door. I was in the process of putting the gun from under the car seat into my purse. That was when he opened the car door. When I saw who it was I froze for a second. He told me to move over so he could drive, but I refused. He put his hand in his pocket and I was sure he was reaching for a gun, so that's when I shot him. It pissed him off so he jumped in the car and tried to get my gun, but I was able to fight him off. That was when he hit me with what I guess was a stun gun. I don't remember much after that."

Tears of anger filled Ky's eyes. Hearing how it went down told him how close Reece had come to losing her life before she was ever taken to the bayou. He was glad she'd fought.

He swallowed the lump in his throat and said, "I don't know what's wrong with that kid. People are out on the street protesting for black lives and he's out in the street proving critics right. He needs a rude awakening and stiff punishment, and so does Yale."

Reece looked up at him in shock. "Did she put him up to it?"

He kissed her forehead and said, "I'm not sure, but I believe she had some involvement."

She laid her head on his chest without responding. The fact that Yale could be involved and go to these lengths to get her out of Ky's life was unbelievable.

"Babe, do you know what happened to your gun, purse, and cell phone?" Ky asked as he pulled out his cell phone. "I got this text from your phone. That's what made me start looking for you."

Reece looked at the text message on Ky's phone. "You know I would never send you anything like that and I have no idea what he did with them. The last time I saw everything, they were in my car. For all I know he threw them in the river."

He sighed and put his cell phone back into his pocket. "You know for a split second it crossed my mind that things were moving too fast and you might've gotten cold feet."

Reece sat up and looked him in the eyes. "Let's get this straight, Ky Parker. When I said yes to your proposal, I meant it. Nothing or no one could ever make me feel or think differently. Got it?"

He kissed her forehead, and with a smile said, "Yes, ma'am."

She snuggled up to him and it wasn't long before she drifted off to sleep. Happy she was able to sleep and put his fears to rest, Ky enjoyed watching TV over the next hour with Reece by his side. She looked like an angel sleeping. The more he thought about losing her, the more his heart ached.

He could not let Yale get away with almost causing Reece's death. He would give Reece some peace of mind by confronting Yale one final time. It would be perfect if Yale actually said or did something to implicate herself in the kidnapping, so she would go to jail too.

As Ky continued to sit with Reece as she slept, he looked at his watch and waited for someone from the family to return from dinner. Once time started to slip by, and no one had returned, he texted Dani to see if she could swing by to sit with Reece until someone else returned from dinner. She agreed since she was only a few minutes away. Once Dani arrived, he thanked her and texted Alston to let him know he had to step out, but that Dani was sitting with Reece until they returned from dinner.

Ky decided not to answer Yale's text. Instead he would just show up unannounced to hash out everything without her having time to prepare. When he arrived he found her male friend sitting on the porch smoking a cigar. He knew he was taking a chance approaching him, but it just might give him the chance to have a heart to heart talk that could work in Ky's favor. He just hoped the friend wasn't as confrontational as he was the last time they were face to face. As soon as Ky exited his truck, Quincy immediately recognized him.

"What the hell are you doing here?" he asked as he stood.

Ky put up his hands and said, "My beef is not with you. I'm here to settle things with Yale once and for all."

"She's not here, and if you have a beef with her, you have a beef with me."

Ky laughed. "Seriously? Let me tell you something. You don't know Yale like you think you do."

"I know her well enough, and it's best you leave before she gets here."

Not wanting to get into a physical altercation Ky said, "OK, I'll leave, but before I go, there's something you need to see."

"What?" Quincy asked defiantly as he put out his cigar on the corner of the porch.

Ky sighed. "There's something I want to show you on my cell. Is that OK?"

Quincy approached him and said, "As long as that's all you're pulling out of your pocket."

Ky pulled out his cell and opened up his text messages. He showed Quincy the text he had received from Yale asking him to meet her.

Quincy looked at it and said, "So what?"

Ky then showed him all the previous text messages from her begging him to give her a second chance. He also played a couple of voice messages she had left him. It was obvious that Quincy wasn't too pleased to hear his woman begging her ex to take her back. It made him wonder where he actually stood in her life.

Ky could see the look on Quincy's face and said, "I get it. I've been there. Yale is a beautiful woman and she has a way of making you feel special, but I also know how selfish, vindictive, manipulative, and inconsiderate she can be. She doesn't care about anyone but herself."

"You guys had a bad breakup," Quincy replied. "It takes some people longer than others to get over it."

"Listen, I don't know you, and you're probably a nice guy. I'm only here because there's a strong possibility that Yale got her cousin to kidnap my fiancée, and she nearly died. He's in jail and I'm pretty sure he was acting on her suggestion to get my fiancée out of the way so she could try to get back with me. She's been harassing me and my lady for months now and I'm tired of it. I've talked to her multiple times and I've told her we're done. I had the police talk to her and nothing is getting through her thick skull. My next step is taking out a restraining order on her. Now if you believe Yale is not that kind of girl, prove me wrong."

At that moment, Ky showed Quincy the mysterious text message sent to him from Reece's cellphone saying she was leaving town and couldn't marry him and to go back to Yale.

"I know for a fact that my fiancée didn't send that message because I found her tied up in a goddamn fishing cabin out in the damn bayou. My lady never broke off our engagement, but somebody wanted me to think she had, and who would benefit the most from a broken engagement?"

Quincy put his hands over his face and said, "She can't be that crazy. She has everything going for her. She's gorgeous, smart, and has a great job. Why the hell would she risk everything over you?"

"Because I said no," Ky replied. "Yale doesn't like rejection. She's a good liar and she loves trying to control people. I'm going to show you how far she will go if you help me."

Quincy thought for a moment and then reluctantly nodded. Quincy realized he needed to know much more about with whom he was dealing.

Ky decided to give Quincy a little more insight, so he dialed Yale's cell phone and put it on speaker.

"Hey, it's me," Ky announced. "I got your text."

Yale answered with excitement in her voice and said, "I'm glad you call. We really need to talk."

"I need to talk to you as well," Ky answered. "We can't keep going in on each other. It's not cool. We've known each other too long for this foolishness."

"I agree. God knows it's been exhausting and stressful on me as well," she replied. "You didn't have to call the cops on me though."

"Yes, I did because you won't listen and you keep involving Reese," Ky answered. This is between you and me."

"OK, OK, I admit I took it to far but you know how much I love you," Yale revealed. "The thought of you touching that woman drives me crazy. Let's meet and talk through this because I hate feeling like this."

Quincy could hear the excitement in her voice as she discussed her meeting with Ky.

"Are you sure you're available now? I know it's getting late, so if you already have plans we can reschedule," Ky said.

"Now is fine, Ky. You know me, I don't have any plans and I'm a night owl anyway."

"Cool," Ky replied before testing her. "Why don't we meet up at your house?"

She quickly shot that down because knew Quincy was probably there waiting on her.

"Why don't we meet at the cafe where we last saw each other?" She suggested.

"That will work. Just give me about fifteen minutes to get there. OK?"

When he hung up, Quincy's cell phone immediately rang and Yale lied to him.

"Babe, can we get together another night? Anniston drank too much and now she's sick. I'm going to hang with her until she's feeling better. I promise I'll make it up to you, OK?"

Quincy played along even though he knew what her motives were.

"I understand, Babe. Just text me when you get home so I'll know you're safe," he requested as the realization hit him that Yale had been playing with him all along. She was waiting for an opportunity to try and get back with Ky and now she was taking advantage of it.

"I'll call you the moment I get home," she answered.

When he hung up his cell he was overwhelmed by what he had seen and heard. He asked Ky for the address of the cafe and he planned to confront Yale by showing up a few minutes behind Ky.

Yale was super excited that she would finally get to make what she hoped would be her final move on Ky. Before getting out of the car, she freshened up her makeup and reapplied her lipstick. She made her way inside the café where she found Ky already sitting at a booth. As she walked over to him, several men couldn't help but admire her shapely body in that sexy red dress.

Ky stood. "I'm glad you could make it. You look great."

She sat down and said, "Thank you. So do you."

At that moment a waitress came over to take their drink order. Once she left, Yale said, "You know we've been close for a long time and like I've told you before, I'm still madly in love with you. It makes my heart ache seeing you with that other woman. You don't know enough about that woman to marry her. I understand I messed up and why you hate me so much. We had a great relationship, Ky. It was passionate and we had a lot of fun. That's why I've made such a fool of myself over the past few months but I hope you can overlook my mistakes and forgive me. Please give me another chance. I know I can make you happier than you ever dreamed."

The waitress returned with their drinks and Yale hoped for the opportunity to slip the drug into his drink but her hopes were dashed and Ky completely blindsided her.

He took a sip of his drink and said, "I appreciate and understand everything you said, but it's not enough. You have no idea how bad I want to hurt you right now."

"Why?"

"Are you going to sit here and tell me you don't know your cousin, Andre`, is in jail?"

She sighed. "I told that boy to stop robbing people. I gave him some money, but he keeps doing it."

He leaned closer to her and said, "You really don't know?"

"Ky, I don't know what you're talking about."

"Your cousin kidnapped Reece and left her for dead in the goddamn swamp."

"What? I know you don't think I had something to do with it, do you?"

Ky grabbed her wrist and forcefully pulled her arm. "Andre` told the police he did it for you. He said you wanted Reece to disappear. Lucky for you, she survived and will be OK because if she hadn't, I would choke the life right out of you."

"I don't remember saying anything about making her disappear. I say a lot of things. You know that. Ky, you're hurting my arm," Yale said as she tried to free herself from his grasp.

With her wrist still in his grasp he said, "You didn't give a damn about Reece or what could've happened to her. Where's her cell phone?"

"I told you I didn't have anything to do with what happened to Reece!" she answered. "Why would I have her cell phone?"

At that moment Quincy sat down next to her, forcing her to scoot over. Ky released her arm and Quincy answered, "Because his girl doesn't have it, and someone's been texting him like they're her. So where is it, and don't lie because that's all you've been doing to me lately."

Yale knew she was cornered and she was startled to see that Ky and Quincy seemed to have formed some type of alliance against her.

"Quincy! You're against me too?"

"You broke a date with me so you could meet with him. How am I supposed to feel?"

Yale was speechless as Quincy continued.

"I saw all the text messages and heard all the voice messages you left him over the past few weeks. I feel like everything we've shared since we met has been a lie."

She cupped his face and said, "I told you I wasn't over him, but that doesn't mean I'm not into you too."

He removed her arms and said, "I clearly see you only love yourself. Now, do you have his girl's cellphone or not? If you continue to lie and I find out, you're going to dig yourself into deeper trouble. Not only with me but with the police."

"The police?" she asked.

"Yes, the police," Ky repeated just as the detective came over to their table.

"Miss Spencer. My name is Detective Craig Williams and your name has come up in our investigation in the assault and kidnapping of Reece Miller. I have a search warrant to search your car, home, and personal effects, and I need to read you your rights before we go downtown for questioning."

Shocked, Yale sat there as the detective waited for her to get out of the booth. She looked at Ky and Quincy and asked, "Are ya'll serious?"

Quincy stood so Yale could slide out of the booth. "You need to do everything you can to help yourself. Starting with the truth."

After the detective finished reading Yale her rights, he asked, "Miss Spencer do you have anything in your possession that belongs to Miss Miller?"

With tears stinging her eyes, she willingly opened her purse and said, "No, detective, I don't."

Ky stood. "Just because you don't have Reece's cell phone on you now doesn't mean you didn't have it before or that you're not involved. You're the only person who would think they had anything to gain by it, and whoever sent me those text messages from Reece's phone did it for your benefit. Reece would never break off our engagement and there's nothing you could do to make me stop loving her. To be honest, Yale, I hope you're not involved with this, but either way, you need to get yourself together and forget about me."

"I don't know what to say to convince you I'm not involved," she replied. "My cousin is a hot head and we're very close so he would do anything for me, but I swear I didn't tell him to hurt her."

"I still need you to come down to the station with me so I can ask you more questions," the detective said.

Yale nodded and then looked at Quincy and Ky. "You're both wrong about me. My only fault is that I love hard and I don't like to lose."

With that statement, Ky was done, but before leaving he shook Quincy's hand and said, "I'm sorry about this and I appreciate you being cool about this whole thing. I really pray Yale wasn't involved. I don't know what happened to her. I've been pleading with her to move on with her life for nearly a year."

"I was really falling hard for her," Quincy replied. "I don't know what I'm going to do about her. I have some thinking to do for sure. I don't want to see her life ruined, but if she had anything to do with what happened to your fiancée, she has to pay. I hope she's OK."

Ky left some money on the table for the drinks and said, "Thankfully, Reece is going to be fine. I wish you well with whatever you decide to do about Yale, and believe it or not, I hope she wasn't involved too. Good luck with whatever you decide."

At that point Ky left the restaurant and headed back to the hospital to be with the love of his life.

CHAPTER 25

Ky arrived back at the hospital before Reece woke up. When he quietly entered the room, Reece's mother and Dani were there.

Ky gave Dani a hug and said softly, "Thanks for hanging out until I got back. Did she wake up?"

"No, she's been asleep the whole time. It gave me and Mrs. Miller the chance to get to know each other."

He took off his jacket and said, "Great. Mrs. Maxine, are you OK? Can I get you anything?"

"No, I'm fine. Thank you."

He sat down. "You don't have to stay here tonight. I'm not going anywhere else. Dani can take you back over to my parents' house so you can sleep comfortably."

She picked up her purse and asked, "Are you sure? I have no problem staying."

"Reece is doing really well and the doctor said she can probably go home tomorrow."

Maxine stroked her daughter's hair and said, "I'm glad. She will be able to rest better in her own bed. OK, I'll go, but you call me if anything changes or you need me."

Ky hugged and kissed his future mother-in-law. "I will. Dani, thanks for dropping her off."

"Anytime. You ready to go, Mrs. Maxine?"

She nodded and they left Ky alone with Reece. As he settled into the recliner he sent Alston a text updating him on Yale being taken in for questioning. He also called his father to let him know. Since he was Yale's pastor, there was the possibility that she would reach out to him for spiritual guidance and comfort even though he was Ky's father. He knew his father would do his duty as pastor, regardless of the connection to his son.

The next morning Reece was given her discharge papers. When they arrived at the house they were surprised to see that the women had prepared a nice brunch to celebrate Reece's homecoming.

"You all didn't have to do this," Reece stated. "I'm just glad to be home."

"We did it because we love you, Reece," Ky's mother announced. "We're so happy you're OK."

The family fellowshipped together and gave thanks for Reece's recovery.

That evening, seeing that Reece was doing well and was in good hands, and after plenty of hugs and kisses, Reece's family boarded their flight back to D.C. Their departure was bittersweet for Reece, but she was happy for things to get back to some normalcy. The good thing was that she would be seeing them in a few days when she went home for Thanksgiving and the final fitting for her wedding gown.

As night fell, Reece got ready for bed. Since getting home, Samson wouldn't leave her side, and she could tell he had missed her. He laid down on the floor next to the bed. Ky showered and eased into bed feeling like he could finally exhale. He had been exhausted over the past few days since their ordeal began. Now all he wanted to do was hold her and never let her go, but surprisingly Reece had something else in mind.

She snuggled her body up to his and said, "I'm so glad to finally be home and alone with you. I've missed this."

His body immediately responded as he stared into her loving eyes. Without saying a word he ran his hand down to her backside and pulled her hips against his. Reece slid her hand under the comforter and caressed his lower body.

"Do you think this is a good idea? You just got out of the hospital."

She ran her tongue over the tattoo on his chest and said, "I feel just fine, but you can make me feel so much better."

He smiled and wasted no time showering her body with heated kisses, especially that special spot on her neck that always caused her to let out soft moans. Knowing how close he came to losing her made him want to make love to her, but he knew she was still recovering, and he didn't want to overwhelm her. It was Reece who continued to beg for more.

"You are the love of my life, Reece," he whispered before giving her a tender kiss on her lips. "I can't wait to marry you but tonight you need to rest."

Reece sighed. Their love for each other was undeniable and they couldn't wait to make it official in a couple weeks.

He held her tightly and said, "Don't worry, I'll definitely make this up to you so rest up."

She snuggled against his strong body and whispered, "I love you, Ky."

He caressed her body and said, "I love you more."

Yale was freaking out after being interrogated at the police station. Luckily for her, the detectives could find no direct evidence tying her to the kidnapping, so she was allowed to go home. She wanted to visit Andre` to see if he had an attorney and find out what happened. She mainly wanted to make sure he was OK. He was still a kid, and she hoped to get him some type of plea deal. The last thing he needed was to have a felony on his record. He would never be able to have a decent life with that over his head. It saddened her to know that he went that far because of their family bond and she wanted to let him know she supported him.

It had been a tough twenty-four hours, but after a hot shower and some sleep she woke up refreshed and ready to visit Andre` to see if she could help him. She entered the jail, signed in, and made her way to the visiting area to wait for her cousin. Once he was brought in, he sat down on the other side of the glass and picked up the telephone.

"Cuz, what are you doing here?" He asked.

Yale gripped the telephone and said, "Did you do what they said you did?"

Andre` leaned back in his chair and said, "Man, I don't know what you're talking about. Cuz you have to get me out of here."

She looked into his eyes and asked, "Are you OK?"

"I'm as good as I can be," he replied.

Tears welled up in Yale's eyes.

"You're better than this life you're leading. It has to end if you want to survive in this world. I'm sorry if the way I've been behaving influenced you in any way. It's my fault you're here. I'm going to do everything in my power to help you, Dre`"

Knowing the phone lines were recorded, she didn't want him to say anything that would incriminate him. His arraignment was going to be later that afternoon and she needed him to know that she would be back to support him.

"I know you're down for me, Yale. I've always been down for you too. I appreciate your help."

Yale could see that Andre` was thankful and she could see some remorse in his eyes as well. An adult prison was not where he needed to be, and she prayed the attorney or some type of divine intervention would help him in some way. He thanked her and told her he was sorry.

Once Yale returned home she found Quincy sitting in his vehicle waiting on her. She was surprised he was even there because the last time they saw each other he was extremely upset and disappointed in her. She invited him inside.

"Quincy, I know you're pissed and I'm sorry I lied to you. It seems like everyone hates me."

He sighed and said, "Hate is a strong word. I don't hate you, Yale. I'm hurt."

"Why do you feel like you have to beg someone to love you? Why can't you see the possibilities between us?"

Yale dapped the tears in the corner of eyes and said, "I don't know."

He stroked her hand and lovingly asked, "You're a Christian, right?"

"Yes," she softly answered.

"Don't you realize that people come in and out of our lives like seasons?"

"I guess," she replied.

"Babe, then you have to know that Ky Parker was a season. Your time with him has come and gone. Stop trying to hold onto something God has removed from your life. I'm right in front of you. Why can you embrace a new season with me?"

"I don't know," she replied softly. "I guess I'm not lovable."

"Can't you see that I've fallen for you?" He asked curiously. "I love you."

Stunned by his admission, she repeated, "You love me?"

He smiled and said, "Yes! I've been trying to bring it to your attention for a while now, but your eyes and heart has been so clouded because of your fixation on Ky."

Yale burst into tears and said, "I can't lie to you or myself anymore. There's some things you need to know about me."

He held her hands and said, "Babe, you can tell me anything. You need to unburden your heart because I can see it's eating you alive.

It was then that Yale revealed that she had been molested by her uncle for several years when she was young. He also found out that her drug addicted mother often left her at home alone for days at a time. Hearing this information saddened Quincy and caused him to want to help her even more. Now he sort of understood why she hated rejection and was obsessed with being loved. He knew there was a good person inside her. He just needed to help her to come to terms with her dysfunctional childhood and fear of abandonment. Yale had been through hell and back, and all she needed was love and understanding. He hoped he would be able to help her get the therapy she needed to let go of her past and face her demons.

That afternoon the prosecutor alerted the judge that a plea deal had been reached with the defense attorney for Andre'. He pled not guilty to kidnapping and grand larceny; however, he did plead guilty to unlawful imprisonment and assault. The deal included Andre` serving a year in juvenile detention with ten years' probation once he got out. The prosecutor wanted him to serve more time, but he decided to offer Andre` the plea with the urging of Pastor Parker, who assured the judge he had a team of people in his congregation ready to take Andre` under their wing when he got out of juvenile detention. He hoped to save Andre' from himself and give him one final opportunity to change his life for the better.

As Andre` was being led out of the courtroom to start serving his time, Yale noticed Pastor Parker sitting in the back. They knew each other very well, and unbeknownst to Ky, he had had several sessions with Yale over the course of her young life regarding her abusive childhood and was instrumental in getting removed from her mother and into the arms of loving family members who raised her.

He walked over to her and gave her a hug. "Yale, it's good to see you. May I speak to you for a moment?"

"Sure, pastor," she replied as she excused herself from Quincy after introducing him to her pastor. She followed him out into the hallway to a quiet corner where they sat down on a bench. Once there, he prayed over her and assured her that everything was going to be OK. He explained to her that he heard about some of the things that had happened between her, Reece, and Ky, and while he expressed his disappointment in her behavior, he forgave her.

She thanked him for forgiving her and said, "I'm so sorry, Pastor Parker. I never thought anyone would get hurt because I was in pain. It's just that I love Ky so much that it's hard for me to let go, especially when I see him so happy with someone else. I'm also sorry for my behavior at Ky's house a few weeks ago."

He held her hand and said, "I know you didn't want things to end up like this, but unfortunately someone did get hurt. Andre` is lucky he has a good attorney and that both of you have a pastor who cares for his flock."

Yale lowered her head in shame. "I know, pastor, and I appreciate everything you've done. Is Ky aware that you're here?"

"That's not important right now. What is important is that I'm here to help both of you. Things are not going to change for the better until you accept that your relationship with my son is over. Are you ready to do that?"

"This is so hard for me," she admitted. "My mind tells me one thing, but my heart keeps telling me something else."

Pastor Parker put his hand over hers. "Yale, I'm not giving you a choice. You have to accept this. If you don't agree that your relationship with Ky is over and get the professional help I've been trying to get you to accept for years, I won't be able to help you any further. I love my son, and his happiness means everything to me, so my terms are non-negotiable. The police still think you are involved with what happened to Reece, and it wouldn't take much for them to build a circumstantial case against you and throw you in jail. Is that what you want?"

She shook her head. "Of course not."

"Then you need to listen to me," he said as he pulled a business card out of his pocket. "Here's that friend of mine I've been trying to get you to go see. She's a great therapist and can help you through all your issues, past and present. She'll be giving me progress reports on your sessions, so don't disappoint me."

She took the card out of his hand and said, "Thank you. I'm sure Ky and Reece are not happy with you helping me, Pastor Parker."

He tilted her chin, looked her in her tear filled eyes, and said, "My son was raised to have a forgiving heart. I don't know all of the dirty details of what went on between you two, because he hasn't shared everything with me, but the few things he did reluctantly share with me were disappointing. He is extremely angry and hurt over what happened to Reece, but I'm sure he'll eventually get past it. You need to concentrate on getting well and moving on with your life. God has closed the door on your relationship with Ky, but by the body language I picked up on that young man sitting with you in the courtroom, it appears that he really cares about you. You need to embrace him and move on. Do you think you can do that?"

Yale tucked the business card into her purse and gave her pastor a hug.

"Looks like I have to, pastor. Thank you for not giving up on me, and if there's anything you can do to help my cousin, Andre`, I would appreciate it as well."

He stood. "I've already put my two cents in with the prosecutor on his behalf. It wasn't easy since he has a history in juvenile court, but I serve a higher God and he's been given a chance to get his life together. If he messes up, he'll have to face the original consequences."

"Yes, sir," she replied as she wiped away her tears. "Thank you again for everything."

Before leaving, Pastor Parker prayed one more time over Yale and told her he would see her in church.

On the way home, Pastor Parker stopped by his son's house to check on Reece. Once inside, he followed Ky downstairs where he found his future daughter-in-law sitting on the sectional sofa with her laptop, catching up on work. He gave her a kiss on the cheek and asked her how she was doing before sitting down across from her.

With her leg elevated to help reduce the swelling, she answered, "I'm getting there. I'm not as sore as I was and the swelling is slowly going down."

"That's great news. Make sure you continue to take it easy."

"I will. Ky has me on lock down and won't let me do anything."

"He's doing right. Let him take care of you," he said before turning to Ky. "How are you holding up, son? You all have everything you need?"

"I'm fine," he replied before changing the channel on the TV. "And the only thing I need is to get the wedding behind us."

Gerald smiled. "Well it's just around the corner. I'm sure you two are anxious and excited."

"We are," Reece replied. "Are you excited about performing the ceremony?"

"Of course I am. I'm finally marrying off my first born."

"Daddy, you talk like you didn't think it would happen," Ky pointed out as he chuckled.

"Well, I was beginning to wonder, but I knew God was in control and would make it happen when he saw fit."

Reece smiled. "I'm glad God waited for me to come to town to meet Ky."

Gerald watched the interaction between his son and Reece and he could see their undeniable love.

"Listen, guys, there's something I need to talk to you about," Gerald announced. "I went to the courthouse today to see Yale's cousin get arraigned. She was there with her male friend and a few family members. I didn't want to see another young black man's life ruined over bad choices, so I helped break a deal with the prosecutor to give him a year in jail and ten years of probation. When he's released next year, he'll enter our Father and Son Mentoring program at the church where he'll get the structure he's been missing in his life. He's going to be required to wear an ankle monitor for six month, finish high school, keep a job, and report to his probation officer. If he gets into any trouble and violates his probation, he'll go back to jail for six to ten years. Can you guys live with that?"

Reece looked over at Ky and saw the frown on his face. She rubbed his arm and said softly, "It's OK, babe. Rev. Parker, I trust your judgment and support your work in the community, but what I went through in that swamp traumatized me. I still have nightmares about it and what could've happened to me. If I didn't have Ky and all the loving support around me from you and our families, I probably wouldn't be doing as well as I am."

Ky sighed. "Hell! I'm traumatized too, and I want him to suffer all the consequences of his actions."

Reece held her fiancé's hand and said, "Ky, I know this affected you too, and I love you so much for saving me, but I don't want to see another young black man's life wasted. So as long as he's punished in some way that will give him the opportunity to think about his actions, and he follows the stipulations of his plea deal, I'm all for rehabilitation. Hopefully this will help him become a productive member of society."

"What about Yale? What happens to her for her role in this mess?" Ky asked.

"You know as her pastor it's my job to support her too, even though she caused you two a lot of anguish over the past year. It doesn't take away from how much I love you, because you're my blood. It's also my job to do whatever I can to help my congregation. So I told her if she didn't go see the therapist I recommended and accept that her relationship with you was over, I would help the police build a circumstantial case against her, and she would end up in jail too. She accepted my terms and I'll be getting regular updates on her progress from the therapist. I pray she can heal from her past and get on with her life. The young man she was with was acting like he was emotionally attached to her in some way."

Reece glanced over at Ky who was in deep thought as he listened to his father.

"I understand what you have to do as a pastor to help your congregation. If you're sure she's going to get mandatory treatment and leave us alone, I can live with everything you worked out," Reece revealed. "As far as her cousin, I hope he suffers a lot more and is at least remorseful for what he did to me."

"Son, what about you? Can you live with this?"

Ky got up from his seat and started pacing. Reece and Rev. Parker could clearly see that he was struggling with all this information.

"Ky?" Rev. Parker called out to his son.

"Daddy, Reece could've died had we not found her when we did. I can't forgive as easily as you and Reece can, and Yale gave me hell this year. I'm sick of it."

Reece got up and hugged his waist. "Babe, I don't want you to feel pressured to do something you're not ready to do. You'll know if and when you're ready to get past it. Do you remember the words you told me when I was struggling with my past? You told me I had to eventually love past the moment. With you by my side, I was finally able to do that. In time I hope you'll be able to get past everything Yale and her cousin put us through as well."

Rev. Parker stood. "On that note, I'll get out of your way. Son, I don't want you to be in turmoil over this. You found the right woman. You'll eventually find your peace too."

He gave Reece another tender kiss and his son a loving hug before letting himself out of the house.

Once his father was gone, Reece looked at Ky and asked, "Are you angry with me?"

Ky pulled Reece into his arms and said, "Of course not, but I don't see how you can be so forgiving after what happened to you. Then again, you are an amazing woman and I see why you're in my life. I love you so much but you're going to have to give me some time. I never want to feel that helpless and terrified again."

She kissed him. "I get it, and I understand, but don't let it destroy the man I fell in love with. OK?"

He stared into her eyes and said softly, "You are going to be an awesome wife."

"And you are going to be an awesome husband."

CHAPTER 26

It was going to be a magical evening in D.C. The weeks had gone by fast with a bridal shower, bachelor and bachelorette parties, and the rehearsal dinner. The couple had been on fast forward since they'd landed in D.C. Now it was the wedding day and Reece couldn't be any more calm. Ky, on the other hand, was feeling a little nervous. He couldn't believe the day had finally come, and he was starting to get emotional about it. Thankfully he had the men closest to him by his side to support and help him hold it together.

Maxine buttoned her daughter's wedding dress and struggled to keep her tears from ruining her makeup.

Reece's grandmother smiled and said, "You look like an angel."

"Thank you, Grand Momma."

"Reece, you look absolutely stunning, and you picked the perfect gown," her mother added. "It's vintage, elegant, and sexy."

She kissed her mother. "Thank you."

"Ky is going to faint when he sees you," Maxine pointed out.

Reece giggled as she admired her reflection in the floor length mirror. "I hope not. I think he'll be emotional, though."

"Baby girl, I have something for you," her grandmother said as she opened a wooden box. "You know you have to have something old, something new, something borrowed, and something blue. I know you have the blue garter, but I want you to wear or carry this diamond broach given to me by my grandmother. This is your something old and it's very valuable."

Reece's eyes widened at seeing the large diamonds sparkling on the broach. It was gorgeous and she couldn't be more honored to wear it on her wedding day.

She kissed her grandmother and asked, "Is it OK if I attach it to my bouquet?"

"Of course. I'll help you."

Reece held her bouquet while her grandmother attached it to the ribbon wrapped around the bouquet.

"It's perfect," Reece said, admiring it again.

"What about your borrowed item?" her mother asked.

"Reece pointed to her earrings and said, "These are Gabriella's diamond teardrop earrings she wore in her pageants. The only thing I need now is something new."

At that moment there was a soft knock on the door. Maxine walked over and opened it to find her husband in his tuxedo standing in the hallway holding a small, gift wrapped package. She let him in and he smiled when he laid eyes on his beautiful daughter.

"Oh my God! My baby is so beautiful," he said, choking back tears.

Reece kissed her father. "Thank you, Daddy. What's that?"

Seeing his daughter had almost made him forget why he was there. He handed Reece the gift and said, "Ky wanted me to give this to you."

With a huge smile on her face she opened the gift to find a diamond journey pendant with five stones in ascending sizes. Inside was a note that read: *Here's a little something for you to wear that represents the five months I've been in love with you. I can't wait to marry you. With all my love, Ky.*

"Wow! It's gorgeous," Reece said as her father helped her put on the necklace.

"Well, I guess you have your something new," Maxine pointed out. "You're all set now."

Seconds later there was another knock on the door alerting them that the wedding was about to start.

Reece took a deep breath and said, "This is it. Daddy, can you say a prayer before we go out?"

Reece's father, mother, and grandmother held hands and surrounded Reece so they could pray. It was a picture the photographer would capture that would always hold a special place in Reece's heart.

Ky's nerves were getting the best of him as the bridal party marched down the aisle in front of a packed congregation. He was anxious to see Reece, and when his seven and four-year-old cousins entered as flower girls, he knew his wait was over. The moment he saw Reece and her father coming down the aisle, his heart thumped hard in his chest. It was a struggle for him to contain his emotions. He felt his whole body trembling. Ja'el could see his cousin struggling, so he patted him on the shoulder to support him, but Ky lost the battle with his emotions as tears filled his eyes.

Reece was radiant. He had never seen her more relaxed and beautiful. Her long gown was stunning and it fit her sexy curves to perfection. He was proud to see her wearing the necklace he had given her and it went perfectly with the other jewelry. All he could do was thank God for blessing him with the perfect woman and soul mate.

Once Pastor Parker began the ceremony, Ky was able to exhale a little bit, but he couldn't take his eyes off his bride and she couldn't take her eyes off him. Ky was extremely handsome in his tuxedo that fit his broad shoulders and chest magnificently. As he stood there with his bride, he just hoped he wouldn't forget his lines or become so overwhelmed that he would be unable to speak. Lucky for him, the moment he was given Reece's hand by her father he calmed down. The ceremony was beautiful and it wasn't long before he was finally given permission to kiss his bride to the thunderous applause of the guests.

A short time later, after photographs had been taken and the wedding party made their way to the ballroom of a nearby hotel, the reception got off to a wondrous start. The wedding planners created the couple's colorful vision for the reception hall down to the smallest detail. The dinner menu and choice of entertainment was all perfect, and their five-tier wedding cake was not only delicious, but it was a piece of artistry and elegance. The evening couldn't have been more joyous.

It was a magical night of love, dancing and joy with family and friends from the couple's first dance down to the father, daughter dance. Ky also got to shine in the spotlight with the mother-son dance, but it was Ky's toast to his new bride that didn't leave a dry eye in the room as he professed his undying love for her. As the festivities continued the bride tossed her bouquet and Ky took pleasure in throwing Reece's garter to the eligible bachelors in the crowd. With all the ceremonial moments out of the way, now it was time to party.

Reece finally decided to change into her reception dress after remembering that she had bought it as a surprise for Ky. With Gabriella's and Savoy's help, she excused herself from the festivities to change into the dress and then rejoined her groom. His jaw dropped when he saw her in the gorgeous pink mermaid dress. The shimmering beading sparkled against the lights and their guests were in awe of her beauty.

"Surprise," Reece said to Ky before kissing him.

He gazed over her body seductively, pulled her into his arms to dance, and whispered, "You look breathtaking and you are in so much trouble when we get to our room."

"So are you," she replied.

He laughed and kissed her again before dancing alongside their guests late into the night.

Hours later, the couple bid farewell to their family and friends. On the elevator ride to their suite, Reece snuggled up to her new husband and said, "We did it, babe."

He ran his hand down her backside and said, "Yes, we did, and I couldn't be happier. You are the most beautiful woman I have ever seen, and you are wearing that dress. I can't wait to get you out of it."

She giggled and nuzzled her face against his warm neck. "Thank you. I wanted to surprise you. Our wedding was beautiful, wasn't it?"

They stepped off the elevator together and Ky said, "It was more than I could've imagined. Everyone is having a great time and our families are getting along so well. The wedding planners deserve every penny they charged for putting this together on short notice."

As they made their way down the hallway, a few people couldn't help but stare at the handsome couple, especially Reece in her spectacular dress. Once in their room, Reece was surprised to find it filled with candles, rose petals, and champagne. Their large soaker tub was also filled with hot bubbles and rose petals. There was a serving table filled with chocolate covered strawberries, miniature grilled cheese sandwiches with tomato soup shooters, a variety of cheese and crackers, and a couple of yogurt parfaits filled with blackberries, raspberries, and granola.

"This looks delicious. Did you arrange all of this?" Reece asked as she picked up a strawberry and held it up to his lips.

"Of course," Ky said before kissing her and taking a bite of the strawberry. "I thought we might get a little hungry after all the consummating we're getting ready to do."

Reece laughed and caressed his face. "Well, I'm glad you thought ahead. Do you think you can help me out of this dress now?"

He kissed her neck. "Turn around."

Once out of their formal attire, they snacked on some of the food before climbing into the hot tub. Ky filled their glasses with champagne while Reece caressed his masculine legs.

"So where is this mysterious place you're taking me for our honeymoon?"

He took a sip from his glass and said, "I told you it's a surprise. I'll let you know when we get to the airport. I will tell you it's tropical and you won't need many clothes."

She nibbled on his earlobe. "Sounds like paradise."

Ky kissed her soft lips. "No, being with you every day is paradise."

Over the next hour, Ky and Reece expressed their love for each other. He wanted every nerve of her body to react to his touch, and he was more than successful. His hands and lips were all over her and she couldn't contain her moans as he feasted upon her. He was about to explode upon hearing her reaction, so he mounted her soft, shapely body and kissed her hard on the lips before he thrust his muscular body deep into hers. She held on to him tightly, wrapped her legs around his waist, and loudly professed her undying love for him. Ky was overwhelmed with love and pride as he continued to love his new bride. Several minutes later, he felt electrical sensations consuming him.

Reece looked into his emerald eyes and with tears spilling out of hers she whispered, "I love you, Ky Parker."

He let out a loud groan and shivers hit him like a ton of bricks as he gave in to his release. Exhausted, he lay on top of her and struggled to regain his breath.

He kissed her firmly on the lips and whispered, "I love you too, Reece Parker."

Overcome with emotion, she held on to him tightly as tears spilled out of her eyes.

"You are an amazing lover," she admitted while kissing his neck.

Ky winked. "Babe, this is only the beginning."

Reece held tightly to his body and while kissing his neck and lips she whispered, "I wish we could stay like this forever."

He caressed her cheek. "I'll see what I can do to make your wish come true."

She giggled as he rolled over onto his back and pulled her on top of his chest where he held her close. He ran his hands down her back and rested them on her round bottom. Reece stared at her husband while she ran her finger over the lines of one of his tattoos.

He noticed the look on her face and asked, "What are you thinking about?"

"How easy you made it for me to fall in love with you."

He smiled. "I agree. The crazy thing is that I never expected this. You kind of blindsided me, but in a good way, and I wouldn't change a thing. I can't wait for you to have my babies."

"If it's OK, I would like to wait at least a year, but if you want to start sooner that's fine too."

"A year is cool with me," he replied. They spent the rest of the night making love in each other's arms, and it wasn't until the wee hours of the morning before they finally fell asleep.

The couple planned to return to the Gulf Coast the next evening after a large family brunch at the hotel. The second reception would be taking place the following weekend before they spent a week in the South Pacific. Ky made detailed plans to take her somewhere beautiful, exotic, and private, and Bora Bora seemed like the perfect spot.

After spending Sunday with family and friends for brunch, the newlyweds spent the rest of the afternoon at Alston's house before returning to their hotel to prepare for their flight out the next morning. The couple finally returned to their home and settled in quickly. They were going to work from home the rest of the week because they wanted to rest up before attending the reception at Ky's church. They would be out of town for the next week and a half for their honeymoon, getting back just in time to celebrate their first Christmas together.

While Reece played with Samson, Ky checked the messages in his office.

"What would you like for dinner?" she asked as she poked her head into the office.

"I'll take care of dinner," he said as he wrapped his arm around her waist and they walked back into the family room together. "You can go relax, and after dinner we can decorate the Christmas tree."

"I can't wait, babe. I already have a few things to go under it."

Samson brought a toy over to Reece, dropped it, and barked.

She picked up the squeaking toy and tossed it across the room before returning to the sofa. She sat down and started going through the gift cards they had received as wedding gifts in lieu of actual presents since they had to travel. She wanted to get an early start on writing out thank you cards because she knew they would have more gifts after the upcoming reception.

Yale had been texting with Anniston for several minutes. She had neglected her friend for several weeks as she struggled to come to terms with everything that had happened. In the meantime, she was using the time to reflect on everything she had done and to be thankful that Quincy hadn't given up on her. She had started seeing the therapist Pastor Parker recommended and her sessions were going well. The therapist told her she couldn't move forward until she was able to break free of all the pain of her past and present. Yale was finally seeing life differently, but there were still some things that she felt like she needed to take care of before she could move forward.

All the lies, manipulation, and threats had sucked her soul dry and turned her into someone she wasn't proud of. She had been on Instagram earlier and saw pictures that members of Ky's family had posted from the wedding. It was painful to see Ky and Reece so happy when she was still in turmoil. She scanned through every picture and looked at the details in each one. She had to admit that Reece's dresses were spectacular and she looked amazing in them. The couple really looked like they were in love and it made her heart ache. People talked about having a legacy to pass on to their children. She thought one day that would be her in a wedding dress standing next to Ky. It was her plan for them to be a power couple, but she ruined any chance of that happening because she got greedy and paranoid.

"Yale, where are you?" Quincy asked as he entered her house and called out to her.

"I'm upstairs," she replied as she turned off her iPad and texted Anniston to tell her she would get back with her later. She climbed off her bed and stared down the stairs at Quincy.

He walked upstairs to meet her, pulled her into his arms, and gave her a kiss. "I've been thinking about you all day. You good? You look tired."

She smiled. "I'm fine now that you're here. How was work?"

He took her hand into his and walked back over to her bed where they sat down. Yale looked into Quincy's eyes and saw him as the great man he was. He was handsome, nurturing, loving, and attentive.

With a huge grin on his face he said, "Work was great. In fact, I have some news I hope you're going to be cool with."

"What is it?"

"Well I put in for a promotion a few months ago and today I was told I got it."

Yale gave him a kiss. "That's great, Quincy! Congratulations!"

He looked her in the eyes. "Thank you, baby, but there's a catch to this promotion."

"What kind of catch?" she asked as she made her way over to the mirror where she began to brush her hair.

He walked over to her and stood behind her, admiring her beauty. He hugged her waist and said, "The new position is in Miami."

"Miami?" she replied as she looked at his reflection in the mirror.

"Yes, and I want you to come with me. It's a beautiful, sexy city and it will give us a fresh start. Say you'll come with me, baby?"

She stared back at him through the mirror and said, "I don't know, Quincy. I've lived here all my life. All my family and friends are here. I never imagined living anywhere else."

He hugged her tighter and said, "I can't accept the position if you don't go with me because I'm in love with you. I really want you by my side."

She turned and hugged his neck. "When do you have to let them know?"

"By Friday," he replied as he lovingly caressed her face.

"Can I sleep on it?" she asked.

Quincy kissed her forehead. "Sure, but I pray you decide to go with me."

"I know you do, but you also know I'm still dealing with a lot here and I'm seeing a therapist."

"I know, sweetheart, and I'm sure we can find you a great therapist in Miami. I want you to go with me so we can start a new life together. We can always come back and visit any time you want."

"I appreciate you asking me to go with you. I know I'm a hard person to love."

He kissed her on the cheek and said, "Not for me."

Tears filled her eyes and she smiled. "Are you hungry?"

"I'm starving," he replied as she took him by the hand and led him downstairs to the kitchen.

"Good, because I cooked country fried steak with gravy, biscuits, mashed potatoes, and broccoli cheese casserole."

Quincy could see that Yale's therapy sessions were having a positive effect on her. He was impressed with the woman she was becoming, but knew there was so much more to her. He sat down with his woman and prayed this would be one of many future dinners to come—in Miami.

EPILOGUE

The reception at Ky's church was just as exciting as the reception in D.C. It seemed like all the congregation and most of the city as well as some notable dignitaries had come out to celebrate the couple's nuptials. It was a blessing to Rev. and Mrs. Parker and Geneva to see Ky so happy with his new bride. Reece and Ky, along with their family members, recreated the look from their wedding by wearing their wedding attire to give his church family and hometown friends the vision of what took place in D.C. a week earlier. They served dinner, cut the cake, and went through the traditional rituals just like they did at their original reception. Anniston attended the reception but Yale chose not to. Anniston knew her friend was still struggling with Ky's marriage, so she decided not to report anything to her unless she asked.

Across town Yale felt like she had made a lot of progress with her therapist but she still had some personal issues to work through. She had turned in her resignation at her job and made the decision to join Quincy in Miami, and he couldn't be happier. Tonight he was working the late shift and wouldn't be coming by until around midnight. If all went well, it was his plan to make his relationship with Yale more permanent and ask her to marry him once they settled into their new home in Florida. She had actually started packing to get a head start on their move and her house was going to be rented out in a couple of days.

To help pass the time and get through the evening, she decided to make herself a drink. When she opened the freezer to get the ice, she noticed the baking soda box she had stuffed behind a couple bags of shrimp. She stared at it for a moment and then pulled it out of the freezer and set it on the counter.

"Lord, give me strength," she whispered before she pulled a small, plastic container out of the box.

What she was holding was something that could make her extremely happy, but it could ruin the lives of others in return. She had held on to it for a long time. Now she wondered if she should attempt to use it or destroy it so she could start her new life with

Quincy. She realized she loved Quincy and knew he would have no problem giving her a wonderful life, but deep in her soul she was still in love with Ky.

She closed her eyes and with tears running down her face she prayed out loud before she carried the container holding Ky's frozen sperm, stolen from one of his disposed condoms, upstairs to her bedroom. Maybe the destiny she really wanted was in God's plan all along. Only time would tell.